13
TO
LIFE

13 TO LIFE

Shannon Delany

St. Martin's Griffin
New York

13 TO LIFE. Copyright © 2010 by Shannon Delany. All rights reserved. Printed in the United States of America. For information, address St. Martin's Press, 175 Fifth Avenue, New York, N.Y. 10010.

www.stmartins.com

Library of Congress Cataloging-in-Publication Data

Delany, Shannon.
    13 to life : a werewolf's tale / Shannon Delany.—1st ed.
       p. cm.
    ISBN 978-0-312-60914-6
   1. Teenage girls—Fiction.   2. Werewolves—Ficiton.   I. Title.
II. Title: Thirteen to life.
   PS3604.E424A15 2010
   813'.6—dc22

                               2009046740

10   9   8   7   6   5   4   3

Dedicated to my mother, Cecile Plott Reinbold, and bold and humble women like her everywhere. Cancer may have stolen your life, but it could never dim your spirit. Your strength, wit, faith, and courage in the face of adversity inspired me. Then. Now. And always.

ACKNOWLEDGMENTS

Hang in there, folks, this'll be a long one because so many people helped me along the way. Writing can be a solitary struggle, but you helped make my writing life full (and lively). And (just in case) I leave someone off my list here, keep in mind this is a series. Woot!

Oleg and Dmitri, who stayed with my family briefly one summer while the Iron Curtain between our two nations still hung heavily: Your stories, curiosity, and fears inspired my fascination with your language and culture. I hope these stories inspire others to appreciate Russian culture more.

Dr. Warzeski of Kutztown University, whose classes on Eastern European history and Russia cemented my love of all related topics, and Dr. Theiss of Kutztown University, who taught Russian language classes with great humor.

Stan Soper, founder of Textnovel.com, willing tweaker of contracts, great beta, fine agent.

Leslie DeBauche, for being excited about all my projects and giving me an opportunity to try something truly inspiring with her classes at University of Wisconsin-Stevens Point. Point Pirates rock! Returning from Wisconsin I got the idea for the title of this book, from which the story sprang (you are all somehow to blame). Werewolves now—maybe pirates later—I have an idea. . . .

My husband, Karl, for not only putting up with my bizarre need to write, but also encouraging it, bouncing ideas around with me on car rides, and allowing me the time (and mood swings) a writer needs to push forward.

My son, for giving me time to write and interjecting his ideas throughout the project. I promise, there will be a story with potion-drinking werewolves just for you eventually!

Lauren Manzer, for encouraging pack members to vote in the Textnovel competition (and being an awesome supporter and fan—you'll love what happens in books two and three. . . . Bwa-ha-ha!).

My aunt Dorothy Reinbold, for making sure there were always books—in my childhood home and in the Waynesboro Public Library.

Ellen Dwyer, for spreading the word about the story even though you had little computer time—your support means so much.

Joey Holling for being genuinely excited for me.

Jennifer Holling-Blake for reading the first full manuscript when other betas suddenly had full plates. And for asking me for more from Amy. Books two and three are in part a reflection of that request (let's cross our fingers for more Amy in the future, too).

Annette Fitzgerald, owner of The Book Exchange in Ohio and friend to authors everywhere, for printing out the whole manuscript, reading and commenting in record beta time, and telling me over the phone: "You suck!" because she wanted book two right then.

Deborah Blake, CP, beta, and friend with a great eye for detail, a sharp wit, willingness to admit when she's wrong (and hey, she's not often wrong), and a talent for writing that will land her great gigs in fiction.

Robin Wright for talking me back from the ledge. Now that you don't have to read it on a screen, I hope you have time to fully read it (while raising two kids, supporting a busy guidance counselor, and writing your own fiction. Oh, heck. Never mind.)

Morgan Dirk Reinbold, creative brainiac brother who said something that stuck with me: "I believe that if someone writes a good story, it'll get published." That became my mantra.

Morgan David Reinbold, best dad I could have and the guy who willingly listened to the audio recordings of the manuscript on long drives to make sure it wasn't "sucko."

P. C. Cast, who said to me at the party in Bardeo, "Don't let anyone stop you." That got added to the previous mantra.

Thanks to my Textnovel readers, blog followers, Textnovel voters, and members of my 13 to Life Private Writers Group, specifically: James Powel, who made sure I maintained Pietr's animal grace at a key moment; Jenna Bufano, who gave wonderfully specific input on an early draft; Sarah Flinders, who understands the importance of specific praise; Alisha Sizemore, who reminded me how to dream; Kimberly K. and Annabelle—great supporters and fans.

To the amazing people who make up St. Martin's Press: Michael Homler, best darned editor I could have; Matthew Shear, publisher and signer of my contract, who had me change my name but not my title (hey, life's about compromise, and

I'm cool with that); and Anne Marie Tallberg, who was excited to have my novel on her e-reader (along with P. C. Cast's—talk about being in good company!).

To my Twitter followers, Goodreads group (and Carla Black for reminding me I needed one), and Facebook fans—your support keeps me (closer to) sane!

To small-town folks and American immigrants from everywhere—our success in this country has always been built thanks to your hardworking contributions.

Very, very important: To all the students I had the opportunity to teach over the years, from my first tentative steps at Southern Reading Middle School under the guidance of Richard Christ to my years teaching social studies and drama at Burnett Middle School in Seffner, Florida, where a big chunk of my heart still resides. GO WOLVES!

Last, but not least—the small towns I've loved: Oley, Bryson City, Gilbertsville, Brandon, Seffner, Oneonta, Rising Sun, Waynesboro, and Nottingham—all these and so many more have gone into developing Junction.

PROLOGUE

Rio stiffened beneath my touch, striking a glossy hoof against the floor.

"What, girl?" I asked, still fighting the tangle that snarled her ebony mane. She snorted, nostrils turning the red of fresh blood. She shook, long neck yanking the brush out of my fingers. It bounced off the opposite wall with a thump. "Rio!"

Keeping a hand on her, I walked around to her other side and leaned down to search for the brush. For a moment everything was eerily still—completely quiet. Then my dogs, Maggie and Hunter, leaped up from where they'd been dozing, snouts propped on a bag of feed. They rushed the barn door, exploding in a fit of barking.

The other horses whickered, voices filled with equal parts concern and frustration. Hooves stomped, crackling hay.

"What the—?" My fingers danced down Rio's velvety nose. "Shhh. It's okay, girl." Slipping out of her stall, the fine hairs on my arms stood as if lightning charged the autumn air. "Everything's okay," I insisted as I marched over to Maggie and Hunter.

They were not convinced. Wedging myself between them, I snaked my hands around their collars and peered through the narrow opening separating the barn's huge doors. The barnyard was strangely silent, as if everything simultaneously shut its mouth to stare with fearful wonder at whatever stalked the shadows. The dogs pulled, pawing and growling.

The unnaturally white expanse where the barnyard floodlight lit the space between the first barn and the house stretched out like a broad scar before me. Never before had it seemed so ugly and bare—or such a great distance. A cool night breeze pushed the faint noise of television to me. Dad was watching reruns of that crazy video show. Would he hear us over the blare of television if we needed help? The answer hit like a rock dropping into my stomach as Dad's laugh punctuated the suddenly calm air and he cranked up the volume.

I glanced down at the dogs. *Crap.* I was on my own with only Dumb and Dumber to help.

My gaze scraped across the yard from the reassuring glow of my home's windows to the tall floodlight. I whispered calming words to the dogs—vague promises of tasty snacks. *Huh.* Usually gobs of moths fluttered in the glare of the floodlight, bats darting in and out to catch dinner. Tonight there was nothing. The air had gone still, but my apprehension made it seem to buzz with electricity.

I swallowed. A shadow sliced across my field of vision, briefly blotting out the light, and I stumbled back, fingers slipping free of the dogs' collars. Maggie's and Hunter's voices blended into a single thin and wavering whine. I grabbed a pitchfork leaning against the wall and held it before me.

Something shoved at the other side of the doors. Nudged them so they wobbled. The creature whuffled the air like a hound searching for a trail. Its nose, nearly as broad as my palm and as black as the shadow its body cast, thrust between the doors, nostrils stretching as it sucked down our scent. I could see just a hint of reddish fur. The dogs slinked back to me, tails tucked and bodies trembling as I brandished the pitchfork.

But far more frightening than the huge nose (at the height of my chest, I realized) was the line of teeth visible between dark, rubbery lips. Long and jagged, they left no doubt they were designed to shred.

The beast snorted, a sound that rivaled Rio's, and then—as suddenly as the thing had appeared—it was gone. I gasped. Trembling like my dogs, I looked at the pitchfork in my hands and laughed. Add a torch and I'd be set to join the mob in Mary Shelley's *Frankenstein*. What did I think was out there? A monster?

I winked at Maggie and Hunter. "Probably just old Monroe's dog Harold anointing everybody's fence posts," I assured. They wagged their tails but knew better than to trust my words.

I set the pitchfork back in place and busied myself tidying the barn, too aware I hesitated to switch off the lights and cross the bare and bright white expanse between here and home. Too soon there was nothing left to clean or rearrange. And tomorrow was a school day.

I steeled myself for the walk back to the house. "Come on, Hunter. That's a good girl, Maggie." Dread clenching my heart, I remembered the strange stories that came out of the city of Farthington last year. Flanked by my dogs, I walked swiftly to the house.

I only relaxed when the door closed and the bolt slid into place. Hunter looked up at me expectantly, sitting like the gentleman he was far from being. And very happy to remind me with a solemn look from his soulful golden eyes of the snacks I'd recently promised.

CHAPTER ONE

I closed the door behind me, heading down the hallway and straight to Hell. The hall glowed eerily in the morning light. Outside, the wind snarled and threw a kaleidoscope of dry leaves against the large windows. I was sure whoever summoned me had very good intentions, but that only encouraged the gnawing sensation in my gut. Wasn't the road to Hell *paved* with good intentions?

My feet dragged the whole way to Guidance. The call had gotten me out of Ms. Ashton's literature class—not gym. Nobody *ever* got called out of gym.

The whole thing made me suspicious. Why did Guidance need *me*? Had they finally figured out who wrote that scathing editorial about the double standards between the jocks and the nerds? Considering what I knew of Guidance, I could be fairly certain they hadn't—at least not without assistance.

When the call came rattling through the intercom system, I'd shot a look at Sophia, a fellow editor. She'd shrugged. I presumed I hadn't been ratted out.

Then why was I being summoned? Sure, I was perpetually late handing library books in, and there were at least three times I'd signed in tardy with the nurse and accidentally taken her pen. But, seriously. If Guidance wanted to summon a troublemaker, they had the wrong girl. Well—pretty much.

My sneakers scuffed along the oatmeal-colored tile floor and I sighed. *God*, I asked, *don't let them be holding some stupid intervention for me about Mom.* The thought stopped me cold. I looked at the flimsy blue pass in my hand. How bad would it be to forge a time and signature on it and go back to class? Would Guidance remember they'd called? It was the middle of first quarter, progress reports were due soon, so wouldn't they be scrambling to organize last-minute study sessions with the kids slipping (or *diving*) through the cracks?

I glanced up the hallway; its cinder-block walls seemed to tighten around me. *Breathe* . . . The walls retreated. There was no witness to see me scrawl the signature Mr. Maloy joked was proof he could have been a doctor. I could make a quick U-turn and head back to class. . . . I chewed my lower lip, considering the odds I'd get caught. Hmph.

I turned down the hall and opened the door to Guidance; scanning the waiting room, I looked for a coat or hat belonging to my dad—anything to warn me to leave before someone with a master's degree decided it was best for me to talk about my innermost feelings—again. But there was no sign of Dad.

A poster hung on one wall, obviously an art project, raising awareness about the rash of teen suicides occurring on the train tracks between Farthington and Junction. Could things ever be so bad I'd willingly jump onto the tracks before an approaching train? The tension fell out of my shoulders. No. I wasn't a suicide risk. I'd witnessed the worst and I was still here. I exhaled, surprised to find I'd been holding my breath.

The secretary was focused on a magazine. Its blaring red cover featured titles including "What Type of Tree Would Your Lover Be?" and "When to Worry About His Psycho Ex." I cleared my throat. She looked up, said, "Oh. Jessica," and pointed a carefully manicured finger toward the conference room. "Mr. Maloy's waiting."

"Fabulous."

She smiled, big eyes pleasantly blank. Clueless. I figured it was best to have someone like her greeting folks as they entered Guidance. She'd never panic if bullets started flying. She probably wouldn't even notice unless they clipped her stylish hair.

I knocked on the conference room door, goose bumps raising the fine hairs on my arms. I'd been here before, sitting on one of many hard plastic chairs pulled in a tight circle as counselors and teachers told me how much I still had to look forward to in life. How great it would all still be if I only tuned back in . . . How they all cared for me and were there to support me . . . And I'd hated it. None of what they said mattered. They were paid to say stuff like that. Probably contractually obligated.

Besides, I always hated things that made me cry. And I knew I was strong enough to cope with what had happened. Without help.

As the door opened I saw a group of people I didn't recognize, along with Junction High's head counselor and a police officer. Weird, but a relief. No intervention, then—obviously this party wasn't for me; I was merely a guest.

"Miss Gillmansen," Mr. Maloy said, rising from his spot at the far side of the table.

Sipping from a coffee mug, the cop leaned against the wall by the window.

The others turned to face me. They were tall and well built, with high cheekbones and strong jaws—even the single girl standing with the three guys. They had thick dark hair, glinting eyes—and name tags.

"These are the Rusakovas," Mr. Maloy said, motioning to the group.

Out of the corner of my eye I watched the cop set down his mug and pick up a brochure on the windowsill. It had to just be coincidence he was here. Just more bad timing—typical stuff at my high school.

I turned my attention back to the Rusakovas. I smiled encouragingly.

They did not.

Mr. Maloy rounded the table and, peering none too subtly at their name tags, pointed to one of them, announcing, "This is Peter Rusakova. He's in eleventh grade this year. A junior, just like you."

I kept the smile plastered across my lips, groaning inwardly. So *that* was what this was about. "Hello, Peter." I couldn't help my uninspired tone. I wasn't a girl who liked being saddled with the responsibility of escorting newbies to classes.

Mr. Maloy slid his glasses back up the bridge of his nose and gave me a warning glance. "Here is Peter's schedule. Show him around and make sure he's not late."

The police officer glanced at me, saying slowly to Peter, "Got that, Rusakova? Don't be late."

Something prickled along my spine at his tone.

The eldest in the group smiled broadly and wrapped his arm around Peter. "Of course he won't be late, Officer Kent," he guaranteed. "Peter is very glad to be at Junction High."

Peter did not seem so convinced.

Officer Kent said, "We can't have people *avoiding* an education."

"We were *getting* one," the other boy—according to his name tag, Maximilian—muttered.

The eldest cuffed him on the back of the head, attempting comedy, but I sensed a threat in the display.

I took the slip of paper and quickly compared it to my own. I looked from the officer to Peter and back to the schedule. Handing my pass over for a signature, my eyes paused on Peter again. He glowered darkly before me, a sharp contrast to the eldest male's bright smile.

I should have forged Mr. Maloy's signature after all.

"Okay," I said, more to myself than to my silent ward. "We're both in Ashton's lit class. Let's head in that direction, for starters."

Peter gave one brief nod of his head, but his face was a tight mask of disinterest.

Exiting the office, I tried to keep my curiosity in check while I steered him by locations he'd need to know as a student at Junction High. I pointed and explained until my arms were tired and my mouth was dry. He never said a word. Never responded with more than a nod. Bathroom, library, cafeteria, art, shop, band, gym, main office, nurse . . .

In-School Suspension . . .

I eyed him, speculating. Who knew how fast somebody like him could land in ISS? He had that could-be-trouble look. And obviously he came with baggage of the police-escort type. But surely he wasn't dangerous. . . . The cops would never let me lead a real criminal to classes, would they? I continued walking and explaining, gradually increasing the distance between us.

If he noticed, he never mentioned it.

The thought he could be dangerous made me nervous. And when I get nervous, I get talkative. I glanced at his schedule again. "Oh. Your name's not Peter," I said, wondering if I'd been pronouncing it at all correctly. *Huh. P-i-e-t-r.* "It's Pie-eater—"

He winced.

I read it again. "No, Pee-yoh-ter—"

He stared at me.

"Pay-oder?" I tried. I was determined to get it right. Mr. Maloy had obviously botched this like everything else. My mouth twisted, ready to go one more round with the name, but he raised a hand, staring at me like he was in shock. Or maybe pain. I felt my ears go tomato red.

"I have never heard so many—*creative*—pronunciations of my name." He smiled, but only briefly. "Peter," he said. "The pronunciation is the same. Just not the spelling." He tugged off the misspelled name tag and crumpled it up.

"Oh." He didn't *seem* dangerous. . . . "Weird," I said suddenly. "You know, it's actually kind of spelled like my worry stone. . . ." I dug into my jeans pocket and pulled out the large, flat bead I carried. Gold, silver, and milky white threaded through dark blue. "This is pietersite. P-I-E-T-E-R." I held it out in my open palm and thought I saw momentary interest in his eyes.

"A worry stone?"

"My dad's idea. It's also called Tempest Stone. People say it's good for a lot of stuff, like dealing with change and transformation. Oh. And your gallbladder, I think. Or spleen." I shrugged, slipping it back into my pocket. He definitely looked interested now. Maybe he had spleen issues.

"What do *you* think it's good for?"

"Rubbing, when I'm stressed." I shrugged again. "Besides, like Shakespeare said, 'What's in a name,' right?"

He looked past me. "*Romeo and Juliet.* I *hate* that play."

"Well." How could *anyone* with a brain hate a classic like

that? "A good writer should get people to feel *something,* I guess."
I started walking again, hoping to catch his attention. Even
when he spoke directly to me, he seemed distant. Unreachable.
Like this wasn't important.

What was it with him? Was I being blown off?

"So, um. Why the cop?" I figured I'd just go for it. Ask the
question about the elephant in the room.

Pietr didn't pause, just continued walking beside me. "We
went to Europe last year and didn't tell the school."

"Oh." My brain reeled at the thought of just going to Europe. "So you basically skipped school for a few—"

"Months."

"Oh."

We walked for a while in silence, down the long corridor of
tall windows leading toward the English department's classrooms. There was just the noise of my shoes squeaking on the
tile floor. His sneakers never made a sound, and I looked over
more than once to make sure someone was actually walking
beside me.

I hoped I hadn't suddenly suffered a psychotic break and
imagined the meeting in Maloy's office. Although I wasn't
sure why I'd conjure someone like Pietr during a psychotic
episode. . . . That was probably just it, though. You couldn't
know what to expect if you snapped. Or when it would happen.
You just knew everyone expected you to snap and eventually
have one. At least, if you were me.

To relieve the silence I asked, "Where are you from?" If he
wasn't going to talk, maybe I shouldn't keep encouraging conversation. But I was determined to give him a chance. Coming to a
new school was bound to be difficult. Coming with a cop in
tow . . . and then, not making friends—or even acquaintances—
wouldn't make it any easier.

He looked over his shoulder and said, "Farthington." He seemed to regret even the single word.

I paused, stopping in the hall to look at him. "Wow. I would've totally left that place, too. You guys had all that weirdness with that wolf attack."

He nodded.

"I didn't even know there were wolves that close until I heard it on the news. I mean, you occasionally hear about a rabid raccoon leaping onto somebody's porch and biting them, but . . . wolves?"

He remained silent.

"Did they get the wolf that did it?"

"They think so."

From Farthington *and* reprimanded by a cop? There had to be a story here, and I was starting to feel like I had to be a code breaker to piece it together. "I'm with the school newspaper— I'd love to interview you about it."

"No, thank you," he said with absolute conviction.

My reporter instincts made me twitch. Even a reporter for a small school paper has to react when a student admits to being from the site of the bloodiest, goriest, most mysterious and bizarre wolf attack in a century and the guy doesn't want to talk about it. It was an eye-poppingly big story. And Pietr summarily turned down my shot at writing the article—writing something far more exciting than "Students Struggle with New Library Filing System."

Okay. He'd rejected my request about the Phantom Wolf of Farthington. I wasn't beyond trying again.

But something about him was bugging me, and it was more than the fact he came from a place where things actually happened. Living in Junction made you aware the grass *was* greener everywhere else. I wanted to live someplace exciting, too—okay, maybe not Farthington, because the idea of a rampaging beast freaks me out. I shivered, remembering last night's strange encounter at the stables.

I refocused on my more immediate problem. Pietr. It wasn't that he was shy—I've been shy, so I can read that vibe like reading the alphabet. *Shy* was nothing like what he put out.

I squinted at him, trying to figure out what his problem was while he looked everywhere but at me. He was handsome enough. His dark hair spiked up and out in an unruly shock, a strand or two shadowing eyes that seemed nearly navy. Comparing him to Derek (whose stats I absolutely knew by heart), I estimated he was five foot ten or so and probably growing by leaps, considering the other family members I'd just seen.

He didn't look like he had a reason to be mysterious. He looked like he could actually *be* somebody. Probably another snotty out-of-towner who thought he was too good for a small town. Maybe Farthington with its bizarre news made him immune to what was important to folks in an old railroad town like Junction. Maybe it was simply beyond his capability to care.

But that couldn't be true. If I could still care about something—anything—anyone else could, too.

He just stood there. Silent and absolutely inattentive.

"You're not really interested in any of this, are you?" I said, waving my hands to encompass the whole school.

He looked down at me for the briefest moment. Our eyes connected, and I caught my breath. His eyes were so much more than *nearly navy blue*. Looking at them was like looking at the variations in the pietersite in my pocket. He tore his gaze away coolly and simply stated, "I'm not interested in much."

He shrugged, not bothering to look at me again.

Had that been a complete dismissal of me? Was it *me* and not the school or my hometown that he thought he was so much better than? I *was* being blown off.

Fuming, I began walking again, lengthening my stride to close the distance between us and our first real destination quickly. He kept up easily. "Well, you'll have to care about *school* if you ever want to get out of *here*," I snapped, turning the door's handle. "Welcome to lit."

CHAPTER TWO

I stalked into the room, my peers' eyes trying to catch a peek at my expression. I released the door, letting it—and hoping it would—smack into Pietr's face.

He didn't even glare in my direction. I made my disappointment obvious: Handing my pass to Ms. Ashton, I rolled my eyes. But she didn't notice, letting the pass slip through her fingers as she crossed the floor, apologies to Pietr falling from her lips—for *my* behavior!

"I'm so sorry Jessie let go of the door too soon—are you okay?" She scanned his face, her eyes bright and oddly eager. I took my seat and watched the other students' reactions to our arrogant new class member. The girls were all sitting— literally—at the edge of their seats, fingers white around the knuckles as they gripped their desks and made mooneyes at him.

I couldn't believe how they all seemed so blatantly and suddenly obsessed with Pietr. I mean, okay—I looked him up and down without feeling a hint of self-consciousness, measuring and weighing what I saw there. Yep. Not bad looking, sort of had that catalog-model look, good enough for print but not typical runway material.

But he simply didn't care. It made me want to scream. But I remembered: Most girls go soft over guys with that dangerously arrogant edge—that distance that marks them as unattainable. I sighed.

Ms. Ashton was still rambling on about the importance of literature to civilization and, of course, to the class. Pietr occasionally said something softly in that too-cool way of his, and all the girls giggled. Even Ms. Ashton. She had taken Pietr by the hand to better lead him to his desk. I was astonished by her utter disregard of teacher-student protocol.

I ruffled the pages of my lit book, feeling a heat growing on my back. I turned and nearly choked on my own surprise. Derek was watching me. He winked at me and motioned with a jerk of his head at Pietr. I rolled my eyes, my insides melting at this small communication with my old crush.

Derek chuckled silently and pointed to get me to turn back around in my seat.

"So, Jessie," Ms. Ashton was addressing me. "How did you manage to get the assignment of showing Pietr around?"

The girls all turned, glaring at me and yet seemingly hungry to know how they could get their very own new-boy-at-school, too.

"Just luck," I muttered. *Bad, dumb luck.*

I felt Derek's eyes on me again. Pietr didn't bother to acknowledge my statement.

Ms. Ashton closed class with a homework assignment. There were groans in response. Someone stated the obvious: "It's almost Homecoming!"

Ms. Ashton was unrepentant.

I didn't groan. Homecoming wasn't my thing. I barely followed our football team's adventures (other than staring at
Derek and listening to people recount his exploits on the field—
that I could listen to for days). The idea of going to a parade,
bonfire, and dance . . . well, what did it matter if I was curious
about it? Who would ask me, anyhow? Besides, there were always things to be done at home. A horse farm always had
something that needed doing.

The bell rang—a sound even more obnoxious and less bell-
like today because I had a special assignment. An especially
unpleasant assignment.

I stood and gathered my things. I was annoyed to find a mob
of girls hanging around Pietr's desk. They seemed oblivious to
my presence. Nearly as oblivious as Pietr was to me. I cleared
my throat.

No response.

I elbowed Izzy aside, pushing my way into their giggling
midst. "Come on, Pietr. We've got math."

He rose, slipping his newly acquired lit book under his arm.

"Math?" Izzy sighed. "Who does he have, Jessie? Mr. Belden?"
She never once looked at me—his guide and holder of the evidently royal schedule.

"Yeah," I snapped. "Beany Belden." Now I *did* groan. Escorting Pietr was making me less pleasant about everything. "*Now,*
Pietr."

"I'll walk with you," Izzy offered.

"Good." I headed for the door, saying over my shoulder, "I'll
lead."

I did my best to distance myself from the pair of them, but
occasionally I'd hear Izzy say something entirely insipid, and
it seemed as if she'd shouted it down the hall. She was entirely too easy to impress. Her brightest moment in the very

one-sided conversation was when she said, "You even *smell* good!"

I found myself rolling my eyes so often I nearly walked into a wall. Okay, the new boy was cute. So what if he smelled good? I mean—seriously. I totally get the idea that new things are attractive. New toys are shiniest. New cars smell best. But a new boy? Big deal.

Pietr finally returned her compliment. "You smell—delicious."

Odd. I sniffed. Well, Izzy did tend to pour on the perfume. I guessed anyone walking with her would eventually notice her scent, probably along with the slow burning of his or her nose hair in response to the olfactory assault. But that didn't matter because there was no amount of perfume in the world that could overcome the strange smells lurking in Belden's classroom. The man hadn't gotten the nickname "Beany Belden" for his choice of hats. At least Pietr would have a different smell to comment on. Maybe then he'd start an interesting conversation.

Pausing by Belden's door, I reassured myself that at least this weird fascination Izzy had couldn't last. Everything loses its luster eventually.

I turned to Pietr and Izzy. And saw four other gawking girls vying for Pietr's attention.

I didn't get it. What was it about him that they found so mesmerizing? Why didn't I see it, too?

When Derek came up behind me, I nearly jumped. "What do they see in that guy?" he asked, eyes fixed firmly on my own. I concentrated on breathing. *In-out-in-out-in* . . .

"I don't know," I admitted sheepishly. *Good. That was at least coherent.* I tried an endearing smile, but I could feel my lips stretch into a crazed grin. *Oh-god-oh-god-oh-god* . . . I forced my lips back into a less maniacal look, hoping Derek had somehow overlooked my stalker-like smile.

I felt someone watching us and glanced briefly away from Derek to figure out who. . . . Still ringed by my female class-mates, Pietr was glaring our way. No. Not *our* way—Derek's way. Weird. And it wasn't the glare a guy shoots a rival guy over a girl (not that I've seen one personally, but I've read about them plenty of times). No, it was like: *I hate that guy and always will.* Like Pietr already knew Derek.

Derek missed it. "So, I'll bet every girl in class is hoping he'll go to Homecoming with them."

I shrugged. "He's just some guy," I countered, maybe a little loudly. "But yeah, he seems to have attracted a flock of followers."

"Not you?"

"What?" I blushed.

"You don't seem too impressed by him."

"Yee-aahh." I tore my eyes away from Derek's face and looked Pietr over skeptically. Our eyes met, and I thought I read a warning in them. Weird. "Nope." I shrugged again. "I just don't get it."

"So you won't be going to Homecoming with him?"

"Of course not."

"Are you going with someone else?"

I blinked.

"Are you going with somebody else?" Derek repeated.

"N-no."

"All right, children, let's break it up. We have things to learn, not time to burn. Inside, inside!" Belden herded us into the room, using his yardstick to round us up and break up my con-versation with Derek.

I never hated math as much as that day. I watched Derek take his seat in the back and I took mine in the front, Pietr be-tween us.

What had Derek been getting at, out in the hallway? Guys like Derek didn't waste time on girls like me.

That day in math, nothing seemed to be adding up.

By the time math class wrapped up, my mind was swimming with questions. Most of them had nothing to do with mathematical equations. I packed up my things, noticing out of the corner of my eye that Derek hadn't passed by yet. I took a moment to arrange my pencils neatly in my backpack, blushing at my sudden and probably pathetically obvious attempt at subterfuge.

I looked up when I heard someone pause beside my desk, but my lips pursed when I realized it was Pietr. And his gaggle of girls.

Derek skirted the group, shooting me a glance I couldn't quite read as he left class. Left *me*.

I nearly growled at Pietr as I rose. His eyes narrowed, accentuating their oddly exotic appearance, and he seemed to weigh me for a moment. I hadn't realized how distinctly his dark pupils were rimmed with brilliant gold—a bold barrier before the blue. His eyes nearly glowed, giving him a disconcertingly feral look.

The hairs on my arms stood up, but *I* would not back down. "Let's go," I snapped, pushing past the girls he'd inexplicably gathered. I knocked into two of them with my elbows out. It was absolutely calculated.

But they didn't notice, reacting only when Pietr moved to follow me into the hall.

"Where are we headed?" Pietr asked.

What? Was he actually taking an interest in his new school? I glanced at him. "Lunch," I said shortly.

"Oh, Pietr, that's awesome," Izzy, obviously the self-appointed leader of his flock, exclaimed. "We share a lunch period—we can sit together!"

I half-expected that strange "ee-eee" sound hysterical girls make, when spotting this week's pop star, to stream from her lips, but, mercifully, she just grinned like a psycho.

Pietr gazed at her with a look you'd expect from a doting sitcom dad. Then he turned his strange eyes to me. "Where do *you* sit?"

"With my friends." I couldn't imagine such a phrase would attract more trouble, but it seemed I had a magnetic personality in just this one way.

"Excellent," he said softly. "I would like to meet them."

"Our table is normally full," I countered. It was true. Most days *I* had trouble finding a seat if I was running behind.

He smiled, and I felt the girls around him try to set me on fire with their eyes. "Has today been normal for you?"

"No." I crinkled his schedule in my hands. As much as I didn't care for his attitude, I realized there was something— *indefinable*—about him.

I caught a glimpse of Derek as he sauntered by with his fellow members of the football team. He shot me a look that made my heart stop. But I still couldn't interpret it. Maybe that was the key to a crush: You had it, but you never understood it.

Pietr slipped the schedule out of my hand, his fingers touching mine and jarring me out of my speculation. My hand tingled where he'd touched it, the same way it had tingled after I accepted the dare to touch the Monroes' electric fence one wet spring day. I never thought the touch of another person could make the nerves jangle and dance beneath my skin. It was like I had slept the last few months away and now, suddenly, I was waking up.

CHAPTER THREE

"We only have thirty minutes," he pointed out as I rubbed sensation back into my hand. He glanced at the clock and handed back the schedule. "Twenty-nine. Perhaps your normally full table will have an opening today."

I grimaced at the possibility and led Pietr and his mob toward the writhing mass of teenage bodies we referred to as the lunch line.

Considering the lunch line's length, for once it moved at a tolerable pace. I was able to separate myself from Pietr, buffering my location with some of the surrounding girls. I spent my time in line wondering about Derek—the same way I wondered about him nearly every minute of every day for the last two years.

I had been obsessed with Derek in ninth and tenth grade and he hadn't even given me a second glance. Wondering what had changed, I looked down at my hands and encountered my boobs along the way. Yep, that had definitely been a change, I realized, blush stinging high on my cheeks. In tenth grade I'd still been as flat as a board and then, in summer, more than wild-flowers had sprouted. I pulled out my worry stone and rubbed it.

So was *that* it then? Had my sudden—developments—been all that had caught Derek's attention? I squashed the doubt down. Surely there was more to me that he'd noticed.

He had dumped that prima donna Jenny. . . . Everyone knew there was nothing to her but bleach, makeup, and some well-structured bras. Maybe Derek realized he wanted a more complete package—someone with a brain. But in the back of my head a voice kept whispering, *Does it matter why he's interested? Be happy he's actually interested!*

My lunch tray made a clicking noise as it hit the rails in front of the steaming bins of what passed for food at Junction High. The scents blurred and blended—macaroni and pizza, Salisbury steak and meat loaf, shepherd's pie alongside over-cooked peas and rubbery carrots. . . . It all became a nauseating blend of substandard fare. I grabbed a questionable salad plate and a yogurt, pausing briefly to check the stamped date—expiration was imminent, but at least the yogurt and I still had today.

I slid my tray to the end of the line, where Madge waited at the cash register, hairnet pulled tight around her shocking red hair and squeezing her meaty ears, giving her head the appearance of a ham. She tallied my tray's contents and announced what I owed.

"See you at the Home today?" I asked as I paid up.

"Yep, job number two. I'll be bringing a new little helper." She grinned.

I said, "Cool," and a moment later I was free of the food sauna and heading for my table, forgetting Pietr in my need to discuss the Derek situation with my girlfriends.

I smacked my tray down, wiggling in between Amy and

Sarah on the lunch table's bench. Sarah set down the copy of *Sense and Sensibility* she was nearly finished reading and smiled supportively in my direction.

Stabbing my milk with a straw, I introduced my plight. "I just don't get it. Derek actually *spoke* to me today." I jabbed a cucumber slice with my fork and wondered which of us was older.

"Go ahead," Amy urged, her eyebrows tugged together in the gravest of expressions. Almost across from me, Sophia dabbed at her mouth with a napkin—her signal she was bowing out of the discussion. She had gone out with Derek once and never again. She wouldn't talk about it. Ever.

A tray clicked down at the one open spot at our table—directly in front of me. "What don't you get?" a male voice asked coolly.

I looked up and groaned.

Pietr had found me. He sat down casually, ignoring the frowns of his throng as they were forced to find other seats.

I tried to ignore him, but Sophia's eyes slid wisely from him to me and back again. "Sophia"—I pointed to her—"Pietr." I pointed to him. "Sarah. Pietr." Again I jabbed a finger in their directions.

Amy didn't wait for an introduction. "I'm Amy," she said. "I hear you're Pietr."

He smiled. Sarah and Sophia giggled at me. *Some friends.*

Pietr speared a piece of mystery meat loaf with his fork and popped the first bite into his mouth, chewing like eating was an exercise in efficiency, not something to be enjoyed. Well, *that* I understood, looking at my own wilted lettuce. "So, what don't you get?" he asked again.

I refused to answer, trying to seem absorbed in the search for a crouton with some crunch. I was absolutely unlucky today.

"There's really nothing *to* get," Pietr continued. "He's out of your league." Stated with such simplicity it sounded undeniable.

My eyes must have gone saucer-wide at the insult. Amy's hand grabbed my wrist; my fingers were tight around the fork I was ready to launch at my newest nemesis. *"What?"* I demanded, narrowing my eyes.

He hadn't paused in his eating but had nearly finished his meat loaf and was preparing to move on to a double helping of Salisbury steak. He glanced over my head. "Jess." He fixed his glinting eyes on me. "You are a thinker. You probably get good grades and may even be on the debate team and school newspaper staff, but you aren't that guy's type. He's a jock." He chewed and swallowed. He glanced over my head again. "A popular jock, from what I can tell. And they don't date your type without a reason." He looked at me, his eyes gleaming boldly. "So what do you think a guy like *that* wants?"

My hand shook, holding the fork. I could tell without looking that Amy's fingers had gone white in her effort to restrain me. It was the most Pietr had spoken to me, and every word sliced like a knife.

Because he was right: Derek definitely wanted something.

Pietr was well into his Salisbury steak when I finally said, "What business is it of yours?" Amy released her grip on me, patting my hand. Sarah's eyes stayed on my fork, mindful there might yet be bloodshed. She freaked out pretty easily now, even if she didn't remember exactly why.

Sophia simply sucked on her straw, listening intently.

"I guess it isn't," Pietr admitted around another mouthful of meat. "I just thought a male opinion . . ." He looked beyond me *again*.

"What? Because we can't figure this sort of thing out on our own?" I leaned across the table, making it clear I could be just as much the aggressor as he could be the transgressor.

He leaned across the table to meet me, his nose nearly touching mine. The strange and nearly minty crispness of pine made my nose tingle. He smelled like the northern woods in winter. Clean, sharp, and full of mystery.

He stopped chewing, his eyes holding mine—and glittering dangerously. He swallowed. "Perhaps you should consider the motivation of people a little more honestly." He glanced again at something behind me.

I turned in my seat to see what kept taking his attention from our brutal conversation. Was it someone? No. He kept looking above. . . . The clock? *Ugh.* Did he think he was wasting time here? I faced him once more. "So what's *your* motivation, Pietr? You don't even know me!"

He pulled back, a slinking move like shadows sliding. "Good point." He smiled, a sudden slip of his lips across startlingly beautiful teeth. "I try to look out for people who look out for me. It can be a fatal flaw in my family, I suppose." His eyes seemed to cloud with memory. A blink cleared them, and he added, "You are my guide, aren't you?"

"Maybe I *shouldn't* be the one guiding you around Junction. There are a dozen girls who'd jump at the chance." I dropped the fork onto my tray so it clattered, and, reaching into my pocket, I brought his schedule into view. I slapped it down in front of him. "Just hand one of *them* your schedule, okay?"

"No." He slid the schedule back without giving it a glance. "You were assigned a job—"

"A penance, probably," I muttered.

"Whatever." He swept the last bits of food onto his fork and chewed thoughtfully. "I'm *your* problem."

"You got *that* right." I stood, leaving to empty my tray.

Pietr shadowed me as I slammed my tray into the trash, knocking it around loudly to reinforce that I was angry. Withdrawing my tray, I smacked it down on a nearby stack.

Pietr followed suit, unfazed.

"What?" I asked, pausing back at our lunch table. "Afraid I'm gonna ditch you?" I grabbed my backpack, a pencil falling out and skittering over the table.

"No. I'm not afraid." He reached past me, brushing against me as he retrieved the pencil. I shivered, a sort of static electricity snapping along the edges of my body.

As he straightened back up to offer me my pencil, I could swear he *sniffed* my hair. *Totally inappropriate.* "I could find you, regardless."

"And how do you think you'd do that? I know this school way better than you."

He glanced at my hair long enough that I fidgeted with it. "I'd find you." He was so self-assured it angered me more.

"Fine," I snapped, grabbing my pencil and glancing at the clock on the wall. "Let's just see how easy that'll be. I'll be at your next class," I added, folding his schedule and slipping it into my back pocket. "Meet me there."

He blinked at the challenge and before he could speak, the bell rang, four hundred students leaped up from scattered tables and rushed toward three sets of doors. I allowed myself to be swept away by the mob, drifting and dodging along and keeping my head low as I raced through the corridors and took stairs two at a time.

I paused on the landing between floors, certain I'd lost him. But he was suddenly at the base of the stairs. I pulled back from the banister and watched. It was odd, observing him. He swung his head from side to side, like he was searching for some invisible clue to my path.

I thought about how he'd smelled my hair. I gave it a cursory sniff. Mmm. Super-Stress-Free Mint Shampoo. Yeah. Even *it* wasn't helping my peace of mind. Maybe I needed the conditioner, too.

Pietr started up the steps, and I lurched into the jostling crowd and continued trying to evade the guy I should have been guiding.

CHAPTER FOUR

I zipped into the classroom, nearly sliding into my seat. Mr. Miles gave me a curious look. I chuckled. I had covered a vast and winding route to get to the proper social studies class. I pulled out my notebook and fumbled for a pencil. Hadn't I organized them in math? Yeah, and dropped one at lunch. I promised myself, as I continued rooting around, next time I'd actually zip up the compartment I put them in. Anyhow, I was victorious! Pietr surely would learn a lesson in humility by getting lost, and now I just needed a pencil. . . .

People began taking their seats. I could hear the groans and squeaks of the seats even with my head nearly in my bag.

Someone tapped my desk.

"What?" I asked, not looking up. Someone sat beside me. I pulled back from my backpack, only to see Pietr holding out a pencil for me.

Defiant, I thrust my hand into my bag one last time and— aha! I withdrew the pencil and held it high in triumph.

Mr. Miles boomed, "Whoever pulls the sword from the

stone, wait—the *pencil* from the backpack—she shall be . . ."
He paused dramatically, cupping his ear with a hand to signal
us to reply.

"Prepared," Pietr offered, never looking away from my face.
My sneer melted under the heat of a fierce blush.

Mr. Miles laughed. "Good enough. Pietr, right?"

Pietr nodded.

"Very good. Everyone's been talking about your family already. Not much else to do at Junction High, I guess." Mr. Miles
clapped his hands together.

"Today, students," he began, "we will be examining a mystery of World War II. Wait! Before the groans start, let's remember that World War II defined the roles many countries still play
today. Although it was a relatively recent war—I know, I know,
it was forever and a day ago, to you *whippersnappers*." He
stooped, squinted, and teasingly wheezed out the term before
continuing with a wink, "There are portions of it that we histo-
rians still eagerly research. History is not dead!" He glanced at
the room full of students and said, "Now that I've delivered our
public service announcement, you may all groan."

Everyone but Pietr and I did. Pietr watched Mr. Miles and
then glanced at me to judge my reaction. I loved history class
and would never say otherwise. Mr. Miles was so sarcastic and
quirky I felt I understood him best of all my teachers. He examined things from all angles—even the improbable ones. Like a
good reporter should. I flipped open my notebook and prepared to take a lengthy amount of notes.

Mr. Miles turned to the board and scrawled *Porrajmos*. "This
is the word that is equated with the genocide of Gypsies during
World War II. It translates to "the Devouring." We've spent
quite a bit of time on the war, the Holocaust, and its victims,
but today I think we should deal with one of the oddities. . . ."

He wrote: *Fearing the Forest*. "Man has always tried to tame the wilderness. We timber ancient forests, we strip-mine. . . . We have an instinctual fear of wild places and wild beasts, so we have historically tamed them so we feel more in control. This primitive fear impacts how we live and how we react in strange situations."

Pietr's foot began to tap softly. He glanced at Mr. Miles, then at the clock, then at his notes. Then the clock, his notes, and Mr. Miles.

Mr. Miles told us how, as Hitler sent extermination squads out after the remaining Gypsies and Jews, his troops balked at the idea of entering one forest. It was reportedly haunted, and the SS was superstitious. But Hitler didn't grasp the meaning of *no* and made them go in.

Pietr continued to fidget. He may have had a gift for attracting girls, but he also had the ability to make someone nervous. His leg began to shake, and then he began to drum the fingers of one hand on the desk softly as he wrote with the other.

"Pietr," I warned.

He stopped and focused on taking notes. For six solid minutes.

Mr. Miles explained that only two soldiers survived, and one didn't last long. The accounts they gave were so garbled they landed the sole survivor in an asylum.

Pietr was tapping again. Maybe *he* needed some time in an asylum. But an asylum might be quieter, calmer than here. I sighed, thinking about a quiet padded room with no drama. . . . Maybe *I* needed to be committed.

I set down my pencil, flexed my hand, and refocused. Mysteries and oddities of history made great fodder for stories later. I didn't intend to be a school journalist forever. And someone in an asylum was a person journalists wrote *about*—not a person who did the *writing*. I probably shouldn't view an asylum as a comfy vacation spot. Counselor Maloy might just be willing to provide me with a ticket to one.

"What do you think wiped out so many soldiers in that forest? Why did the last man go insane?" Mr. Miles tapped the board. "Let's brainstorm. Call out ideas—nothing's stupid and nothing's wrong in a brainstorming session," he reminded us.

Mr. Miles wrote *ambush, Special Forces, armed Gypsies,* and *traps* as fast as students said them. Then, as we loosened up and remembered Halloween wasn't too far away, *ghosts, vampires,* and *werewolf* made the list. Mr. Miles paused. A few girls were giggling, a thin echo of the boys chuckling in the back.

Mr. Miles said, "You may find it interesting that the one soldier who was questioned claimed things flew out of the trees and reported giant wolves swarmed out of the shadows."

The giggling gave way to "No way" and "Nuh-uh . . ."

"Uh-huh." Mr. Miles smiled. "So of course they locked him away. Now let's look here. . . ." He turned back to the brainstormed list. "These were all interesting possibilities. Let me just clear up a couple minor things. . . ."

Special Forces weren't in the area at the time, and although an ambush appeared to have happened, Gypsies would have been hard-pressed to get weapons sufficient to take out so many armed soldiers. "So these—quite ironically," Mr. Miles commented, circling them with red, "make our *impossible* list. And we all know that once the impossible is ruled out, all that remains, however improbable, is the truth."

At *ghosts, vampires,* and *werewolf,* he paused. "Only one I'd change here." He erased the end of *werewolf* and made it plural. "Think of it like this—if werewolves existed"—he winked— "wouldn't they follow a social structure somewhere between that of wolves and humans? Wouldn't they hunt and work as a team whenever possible?"

"Wait—so are you saying monsters wiped out the SS?" someone called out from the back of the room.

"Absolutely." Mr. Miles grinned. *"Monsters* destroyed the SS. Maybe not monsters like werewolves, maybe not like vampires or ghosts. Think about it. The SS was filled with—and led by—some of the cruelest monsters in history. And they were all purely human."

"So what really *did* happen in the forest?" someone else asked.

Mr. Miles shrugged. "You tell me. History's not really dead as long as the living wonder about it. And that"—he pointed to the clock, and the bell sounded—"would be the bell. Quick reminder," he added as the class began to rise. "Today you all will be heading out to your Service Learning assignments. Vans will roll out five minutes after the dismissal bell. Don't be late."

Pietr had already leaped out of his seat.

Mr. Miles ruffled through a few papers on top of his desk before saying, "Oh, Pietr. You'll tag along with Jessie. Her group could use an extra member."

Pietr nodded, accepting his fate without question. I nearly smacked my forehead on the desk in frustration.

I jostled my books and papers together, shoving them unceremoniously into my backpack as I kept an eye on the clock. My Service Learning assignment was the one place I could forget about everything else that was (and had been) going on. I was assigned to the Golden Oaks Adult Day Care and Retirement Home in town. Brimming with people who averaged twice the age of my parents—my parent, I mentally corrected myself—I could focus on the idea that people could grow old without tragedy.

Sure, Golden Oaks wasn't the happiest place—there were lots of people whose relatives avoided them as if old age were catching—but that's where my Service Learning group came in.

I hopped to my feet, dodging out the classroom door and down the hall. I paused at my locker, spun the dial, and yanked the handle. Another moment and I'd made the exchange of class stuff for home stuff and slammed my locker shut. There was Pietr, his backpack slung carelessly over one shoulder, glancing from me to the clock hanging in the hallway and back.

"Gotta hot date?" I asked.

"What?"

"The way you're always watching the clock. I figured there was someplace you'd rather be."

"Maybe," he said.

"Let's go," I muttered, heading out. Our van was already idling outside along with others.

Sarah was in the distance, getting ready to do her part. I felt sorry for her immediately. She always looked so out of place now if she wasn't with Amy and me. Jenny and Macie were beside her, sweeping her along with them into their waiting van. It was one thing I hadn't been able to fix for her: Service Learning assignments were basically set in stone.

Amy waved to me from farther down the line. With a grin she slid into the van, her off-and-on boyfriend, Marvin, with her. She didn't often talk about her assignment. There were certain restrictions, including maintaining strict confidentiality, placed on everyone in her program.

Participants in Amy's assignment couldn't give clients' names or interact with any of the people they helped outside of the program's scheduled hours. I couldn't handle that. I had to get everything out. Well, at least, I used to. Although Amy couldn't say much about helping specific "clients" get their emotions out through art, when she *did* talk about what she was allowed to talk about, she glowed with satisfaction.

I glanced over my shoulder. Pietr was there. Of course.

I motioned to the van, and we both climbed in.

"Cool, Jessie brought us the Russian," a voice from the back proclaimed. Jaikin snapped shut his magnetic chess set and stared at Pietr as if viewing a new species of animal. Hascal, my favorite gamer with absolutely no game of his own, and Smith, captain of the debate team, chuckled at Jaikin's overt enthusiasm.

"I'm concerned that this addition to our group will negatively impact my odds of getting to take you to the senior prom, Jessie," Smith said with a sniff.

I turned in my seat and saw him leaning across the back of it, arms hanging over my side as he smiled impishly at me. "Oh, Smith." I patted his cool, pale arm. "You know an amazing brain does far more for me than a nice face and a hot body."

His smile grew into a grin, but the geniuses sitting as his bookends piped up with, "Ohhh, she thinks Pietr's got a hot body!"

"That was *not* what I meant." I seethed. I tried to get myself back in control, modulate my tone and my pitch, and think of a snappy comeback, but . . . nothing.

On the bench in front of me I noticed Pietr's shoulders going up and down. He was chuckling.

"Besides," I said, "dear, dear Smith, you know I only have eyes for one man." I glanced toward Pietr. His chuckling had stopped and he seemed somehow stiffer, knowing I wasn't talking about him.

Jaikin followed it up with, "Oh, yes—the power of unrequited love."

Hascal sneezed. "'Scuthe me," he said, reaching into a pocket for a tissue.

"Allergies?" I asked, although I knew the answer.

"Yeth," Hascal admitted. "But ith highly improbable. I only react thith way to thertain memberth of the canid family."

"Canid?"

"Dogth, jackalth, wolvth . . . ," he muttered, trying to be nonchalant. I barely kept from laughing as his every *s* became a *th*.

"Jessie, you're way too good for Derek," Smith jumped in. "I admit I can understand the attraction—"

Hascal and Jaikin spun and looked at him, eyes wide.

"No, not like *that*—I mean, not that there's anything wrong with that," he qualified. "But as a strictly objective observer aware of what the average adolescent female finds attractive in a male of the species, I can understand what Jessie might presuppose about the masculine attributes of Derek Jamieson," he specified, wiping his brow and taking a deep breath.

"Oh, now stop talking that way, Smith. You know it just makes me *desperate* to hear more . . ." I grinned at him.

Jaikin and Hascal started cracking up.

Smith looked slightly peeved.

From the front I heard Pietr turn around to watch the show. I tried to ignore that fact. The boys and I had been playing the flirting game since the start of freshman year, when we were lumped into this assignment together. I tried out my most ridiculous material and moves on them, they returned the favor, and we were usually rolling with laughter by the time the van pulled in to the lot at Golden Oaks.

The boys took my mind off everything else. They were brilliant and awkward but, most important, they were safe. After graduation they'd be off to Silicon Valley, and me—I'd be trying to find life beyond Junction.

"Go on, Smith, say something else—say *algorithm*," I purred, rolling the *r* and leaning across the seat. Jaikin and Hascal collapsed in hysterics. The corner of Smith's mouth twitched into a smile.

The van stopped.

"We're here," Pietr announced, stepping out.

"Does he always state the obvious?" Smith asked, adjusting his glasses.

"So far," I said with a shrug and a glance at Pietr.

He looked down at me. "I've found the obvious is too often overlooked."

Hascal grinned. "Like common thenth being quite uncommon." He snorted and blew his nose again.

"Yeah, yeah," I said, waving a hand dismissively.

"Thank goodneth for fresh air," Hascal whispered.

"You're looking better already," I encouraged.

Pietr paused in the parking lot, his eyes roaming the brick structure that comprised most of Golden Oaks' living quarters. I wondered briefly what he was really seeing as he looked and I turned to examine the building again myself. It was standard 1970s construction, from what I'd been told, and as red as brick could be. Some of the details were starting to smudge under the thumb of time; corners and ledges weren't as sharp or strong as they were in their prime. But the facility was well maintained and its people well loved. I hoped Pietr would see that, too, once we started inside.

"So what do we do here?" Pietr asked. He looked at the face of his cell phone. Another clock.

I blinked at him. "Help improve people's quality of life."

"Is that on some brochure?" he asked. "It's catchy, but what do we really do? How long do we have to stay? There are things I'd rather be doing—"

"I hope one of them is shutting your mouth and realizing we don't just . . . ugh!" I exclaimed in frustration, "We don't *just* live our lives for ourselves," I retorted.

Hascal wrapped an arm around my shoulders, dragging me forward. "That's Jessie's new motto," he explained.

I immediately understood that to Hascal "new" equated with "since the accident."

"What was your old motto?" Pietr asked.

Annoying Pietr. "I didn't have one," I admitted.

Madge greeted us by the local animal shelter's van, where it was parked near Golden Oaks' main entrance. The shelter loaned us a few of its permanent residents each week so we could make our rounds. Madge looked far less ham-like. She smiled and tugged gently on a leash wrapped around her legs. "This is Tag," she said as a little pug waddled out from behind her.

"Wow!" I said, looking at its bulging eyes. The tip of its tongue stuck out beneath its squished nose, giving Tag the look of something that had run head-on into a fence post. More than once. "He's so—"

Pietr jumped in with, "Ugly, he's—"

"*Adorable,*" I snapped. I glared at him, patting Tag. "I'll take Tag," I offered, accepting the leash and scooping him into my arms. He felt like he was lead-loaded. I silently hoped he was absolutely *not* loaded. With anything. I readjusted my grip. "Did you bring Victoria?" I asked.

Hascal, Smith, and Jaikin stepped back.

I looked at them skeptically. "With all the allergies you guys have to different stuff, I'm surprised any of you can handle anything other than fish and reptiles."

"Amphibians are cool, too," Jaikin insisted.

"Literally," Smith quipped.

Hascal pouted. "Speak for yourselves," he said. "They give me hives."

"I have Victoria," Madge confirmed. She reached into a cat carrier and extracted an adorable kitten. As she held it out for Pietr, what had been a cute ball of colorful fur unrolled to become a spitting, hissing, absolutely insane calico kitten. A calico kitten capable of starting bloodbaths and devastating humanity like a fanged plague.

Madge looked shocked as Victoria tried to maul Pietr with paws no bigger than his thumb. And tiny, razor-sharp claws. "I think she just needs to be better socialized," Madge suggested.

"And you accuse *me* of stating the obvious," Pietr muttered in my direction.

"Dude," Hascal whispered, "I think you're bleeding."

Madge handed him a pack of Band-Aids. "She's always so sweet to the old folks. . . ."

Pietr carefully held Victoria by the nape of the neck, up and out in front of him.

She twisted and batted. Snarled. Spat—she was a whirlwind of fur and whiskers.

Pietr looked her directly in the eyes and said, "This is ridiculous behavior," in a totally parental tone. I heard the faintest hint of an accent in his carefully chosen words. "I know you don't like me, and—and frankly—you aren't doing anything to encourage my potential interest in cats."

Victoria spat again.

"But we have a job to do," Pietr pointed out. "I would appreciate your assistance." He blinked at her. Once.

And then Victoria just stopped hissing and growling and, instead, mewed. She turned from crazed to cute in a heartbeat.

Pietr said, "Thank you," and, resting her in the crook of his arm, suggested we get started before she changed her mind.

Madge said, "If you can do that consistently, boy, do I have a job for you."

Pietr shook his head as the other guys chose animals, too.

Once inside, we boarded the elevator to begin our rounds. My boys got the first two floors; Pietr and I got the third and fourth. As the elevator doors opened, he wrinkled his nose.

"It reminds me of a hospital," I confessed.

"I hate hospitals," he replied.

"As much as you hate *Romeo and Juliet*?"

He smiled at the comparison. "Almost exactly."

"Let's start at Mrs. Feldman's," I said, leading the way. I knocked on her door.

"Come in, come in!"

I ran my hand across the chimes that hung from her door-jamb, enjoying their sparkling sound. "I just don't understand why you hate *Romeo and Juliet*," I said as we entered.

Mrs. Feldman's eyes grew wide. "Who hates *Romeo and Juliet*?" she asked, her gaping mouth accentuated by the stretched and ghostly wrinkles of laugh lines. She set aside the strange cards she was shuffling, tucking them into one of the folds of her voluminous and colorful skirt.

I looked at Pietr accusingly, then moved a small, wheeled table covered with a variety of stones and colorful crystals out of my way to stand beside Mrs. Feldman so she could pet Tag. "*He* hates *Romeo and Juliet*."

"Well, finally!" she exclaimed. "A sensible young man!"

Pietr beamed.

"Close your mouth," she instructed me. "You'll only catch flies that way."

I obeyed.

"Why anyone finds that play romantic is beyond me. Both Romeo and Juliet are so"—her jaw worked silently, pushing her expression around until she found the word—"naïve! Instead of enlisting their friends' help, they go behind everyone's backs, lying." She snorted.

"The cat, please," she said, her fingers twinkling with gaudy rings set with chunky stones. "Why you must always bring cats and dogs eludes me," she whispered as Pietr stepped to her other side. "Why not a little bunny? They're so cute and inno-cent. Cats are always thinking up trouble." But she petted Vic-toria, her hands relaxing at the feel of plush fur. Victoria purred so loudly Tag wiggled around to watch.

"Hmph. Romeo and Juliet. The boy—Romeo!" Mrs. Feld-man shook her head. "Hardly a romantic hero. He was head over heels for Rosaline, and then—poof! She's out-of-sight-out-of-mind as soon as Juliet comes into view." She grimaced. "And why does he really want Juliet?" She looked at me, waiting for an answer. "Why?" she prompted.

"He thinks she's beautiful," I said softly.

"Pah! She's unattainable! He knows he can't truly have her, so he wants her even more! They're so blinded by hormones—*hormones!*" She set Victoria on her lap and petted her. "They think love will be *easy*." Putting her lips together, she blew, re-minding me of my horses. "Pah! They wouldn't know love if it—if it"—she held Victoria out, giving her a little shake in emphasis—"*bit* them."

CHAPTER FIVE

Pietr flinched when the kitten was thrust into his arms, but Victoria simply curled back up.

"I like you, boy," Mrs. Feldman said. "You're not like those other ones she traipses around with. Simpering, lily-livered fools. What's your name?"

"Pietr Rusakova."

"A Russian?" She peered at Pietr more closely, her milky blue eyes glittering. "Are you a Commie?"

Pietr looked wary but answered nonetheless. "I'm not sure of my particular political affiliation yet."

Mrs. Feldman snorted again. "Good for you. This one's got balls, Jessie. Those others would have wheezed out whatever they thought I wanted to hear."

A nurse entered, smiling as she held out a tiny cup of pills. "It's time for your medicine, Hazel," she said gently.

Mrs. Feldman grasped the plastic cup and squinted at the pills. "Hormones!" she proclaimed conspiratorially. She grabbed the flowery cane resting by her bed and pointed it toward the nurses' station. "It's because that young doctor"—she shook her cane at a man in a long white coat—"likes older women."

With a wicked smile she slugged back the pills and chased them with water, insinuating that it was fine with a quick move of her eyebrows. She winked, saying, "But that's all right, because I like younger men!" She laughed as the nurse scooted us off to another room.

"Well," I said. "That was—" I wanted just the right word . . .

"Educational?" Pietr tried.

I smiled despite everything. "Yes," I agreed.

We walked the rest of the third floor, letting people who often had too few human visitors enjoy a little companionship of the animal kind.

In the elevator I was silent as Pietr shifted from foot to foot, glancing at the cell phone in his hand.

"Cell not getting a signal?" I asked as the elevator doors slid open.

"What?"

"Or are you just watching the time again?"

"*Prosteetcheh*," he said.

"Pro-what?"

"*Sorry. Da.* I don't like feeling caged. Makes me nervous," he said, pocketing the phone again.

"Taking the stairs is healthier, I guess. We'll take them on our way out." Greeting patients on the fourth floor was easy until we got to the last two rooms. "Oh."

I stopped at room 427. The door was open a bit, and I could see two empty beds. A nurse came up behind me to explain. "Mrs. Maier died on Saturday, and Mr. Maier followed on Sunday." She patted my shoulder. "It happens—dying of a broken heart."

"I didn't expect . . ." But my sentence died, too.

Pietr nudged me. "Come on," he said, "before Victoria forgets our little talk."

I tried to smile, but it was halfhearted.

"No one lives forever," he said.

He had no idea how well I understood that most simple and cruel fact. His hand on my shoulder, he steered me away.

I saw how comfortable Victoria looked, resting in the crook of his arm. If *she* could trust him, he wasn't too bad.

"You two look chummy," I commented.

His brows furrowed. *"Da,* surprising," he murmured.

"Not an animal lover?"

"Nyet . . . I love animals," he said, but his tone made me think of the way I'd say *I love pizza.*

I glanced at the next room number on our list. "This is our last one today. Everyone else either has allergies or objections to animals." I knocked on the door. "Hello?"

"Come in, child."

"Oh! Ms. Fritz! I didn't expect *you* here." I shivered. "Aren't you cold?" A breeze pushed through a window at the far side of her room, tugging her curtains and tossing around the "Get Well" cards on her bureau.

"A little." She smiled, wrapped in a blanket she was knitting. "I got moved up here a couple days ago," she explained. "They won't let me out to enjoy the autumn air. Not since I did this. . . ." She pulled up her pant leg, revealing an ankle cast.

"Ms. Fritz!"

"I was out power walking late," she explained, glancing down before continuing. "I got startled and fell."

"Oh, Ms. Fritz." I moved Tag into proper petting position. "What—" I tried for a synonym and failed. "What *startled* you?" She seemed embarrassed by her fall, but I hoped by talking about it she'd get over it. I nearly ground my teeth at the thought—it was the same theory Guidance tried on me. As if just talking about something lessened the pain.

"Oh, Jessie, are you trying to scoop a story?" she teased. "Jessie is quite the writer," she addressed Pietr.

He raised his eyebrows.

"Now, Ms. Fritz, nobody cares about that. Besides, how good can I be as often as I fumble for the right words?"

"That's when you *talk*. When you write, you are eloquent."

"Oh, my writing's horrible, too. It's in editing where I excel." I grinned. I got the sense Pietr was amused by the way we bantered. "So what was it?"

"Some animal in the woods. It growled—" She shivered.

"Pietr, get the window," I requested.

"It sounded big, like a large dog. And I remembered what I'd heard about what happened in Farthington. . . ."

I heard Pietr stop.

"The window," I urged. "What happened then?"

"Well, I tripped. I must have made an awful racket falling, because this young man—a jogger, I guess—came running to help me. He picked me up and carried me to his car"—she paused, relishing the memory—"Full-leather interior," she detailed, "and drove me straight here. Amazing vehicle—the engine snarled and purred more smoothly than Victoria's very finest."

"I didn't know you were a car fanatic, Ms. Fritz."

She smiled. "The driver was a handsome devil, too," she added. "Dark hair and absolutely brilliant eyes." She sighed. "I was lucky he was so close."

I turned to see what progress Pietr was making. He set Victoria down to unstick what was obviously a stubborn window. A pigeon landed on the ledge outside, twitching its feathers before it began to strut. It cooed, evidently looking to coax a little love from a bird yet unseen.

"Uh—" Victoria uncurled and, as Pietr pressed once more against the window's edge, preoccupied, she leaped after the self-involved bird. "Oh, my God! Pietr!"

He ducked out the window just behind her.

I dropped Tag into Ms. Fritz's lap and raced to the window. Sticking my head out, I saw Pietr crouched on the narrow, crackled brick ledge, Victoria just a little over an arm's length beyond. The pigeon had flown away, leaving Victoria and Pietr without a similar option. "Holy crap, Pietr," I admonished, but quietly, so I didn't startle either of them. "Leave the cat out there. Come back inside."

"I can get her," he insisted, the purr of his accent returning as he concentrated.

"We'll lure her back with food." I made the mistake of looking out the window and down. Straight below was the main awning and sidewalk. Four stories straight down. The breeze picked up again. "Come back in."

But instead of obeying, he leaned forward, stretched out his arm, and wiggled his fingers, inches from the nape of Victoria's neck.

"Pietr," I whispered to his back.

And as he stretched forward I heard a crunch and a crack and watched in horror as the ledge gave way and Pietr—

—fell.

I couldn't watch. I must have screamed, and I tore back through Ms. Fritz's room babbling incoherently at the nurse's station. They called for a doctor even as I bounded down the four flights of stairs. I wouldn't have made it in the elevator— talk about feeling caged! I was out the doors and on the side- walk—as were gawkers, nurses, and doctors.

Stunned and still in the full grip of horror, I couldn't stop walking forward. I had to see what was left of the new guy at Junction High. Peering over the shoulders of the crouched doctors and nurses, my fist wedged between my teeth, I saw him.

Laughing. And holding Victoria.

"What the—"

A doctor turned, shaking his head. "Dislocated shoulder, possibly a broken arm. Caught himself on the awning and somehow used its metal frame. He's a lucky S.O."—he caught himself—"a lucky, lucky boy. Cat's probably got two less lives, though. Had to spend them saving the boy and herself."

Evidently I wasn't the only one stunned.

"Jess," Pietr called. "Take—" he winced. "Take the cat, please. I think we've been through enough together."

He was being helped to his feet.

I blinked and accepted the kitten.

He gritted his teeth and reached one hand into his jeans pocket and pulled out his cell phone. He flipped it open. "Alexi. Pick me up at Golden Oaks Adult Day Care. *Da*. Now's best. *Da*. I'm definitely done for the day." He clicked it shut and slipped it back into his pocket, wincing again.

A nurse suggested, "You should really have an X-ray and get the bone set if it's broken."

He just smiled at her. "My brother will take care of it."

"Aspirin?" she asked.

He blinked. "*Da*. Two, please."

I stood there on the sidewalk as the crowd cleared. I just petted Victoria. And stared at Pietr.

"What?"

"I thought—"

"What? That I'd died?" He looked back up the way he'd fallen. "I didn't."

"There you go, stating the obvious again."

"Well, you're the one who said we don't live our lives just for ourselves."

"It wasn't like I was giving you an order. Seriously." I rolled my eyes and focused them back on him. "Really? So you walk out onto a ledge after a kitten with anger-control issues?"

His smile slid into a full-sized grin. "Not my brightest moment."

"Yeah. That's an understatement."

"Guess it's catching," he muttered.

"What?"

"Stating the obvious."

I opened my mouth to respond, but there simply were no words. So I shut it again.

Behind me I heard the hoots and hollers of Hascal, Smith, and Jaikin as they raced outside and put the whole scene together with what they must have heard. "Holy Hell," Hascal shouted, "That was totally bad-ass!"

I heard a car squeal into the parking lot, sliding to a perfectly positioned stop as if it had been carefully parallel parked at the edge of the sidewalk beside Pietr. It was a beautiful cherry red convertible. Not something many folks near a town like Junction would have. *Could* have. The engine settled into a purr as the passenger's door swung open, revealing a full-leather interior and a handsome young man with dark hair and brilliant eyes.

My mouth gaped open again and in the back of my head a small voice proclaimed thanks for few flies to catch in autumn.

"Get in, idiot," the driver said to Pietr.

I looked back up toward the open window. Ms. Fritz leaned out, waving frantically at the spotless red convertible. "Oh! Hello, Alex!" she yelled. I could just see and hear a nurse saying,

"Come away from the window now, Ms. Fritz. You shouldn't be on your feet."

Ms. Fritz responded, "That's my Alex. He's everybody's hero, I guess."

Pietr looked at the car's driver and then up to Ms. Fritz. "Small town," he commented.

"*Da*, small town," the driver agreed.

"My ride," Pietr said, looking over his shoulder at me. "Tomorrow?"

I nodded, and continued standing there, slack-jawed, Victoria in hand.

Pietr smiled at me, and then, carefully, got into the car. "So I hear you've started jogging," he said to Alexi.

Alexi snapped, "Let's go," in reply before the car peeled away with a snarl.

I stood there, watching it zip out of the lot. The nurse returned with a cup of water and two aspirins. "Oh," she said. "I guess he didn't need these after all."

I stuck out my hand. "I'll take them," I said softly. "I feel a headache coming on."

Back home, I saddled Rio and went riding. Always up for an adventure, Maggie and Hunter accompanied us until their tongues neared purple and their sides heaved. As Rio wound her way along the farm's outskirts at a trot, I considered the odd new guy at Junction High.

I had to admit it: He definitely had me flustered. He was utterly disinterested in everything and ticking me off. And maybe I needed to be more like my mother and just forgive people's faults. I was certainly doing my damnedest to forgive when it came to Sarah. . . .

I pushed away from where that line of thought led and nudged Rio into a gallop, thoughts of Pietr returning. When he was focused, for even a minute, his intensity startled me. There was a quality about him I couldn't quite define, something beyond the new-boy mystique and even the foreign feel of everything he did. It went deeper than him being of Russian heritage. He was out of place in Junction, but I had no idea why it seemed he was even more out of place than I normally felt.

Rio's head snapped up, her neck stiffening as the reins went slack in my hand.

"What?"

She stopped in the middle of our regular trail and pawed at the path. I looked around. All along the trail's edge the briars, brush, and brambles sported leaves in autumn's colors. A breeze stirred their branches and canes. And then I noticed what made her body tense beneath me.

A hole was torn in the trail's edge, as if something large had ripped right through the thorns. Something strong. Not as big as a horse or— "Steady, girl," I whispered as I slid off the saddle. I wrapped her reins around my fist. Rio followed.

"Wow." Whatever had rocketed through here had uprooted whole plants. And . . . I reached out to grab the thick tuft of fur still wrapped around one particularly sturdy berry bush. It had left a little of itself here, too.

Rio rolled her eyes.

"Rio, it's just fur." Thick fur. Auburn and long like the darkest color on a collie. But collies didn't bust holes in thorny underbrush. I rubbed it between my thumb and fingers. It didn't have the slightly greasy feel of most dogs' hair, either. I sniffed at it, remembering how Pietr had sniffed my hair. Seriously? I sniffed again. It smelled nearly sweet, like its owner had been recently deodorized or spritzed with perfume. Way too fancy for a simple farm dog. "There's definitely something strange going on around here," I confirmed to my nervous equine companion. I tucked the wad of fur into my jeans pocket and climbed back onto Rio.

Pulling the reins, I turned Rio's head toward home. What was going on? Strange dogs, bizarre boys . . . I tried to clear my head. My thoughts returned to Pietr. Definitely weird.

Had I ever felt so off balance with Derek? I shook my doubt away. I absolutely adored Derek. Didn't I? Of course! He was spectacular. And he might finally—finally—be interested in *me*.

But how bizarre was surviving a fall like that?

I dismounted and walked Rio into the barn and down the broad aisle to her stall. A few of the other horses whinnied and snorted greetings. Hunter and Maggie milled around a hay bale, digging at its edge. A mouse squeaked and the dogs redoubled their efforts to drag it out.

I slipped the bridle over Rio's ears and off her head, rubbing the places it had pressed her hair down. I froze and she snorted.

"Hello?" I called.

No answer. I got the undeniable feeling I was being watched.

The dogs stood and looked at me, tongues lolling, the mouse forgotten.

The evening breeze shifted, scattering bits of hay and a puff of dust. Carrying scents from outside. The fur on both Maggie's and Hunter's backs rose into crests.

"Who's there?" I demanded, my voice bolder than I felt.

And then the sensation of eyes on me faded and the dogs relaxed, their fur settling, tails wagging once more.

"Things are getting way too weird around here," I confided as I unsaddled Rio and quickly brushed her down.

With Rio back in her stall and her tack away for the night, I headed inside. I stepped into the kitchen briefly and grabbed a sandwich bag. Sneaking past Dad dozing in his recliner, I thought better of it. I crept over beside him and gently kissed his wrinkled forehead; it was starting to smooth only in sleep.

I climbed the stairs to my room and unlocked my door, locking it back before turning on the lights. My little sister was a snoop and a rat—at best. I did a quick check to see if Annabelle Lee had managed to pick the lock and mess with my stuff. Frankly, the search probably wasn't worth my time since she had such an eye for detail. Nothing would be left out of place unless it served some purpose.

But I did my visual inventory anyhow, reading each of the headlines that crowded my small bulletin board, hoping to quiet my undeniable nerves:

"Russian Mafia accepts Moniker of 'Werewolves' from Newly Envisioned Mafia Card Game."

"Dog-Eat-Dog World of Russian Mafia."

"Phantom Wolf of Farthington: Paw Prints Too Big for Gray Wolf."

"Crazy Cryptos at It Again: Cryptozoologists Proclaim Phantom Paw Prints Prove Bigfoot."

They were exactly as I'd left them. Sighing, I reached into my jacket pocket and pulled out the newest addition, carefully unfolding it.

I read it out loud as I pinned it to the corkboard. "'Werewolves of a Different Breed: Sinister Links to Russian Mafia Found in Farthington.'" Excellent. Even if the new guy at Junction High wasn't forthcoming about Farthington, I could still do research.

I dug the strange fur sample out of my pants pocket and slipped it into the plastic Baggie. I pinned it to the bulletin board, too.

I sat on my bed and yanked off my sneakers. Tugging off my socks I noticed my big toe was nearly peeking through one.

Well, at least it wasn't like anyone else knew. Reaching up, I opened my sock drawer. My hand patted along the bare bottom of the drawer. Nuts. Definitely laundry day. I stood to get a better look, reaching past my old shooting medals cluttering the drawer as I attempted to find a pair of socks without holes.

Dad sometimes asked why I didn't hang up the medals from my brief stint with competitive pistol shooting—give them pride of place since I'd earned them with hours of practice. But every time I looked at them I ached knowing that for every hour I had practiced that solitary sport I had lost an hour with my mother. Forever.

In my opinion, life passed too quickly to spend it holed up on a pistol range shooting holes in paper targets—alone.

The nightmare greeted me as invitingly as any night—beautiful and innocuous as a jack-in-the-pulpit, and just as foul a trap. It always opened the same way, with me standing under the dogwood tree as the sun faded into a glorious glow of pink, orange, and purple. I hit SEND on my cell phone, Mom looking radiant as an angel when her picture automatically popped up on the tiny screen. "Yeah, I'll be under the dogwood," I confirmed. "On your way? Awesome." Then I flipped it shut. No "I love you" or "Thanks a bunch."

That small part of me that knew I was deep in the grasp of the nightmare tensed, urging me to change some detail . . . to lessen the pain it knew was coming. But I couldn't. I struggled; my body surely twisted in my bed, but the connection of my real self to my dream self was just strong enough that dread and anguish felt real and inseparable to both.

And then, as quickly as I'd realized I was too weak to change the past, I saw Mom's car turn into the parking lot. I heard the squeal of tires . . . the crunch and shattering noise of two equally matched titans meeting, the chattering sound that comes when two things that shouldn't rub together *do*. . . . I screamed, choking on the smell of burning rubber.

I felt eyes on me—strangely brilliant eyes—watching with an odd detachment equally distant and fascinated, like an alien observing human tragedy for the first time and not knowing how to dull the victim's pain. Not knowing if it *should* be dulled.

I woke, my pillow strangled in my arms, my chest heaving. I repeated my mantra: *I can get through this. I will get through this.* This was the normal part of night for me. I sat up, glancing around my room, half-expecting the eyes to be there, glowing back at me. They were a new addition to my nightly terror, and I wondered what they meant. Or if they meant anything at all.

CHAPTER SIX

I was glad to get back in the normal swing of things the next morning. The weirdness surrounding the new guy at Junction High left me feeling totally off balance. My dreams had been different—not a bad thing, really, when I considered what usually greeted me in sleep—but it was so exhausting.

That morning on the bus Stella Martin (the local gossip-queen wannabe) leaned across the aisle to talk. Life just kept getting better and better. "Those Rusakova boys are pretty hot," Stella said, as if it were a natural way to open a conversation.

I shrugged.

"Seriously?" she asked. "I mean, I know you're still crushing on Derek—*everyone* knows that—but I think Pietr really likes you. I saw the way he watches you," she added to justify her assumption.

I sighed. "Stella. He hasn't been here long enough to *really* like anyone," I protested.

She snorted. "Haven't you ever felt a crazy attraction to somebody? You know, like something that defies explanation?"

"You mean love at first sight?" I smirked.

"Not *love* at first sight. Lust at first sight. Haven't you ever just wanted something?"

"Yes. Yes I have," I admitted. She leaned closer. I looked into her pale blue eyes and said, "Every time a new vampire novel comes out I *want* it."

Stella groaned. "I don't get girls like you."

I laughed. "I've heard that before." It was one of the phrases signaling the death knell of many of my relationships. That and: *It's not you, it's me.*

"Have you ever thought that instead of reading about exciting stuff, maybe you should make some excitement yourself?"

I blinked. "I've had enough excitement recently, thank you." I turned to the window just as the bus rolled into the parking lot, ignoring the way my stomach quivered. Because, like it or not, there was something about Pietr Rusakova that excited me. So it was even smarter for me to stay away and regain my emotional balance instead of being swept up in some crazy infatuation about the new boy.

The best way for me to regain my balance, as lousy as it was, was to recommit to my education. Even if it meant actually *trying* in gym class.

I caught up to Pietr in the hallway before homeroom, still not relieved of my guide duties thanks to Junction's hectically switching A-B schedule. "Huh. You're here."

"*Da*. I don't have a choice," he said.

I wondered if that was a clue about the cop accompaniment yesterday but didn't want to bring it up. It was surprisingly easy to forget that Pietr had a past that somehow included law enforcement. Oh, well. I could ask about it later and maybe try again for an interview about the Phantom Wolf of Farthington.

"Wait right here after homeroom," I instructed in my most authoritative voice, pointing to the glossy floor.

He nodded, the same curt movement as yesterday, but his eyes glinted in response.

"Unless you're ready to give me an interview about Farthington . . ."

He shook his head, a clear *no*.

Fine. I wondered if he'd noticed the way I'd looked him up and down. No cast. No sling. "Arm's okay?"

Again, he nodded.

Total weirdness. Shaking my head, I realized an arm in a cast would probably only have improved Pietr's popularity. The whole sympathy angle of attraction would be invoked. Disgusting.

I headed to the library. Ten minutes before homeroom started. No problem. The topic I was researching was one I'd followed forever. Although I'd exhausted all resources directly related to the Phantom Wolf attacks, I was certain there was something I was overlooking. Something else must have happened before the wolf attacks. Something weird.

I pulled up Google. Farthington plus wolves, coyotes, fox, and bear—I'd zipped through reports on all of them. Any strange animal activity in Farthington that hit the Web had my eyeballs all over it. I'd even collected the weird stuff—things from folks dismissed as wackos. Werewolves, Bigfoot, even Mafia references dotted my bedroom walls. There had to be an answer to the whole Phantom Wolf fiasco. Maybe I needed to broaden my search. Look outside of Farthington. What else weird had happened—maybe before the first Phantom Wolf prints were found? Weird news, plus . . . I added a year to the search.

"Man Swallowed by Goat."

"Elvis Alive and Making Pizzas in Nevada." Okay, weird, but not *my* kind of weird . . .

"CIA Swamped by Tons of Russian Documents." *Huh*. I clicked the link. Wow. That *was* lots of paperwork! The photo showed a warehouse filled with stack after stack of file boxes, each label reading C.C.C.P.

At the right side of the photo stood a female agent—just her back, from head to waist, hair pulled back in a startlingly severe ponytail. The edge of her face was visible enough I could see determination and satisfaction firming her jawline.

The caption read:

> Enough Russian Cold War research shared with U.S.A. to bury Agency for years. Agents overwhelmed as they try to find important documents amidst piles of questionable resources.

Well, it wasn't what I was really looking for, but keeping it might remind me to quit complaining whenever I felt buried in homework. I hit PRINT and snagged the single page it spit out before rushing to homeroom.

Homeroom was the same as always. Dull, dull, dull. I didn't mind. I pored over the printout. It seemed the Russians had shared nearly every one of their coveted documents from the Cold War period in a show of friendship that some felt was suspicious because it happened as U.S. agencies were spread thin dealing with the Russian mafia. Hmm. I folded up the paper and slid it into my pocket to be hung on my bulletin board later.

Already standing outside his homeroom door, Pietr watched me come down the hall. He raised one eyebrow and looked at the floor with obvious dramatic intent. He glanced up at me and took a careful step to the side. "Right *here*, you said," he stated, his smile sly.

I pursed my lips to stop from falling into his trap and smiling. "Where's your gaggle of followers?" I asked, like it mattered. And it didn't. Really.

He shrugged, but I noticed him touch a thin silver chain hanging around his neck. I hadn't noticed it before.

"Cool chain."

He nodded and tucked it a little more effectively under his shirt.

Down the hall we went. "Nuts!" I exclaimed. "I forgot something."

"To your locker?" he suggested. "We still have four minutes."

I nodded. "Coach isn't a stickler about being tardy, anyhow."

"Hey," Amy greeted me in the hall, and turned away from the door of her class to follow me. "Hey, Pietr," she acknowledged.

He smiled at her.

Students still milled around·in the hallway, procrastinating all the way to their classrooms.

I was digging in my locker when Pietr leaned toward me and spoke again.

"You look really nice today."

My breath caught. Probably because I'd stirred some dust up in the bottom of my locker. I really needed to clean it out soon.

"That's a pretty lame compliment," a deeper male voice rumbled behind us.

I turned around to see Pietr's brother—was his name Maximilian? I tried to remember the name tag he'd been labeled with in the Guidance Office yesterday.

"Max." He introduced himself with a bold grin.

He had Pietr's attention. And Amy's. Giving myself a moment to look at him, I could understand why. He was tall and broad across the shoulders with a mop of hair so dark it was nearly black. Certainly not hard to look at. I had to give Stella credit. The Rusakova boys were pretty hot.

"The proper way to hit on a girl," Max was saying to Pietr, who looked like he would sink into the floor, he was so embarrassed, "is like this."

Max turned all his focus to Amy. "Hey," he said with a nod of his head.

She froze like a deer in the headlights of an oncoming car.

Max slowly let his gaze wander the length of her body before his eyes came back to hold her own. "You have to let them know you're looking," he whispered to Pietr. As if we'd gone deaf.

Pietr squeezed his eyes shut, his brow wrinkling. He groaned—an apologetic sound.

Max raised his arm and rested his palm flat on a locker, leaning over slightly. "Getting an arm up to shoulder height or higher," he whispered to Pietr, "helps accentuate the triangulation of your body. Girls like that."

Amy certainly didn't seem to mind.

He grinned at Amy. I'd read enough romance books parading as paranormals to have stumbled across dozens of descriptions of roguish smiles. They all paled in comparison to the dangerous twist of Max's lips. In this case, words were not enough. "You look absolutely rockin' in that shirt," he said.

Pietr raised an eyebrow.

"Lowering the pitch of your voice," Max continued coaching, "makes you sound even stronger. And whispering"—his voice grew softer—"is a way to get her to lean in closer."

His gaze drifted away from Amy's eyes and past her lips. Falling down.

The crack as her hand slapped Max's face made both Pietr and me jump.

"And staring at my boobs'll get you smacked," Amy replied with a grin of her own.

Max rubbed his jaw but never stopped smiling. He chuckled as he straightened, looking at her with newfound respect. "Sorry, Red."

"The name's Amy," she corrected, rubbing her hands together. She winced. "Thickheaded," she muttered. "Here are a couple tips for you, Max. Learn a chick's name first. Focus on a girl's face. Eye contact? *That's* hot."

"Hey, Max." Stella had found us. She slipped her arms around his waist and peered at Amy.

Max didn't even seem to notice her until Amy did.

"Of course," Amy clarified, "it depends on what you're really after." Her eyes settled on Stella for a moment before she narrowed them in a glare at Max. "Some people will settle for less than they deserve. I won't let Jessie do that."

I blushed at her protective tone.

"You're a good friend," Max assessed correctly.

"The best," Amy stated.

"Come on, Max," Stella urged. "I'll walk you to class."

He followed Stella. But he nearly turned all the way back around once to look at us. Well, at Amy.

"What an ass," I said.

"Yeah," Amy muttered, staring as Max walked away. "What an a—"

"Amy!" I scolded with a laugh. "God, Pietr. Is he always like that?"

"More often than not," he admitted.

"He was kind of funny, though. Thinking you were hitting on me," I added.

Pietr's jaw tightened, but he nodded. *"Da.* Funny." He paused. "We're going to be late," he said. "Now."

The bell rang and I jumped, startled by his accuracy.

"Gotta go," Amy agreed as Pietr and I hurried off toward the gym, just the pair of us walking together in the scattering crowd, and I wondered if perhaps the new-boy mystique was already wearing thin.

"Hi, Pietr!" someone shouted from across the hall.

Izzy. Evidently Pietr had impressed Izzy beyond being brand-new to Junction. Fabulous.

"Boys' locker room." I pointed down the hall a little, hoping to avoid any Izzy-related annoyances.

"Girls' locker room." He pointed to the door directly before me, giving me a sideways smile.

I smiled back before I could stop myself. So now he was being playful about pointing out the obvious. I entered the locker room, one of the last to arrive. I wiggled out of my jeans, slipped off my T-shirt, and exchanged it for my gym uniform, emblazoned with the Junction High name and mascot.

The Junction Jackrabbit glared out from my shirt, hind legs twisted to kick an unseen opponent, the rabbit's teeth so big and pointy my dad had proclaimed it a beast worthy of a Monty Python sketch. Although I never considered myself a morning person—most mornings I felt I wasn't much of a person at all— the morning was progressing nearly normally except for the additions of Pietr and Max.

I slipped my necklace over my head and set it on the locker's top shelf and gave my jeans pocket a squeeze to reassure myself that my worry stone was still there. I hated not having it, but gym class had rules about jewelry and "accessories."

Sarah caught up to me and I asked what she was reading today. "I'm already deep into *Great Expectations.* Have you read it?"

I said, "No," although I thought I had.

Even at my fastest, I couldn't consume books as she now did. Something had flipped a switch in her brain after the accident and she'd come out of it hungry for words.

"It's amazing. It's all about moral self-improvement. The character Pip wants to be a better person and works really hard at it," she said, glowing.

"Sounds great," I said. "I'm all about the self-improvement." More important, I hoped Sarah was big on that same theme. We exited the locker room and entered the broad and open expanse of the gym. Coach Mac took a shot from the foul line with a basketball, Pietr in his shadow.

Pietr nodded at me. Girls glared in my direction, eyes daggers at the idea Pietr might have found some special connection with me. At least there were fewer of them stalking him today than yesterday. Popularity like he'd had earlier neared paparazzi-level.

The ball swished into the basket, and Coach Mac said, "Yep, Petey, that's the way we do it at Junction. *Sswish!*" Coach squeezed Pietr's shoulder before pointing to the locker room. "Derek!"

Derek swung around. "Yeah, Coach?"

"Get the fresh meat a uniform and assign him a lock."

"No problem." Derek smiled in a way that left me wondering, even as Sarah maneuvered me to the stands.

I watched Derek and Pietr disappear into the locker room together. Sarah said, "Sit," and I sat, eyes stuck to the locker room door. "What's going on with you?" Sarah waved her hand in front of my face and I gasped, jolted out of my trance.

"What?"

"What's wrong with you, Jessica? I've never seen you like this before."

"Sure, you have. Everyone has. You probably just don't re-member," I said gingerly. I ticked the times off I'd been precisely like *this* on my fingers, "Bobby Constantine in fifth grade, Aaron Johnson in sixth grade, Matt Greene in seventh grade, and Derek—"

Sarah shook her head in denial. "Yeah, you probably got a little nutty over each of your crushes, sure. But you're, like— like—" She searched for the right word, and I knew a snappy piece of vocabulary was going to be thrown my way. "You're totally *vacillating* between love and hate." She smiled.

"What?"

"You're totally up and down over him. You can't decide to love him or hate him."

"*What?*" I tried again. "I *totally* adore Derek. You know that." I rolled my eyes.

The locker room door popped open, and Derek strode out, looking sour.

"I'm not talking about *Derek*," Sarah insisted.

But I didn't pay attention because Pietr threw the door open and stepped into the gym, a dark look twisting across his face. Even so, I never thought a person could look decent in our gym uniform, but Pietr had pulled it off.

"What do you think they talked about in there?" I asked, leaning into Sarah's shoulder.

"What do guys ever talk about? If it's not about themselves, or sports, it's girls."

Stella Martin leaned forward, wedging her face between us. "Maybe they whipped out their *stuff* and compared sizes." She giggled.

I raised an eyebrow at her intrusion, but Stella always tramped around outside the bounds of common social graces and never took a hint.

Sarah blushed at the suggestion but surprised me by adding, "So who do you think won *that* competition?"

"I heard you could tell by their shoe size," Stella mentioned.

I couldn't help it—I found myself comparing sneakers in curiosity.

Sarah nodded in sage and silent agreement.

Stella crossed her arms and leaned back in the stands, out of the bubble of what I'd thought was a private conversation.

"Ridiculous," I muttered.

Coach was speaking. "So, since we're playing shirts and skins in b-ball today and Admin frowns on shirtless girls—" He winked at Amber Fox in a way that made me shiver. Amber just beamed. "You girlies are going to be on one team, but don't worry your pretty little heads, 'cause I'm also giving you our two best guys—best at any sport—Derek *the man* Jamieson and Jack *desperado* Jacobsen."

They jogged onto the court, Coach clapping.

"Come on, laay-deez!" Jack whistled what he must have thought was a rallying signal. I thought it was an insult to any self-affirming young woman. But Amber bounded out to the court as if answering a language only she could understand.

Sarah and I groaned and stalked out onto the court as well.

"Let's get everybody into position, Jack," Derek called over his shoulder as he approached me. His scowl from earlier had eased. "Jessica," he said, smiling again. He put one hand on my waist and one on my wrist to steer me into position, his eyes never leaving mine.

Warmth crept out of his fingertips and I struggled to focus. For a moment I could almost imagine we were dancing . . . but the sensation dropped away when he let me go. My face felt as if it were on fire. A sudden dizziness made my knees tremble.

Derek's fingers swept under my chin, tilting my face up. My eyes fogged, seeing only him. "I want to talk to you about Homecoming."

I nodded, mute.

"Later," he assured, leaving to help Jack.

I noticed he didn't touch any other girl the way he'd touched me. Not even his ex-girlfriend, Jenny. And she noticed, too.

Coach rattled on, one moment complimenting Derek and Jack's emerging strategy, the next teasing the remaining ragtag group of guys. I tried to remember to be disgusted at such blatant favoritism of the jocks, but Derek winked at me and I couldn't remember anything anymore.

The other guys were climbing out of the stands and peeling off their shirts. There was a sudden glare as fluorescent light bounced off white skin as first one debate team member and then a chess club guru shrugged off their cotton tees and revealed their thin frames. It was like watching vampires disrobe, but none of them looked as healthy as the undead I'd read about.

A wall of white flesh formed with Pietr lost somewhere on the other side of it. I heard a gasp. The white wall shifted. It was then I caught a glimpse of Pietr, surrounded by the smartest guys in school as they hypothesized about something beyond my view.

Pietr stood frozen, uniform shirt in his hand, mouth tight. Not nearly as alabaster as his observers, Pietr's skin looked like someone beginning a tanning regimen. He looked . . . warm.

Pietr stood as still as stone while the other, shorter boys pointed and speculated over something on his back.

Smith, always my favorite debater and member of my frequent flirters club, said, "It looks as if you have a peculiar birthmark." His eyes narrowed behind the frames of his thick glasses.

"It's a tattoo," Pietr countered. "My whole family has them."

Jaikin jumped in, trying another tactic. "It is a very *natural* color for a tattoo." Just because the boys had bonded a little with Pietr at Golden Oaks didn't mean they'd stem their natural curiosity for the sake of his comfort. I loved my nerds and their boldly awkward ways.

"Amazing what they do with dyes," Pietr quipped.

"It *does* have a very well-defined shape to be a birthmark," Smith agreed. I nearly smacked my forehead, suddenly too aware of why our debate team was on a losing streak. Mrs. Feldman had been absolutely correct: Sticking to their guns was not my nerdy boys' greatest talent.

By now, even Coach Mac was curious about the symbol marking the new student.

As he moved in to take a look, the rest of us drifted from our assigned positions. From my spot in the curious mob of uniform-wearing students I could see the tattoo clearly. So clearly that I had to agree with my boys' first instinct: It was not a tattoo marking Pietr's left shoulder blade.

Someone asked the question I didn't because I didn't want to appear too interested.

"What is it exactly?"

"A sword," Pietr said, flipping his shirt over his shoulder to try to end the debate.

But Hascal added his own perception, which, oddly enough, made Pietr even more uncomfortable. "It looks like a saber."

I circled the group of them, taking the opportunity to look at Pietr shirtless. He was slender but not thin, his muscles moving sleekly beneath his skin as he turned his torso slightly, seeking to end the crowd's curiosity. His arms and shoulders were well defined, his chest broad and strong, as if he spent mornings helping on a local farm. But I knew better. Because I knew Pietr's family came from Farthington.

And there were no farms there.

"A saber is a *type* of sword," Pietr nearly groaned.

"Hey—the last name's Rusakova, right?" Hascal knew he was right. He seldom said anything he doubted was correct.

Pietr's lips thinned and paled, but he nodded.

"Was your family in the Russian military?"

"Somewhat."

But that was when I saw the thing that made the mysterious tattoo fade to nothing in my mind.

"Somew . . . ?" Hascal floundered. I could almost hear the cogs in his brain shift to interpret the cryptic answer.

I stepped forward, slipping between observers until I stood intimately close to Pietr, and before I realized what I was doing, my hand was touching a wicked-looking scar that started at his side and twisted cruelly, racing raggedly across part of his abdomen, just below the ribs. Pietr was as warm as he looked. "And what's this?" I whispered, startled that someone could be cut like that and stand before me—in gym class—alive.

"Appendix." His hand took my wrist, my nerves jangling at the contact. His eyes were a smoky blue, clouded, distant, and stunning as a sandstorm rising against a perfect desert sky.

Coach Mac snorted. "Sue your doctor, then, Petey, 'cause that's the wrong side for your appendix."

Just then a basketball slammed into Pietr's chest. He didn't blink, couldn't have seen it coming, but he caught it, his eyes never leaving my face. He had released my wrist.

My fingers were all pins and needles. My spine only jelly.

"Let's play ball!" Derek roared, rallying us all from our

focused fascination. Coach echoed Derek's sentiment with a fierce blow of his whistle.

I made it back to my position only when the game officially started, mysteries on my mind.

Basketball has always been a blur to me, whether I'm a hesitant member of the crowd or an unwilling player. I know (and usually remember) the basics: You can't carry the ball when your feet are moving, you have to stay in bounds, and you can be aggressive, but you can't smack your opposition around or blatantly trip them (although it happens all the time—refs *do* have only two eyes).

The game was like any other: I moved around and waved my arms in a simian sort of way, trying to keep up my class participation grade without actually touching a ball. My interest in trying in gym faded as soon as my curiosity about Pietr ratcheted up.

Derek did his best to help, dodging in front of me anytime a ball neared, like he was some white knight (albeit in polyester gym trunks). And every time he intercepted the ball (on my behalf), he smiled or winked at me. Although I knew I should be offended by his willingness to make me an unnecessary presence on the b-ball court, I didn't mind. He had a brilliant smile. Even his teeth were perfect. He was paying attention to me—how could I complain?

But in the midst of all the chivalrous ball-handling, Pietr bumped into Derek. It wasn't intentional—wasn't a *foul*—but it set Derek off. Snagging the ball from Pietr, he leaned in and snapped, "What? You think you're a bad-ass because you've got a *tattoo?*"

Derek body-checked Pietr with a force that would have sent anybody else onto the floor. Pietr wobbled but didn't even move his feet to compensate. His jaw jutted forward, and his eyebrows lowered menacingly. He bristled at the attack.

Coach never made the faintest *tweet* on his whistle.

A minute later Derek skidded across the gym floor. Pietr was almost motionless; the only parts of him moving were his hands as he methodically dribbled and passed the ball between them. I thought I saw him mouth the phrase *"That's why I'm a bad-ass"* in Derek's direction, but I couldn't be sure. Derek thrust a fist out, pointed at Pietr, and Coach's whistle blew like he'd witnessed a double homicide.

Pietr sat out the rest of the game. I was envious. And more than a little mystified.

I hit the locker room door with palms flat, shoving it open with a grunt. No need to shower—I'd barely done more than raise my hands and shift my weight from foot to foot the entire game. Sarah followed close behind me, probably planning our next conversation so she could insert as many fresh vocabulary words into it as possible. I didn't mind; I liked listening to her enjoy words, especially considering what she'd suffered in June. She'd come a long way since then, and I was glad to be instrumental in her recovery effort.

But then, June had sucked for a bunch of us.

CHAPTER SEVEN

I popped open my lock and was pulling off my gym shirt when the note fluttered off my locker's top shelf and headed for the floor. I couldn't untangle my arms in time to yank it back in midair, so I watched, sickened, as it hit the floor. At Jenny's perfectly pedicured feet. Size five.

As graceful as a ballerina, she swooped down and picked it up, crinkling her professionally sculpted nose at it before turning to Macie.

I didn't know what to say. Or do. My heart stopped the moment she picked the note up off the grimy locker room floor. It was an old note—from my mom to me when I was headed off to what I had feared would be an extremely difficult day in third grade. I had found it again in July and carried it with me frequently. It was a touchstone most days—a lifeline others.

I knew it by heart, even the shapes of the letters. I thrust my hand out and said, "That's mine."

They snickered.

"Give it back . . . please."

By then Sarah was beside me. She must've heard something in my voice. Something desperate.

Jenny and Macie smiled, knowing they didn't need to read it. But that's exactly why they did—out loud. I stood there in only my bra and gym shorts, more exposed than if I'd been naked.

"'Sweetie Pie,'" Jenny began, her voice an even higher pitch than usual, "'I know school can be tough sometimes'"—Macie pantomimed crying—"'but you're my little trooper. You can do anything if you put your mind to it. Forgive the kids that treat you badly. You're better than that. I'll always be proud of you. Love, Mama.'" Jenny was laughing so hard by the end of her overly dramatic reading she barely got the last words out.

Sarah ran to get Coach. I thought later she knew before I did what was coming next and evacuated. Sarah was not keen on violence.

"Give the note back," I said.

"Geeeeez," Jenny said, turning back to Macie and blatantly disregarding my request. "Do you think she was ever dumb enough to believe it?"

"What part?" Macie asked, rubbing her chin in fake speculation. "The part about being able to do *anything?*"

Jenny grinned. "No. That her mama ever *loved* her." She turned to face me, her eyes beyond cold, lips hard. "Because *that's* not what I heard. I heard she was on her way out of Junction. *For good.*"

"Didn't get far," Macie added slyly.

I glanced toward the door. *Where the hell was Coach?*

"No, didn't get far at all," Jenny chided, her face going soft and deceptively innocent.

I tried to hear my mother's voice in my head, the reassuring phrases she'd say, like, "They're mean because they're jealous of you, honey. You have to have compassion for them. Their mamas should have taught them better. *Forgive them.*"

But all I heard was my pulse pounding in my ears. And then Jenny held the note up, fingers positioned to tear it in half.

I snapped.

I honestly don't recall how it happened. One minute I was standing there. Taking it. I remembered moving forward. . . . The next minute I had my mother's note back and Coach had me under one arm—Sarah shoving my gym shirt back over my head and gently guiding my rage-stiffened arms through the sleeves.

Coach muttered something about girls only fighting girls in Jell-O wrestling, and Amber dashed off to fetch the nurse.

I glimpsed Macie and Jenny on the floor, holding their faces and crying as I was toted out the locker room door and toward the office, bloody but victorious.

"Can't go around hitting people, J-bird," Coach muttered. He set me on my feet outside the locker room door and, holding my shoulders, turned me to face the office. "I know your mom—"

I spun back, throwing enough hate from my eyes to silence the affable Coach Mac. "You *don't* know."

Someone approached, but they kept their distance, never interrupting, although I felt eyes travel the length of my body and come to rest again on my face. Somehow I knew without looking it was Pietr.

Coach rubbed his broad forehead, the sudden turn of events surely setting his brain ablaze. "J-bird," he said in a tone I'd never heard him take before, "I know you're struggling. You're right—I don't totally get it. I never lived it. But you've gotta keep it together. You can't just attack somebody. . . ." He shook his head.

Sarah came and held my hand, stroking my arm in an attempt to numb me into a stupor.

I shook free of her grip, only more irritated. "I—"

Coach Mac turned me around once again to face the hallway leading to the office—and judgment. "You threw the first punch, J-bird. You *never* throw the first punch."

I chewed my lower lip. What would it mean, a fight with cheerleaders—the rich girls? Wasn't Macie's mom on the school board and always busy cutting general arts funding to provide professional choreographers for the cheerleading squad? Jenny and Macie were powerful enough, but their moms . . .

My head ached. My high school records were supposed to be my ticket *out* of Junction, not the start of a police record that would block me from attending the college I really wanted.

I heard Sarah speaking softly. With her I knew Pietr kept pace. Didn't he know to ask one of the girls to get his schedule back? Surely one of them would eagerly guide him around school. He didn't need to follow me like some puppy. I forced my eyes to the floor, unwilling to meet his own accidentally. I wondered why what he might think of me mattered but my stomach clenched at the thought he'd think less of me.

I shook my head, trying to clear it. I needed to formulate a defense, not get weak-kneed over some guy. Man, I wished I had my worry stone. I'd be rubbing it to a high gloss, attempting to calm myself.

The nurse rushed past us, scowling at me as Amber begged her to hurry. She carried a cooler, probably full of ice and bandages. I needed to remember to buy her a few new pens. Although that probably wouldn't change what she thought of me now. Unintentional pen thief was one thing. Bludgeoner of cheerleaders was definitely another.

My stomach swished uncomfortably. Not only could this

get me a criminal record, it could get my family sued. I had finally done it, I realized, passing through the office doors—I had ruined what was left of my family's future.

The door closed behind Coach and he nudged me toward a chair. Through the office's thick plate-glass windows I saw Pietr. Watching me. His eyes were a dazzling blue, shining with concern.

Well. At least I hadn't given him something as big as a deadly fall to worry about. My irresponsibility seemed small compared to his at the nursing home. I turned away from him in a huff but occasionally peeked in his direction out of the corners of my eyes.

Sarah grabbed him by the arm and pointed back toward their next class, saying something. He shook his head and pointed to the clock in the hall outside the office. I turned slightly in my seat so I could have a better (but still relatively inconspicuous) view. Sarah pulled out her cell phone, pointed to its face, and said something else. She had to be talking about being late to class. Pietr looked at me. I pretended I wasn't watching the argument outside.

I caught another glimpse as Pietr shrugged at her, turning the *opposite* direction he was supposed to go. He took off. . . .

Sarah threw her hands into the air and stomped away, headed to the class Pietr should have been attending, too. *Where the heck did he think he was going? Why?*

I crossed my arms, listening halfheartedly to Coach still yammering to Vice Principal Perlson. Alone with my thoughts, I felt desperately uncomfortable.

My temper cooled waiting in the office. I had retrieved my mom's note—intact—and was missing a quiz in science. Working hard to maintain some shred of optimism, I thought things could have been worse.

Vice Principal Perlson listened as Coach glossed over things. The VP responded in his rich island accent, flexing his dark hands. I listened to every word he said—not because he spoke so melodically it was tough imagining my fate was in his hands, but because I always admitted to having a fascination with anyone not from here.

And everything about VP Perlson was a reminder that he wasn't a Junction native. I hoped that would work in my favor, praying a more worldly view would give him better insight into my circumstances. Without me having to explain them while Mr. Maloy took notes and nodded sadly. Again.

Perlson shot me one of his most disappointed looks before disappearing into his office with Coach following behind.

He shamed me with a single look. Probably a prerequisite of being a VP. Or maybe it was some sort of weird voodoo power he had.

I outright refused to consider it was because I cared what he thought of me. He was part of an exchange program, a temporary member of Junction society. He'd probably leave Junction at the end of the year—like anyone with any degree of common sense.

I ran my finger along the edge of Mom's note. She'd had plenty of common sense. But Junction had a way of sapping that, and the will, out of a person. It was like a slow drain on your ability to be both human and humane. I wouldn't have blamed her for wanting to leave. But I knew that wasn't where she was headed the evening of the accident.

Dammit. I felt tears pushing along my eyelashes. I blinked them back, frustrated at my momentary weakness. I tucked the note into my shorts and tapped my sneakers. I needed a sound defense to get out of this mess.

And I didn't want to play the insanity card—even though it would probably be accepted without anyone batting an eye.

That was probably the worst, that they expected me to fall totally apart—waited and watched for it—and I couldn't. I just couldn't let it go. If the whole fight in the locker room were evidence of some psychotic break, they would excuse it. Maybe even murmur knowingly. But I knew that although I had snapped, I hadn't broken. I wouldn't. And not broken equaled no break. *Dammit.*

What could I say to fix things? I leaned over, studying my fingernails and thinking about the few options I had. I was lost in thought; time slipped by.

The office door wheezed open. I saw sneakers. Stylish sneakers—not like my "weekly special" ones gotten from the store that advised you to pay less with its company name. My eyes wandered from the shoes up to the person wearing them.

"Hey." Derek handed me my stuff from gym.

I blushed. "Hey," I echoed lamely.

"So I hear Jenny and Macie really pissed you off." He sat down in the chair next to me.

I rolled my eyes. "That's a bit of an oversimplification."

"You're painfully honest, you know?"

I sat silent at what sounded like a reprimand.

His hand rested on my knee. *My bare knee.* My body tingled and my brain stuttered. I struggled to keep breathing and looked at him, wondering how long someone could go without breathing before losing consciousness. "Don't say much to them," he advised. "Let me do the talking."

I blinked dumbly and had the good sense to follow it up with a quick nod.

"Good." He removed his hand, and my lungs started pumping again. I sighed before I could stop myself. He smiled. "I'm good at this sort of thing," he promised.

I believed him. I had to believe Derek "the man" Jamieson was good at everything he tried. Something deep inside me got soft and warm at the realization I wanted to find out exactly how true that belief was.

Derek ducked out of the office as unobtrusively as he'd appeared. Sure, he winked at the secretaries and asked about their kids—threatening to marry one's daughter when she got into ninth grade—but then he left, leaving the middle-aged women chuckling at being so easily flustered by an eleventh-grade boy. If Derek could work magic like that on my behalf, not only would I get off scot-free, I might be sainted, too.

The office door wheezed open again. Mr. Maloy flopped into the seat recently occupied by my would-be hero. He was holding a set of thick manila folders. With a sinking heart I knew they were labeled with my name.

Counselor Maloy held my life in his hands.

I reached into my backpack and dug into my jeans for my worry stone. I kept my mouth shut. I'd learned early that saying too much to the wrong person was sometimes more destructive than keeping it all bottled up inside.

After three minutes of facing my stony silence, Mr. Maloy spoke up. "You have to talk to me so I can *help* you, Jessica."

I had the sudden impression of him as a struggling defense attorney begging a client to *cooperate*. Maybe that was why he was a school counselor now.

"I want to help you, Jessica. Girls like you—"

I ground my teeth. *Go ahead,* I thought. *Compare me to some case study on grief and adolescence. Tell me how I stack up against other disturbed girls in my age range and socioeconomic class.*

I rubbed my thumb across the pietersite bead, making slow circles on its surface as I focused on staying calm. I rested my cheek on my knee and stared at the floor. And kept massaging the worry stone as if it could erase my problems. Or at least Mr. Maloy.

The door opened again. I saw high heels. Bright red, look-at-me high heels.

My head jerked up.

"Hey, Maloy." Counselor Harnek smiled down at the mousy man with the comb-over as if she were an avenging angel newly descended to save his sorry hide. "I got called in on this one," she explained, patting his shoulder. She leaned over and took the files from him. Slid them right out of his hands and into her arms. With a subtle move of her hand, she opened the top file. One quick glance and she closed it again.

He stood, surprised but equally relieved.

Harnek edged him to the door, speaking in that way of hers that made you think you were in on some confidential information while she let other people in on it, too. "She's a tough cookie, Maloy. You've done a fine job with her—God knows she didn't give you much to work with, probably clamming up on you. . . ."

His nod only fueled her declaration. "Yep, seen it before when she was still in middle school. I have one last trick up my sleeve I'd like to try— No? You don't mind me taking this case from you? You're the best, Maloy. I'll keep you posted," she promised, opening the door and walking him out.

I half-wondered if the Harneks and Jamiesons were related; they were so slick.

The door clicked shut. Harnek plunked down next to me. She moved the stack of folders over to an empty chair and straightened the hem of her skirt before turning to address me. "Hey, slugger." She winked.

I groaned. Still, I felt tons better. It was like I was right back in middle school, popping into her office because she was the counselor anyone could talk to. About anything. Now years separated us. And tragedy. Harnek took it all in stride.

She patted my knee. "So, sounds like you administered some old-school justice in the girls' locker room."

I wasn't sure how to answer.

"Don't sweat it. I kicked some righteous ass when I was your age, too. Here's the thing. Perlson's not going to want to act on this because you're a good student. And everyone's heard some version of what happened on the seventeenth."

I swallowed. Leave it to Harnek to remember the date.

"So you're already a martyr. That works in our favor. But you'll have to be punished because you took down a *pair* of cheerleaders." She whistled, a low, respectful sound. "And although their mamas are no great prizes, they know how to raise a stink, especially over the price of a damaged nose job. So there're a couple options. . . ."

She looked me flat in the face, studying my eyes. "You're not even high—that would have been an easy defense." She tapped her chin. "I'm guessing you don't want to play the crazy card. . . ."

I chewed my lip.

"No, I'd save that one up for something really good, too," she agreed. "Are you opposed to doing some community service?"

"No," I whispered.

"Good. Let's see how this all pans out. But if I have to jump in and save you, I have a totally doable option." She patted my knee again. "Don't worry, Jessie. You're in good hands."

She leaned in close; this time her voice was a whisper marking a true secret. "I'm actually thrilled to be here," she admitted, brown eyes glittering with tiny golden flecks. "I've been waiting a while for those two little chickadees to get a good karmic ass-kicking." Then she sat back up, straight as a rod, hands folded in her lap as if she'd never entertain such thoughts.

She looked at me again rather suddenly. "For the record—"

I sighed. "Yes?"

"You're not feeling—I don't know—a little reckless right now, are you?"

I stared at her steadily, waiting.

"I mean, you just did something really dramatic. Have you—at any other time—felt the desire to hurt someone else?"

"What? No! I didn't even want to hurt *them*. I just wanted my note back."

"Hmm."

"Hmm *what?*"

"Just hmm. Have you recently begun giving away any of your belongings? CDs, favorite clothes or books. . . ."

"No."

"Distancing yourself from friends?"

"No."

"Ever feel like hurting yourself?" she tossed out, as lightly as if she were asking did I prefer Coke or Pepsi.

"No! I am *not* suicidal," I hissed.

"Okay, okay." She waved her hands at me. "I just have to ask."

"Fine."

"As a note—"

"What?"

"You might want to make sure Maloy understands that, too." She flipped open the folder on top.

CHAPTER EIGHT

My school picture stared back at me, my basic stats hugging its corners. "So?"

"Red paper clip."

Again I asked, "So?"

"I worked with Maloy years back." Harnek rolled her eyes. "He sort of uses a code to let him keep up with stuff at a glance"—she closed the folder and turned it on its side so I was looking into its top—"without writing it all down."

"And since it's not written down, if something happens on his watch, he can just remove the clip and claim ignorance," I surmised.

"No! Of course not," she assured, flustered. "Maloy's socially awkward, but he follows up on all his hunches. Even the weird ones."

"I know."

Vice Principal Perlson's voice crackled across the intercom. "Please send in Ms. Harnek and Miss Gillmansen."

I let her lead the way. I focused on keeping my brave face on, all the while hoping no call had been made to my dad yet. The pietersite bead grew warm beneath my frantic touch.

Perlson sat back down when we entered. Coach Mac nodded from where he sat in a chair reading an old sports magazine, feet propped under the lip of the VP's desk.

"Yo, Coach," Harnek said, laughing when Coach dropped his feet from the desk's face and threw down the magazine.

"Well, Nance! They're dragging you out of the middle school cesspool to come help *us* now?"

Perlson watched the exchange with veiled eyes.

"Only a temporary gig, Coach." Harnek smiled. "Take a seat, Jessie." She beamed at Perlson; he smiled broadly back.

"Your reputation precedes you, Ms. Harnek," Perlson said affably.

"That's the nicest way of saying what you really mean, Vice Principal." She winked and settled in next to me. "Shall we cut to the chase, gentlemen?"

"Gladly," Perlson agreed, smiling more pleasantly, although I felt I watched a man swiftly shifting gears beneath a carefully constructed mask.

"We all know about Jessie's recent history," Harnek began.

I ducked my head but heard the men make brief, humming affirmations. My face grew hot under their watchful eyes. I worried about what version of the events they had heard. Some were kinder to my family than others.

"Anyhow, Jessie's been coping with a lot recently. And she's really been there for Sarah Luxom—"

I twitched at the mention of Sarah's name. I hadn't expected her to be brought into this.

"Ignoring her supposed involvement in the June seventeenth accident and instead helping her reacclimate to school."

"Admirable," Perlson murmured. I watched from beneath my bangs as he drew back in his chair, putting more distance between us. "But she is no saint. She *assaulted*—"

I winced at the word.

"Two cheerleaders."

I thought Harnek took a moment to peer at the clock over Perlson's rounded shoulder. "Even Jesus freaked out in the temple," Harnek quipped, shrugging.

The two men stared at her blankly.

"I'm just saying—if we want to draw comparisons between saints and Jessie, we should remember that saints and saviors aren't always perfectly peaceful."

Perlson quirked an eyebrow at her. "Nonetheless—"

The intercom on his desk sputtered. "Derek Jamieson, Jenny Smailles, and Macie Gunders are here to see you, sir."

"Excellent. Send them in." He tapped a button and then looked at Harnek with cool, coal-colored eyes. "Let's see what the girls have to say before we decide anyone's fate, shall we?"

I realized in that moment that even his beautiful voice with its calypso rhythms couldn't sugarcoat my situation now—had he wanted to sugarcoat anything.

The office door opened and Derek walked in, a solemn look across his handsome boy-next-door features. My heart stopped. I wondered if he'd failed in his self-appointed mission to rescue me. He held the door open and Macie walked in, scowling, her upper lip puffed to an outrageous size and slightly purpled. Even with her finest skills in cosmetology she'd have quite a job hiding that. She sat down and glared at me. I wondered if whatever Perlson did to me could possibly be worse than the revenge Macie was already cooking up in her head.

The room grew completely still as Jenny entered playing with her bleached blond bangs, curling them with her fingers into a sweep over the bridge of her pert ski-slope nose (which she covered with an ice pack) and her left eye.

As Jenny turned to sit, the bangs swayed away from her face a moment. I almost gasped. The skin around her left eye was swollen and bruised, leaving the eye barely able to peek out. I wondered if her right eye would do the same. Surely a far cry from the look she was probably going for at Homecoming.

"Ladies," Perlson said softly.

I mentally questioned his choice of the term, but Jenny and Macie seemed to recognize it as somehow applicable to them, and nodded in his direction.

Derek sat down and took Jenny's hand, guiding her into the seat beside him.

I froze.

He patted her hand reassuringly, whispering encouragement into her ear. She smiled at me.

I couldn't even blink. I felt like I'd been socked in the gut—betrayed. My eyes dried up like raisins.

"Miss Gunders," Perlson asked, "could you please tell us about the situation in the ladies' locker room today?"

Macie looked at Jenny. Something passed between them that I couldn't understand. I hated how it seemed the popular kids communicated at a different mental wavelength from me. It was a look laced with hidden meaning.

I knew my fate was hidden in that single glance, but I couldn't read it. I could pick apart Shakespeare, analyze Freud, but understand cheerleaders? No. They were a different species, predatory and lethal.

Derek sat silently at Jenny's side, placidly stroking her hand.

"Miss Gunders?" Perlson tried again.

Macie nodded. Her eyes were cold. "We were all in the locker room after a game of basketball." She leaned around Jenny and addressed Derek. "Good game, Derek."

"Thanks, Mace." He didn't falter stroking Jenny's hand.

Glaring at me with fresh ferocity, Macie continued, "We were all getting changed and we saw a note fall out of *her* locker."

She wouldn't say my name. Was I so far beneath her? I rubbed the stone until I thought my thumb would callous.

"And then?"

"Jenny picked it up."

"Did Miss Gillmansen ask for it back?"

"Yes," Macie admitted. "She even said *puh-leez*," she added. But it was far less a note about my polite behavior than a verbal swipe. As if saying "please" was a sign of weakness.

"Hmm. Who was the note from?"

"Her mother."

"Oh." Perlson paused. "Then what happened?"

"Well, we read it, of course." Macie rolled her eyes.

"Out loud?"

"*Yes.*"

"And then Miss Gillmansen attacked you?"

"No." It was Jenny. She peered at me with her one good eye. "I was going to shred the note." She gave Derek's hand a squeeze. He squeezed back reassuringly. "It was a really bitchy—oops." Her hand flew to her mouth. "Sorry."

Perlson nodded, excusing her faux pas and signaling her to continue.

"It was a really *nasty* thing for us to do. I can't blame her for snapping. I mean, that whole mess with her mom—"

Derek squeezed her hand again, and I saw something different behind his eyes. But Jenny kept rattling on; and Derek kept pumping her hand—to silence her or encourage her? I couldn't tell. I couldn't be sure of anything.

Jenny was babbling. "You know—surviving the sophomore slump, trying to deal with poor mental Sarah"—she set the ice down long enough to spin her finger in the air near her ear—"and the way Derek's been stringing her along just to make me jealous . . ." She shook her head sadly.

Derek released her hand. His eyes met mine. There was no message there—no meaning for me to read. I felt sick. Stringing me along? As much as I didn't want to believe it, every one of my doubts and insecurities agreed until I did. Guys like Derek didn't waste time on girls like me.

"Derek," Harnek said, her tone meant to shame.

He had the good grace to look at the floor.

"But it's all okay now," Jenny said with a pleasant smile. "I don't want her to be punished. Living like she is—well, that's punishment enough." She shrugged.

Macie looked up from beside her and grinned at me. "Yeah. Her life's so miserable, she's suffering enough already," Macie agreed. "I'm over it."

Perlson swallowed, looking stunned. Probably by all of it. "Well, ladies. That's very—generous of you. Will your parents agree, though?"

Jenny and Macie laughed in that strange calculating way they had. "Of course, Vice Principal Perlson." I realized then that they ruled their homes. Ruled their parents. It was a chilling thought.

Jenny and Macie rose as one. Jenny put her hand out and Derek stood, too, taking it. His head hung from his neck like part of his spine had disintegrated. I struggled to understand what could have happened during the time between his exiting the office and his return with both girls. Had his talk with me been simple bravado?

"Then I guess we can wrap things up here," Harnek said. "Wow." She looked at the clock. "Just in time."

Derek opened the door, but Macie and Jenny paused before exiting. "We *forgive* you, Jessica." And then, giggling, they were out of my sight.

Derek didn't even give me a glance as he pulled the door shut behind them.

Harnek patted my knee. "Well, that came out differently than I'd imagined. How about you?"

I groaned.

"You have enough time to get changed and make it to the bus," she said, startling me into action. I'd seen her look at the clock—heard her comment about the timing—but it hadn't sunk in. The whole day had slipped past me. I wondered for a moment if Pietr'd made it to his remaining classes on time. Harnek was speaking again. ". . . going to Homecoming?"

"What?"

"Are you going to the Homecoming game?" she repeated.

"I don't see any point in going now," I whispered.

"Hmph. Well, as your appointed counselor, I suggest you *do* go. Get your mind off everything else."

I shrugged and stood. Indifferent.

Harnek opened the door, and we stepped into the main office's waiting room. "I might want to see you about all this later," she said. "Just to wrap stuff up."

I nodded.

"Hey, look. Someone's glad to see you."

My head snapped up. *Derek*—? But, no. Of course not.

Pietr peered up at me from the line of uncomfortable office chairs. "Oh."

"I'll leave you two—" Harnek said, giving me a puzzled look and exiting before I could correct her misconception.

"Why are you here?" I asked a bit too harshly.

"I'm getting my bus assignment."

"Oh." I surprised myself by actually being a little disappointed. But why should I be surprised? The guy I thought was going to ask me to Homecoming had been leading me on. And *he* had been my self-appointed savior. Pietr aspired to no such station.

One of the secretaries came to the counter. "Bus thirteen," she announced.

"You're kidding me."

"What?" he asked, eyes guiltless.

"That's my bus." Crap. My bus generally had only one or two empty seats on it, so packing in another body wasn't going to make the ride any more comfortable. "I need to get changed."

"Better hurry—time's running out," he advised, pointing to the numbers on the face of his cell phone. "I'll wait for you."

"Don't do me any favors," I said, leaving the office and abandoning Pietr so I could have a few peaceful moments before the ride home.

I left him standing there, head down, looking like my last words wounded him deeply. I was immediately sorry, but I didn't know how to say it. The day's events had confused me.

In the bathroom, I quickly slipped out of my bloodstained gym shirt and shorts and into my street clothes. Today had officially been Hell and tonight would be Homecoming—the bonfire and game.

Hell. Round two.

There was no escaping it. As an editor of the school paper, I needed to attend. Besides, didn't I want to watch Derek on the football field, leading Junction's Jackrabbits to victory?

I sighed and tried to fix my hair in the mirror. "Ugh!" My fingers still trembled from the fight. Why did I bother trying to fix unfixable things? Fixing my mop of mousy brown hair here and now was like a metaphor for my life—wrong place, bad timing, never the right tools to solve the problem. But I kept trying. Stubbornly stumbling forward.

Now my failure was all brought into glaring focus in Junction High's girl's bathroom. Under fluorescent light. Because if I was going to suffer, my suffering should absolutely be illuminated by the worst lighting ever. *Crap.* It was official. My hair couldn't get worse unless it caught fire. The hum of the fluorescents overhead didn't reassure me that wouldn't happen next.

Of course it wasn't as if I'd see Derek before the bonfire—probably not even before the game wound up. All I had to do was wash the last bit of blood off my knuckles. "Out, damned spot," I whispered, quoting Lady Macbeth as I cranked the faucet on to rub the stain away with fierce fingers.

I'd get on the bus and head home. I'd clean up there. Regroup. Figure out what was going on with this Derek and Jenny mess and where I fit in with Derek—if I really did at all.

After the bus ride. After sitting by Pietr, with my luck.

"Crap, crap, *crap!*"

At least Lady Macbeth believed her Hell was murky. My newest version of Hell was crystal clear—lean and handsome, with a soft Russian accent and a frustratingly mysterious past. Ever-present. And yeah, he'd probably be at the bonfire and game, too. And if I compared him to Hell in front of my friends? Amy would just point out that Hell was supposed to be hot.

And Pietr Rusakova was at least that.

When I finally boarded the bus, Pietr was already there. I took the remaining seat across the aisle, nodded to my seatmate, Stella Martin, and began to watch Pietr surreptitiously.

Pinned beside the window by some anonymous freshman, Pietr stared out at the other kids hurrying to their buses. But he didn't react to any of them, didn't seem to actually see them. Then he shifted and turned, looking straight at me. He scrutinized my expression, eyes tracing over my forehead, traveling around my eyes as I felt their edges crinkle in response to his odd deliberation, and finally his gaze rested on my lips. Lips that betrayed me by twitching into a nervous smile. *Dammit*.

He turned back to the window.

"He really likes you, Jessie." Stella's whisper was weighted with happiness and awe. "You two should sit together. . . ."

"No. No, Stella," I protested as she began gathering her things. I wanted to apologize for being rude to Pietr, sure, but sit beside him on the way home? I didn't want to give him the wrong impression.

But Stella was already squeezing past me to stand in the aisle as the bus bounced forward, rumbling to life.

Our driver glared into the rearview mirror at her. "Stella—take a seat!"

"Yes, Stella," I urged, scooting over to the window. "Sit."

"I will in a minute." She frowned at me. "How hard is it to get something good out of life for once, Jessie?"

Pietr watched our exchange.

"Pietr," Stella began, "I would like to sit here. Beside—" She looked pointedly at the freshman. Sweat glazed his upper lip as he realized he was embroiled in the affairs of upperclassmen.

"Billy," he muttered, straightening in his seat. He rubbed at his upper lip. The faintest trace of a mustache grew there.

Stella appeared suitably impressed.

"Beside *Billy*," she said. "Pietr, would you please sit over there with Jessie?"

Pietr bared his teeth in a charming smile. "Billy," he said, "it appears you are getting a much more attractive companion."

Stella beamed at Pietr as he brushed past.

"Sit down, both of you!" the driver bellowed.

He settled in next to me. I wedged my backpack between us like a wall. He didn't seem to notice. The bus lurched along, shuddering as it paused at a stop sign. It was going to be a long ride, like always, made longer by what I now had to do.

We stopped a few times before the edge of town, kids stumbling to the exit as the bus continued running, still swaying faintly even as it sputtered at its appointed stops. The houses spread out slightly, not quite so tight against each other.

A few more stops and scarecrows would decorate small, rock-walled gardens instead of poorly lit porches just off of cement sidewalks. After that there'd be fields dotted with brick-red barns and stacked with the huge round hay bales that marked winter's inevitable approach.

Then, home. And since I didn't know where Pietr lived, I couldn't wait any longer to say what I knew I should. "Pietr . . ."

He nodded.

"I'm sorry about the way I snapped at you in the office."

"It's okay. You seem to be under a lot of stress," he commented, staring into the back of the seat before us like he could drill a hole with his eyes. "It's not a big deal."

Okay. He forgave me. Macie and Jenny forgave me. It seemed like everyone was forgiving my bad behavior and I was the only one still holding grudges. How ironic. Wouldn't my mother have been proud? *Nuts.*

I dug my novel out of my pack. Leaning back, I parted the pages right at my bookmark and began to read. I hadn't gotten far when I felt his eyes on me. Well, on my book, at least.

I noticed one of his dark eyebrows was raised skeptically.

I closed the book. "What?"

"Life Sucks?"

I looked at the title of my book and smiled. "Yeah." My reply was more than an agreement on the title.

He put his hand out and wiggled one finger. "Come on."

I was frozen for a moment, remembering the electric vibe of those fingers. Tentatively I handed the book to him for his appraisal, all the while telling myself I really didn't care.

He scanned the back of it. "Seriously? *Vampires?*"

CHAPTER NINE

I grabbed the book back and shot him a *how-dare-you-judge-what-I-read* sort of look.

He shrugged and tried again. *"Vampires?"*

"Vampires are quite hot right now," I replied matter-of-factly, as if the quality of a book was truly based on its mass-market appeal.

"Hot? I'd always presumed the undead were perpetually cold."

I snorted at his cool delivery of the line. *Dammit. He got me to smile.* I schooled my features, but he'd taken in my reaction.

And was smiling back.

"I keep meaning to read other stuff, like *Anna Karenina"*—his eyebrow rose even higher, threatening to merge with his hairline—"but vampires are all the rage right now," I said. I ruffled the book's pages. "It's a quick read and it takes my mind off stuff," I justified. Although I wasn't sure why I felt the need to justify anything to Pietr.

"I just think it's kind of unfair," he replied.

"What?"

"That vampires get so much time when there are plenty of other—monsters—to choose from."

I turned in my seat to face him. "Like what—or is it more properly *whom*?" I challenged.

He grinned. His smile was as perfect as Derek's. "I think they'd request the use of *who* or *whom*," he advised with a nod. "Werewolves, for one."

I wrinkled my nose at the suggestion. "Werewolves?" I shook my head, trying to imagine them ever really being a challenge to the popularity of vampires. "Why werewolves?"

He leaned back, pressing his legs against the seat in front so his feet dangled free. In their *large* sneakers.

I blushed.

"Think about it," he said. "Life's about transformation, right? We grow, we change, hopefully we evolve into better people. . . ." He shrugged. "Who represents transformation better than werewolves?"

"Okay. Interesting. But vampires—that whole thing of living beyond the life span of those you love . . . it's so tragic."

His eyes darkened, his features masked. He peered past me and out the window again, searching for something. "*Da*. Wouldn't *that* be difficult. Having eternity to figure things out, see the world—to get it right. *Da*. That'd totally suck."

"Besides"—I smacked his arm to pull him out of his sudden funk—"don't werewolves only transform under the light of a full moon? Vamps have to cope with bloodlust all the time."

He looked at me, searching my face. Pietr sighed. It seemed like he hadn't found what he was looking for in my

expression. *"Da.* I forgot." He shrugged again. "You're probably right. Vamps are way more marketable because of that,
too."

"Besides," I teased, "it's not like I believe in either of them."

His lips quirked at their corners. *"Horashow.* Good," he said.
"It's definitely better that way." He stood then, and I noticed the
bus rattling to a stop. "This is my stop," he said. "Oh—Sarah
gave me a note for you." He dug into a pocket in his jeans.
"Here." He pressed it into my hand and I fought not to shiver at
the contact. "See ya."

"Yeah," I called weakly as he walked down the aisle. I flopped
back into the seat, peeking out the window and watching for
him, wondering which road he'd take, which house was his. . . .
But he'd already disappeared.

"See," Stella confirmed across the aisle. "He likes you."

I nodded, my lips in a tight grimace. Pietr was starting to
grow on me, and Derek—could he have really been stringing me
along to make Jenny jealous? Maybe, but I didn't like the idea I'd
just been some pawn in the mind games the popular kids played.
Settling back in to the seat, I unfolded Sarah's note.

OMG. Is Pietr as hot as I think he is?

I flipped the note over. Yeah. It was definitely from Sarah,
but she never wrote—or thought—like that. I started again.

*OMG. Is Pietr as hot as I think he is? He's such a rebel.
I told him he had to get to class on time and he completely
blew me off, racing off to try to help your cause. Of
course, if you're reading this, it means he must have
succeeded, so YAY! He did finally make it to class and*

*he's pretty smart, too. I think I may be developing a
serious crush! OMG—you have to meet me at Homecoming tonight. I think he's going, too.*

I groaned. Two votes telling me to go to Homecoming:
Harnek and Sarah. But if I went, what would I find? Jenny in
Derek's arms? Ugh. Though I couldn't imagine actually going,
the idea Pietr might be there was oddly enticing.

The bus jerked to a stop again and I recognized the long
lane of my driveway. Tossing my backpack over my shoulder, I
slipped Sarah's note into my pocket and sidled down the aisle
and down the steep stairs, promising myself to call Sarah—
immediately.

But evidently *immediately* wasn't soon enough for Sarah, her
mom's car parked and running at the crest of our driveway.
"Hey, Mrs. Luxom." I waved at her through the driver-side window. She waved back, startled. I noticed the car was empty, but
there were two bags in the backseat—Amy's purse and Sarah's
backpack.

So it was an ambush. What was waiting for me in my
house—a full-on intervention with my friends and father?
Yeah, I'd gotten into a fight at school, but did I have to be ready
to defend myself walking into my own home, too?

But if I was going to be inside with them for a while, talking out my troubles, would Sarah's mom keep the car running?

I opened the door, stepped into the mudroom, and hung my
backpack up on its appointed peg.

"Hey, Jessie," my dad called from the kitchen.

"Hey."

Sarah and Amy were seated at the tiny table near the windows. Mom had called it the breakfast nook. Dad always called

it the cheap seats. Sarah set down her copy of *Great Expectations* to focus on the conversation. She appeared to be just a few pages from the book's end. Already.

"Sarah and Amy were just tellin' me about how you all are goin' to Homecoming tonight," Dad explained. He pointed to the tin on the table. "Help yourselves, girls. Those are the factory's newest chocolates—the Starlight line."

Sarah made a comment about chocolate ruining her complexion while Amy dug in.

"You work for the best place, ever, Mr. G.," Amy confided. "All my dad brings home are dented cans of mushrooms."

Dad smiled at her. "Maybe we'll need to work a trade, then, Ames. Jessie can't stand chocolate anymore—"

"And I can't cope with mushrooms." Amy grinned. She nibbled a chocolate in the shape of a jaunty Jupiter. "I doubt it would seem like a fair trade, though—canned mushrooms for fancy chocolates."

"Believe me, mushrooms would be welcomed," I replied.

"Jessie always says you can't top pizza with chocolate," Dad added.

Sarah had fallen to temptation, too, and smiled around an elaborate white chocolate moon. "Oh, Jessica, you need to be more inventive, then. I can't imagine anything that wouldn't be improved by the addition of this chocolate."

Dad stirred a cup of coffee.

"Night shift, Dad?"

"Yep. Nothin' better to do on a Friday night."

"Yeah." Not like he could actually hang out with his kids. Maybe play some cards or watch a movie. Nope. Just work. Like always. "Yeah," I said, looking at Sarah and Amy.

Dad sipped his coffee, turned back to the counter, and added more sugar. "Bonfire and game tonight?"

I looked at the girls, clueless. They nodded in unison. "Yep."

"Who are you guys playin'?"

We all exchanged stupefied looks.

"The Madison Bulldogs."

The three of us spun to see my little sister standing in the doorway, nose in a book. As always.

"Annabelle Lee," I said in greeting.

She stuck her tongue out at me before Dad could smile in her direction. I swore I remembered being twelve, but I was never *that* type of twelve.

"So, Anna, who would you put your money on tonight?" Dad asked.

"Bulldogs are going to wipe up."

"But we have Kurt Anderson, Derek Jamieson, Jack Jacobsen . . . ," I protested.

"Four words for you," Annabelle Lee said shrewdly, enunciating in emphasis, "Bryce-the-Breaker-Branson."

Dad whistled. "I've heard of that boy. Smashed up a bunch of Tompson's kids earlier in the season." He shook his head. "Gonna be a good game. If I knew that, I wouldn't have signed up—"

I winked at him. "Yes you would have, Dad."

"Anna, you gonna be all right all by yourself tonight?"

"I'll call all my crack clients and host a rave," Annabelle Lee said without skipping a beat. She was busy reading again.

Dad twitched a moment and then smiled, dismissing what he often called her "quirky sense of humor." "So. tomorrow night's the parade and dance?"

"Yeah." It only made sense, I guessed. I obviously needed to start listening to the afternoon announcements.

Sarah stood. "So, Mr. Gillmansen, can we get Jessica early to run into town and pick up some stuff?"

"What stuff do you girls still need?"

Amy blushed, Sarah pursed her lips, and I stared at the floor. It was a well-rehearsed routine. And it worked every time.

"Oh. Girl stuff." Dad dug into his back pocket and pulled out his wallet. I wondered when he'd start asking me just how much "girl stuff" one girl could possibly need—or even what "girl stuff" really was. He handed me a few bills, and I kissed him on the cheek.

"Thanks, Dad. Come on," I said. We got to the door, and Dad stopped me, a hand on my arm.

"Go on, girls," he said, waving them on. They ducked out and I stood there, heart in my throat. Maybe he had gotten a call from the office after all. "You know," he began, looking down at the patterned linoleum floor that pretended to be brick, "I'm really kind of flyin' blind about all this"—he waved a hand in the air—"*stuff* that comes with you growin' up. I mean—" he stalled out, and I touched his arm.

"I know you're trying the best way you know how, Dad."

He looked relieved. "Take your jacket. 'Sposed to get chilly tonight."

"Thanks," I said, slipping it off the hook.

The door was closing behind me when I heard him say, "I just wish your mama was here to help ya better. . . ."

I sprinted to the car and jumped into the death seat, slamming the door to close out his last words. "Ready," I choked, my eyes straight ahead as I buckled my seat belt.

The drive to the mall was short. Once you were in Junction's limits it was never far to go to get to anything within Junction. We were the definition of "small town." Junction had gotten its start as a railroad hub. In the late 1800s it blossomed from a few farmsteads into a busy railway town. Main Street filled out, and people started to really settle into the area.

Professionals came to treat the population. And they demanded better things. More land was cleared, more farms established, more people moved in. A few factories popped up, mainly for milling or making animal feed. Folks who didn't want to be "simple farmers" moved into the center of town and worked the same backbreaking hours but with less light and more noise in the factories.

Then the trains stopped coming with such frequency. People could afford cars and trucks. The main railway station got bought out and became the local DMV. The farmers didn't come into town as much once the mill closed. They still came for livestock feed, but they didn't need to come so far in.

The social lines that had been blurred by mutual respect and need sharpened again. The farmers were one group, the townies the other. And so it continued, the townies buying up property that in a stronger economy had *been* farms—all the while complaining about the smells and sights of the nearby livestock and fields. Complaining about the farms that predated them by decades.

The railroad station that became a DMV switched hands several more times before it settled into its current incarnation as a cozy Italian restaurant. My parents' first date was there. My mom, a dissatisfied townie; my dad, a fourth-generation, firmly rooted farmer. They shouldn't have lasted. And Fate guaranteed they couldn't.

The mall was one of the most recent additions to the community, only seeming aged compared to the gleaming and gluttonous Supercenter with its parking lot so large it rivaled the county airport's tarmac. I would always prefer the mall. Things there didn't have the same gloss and mass-produced glare as in the mind-numbing Supercenter.

Inside, Southside Mall was dressed in its Halloween best.

"Ugh," Amy said, looking at the fake cobwebs. "Already? I think it gets earlier every frikkin' year."

But Sarah was watching me try on masks. "So what's appropriate for Homecoming?" I chuckled. "Zombies, since we'd have to be brainless to fall for this blatant jock worship, or"—I yanked off the zombie head and tugged on another rubber mask—"Dracula, because Homecoming's bound to suck?"

Sarah lost control, snorting. Even Amy laughed before leading me away.

"Homecoming's not going to suck," she assured. She looped her arm around mine. "Just because things aren't quite as we expected . . ."

"Yeah, like Derek getting back with Jenny—"

Sarah nudged me. "You're better off without him."

I rolled my eyes. "That's what best friends are *supposed* to say," I protested.

"Hmph." Amy paused, hands out before her as if she were flipping through the pages of a book. She seemed to examine something on one imaginary page. "My official BFF manual says to add: You're too good for that jerk, anyway." Amy smiled and guided us into a colorful boutique.

Sarah stated, "The 2.0 version also suggests: It's *his* loss."

I couldn't help it. I grinned despite the loss of my crush.

A pair of earrings and matching necklace later and I wasn't so concerned about Derek and his renewed relationship with a somewhat pulverized cheerleader. I looked good. Sarah and Amy chose a few things to accent what they'd be wearing to the dance, the whole time telling me I simply had to go, too.

By the time we were back in the car and headed to the big game, they had mentally gone through my wardrobe, verbally inventoried it (finding it severely lacking), and had chosen an appropriate outfit for me to wear to the dance. I knew I was being railroaded into attending, but I just hoped it wouldn't be as bad as I imagined.

Mrs. Luxom dropped us off by the school's main entrance, reminding us she'd wait for a call before picking us up—but no later than ten. We agreed, too happy being in each other's company and not in school to care about a curfew. Besides, we had cell phones, so we had options.

The bonfire burned brilliantly: carmine, copper, and cardinal in the vacated baseball field before us, searing our vision as it flickered and flared, contrasting sharply with the gathering darkness. Arm in arm we headed toward it, scanning the growing crowd for anyone we recognized. But the hungry flames drew our attention again and again until, mesmerized, we simply stared at the ever-changing boundaries of the flames.

It was utterly primal, the fascination we felt. Had we ever evolved beyond those generations in the caves battling each other as much as the elements? I wondered what it might have been like, huddling around a fire and hearing the menacing wails of wolves lurking somewhere in night's dark heart, hungry as they hunted with glowing eyes. The heat of the fire prickled our faces, flushing our cheeks. It suddenly sputtered and popped, pushing us back to a respectful distance.

Amy grunted and proclaimed, "Fire. Bad. Much danger!"

I giggled. Sometimes it was like she could read my mind.

A shout rose up from behind the crowd massed on the opposing side of the bonfire. More people joined in the shouting, and I could see a bulbous shape rise above the crowd, suspended from a thick pole. The cry of "Burn the Bulldogs" became more distinct and I could see the shape was—

"Look, it's a Bulldog in *effigy*!" Leave it to Sarah to get the right word out.

"Burn the Bulldogs! Burn the Bulldogs! Burn the Bulldogs!"
And the effigy was tossed into the bonfire, sparking before
crumpling in on itself with a sickly green flame.

"They must have salted it," Amy whispered, awed. "Makes
the flames colored," she explained.

I just nodded, enjoying the buzz of excitement that seemed
to emanate from the crowd.

He stood on the other side of the hungry blaze. Watching
me with eyes so bright they mirrored the flames and yet glowed
with some strange inner light. Pietr stared at me, his slight
smile lighting his features even more than the fire. The glaring
orange firelight ran across the chain around his neck, bouncing
between it and his gleaming eyes.

I was determined to avoid him. My resolve was strengthened by the memory of Sarah's note. She was crushing on him.
I needed to reserve my teenage angst for other unattainable
targets. Mainly Derek. "Come on," I urged Sarah and Amy.
"Let's get some decent seats for the game."

We climbed into the soaring bleachers, going up and up
until I was satisfied we'd outdistanced Pietr.

"God, Jessie," Amy complained. "Are we trying to outrun
the law or something?"

"No. Just my luck." I looked around. "This is perfect."

"If you brought binoculars," Amy muttered.

"Oh." Sarah sat beside me, a smile twisting her freshly glossed
lips. "This *is* perfect." *Great Expectations* got tucked away, but it
seemed certain she'd finish it tonight.

I followed her gaze and saw Pietr finding a seat five rows
below us. "Oh. Yeah."

Amy looked lost as she took a seat on my other side.

"Sarah has discovered she has an interest in Pietr Rusakova,"
I explained.

"Who doesn't?" Amy asked, leaning around me to address Sarah. "I saw him first," she said with a devilish wink.

Sarah huffed dramatically.

"You seemed more curious about Pietr's brother, Max," I pointed out to Amy, "And you're dating Marvin and, technically—" I added, but Amy jumped in.

"Yeah, technically Jessie saw him first."

CHAPTER TEN

"But Jessica says she doesn't want *Pietr*," Sarah pointed out. "She's still all knotted up about Derek. So he's fair game," she declared.

I flopped forward, fingertips brushing the tops of my sneakers, willing Sarah to be correct. I did still want Derek—didn't I? I mean, just because he wasn't returning my feelings, just because my crush was—

"Jessica's just dealing with *unrequited* love," Sarah said, patting my back.

Yeah. Unrequited. It didn't negate my crush's existence. My heart still ached over Derek. *Stupid heart. Stupid girl.* And things could change, right? My head hurt just thinking about it all. Hope was getting harder and harder to hold on to.

And then there was Pietr . . . Strangely distant, annoyingly arrogant, utterly straightforward, twitchy, witty, and yes, slightly argumentative Pietr. There was plenty about him that got under my skin.

I peered down the rows of bleachers separating us. Ugh. Handsome Pietr. I had to admit that, too. My stomach churned.

Well below us he had turned to glance up the bleachers. He looked directly at me and nodded. Smiling lopsidedly as if we shared some secret. Surely he couldn't have heard us. . . .

Sarah and Amy waved at him. Inviting him to come join us.

I sat up, smacking at their arms. "*What* are you two doing?" I demanded under my breath, smiling at him the whole time as if my reaction had nothing to do with him. Maybe he'd think I was swatting away a sudden onslaught of late-season mosquitoes. Not that I was absolutely flipping out at the idea of sitting beside one handsome guy I shouldn't be attracted to while watching another who might not be attracted to me . . .

"We're inviting him up," Amy said, giving me a look that showed she was being as obvious as possible—what didn't I understand? "Look, I managed to erase an important phone message from the school to your dad today," Amy said. "Let us have some fun, okay?"

"I'm all about fun," I insisted, my stomach twisting as I watched him consider their offer.

Luckily he shook his head.

"Too bad," I said, although my tone was totally transparent.

Then he motioned at the open spaces beside him and signaled to us.

"What?" I pantomimed not understanding, cupping an ear with my hand.

His brows lowered in frustration.

Amy sighed. "God, Jessie. You can be sooo—"

"*Daft*," Sarah snapped, standing and snagging my arm. She nodded and waved back to him.

"Come on. He's got better seats for actually seeing the game, anyhow," Amy pointed out. "Don't you want to *see* the action?"

But it didn't matter. Whether or not I wanted to see the game's action and Derek's involvement didn't matter. Whether or not I wanted to sit near Pietr didn't matter.

I was pushed and pulled by a force far stronger than my own will: the force of two giggling girlfriends.

Amy sat to Pietr's left, Sarah on his right. I shrugged. "Guess I'll go back up," I motioned the way we'd just come.

Pietr looked at me with an unreadable expression. Amy's and Sarah's expressions, though, were absolutely clear. I should have been frightened by what I read in their eyes. It was obvious they wouldn't tolerate my attitude much longer.

Pietr pulled his feet off the bench before him. "Sit," he said.

I looked at Amy and Sarah. They stared back. I could nearly hear Amy thinking up ways to get back at me, so I swallowed my frown and decided not to ruin their evening. I sat, my back warmed by the nearness of Pietr's knees and shins. It was absolutely impossible to ignore his proximity.

Mercifully, the announcer began introducing the starting lineup, his voice booming and crackling from the speakers. Madison's Bulldogs broke through a painted banner held by scantily clad cheerleaders who seemed incapable of controlling impulses to kick up their heels and punch skyward with tiny pompoms. I didn't bother to hide my disgust at their short-skirted display, frowning. I tried not to focus on the fact that the cheerleading squad managed, with their every hop and split, to utterly undermine the hard-won feminine power that generations of women had struggled so hard to achieve.

They did look perfect, though. *Crap.* Even I had to admit that.

The announcer droned on, listing team stats and some upcoming Madison games. Recognizing a name in the enemy lineup, I shivered at the introduction of Bryce-the-Breaker Branson. He was easily six feet tall and 250 pounds, but he moved more like a panther than the clumsy bull I was hoping for.

"Are you cold?" Pietr's breath in my ear made me jump.

"What?" I crossed my arms. "No."

"You shivered," he observed, his words soft and warm, his breath tickling my ear and neck.

"I'm just worried," I admitted, mistakenly leaning back against his legs to intimate the fact. I shivered again, this time at the complete contact with his strong legs, a bolt like lightning racing up my spine.

I was freshly aware of his nearness, of his easy strength, and my not-quite-in-control curiosity. I pulled forward, hunching over my knees and trying to focus again on our cheerleaders and banner. Our marching band struck up the alma mater, trailing it into a rhythmic chant of "Burn the Bulldogs! Burn the Bulldogs!"

Kurt Anderson led the charge, tearing through the flapping banner as if it were tissue paper.

I heard Amy enlightening Pietr: "It took the art class three full periods to complete that thing."

"Hmm," he said.

A jacket flopped across my shoulders and over my back, heavy and warm and smelling of pine-filled forests. "What?" I turned in my seat to face them.

Pietr leaned back and, looking quite smug, stated, "You shivered. Twice." He shrugged.

"And you?" I glanced pointedly at his thin shirt, looking for a gentle way to return the jacket.

Amy and Sarah scooted closer to him, grinning. I tried ignoring their willingness to be Pietr's personal space heaters.

"I'll be fine. Besides, I can't have my guide getting sick, can I?"

I groaned and shrugged free of his jacket. "I think you and I need to have a talk." I stood. "Now." I held the jacket out to him. Silently he took it, slinging it over his shoulder with a non-chalance I envied.

"Lead on," he said, his voice low.

If Amy and Sarah hadn't been my best friends, I think they might have seriously contemplated committing an act of violence against me as I stole their prize away for a reprimand. Yep, looking back over my shoulder at them, I knew I was a dead woman.

My knees felt weak as I jogged down the bleacher stairs, the metal flexing faintly beneath the bounce of the traffic, most of which was headed in the opposite direction I was going. I didn't even pause to see if Pietr still followed me. If there was one thing I did know about Pietr by now, it was that he would follow or find me whether I wanted him to or not.

Jostling down the stairs only made my stomach lurch even more. It had to be that, I assured myself, not some emotional distress. I was still holding it all together. I could *keep* holding it all together. Just because everyone expected me to break didn't mean I *had* to.

I bounded down the final three steps and headed to the left, nearly slamming into a family in my single-minded advance. "Sorry," I muttered, dodging through the bunch of them. Free of the streaming crowd, my feet quickened the pace, leaving me wondering what I was running from.

He grabbed my arm, tugging me into the shadows at the edge of the bleachers, just outside the soft glow of the opening concession stand. "Jess." He moved in front of me, blocking the light, his powerful silhouette shadowing me. "If you want to talk, talk."

"Don't you need to check the time?" I asked.

"No. That doesn't matter right now."

We stood there, together, silent in the dark. The sound of his steady breathing was even more deafening than the marching band's drum routine as they processed off the field. I had missed Derek's big entrance, but somehow it seemed an after-thought.

"Have I done something wrong?" he asked. The silhouette shifted. His head seemed to hang.

"No. Yes—" I groaned in frustration. "I mean . . ." My eyes roamed, trying to find an easy answer.

And then he kissed me. My mind blanked. My spine loosened, and my lips moved, kissing him—impossible Pietr—back. For a moment there was nothing else. My world was forgotten. . . .

"No." I forced my hands between us and encountered the firm warmth of his chest. "No," I insisted, more to myself than to him because he was already drawing back.

He stood, as still as stone—reminding me of that moment in gym class when the boys had spotted his strange saber tattoo.

"I can't . . ." I tried to explain, but words failed me. Like always.

"Because of Derek?" he asked, nearly growling the name. The accent that only occasionally ghosted around his perfect American English became suddenly pronounced. Rich and powerful. "Don't you get it, Jess? You and he—it won't work. It can't be any good for you."

"God!" I was suddenly so mad at him. Why did he always need to state the obvious? "That's not even it!" I raged, realizing I was telling him the truth. "Sarah likes you."

He grunted. "The new kid always gets a lot of attention."

"Seeing what I have, I agree. But it's not that simple," I insisted. "Sarah's my best friend. She's been through a lot recently."

"From what I understand, so have you." I didn't know how his eyes could seem to glow in the dark of the bleachers, but they did—seeking to spear straight into my soul.

I squeezed my eyes shut, trying to close out the sound of his outright concern. "She was in a horrible accident. She nearly died. She was in a coma for almost a week." I paused, remembering. "She had to learn to do everything all over again. There's so much she still doesn't remember. . . ."

"That's terrible," he agreed. "But—"

"No. There can't be a *but*," I explained. "She hasn't shown an interest in anything except words—she hasn't cared about anyone. . . . And now she likes *you*."

"And I like *you*," he stated.

"Aaargh! You don't even *know* me!"

"Sarah doesn't really know me, *either*," he argued.

"Please," I begged. "I just *can't* . . ."

He moved, looking toward the concession stand. I knew he was thinking. And I knew he was hurt. "Do *you* like me?" Handsome, bold Pietr whispered the question.

I knew what he wanted to hear and I knew the truth. And I knew what I could say to fix things. My lips moved to form the right words, even as they tingled from the jolt of his kiss.

But my heart froze even as my mouth moved to say the necessary words to him under the bleachers. My mouth has always been under *just* my mouth's control—there's normally little interference from my brain. But this time I thought the words before I said them. Then I thought them each again as I voiced the phrase "I don't like you like *that*."

I was amazed I'd gotten the words to sound even halfway convincing. *Liar.* Surely he'd call my bluff, remind me how I'd kissed him back a brief moment before. . . .

"Oh."

What? Where was the sentence he was supposed to say—the sentence that would make me admit I was lying to protect poor

Sarah's freshly forming feelings for him? Where was the raging male ego at being told he wasn't "all that"?

My head was spinning. Why didn't he call me out? Why didn't he point out the obvious *this* time, too? Tell me I kissed him back like I *liked* him—*really* liked him. . . . I shoved my hand into a pocket and grabbed hold of the worry stone.

He put his jacket back on.

My heart sank. Maybe he wasn't saying it because every girl he kissed responded that way. What did I know about kissing, after all? I mean, it wasn't my first kiss—that honor had gone to mush-mouthed Marvin Broderick in fourth grade. What an illustrious introduction to one-sided love *that* had been! A few awkward kisses each year thereafter, a grope or two (resulting in well-aimed slaps), a lengthy dry spell, and here I was, seven long years later, bewildered.

He liked me. I liked him. And it still wouldn't work.

"We'd better get back," he said, "before they get the wrong idea."

I nodded, eyes stinging. "I'm going to get some snacks for the girls," I said, stepping into the light. He must have heard the way my voice cracked.

He looked at me, searching my face, concern like a wound in his bright eyes.

But I stayed stoic, dying a little inside. "I'll see you up there."

He nodded, a curt dip of his head.

We went our separate ways, and before buying chips and sodas, I detoured to the bathroom and wiped my eyes with toilet paper, promising to pull myself back together before returning to my friends. And I did. Because although I didn't often lie, I found I had a developing talent for it.

And no, that didn't make me feel any better. About anything.

CHAPTER ELEVEN

It was a good game (according to my limited understanding of football). It didn't help that Amy told Pietr I knew nothing about football and he spent several painfully awkward moments trying to explain the finer points of the game to me. He seemed to know a decent amount about it and was obviously trying to bridge the chasm I'd just torn between us.

He spoke; I nodded, listening to the sound of my stupid heart breaking as much as listening to his every word. He admitted grudgingly to a couple of fine plays that Derek made.

Sarah tucked her book away to watch the game. Or Pietr.

She caught him once when he spitefully admitted, "That was an excellent move."

"Do you have something in particular against Derek?" Sarah asked. "You don't seem to like him and you haven't been at Junction High long enough to really know him."

I silently prayed Pietr didn't look at me when responding. *Don't let it be because of me. . . .* But at the same time, a tiny bit of my ego hoped—even as it dreaded—that it was *precisely* because of me.

But Pietr didn't look at me, didn't give a clue as to why he might harbor some animosity toward our junior football star other than saying, "I've known a lot of people like him before."

He slouched back down, his body so close to mine I felt the warmth of him seeping through my jacket.

"It's fourth and goal," Pietr whispered. "They're close to scoring. The Jackrabbits need to decide whether to kick or pass.

"They can attempt to fake the Bulldogs out—or pass it—or they can get a kick and hopefully make the goal." Pietr's mouth moved beside my ear as he explained, his breath warm. My eyes were glued to Derek's distant form, wondering if he'd be instrumental in this play, too.

He was impressive on the field, quick and powerful, seemingly thinking on his feet and anticipating his opponents. I hadn't appreciated his position as a running back until Pietr had explained it mere minutes before, at my prodding.

"It means he's quick on his feet and good with his hands," Pietr had grumped.

Amy snorted soda through her nose.

Sarah giggled. "That's what Jessica hopes."

I blushed, mad at them all. Equally.

As they got into their starting positions, I could hear Kurt Anderson calling the play—a long line of what seemed to be nonsensical numbers. "They're well enough positioned to kick and make it," Pietr mentioned. But as Kurt fell silent, we saw him spin to his right and hurl a short pass to Derek. There was a groan as the Bulldogs lurched toward Derek, surprised.

Derek dodged and headed for the end zone, but a sudden blur tore across the field—a Bulldog rushing from out of nowhere. There was a bone-jarring crash as pads, helmets, and bodies collided, and for one moment the ball popped totally free of Derek's able hold and I watched him go down in slow-motion, Branson toppling him. . . .

The crowd shouted, seeing the ball leap, taunting, out of Derek's grasp and more players—Bulldogs and Jacks alike—jumped into the fray, becoming a tangle of heavy bodies and clacking helmets struggling for a single prize.

A whistle was blown on the play, the ref rushing forward and waving his hands for attention.

"He's calling everything from *holding* and *face mask* to *block in the back*," Pietr said, his tone slightly awed. "It's a mess."

The ref rounded the group of them, encouraging boys out of the way so he could get a clear look at the ball. "He's determining possession," Pietr said.

A moment passed as the ref examined the situation, and his expression changed. He squatted and suddenly hopped back up. Turning toward the stands, he stretched both his arms out, beckoning.

"That's not good," Pietr said, his voice taking on a confidential tone.

"What?" I asked stiffly. My hands balled into fists on my lap, the worry stone a weight in my palm.

The crowd howled, people jumping up. I heard distressed calls of "oh-God-oh-no-please-God-no" emerge from all around the bleachers as people realized the remaining pile of boys was barely moving.

"He wants both teams' trainers. Players from both sides are hurt." Pietr's voice was calm, his tone distant.

Assistant refs and benchwarmers darted onto the field,

helping carefully extricate players from the heap. The first few players stood and walked off the field to relieved applause.

A stretcher was run onto the field, and Bryce-the-Breaker Branson was loaded onto it and carried off, trainers laboring beneath his hulking size. And just beneath where his body had lain was Derek, still, and surrounded by stunned teammates and his coach. Jenny rushed the field and was held back by a couple of Jack halfbacks as medics ran past her.

"Oh, God," I whispered.

In my ear I heard Pietr's breathing grow ragged.

"Jessie—" Amy whispered from behind me.

I turned to face her, my mind reeling. I couldn't watch. I'd watched before when medics had been too little . . . too late. . . . It was too much and too soon to see something like it happen again.

Pietr's eyes locked on my own and he gripped both my shoulders, his hands hot through my jacket. "Jess." His eyes gleamed. I was present enough to know I was stunned. Terrified. "Jess. He's going to be fine." He turned me back around. "Watch."

"Pietr," Sarah warned.

But he held my shoulders, firmly, letting me know he was there as I watched the madness on the field. Through eyes blurring with tears, I watched the Junction Jackrabbits close ranks around their prone teammate, giving the medics precious privacy before the watchful eyes of hundreds of concerned classmates, teachers, and parents.

The announcer came on and started to ramble, trying to distract us all from staring at the thing we could no longer see but couldn't avoid imagining.

I trembled beneath Pietr's steady hold, feeling the walls I'd built so carefully since June falling to pieces beneath the careful power of his hands. My right hand grasped his, and I started breathing again.

The crowd of Jackrabbits parted. Squinting through tears, I could just make out the two medics, with Derek between them. Walking. I let go of Pietr's hand and rubbed my eyes clear. I wasn't hallucinating. Derek was conscious—walking—obviously wounded and awkward, but . . . I spun around in my seat, breaking Pietr's grip on my shoulders, and Amy and Sarah rushed me, bending awkwardly to hug and reassure me.

From between them I could glimpse Pietr sitting back on the bench, watching me with guarded eyes.

The game resumed, but I didn't care. Without Derek, what was the point of football? My boredom and subsequent twitching became so noticeable that Amy finally said, "I'll be back."

It was part of a code we used.

Pietr must have followed her with his eyes because Sarah ratted us out. "She's going to see if she can get any information on Derek. Or—better yet—if she can sneak Jessica in to see him *sans* Jenny."

"Of course," he said, but I knew he didn't approve. Wasn't I aiming too high with my crush? *"Sans* Jenny," he repeated.

My spine stiffened at his tone. I knew he was thinking.

"Are you going to the Homecoming Dance?"

I turned, temper flaring again. "I already said—" But the words died in my throat.

He was facing Sarah.

She sputtered. Blushed. "Nobody asked me."

"I guess I'm asking you," he clarified.

It was horrible. There he was, exceeding my hopes for making Sarah happy and killing me at the same time. At point-blank range. In a way, he was doing what I'd told him I wanted.

But I couldn't watch. "I'm going to check on Amy," I mumbled, leaving them, but not so soon that I didn't hear Sarah's shy reply.

"Sure, I'll go to the Homecoming Dance with you, Pietr."

I saw Amy at the bottom of the stairs, scoping out the Derek-Jenny situation. "You don't look so good," she said.

"Thanks. This day's gone on for-ehv-er."

"Well, good news is, Derek's just twisted an ankle—or something like that." Amy shrugged. "Sounds like a pretty girlie wound for football, if you ask me."

I just looked at her, pursing my lips.

"Ye-ahh. You didn't ask me." Amy smiled with a wicked twist of her lips. "Jenny should be going to get more ice pretty soon, I guess. That's when I suggest you zip in—and out. Don't forget to get *out* again. Jenny'll kill you if she finds you there."

"I know."

"Are you sure you want to see him? From what I've heard, he's—"

"Stringing me along. Yeah. I've heard that, too. But . . ."

She seized my arm and shook it. "You're kidding. After all you've been through, you've still got a bit of optimist in you?"

I looked down.

"God, I hope he doesn't crush it all out of you. I guess you could try to claim you want to interview him for a story about the Homecoming game. . . . I doubt Jenny'd believe you, though." She let me go. "Shh." She pointed. "There she goes. . . ."

Together we watched Jenny (with her taped-up nose) head for the concession stand, a small cooler in her hand.

"Go, but be quick," Amy advised.

And I did—ducking under the stairs and jogging down

the dim hall to where the locker room door was. I opened it slowly . . . quietly. If he was resting, I didn't want to disturb him.

Derek was propped on a table, sipping Gatorade. He looked good. No, actually, he looked great. "Hey," he said, seeing me.

"Hey. I just wanted to see that you were okay."

He watched solemnly as the words dropped away from me. "Even after what Jenny said in the office?"

I sucked in a deep breath, reminding myself that I trained unruly horses, jumped them in bad conditions in competition. . . . But for some reason I was more nervous being in the same room alone with Derek than I'd ever been before. "Yes." I blushed.

"Good," he said with a sigh. He ran his fingers through his thick blond hair. "Because I told her all that bull so she'd let you off the hook."

"It worked," I whispered, awed.

"That was the whole idea." He smiled, and my stomach did a flip. "Jenny's not the smartest girl—or the nicest," he said. "But she can be convinced to do certain things. . . . She just needs to be able to see how it might benefit her somehow first. What is it you'd say? You can lead a horse to water—"

"But you can't make it drink," I concluded.

"I'm just good at getting that *horse* to take a sip and realize how thirsty she is for more." He winked.

"Oh." He did seem like he could be amazingly persuasive. Convincing without the slickness some people mistook for charm. "Thank you." I looked back toward the door, Amy's warning echoing in my head.

"Yeah." He followed my gaze. "Jenny better not find you here."

I headed for the door, but his words stopped me. "Wait. Come here," he said.

I did. I couldn't stop myself.

"I didn't get to ask you—" He swung his legs off of the table and winced.

"Oh! Are you okay?" My hand went to his knee.

"Getting better." He grinned. His eyes' broad pupils were like twin black holes. I was sucked into their inescapable depths.

I blushed so hard I thought my ears would start to smoke.

"I can't ask you to the dance," he said apologetically. "Not now, with Jenny thinking we're back together."

I nodded. My hero was sacrificing himself for my sake. I held my breath—held back my sigh of enamored contentment.

"But—" He leaned over me, taking my face in his hands. His hands were cool against my burning face and he made me look up at him. I saw his eyes grow near, they closed. . . . I closed mine, too, and then he kissed me—a hard kiss, fast and strong like his performance on the football field. My toes curled in my sneakers. My head fogged. I had imagined this moment for years. And it was so much better than my imagination could even dream up. . . . He drew back suddenly, examining my face, his brows slightly pulled together. He licked his lips and let go of me. He was thinking something.

"What?" I wobbled on my feet, unsteady.

But the strain on his features cleared and he smiled. "I like you, Jessica," he confirmed, as if a kiss like that wasn't proof enough. "But you'd better go."

I did. I raced out of the room and back up the hall and out from beneath the stairs, skidding to a stop. Amy was motioning me frantically to the side.

Just on the other side of the under-stair entrance stood Jenny, tapping her foot and shifting the cooler from one hand to the other. Before her, Pietr successfully blocked her chosen path. Jenny glared at him but didn't seem capable of just brushing him off.

"So the stress and strain from jumping around so much in cheerleading can actually tear your ligaments and wear out your joints well before your eighteenth birthday," he was explaining. Slowly. I mean, *real-ly slow-ly.*

"What took you so long?" Amy asked me. "If Pietr hadn't come down when he did, well, I'd be cleaning up what was left of you after Jenny found you with Derek and tore you apart."

Jenny finally had enough of Pietr's speech and glared at him, pursing her lips before pushing him aside and racing down the hall I'd just emerged from.

Pietr joined us in the shadows. He looked at me like he'd just done something he'd regret. Then his eyes focused on my lips—like he could *see* the place Derek's lips had pressed minutes ago. "I've got to go," he said, his jaw tight. "Thanks for an exciting evening." He paused and added, *"Da. Spahseebuh."* The last word came out bitterly.

And then he walked away. Without bothering to look back.

I went home that evening, a lump in the back of the Luxoms' car, listening to Sarah detail every move Pietr had made, every syllable he'd uttered, and all the ways his super dark brown hair (she proclaimed it to be a delicious dark chocolate) glinted with burnt-umber highlights under the spotlights at the football field. She *really* liked him.

Which made me feel even worse because I *really* kissed him.

CHAPTER TWELVE

Amy and Sarah were still determined to drag me to the Homecoming Dance, but I managed to close the car door between us before they could force a resentful *yes* out of me. I couldn't imagine going to the dance. Seriously—how much did I have to suffer in one week?

Rain began to fall, only deepening my souring mood.

I had walked the new kid around the school, wound up in the office for single-handedly creaming two cheerleaders, watched my crush reunite with his ex, realized I kind of liked the new boy but couldn't have him because Sarah liked him, got kissed by my crush, and almost killed by his girlfriend. . . .

I sighed, standing outside my home, hand on the doorknob. I inserted my key and wondered if I was seriously supposed to watch everyone have a great time at a dance now, too.

With a groan I twisted the knob and nudged the door open. I heard music coming from the kitchen.

"Dad?" I called.

"*C'est moi,*" Annabelle Lee responded.

I joined her at the breakfast nook. "What are you listening to?" I asked, sliding a CD case across the table to look. She had what Dad called his "boom box." I had joked with him that the only way it'd boom was if he let me shoot it. He hadn't been amused. Mom had laughed *so* hard.

"Eighties rock," Annabelle Lee said, not looking up from a well-worn copy of *Pride and Prejudice.* "Dad's putting together a mix CD for your Homecoming Dance—"

"What?" I couldn't hide the alarm in my voice.

"Something about the deejay getting sick or disappearing, or—" She shrugged, unconcerned.

"So why *Dad*?" I felt my nose crinkle as I asked.

"Our father evidently has the largest collection of eighties music in all of Junction."

"What a thing to be known for." I tapped the CD case. Queen. I flipped it over. "Who Wants to Live Forever" and "It's a Kinda Magic" were song names. "They really think people will come to a dance with an eighties theme?"

"It's not just *any* dance. It's Homecoming. It's like the prom—from what I've heard. The theme doesn't matter. It's the event itself," Annabelle Lee patiently explained.

Something suddenly occurred to me. "Oh, God . . . Dad's not actually *going* to go to the dance, is he?"

She closed her book slowly and set it down on the table between us. "Should he?"

I pressed my lips together and narrowed my eyes. "He's not needed there, Annabelle Lee," I said, making my voice as blatant a warning as I could muster.

"Middle names are *very* parental," she warned right back. "You drop the Lee and maybe I won't tell Dad a boy stopped by for you tonight."

"What? Annabelle L—" I stopped and switched gears. "Tell me who stopped by, please." I sat.

She slipped a folded piece of paper from between the pages of her book. "He said his name was Pietr. I had to put Hunter and Maggie in the laundry room while he was here; they were crazy!" She paused. "Anyhow, he brought you an assignment you missed somehow today." She slid it across the table to me.

Crap.

"So how does *that* happen?" she asked. "I mean, you're in school and somehow you miss an assignment?"

"What did Pietr say?"

"He wasn't very forthcoming," she admitted. "Russian, right?" She didn't wait for an answer. "Hope he's not related to the rumors of Russian Mafia the newspapers keep dredging up."

"The *newspapers*? Since when—?" Reading newspapers was not Annabelle Lee's style. She was always quick to point out there must be a reason they were the most readily recycled form of literature.

"There are a few decent columns. Anyhow, Pietr's cute," she admitted, "in that nearly feral Heathcliff sort of way."

"Heathcliff—that cat from the old comic strips Dad keeps?"

She rolled her eyes. "You can be so very *daft* sometimes." She sighed.

"Huh. I've heard that about myself recently," I stated.

"Heathcliff," she tried to explain, "from *Wuthering Heights*."

"Is that nearby?" I wasn't an idiot, but I enjoyed playing one sometimes. Baiting Annabelle Lee was a favorite pastime. And, brilliant as she was, she almost always fell for it.

"Argh!" She picked up *Pride and Prejudice* just to slap it back down on the table. "*Wuthering Heights,* the novel—by Emily

Brontë." Her hands were in her hair, tugging in frustration. "Don't they make you *read* in high school?"

"Oooh. It's a book." I looked at the paper Pietr'd left. Science. The biology of canines. Surely fascinating stuff. "Maybe I'll check it out on Blu-ray sometime," I said, rising from the table and guessing I'd just insulted bibliophiles everywhere. *Biblio-phile.* Huh. Thank you, Sarah.

"Aren't you going to make a request for Dad to put on the CD? A slow dance, maybe," she teased. "Pietr looks like he'd be a good dancer."

"I won't be the one finding out," I called over my shoulder as I climbed the stairs to my room.

I hadn't gotten very far when I heard Annabelle Lee yell up the steps.

"Something's going on outside!"

I bolted down the stairs, trying to listen to any sounds other than the stomping of my feet. Barking. Lots of barking. I slipped my feet into my muck boots.

Annabelle Lee stood by the door, her expression battling between fear and excitement. "I don't know what's going on out there, but I think Hunter and Maggie are going to get them-selves in real trouble."

I pulled on my jacket and Annabelle Lee handed me the flashlight. Opening the door, I stepped outside, but her hand latched on to my arm, and she tugged me back in.

"You aren't seriously going out there?" she asked. "Just call the dogs in."

"Maggie's too dumb to come in once she's spotted something—you know that. It can't be that bad . . ." A shiver raced across my shoulders, proclaiming I lied. I remembered the beast outside the barn. Just a dog, right? God, I hoped so.

The pattering rain blew into a deafening downpour, scattering the powerful flashlight's beam in streaks of silvery water. Scanning the broad yard ahead, I called, "Hunter! Maggie!"

The barking had stopped.

"It was probably nothing! They probably went after a mouse. A raccoon." I sighed. "With my luck it's a skunk. But they aren't barking now." Like that was somehow reassuring. "They must be eating whatever it was."

"Or being *eaten,*" Annabelle Lee whispered.

"You're quite a pessimist," I muttered.

"Takes one to know one."

The rain lessened, merely muting the night noises, not drowning them out entirely.

"Maggie! Hunter!"

Still no response.

"You're seriously going out there?"

"See me stepping off the porch?" I replied.

"Holy crap." She dodged back into the house.

Good to have support. On the porch's lowest step and just below the lip of the roof, I examined the yard again with the flashlight. Nothing. The floodlight between the barns and the house gave no clue about the disappearance of my dogs, either.

In a moment Annabelle Lee returned, leaning out the door, a heavy walking stick in her hand. "At least take this."

"That's a good idea." I could whack something pretty hard with it if I needed to. I pulled up my hood and shuffled away from the porch, searching the area with the flashlight the whole time. "Hunter! Maggie!"

Nothing.

I trudged through the puddles and slick mud, and was nearly at the barn when I heard it: a growl deeper than any noise Hunter had ever dredged up.

My light caught Hunter and Maggie, their bodies low and wet, hair spiked along their shoulders, their faces fixed in the direction of the noise. They didn't notice my presence.

But *it* did.

I gasped as the white beam of my light intersected with bright red eyes—predator's eyes—at a height that made my dogs look small. Shaggy and heavy-headed with colors that blended with the brown mud at its feet, I knew it wasn't the red one from the barn or the brambles. And it most definitely wasn't a dog. . . .

With a snarl it leaped up, springing over the dogs and straight for me. The flashlight hit the ground, spattering me with mud as I raised my stick and took a swing. Massive paws nailed my shoulders, driving me down as my stick connected underneath its broad body.

It yelped.

If it was male, it'd feel my hit fiercely.

In the dark Maggie and Hunter snapped out of the spell they'd been under and came to my aid, whimpering and licking at my face. Hot wet tongues a sharp contrast to cold raindrops. Great. Because what I needed when going head-to-head with a monster was doggy kisses.

I wiped the rain out of my face with my sleeve and pushed them back. "Dammit," I muttered, reaching around in the softening ground for the flashlight.

Back in my grasp, it cut a sharp beam of light around the yard, quivering in my shaking hand. The beast was gone.

But not its tracks. They were huge. Larger than my hand

with fingers spread. The rain was already beginning to blur their edges and I jogged forward, playing the hesitant tracker. Definitely canine and . . .

I froze.

The canine tracks ended suddenly. If not for the smudging effect of the rain and the poor quality of light in the soggy darkness I might have said that where the canine tracks suddenly disappeared human footprints took over.

But that was impossible. I shivered and the rain grew heavier again, weighing down my jacket and slipping into my hood as I stared dully at something I simply couldn't explain. I was tired. Seeing things. My writer's imagination was just running wild.

"Come on, Maggie. Hunter," I said, walking quickly toward the house. They did not argue and nearly beat me to the door. Not guard dogs, certainly.

"What was it?" Annabelle Lee asked.

"Big," I growled, handing her the flashlight and walking stick so I could hang up my dripping jacket. "No more going out after dark until we know what else is out there."

She nodded gravely.

As I climbed the stairs I realized that as good as my hit had been, if the creature had wanted to it could have made short work of me. So it never meant me harm. The fact was almost reassuring. Almost.

That night the nightmare returned to its full ferocity. There were no alien eyes watching my response to distract me. And, as always, my reactions were just as devastating as when it truly happened. I'd lived the nightmare more than a hundred times now and it never dulled my senses, never blunted the anguish of that first horrible moment.

The only mercy the nightmare granted was that it always jolted me awake just after the cars collided. Before the screaming and flames. It left me wondering each morning if I never saw it repeat those last agonizing minutes because I still remembered them so clearly. Perhaps there was no need for the subconscious mind to devastate me when my conscious mind still did it so readily.

I growled at the slender lines of sunlight slicing through my window's blinds, a reminder that morning came early on our horse farm. Even if I'd slept well the night before, I wouldn't have been thrilled about doing all the chores. I stumbled downstairs in my work jeans and an old flannel shirt, rubbing my eyes against the sun that crept through the kitchen curtains.

"Mornin'," Dad said. I waved, eyes narrow with sleep.

The newspaper was dead center on the table, folded in half, headline announcing, "Mafia Spreads to Lytle, Junction, and Kitezh."

"Cereal." I grabbed a bowl and spoon and sat at the small table.

Dad passed me the box. I gave it a healthy shake, following it up with a splash of milk.

He cleared his throat. "I've been thinkin'. . . ."

I looked up at him. Glared at Annabelle Lee. She seemed absorbed in studying the ingredients list of the All-Natural Orange Juice carton. What was there to really study? The list read: orange juice. So she knew what was coming next.

"You work really hard doing all the chores, trainin' and ridin' and tryin' to stay focused on school. . . ."

My chewing slowed. In my mouth the Crispy Os disintegrated

into mush as I waited for Dad's next words. There had been a conversation that started like this at the very beginning of the school year, too. I'd made sure I kept my grades up since then.

"I think it may be too much for one person to handle."

I jabbed my spoon in Annabelle Lee's direction.

"Now," Dad said, "you know Anna's just a little too frail to help with the stuff you do."

It wasn't worth arguing. I'd tried before and all it had done was make Dad sad and Annabelle Lee more unbearable. She had a slight curvature of the spine. Exceedingly slight. Most doctors missed it. But anything that was related even vaguely to anyone's health now sent Dad into fits. I couldn't blame him. We were all he had. I put my spoon back into my bowl.

"I've decided things need to change round here."

I pushed my bowl away; I wasn't hungry anymore. The horses were the last things left of my mother's dreams. She had been a champion rider and a great judge of horseflesh. While Dad worked at the Aphrodite Chocolates Factory, Mom worked training, riding, stabling, and studding. It was where I envisioned my life going, too, if I stayed in Junction.

Besides, I couldn't bear seeing Mom's dreams die, too, even if she wasn't here to watch them be fulfilled. I swallowed the soggy mash still sitting in my mouth. "I'm not ready to sell any of the horses."

"Jessie, I don't—"

Annabelle Lee smiled. Big surprise. She'd always equated the horses with relentless work and none of the joys they brought. She was probably already considering ways to spend the money we'd get selling them.

Someone knocked on our door and startled me; I jumped enough for my little sister to notice.

"He's here," Annabelle Lee sang out, grinning at my puzzled expression as she bounded to the mudroom, opening the door with a grand sweep of her arm.

Pietr raised an eyebrow at her antics and stepped in. "Good morning, sir," he said toward my dad.

I glared at him. He was interrupting an important discussion about the future of the horses. And, hey, it was Saturday. Why was he even . . . My mind only slowly took in what he was wearing. A pair of well-worn jeans, a sweatshirt, and a very sensible denim jacket announced he was dressed for real work. Manual labor. And, I realized angrily, he was even better looking now than he had been last night. When he'd flirted with me. When he'd *kissed* me.

"Pietr," I said dismissively, trying to keep the questions from my tone, "thank you for stopping by, but I'm about to be very busy. I'm sure I can handle the papers you dropped off just fine without help."

Dad cleared his throat. "Jessie. I *hired* young Mr. Rusakova to help with daily chores. He stopped by to drop somethin' off for you, and—well, you know how Anna's always thinkin' . . ."

I looked at her and echoed lamely, "Always thinking. Yeah." Always *plotting* was more like it.

"Well, she had the forethought to get Rusakova's phone number for me."

"How very smart," I said, glowering at Annabelle Lee.

"I figured I'd rather give him a legitimate job than find out some friend of yours is fallin' in with the Russian Mafia."

Pietr focused on the floor.

"Seriously, Dad. The Russian Mafia?" I rolled my eyes.

Dad shot me a look, reminding me to maintain appropriate

respect while under his roof. "You'll still do all the brainy stuff—the trainin', the ridin' . . . but Rusakova will help with feedin' and muckin'—the brawny stuff."

"I·can do all of that, *too*," I whispered. "I always have."

"No one's doubting your abilities, Jessie. I just want you to focus on school and *your* stuff," Dad explained.

I rose from the table and headed to the mudroom.

"For God's sake, girl, accept some help for once," Dad called as I sat and tugged on my boots. I stood and there was Pietr, my ratty jacket in his hand. He held it out for me, silent.

I grabbed it, then threw open the door so I could hear its hinges whine as I strode out. Behind me I heard my father say apologetically, "She's a good girl, Rusakova, just stubborn as her mother. She'll come round," he assured him.

I was a good few yards ahead of Pietr when the dogs rushed out of the barn. They raced around me, eager to join me for the morning's chores. A breeze picked up, cool as autumn at its best, and the dogs froze, eyes fixed on Pietr. Hunter began to bark, ears back, the ruff of thicker fur across his shoulders rising defiantly. Maggie, more bark than bite, sat down in front of me suddenly—nearly tripping me—and started to whine.

I turned and looked back at Pietr, shouting over Hunter's barking. "What'd you do to my dogs?" I asked. "Hunter. Hunter, shut up!" I snapped. He stopped barking, the last yap falling into a questioning growl.

Pietr shrugged. "Some dogs like me. Some don't."

My lips pursed. "You'd better come here and introduce yourself properly, then, if you're going to be working here," I suggested. I slipped my hands around the collar of each dog. Just in case.

Pietr approached slowly. Hunter began to growl again, and Maggie resumed her nasally whine.

"Shut up!"

They did, and Pietr covered the last bit of ground, coming to stand before us. The dogs nearly ripped my arms out of their sockets as they fell to the ground and rolled over, bellies up in utter submission.

"What?" Mystified, I crouched between them, hands at their collars. The breeze picked up, ocher and sienna leaves rolling brightly between us.

Pietr stooped before me, carefully moving a hand out to let the dogs sniff, and then he patted their tummies reassuringly. They whined in pleasure, as if an old friend had returned home and they needed time to recognize him after so many years. I thought about Homer's *Odyssey* and the way Ulysses' dog, Argos, recognized him when no one else could. It was like Pietr belonged here.

"They usually aren't this"—I tried to find a word as interesting as Sarah's—"weird." I sighed, giving up. "We've occasionally hired people but . . . the dogs are acting really weird."

"They're just being protective of you," Pietr reassured. "It's what they—" He paused, gazing into my eyes. Something flapped with a thousand wings in the depths of my stomach. "It's what they're bred to do," he asserted.

Laughing, I stood and headed toward the barn again. "You haven't seen them eat." I chuckled. "Once you do, you'll think *that's* what they're bred to do."

In the first barn, I showed him the hay and grain—and the manure fork. He didn't seem concerned about getting a little dirty. Walking into the second barn and down the aisle of stalls, I murmured to each horse, rubbing their snouts while conceding that Dad would want me to date a guy who wasn't afraid of a little physical labor.

But that didn't matter, did it? *I* wasn't dating Pietr. Sarah was going to Homecoming with him and I should be happy for her. I wondered how long I needed to keep telling myself that before I'd believe it.

I popped a CD into the player and adjusted the volume so the sounds of city traffic bounced off the stall doors. The horses flicked their ears and relaxed again.

"What are we listening to?" Pietr asked, brow furrowed in obvious distaste.

"It's a training CD," I explained. "It gets the horses prepared for weird noises so they don't freak out in competition."

Pietr smiled. "I wouldn't have thought of that."

"Me neither," I admitted. "Mom had the first ones made. I credit that and having the dogs underfoot with being the reasons why our horses are so calm and well mannered. They hardly spook anymore." But they had totally freaked out the night before Pietr showed up at Junction High.

Pietr nodded, reaching a slow hand toward Rio to pet her nose. She blew once through widened nostrils and then accepted his kindness. "I see that."

Pietr cleaned stalls and filled feeders at a remarkable pace. I actually stepped over to see that he was doing it right; I was sure he was taking shortcuts. But he wasn't.

"Everything okay, boss?" he asked with a slow smile.

"Yeah."

He stood beside me, heat pouring off of him. He'd shed the denim jacket a while ago and had pushed up his sweatshirt's sleeves, revealing powerful forearms. I could smell the mingled scents of pine-laced sweat and sweet timothy hay on him and I thought together they made a fine cologne.

"Are you going to Homecoming?"

I swallowed. "Amy and Sarah want me to. I think Sarah wants to show you off."

He grunted and leaned the manure fork against a stall. He picked up a pail of water and began to refill Rio's bucket.

I asked the next question before I could stop myself. "Did you kiss her?"

He froze, mid-pour, thinking. Water dribbled over the bucket's edge and onto Rio's floor.

I righted the pail, taking it from him, my hands brushing his. I shivered at the touch.

"Did you want me to?" he pressed, his beautiful blue eyes dark, hooded.

I blinked up at him. God, he was *so* frustrating. I set the pail down, letting it slosh to show my frustration. "Do what you want," I commanded.

And then he was kissing me again, moving me backward until I was against the wall, bridles and reins rustling against my head and toying with my hair.

I knew that no matter how much I wanted to be kissing Pietr—to be dating Pietr—I couldn't. Not right now. So I dodged beneath his arm. "I *can't* do this!"

He stood back, arms across his chest, observing me coolly. Waiting for a confession. Fine! I could confess, but that would have to be it. There couldn't be any dating for us—not as long as Sarah had a crush on him. Otherwise, what sort of best friend would I be?

I leaned over, hands on my knees, trying to catch my breath and focus.

"Please tell me what you *can't* do," he said, the softest hint of an accent edging back into his voice. "Because it seems like you can kiss me back just fine."

Ugh. So he *had* noticed. Well, it didn't matter. I steadied my breathing and rose, careful not to meet his searching eyes. "Yeah. You're a great kisser." Oh, God—did I actually admit he was *great*? Out loud? I paused, concentrating on not blushing. Unfortunately, that only intensified the stinging stain of red on my cheeks.

He was chuckling, a rich, slow sound.

"Don't laugh at me," I demanded. "Okay, so I do like you."

"*That* way," he clarified, keeping most of the mockery from in his voice.

"Yeah. That way," I admitted. I looked up at him. "But you have to understand. Sarah really likes you, and . . ."

"I get it," he said. "You have to be a loyal friend first." He paused. Picked up the pail between us. "I totally get it. I just don't like it." He moved down the aisle and poured water into Snap's bucket. "It's only one dance, though. Maybe she won't like me after that."

I frowned. "Doubtful."

"It's not like we're . . . what—*an item*?"

"After the dance, you will be." I shrugged, but I didn't feel indifferent about it at all. "It's part of Junction's small-town charm: People assume things, and we all live up—or down—to their expectations." I was madder at myself than I'd been for months.

I sighed. Wasn't I getting what I wanted? I wanted Sarah to be happy, so I made myself unhappy and arranged things just right. And I was *totally* unhappy watching him doing the chores because it was time when he wasn't kissing me. But I was unhappy kissing him because I knew it couldn't continue, and unhappier yet because I knew I couldn't betray Sarah—even though some small part of me was really tempted to.

"Then I'll just have to find a reason to break up with her after the dance."

"What?" My stomach fluttered.

He grinned at me. "I'll date Sarah a while—she'll be happy and you'll be a great friend, and then she'll screw it all up." He took a scoop of grain to Bunny. "I mean, she's bound to do something that'll legitimately tick me off—she's a teenage girl. Like you. And *you* have a gift for ticking me off."

I nodded but was no happier. What Pietr didn't know about Sarah was that she was perfect: absolutely incapable of ticking someone off. I picked up a soft currycomb and stepped into Rio's stall. I followed the gentle curves of her powerful body, realizing that as simple as the solution seemed to Pietr, he had no idea what he was up against.

Sarah was absolutely infallible and completely lovable . . . unless she was dating the guy you liked. I barely stopped myself from groaning. *One* of the guys you liked . . .

CHAPTER THIRTEEN

That evening and the Homecoming Dance arrived far too soon.

I had never seen so many blue, white, and gold balloons as I saw the night of the dance. They filled the gym, long ribbon tails brushing against people's hair whenever one started to lose helium. It was at least vaguely amusing to watch girls in their finest angrily swatting away the ticklish ribbons, their dates occasionally grabbing and popping the offenders as if it were a demonstration of chivalry reborn.

I slid off my shoes, putting them in the growing pile by the gym's doorway. Amy was beside me dressed in a pretty and long-sleeved green dress, equally coaxing and prodding me. I still wasn't convinced I should be there.

But Sarah had sounded like she was on the verge of tears when I'd begun to list my excuses on the phone that afternoon. Considering what I'd already done to support Sarah, watching the guys I liked dance with two other girls didn't seem like it should be such a big sacrifice. It felt big, anyway.

"What is that song they're playing?" Amy asked, wrinkling her nose.

I listened, remembering the songs Dad had been going through the whole afternoon to create the mixed CD.

"Steam in the subway, earth is afire—"

"Hmm." I searched the large room's edges, sadly curious. I spotted Derek dancing with Jenny. She was focused on him like she was obsessed. "Hungry Like the Wolf—" I said, thinking she looked like she could snap him up in one bite. "It's by some British band, I think."

"Woman you want me, give me a sign—"

"So they subject us to eighties music and stuff from overseas?"

"'Across the pond,'" I corrected, smiling. "Oh. It's Duran Duran. Believe me, it could be waaay worse. Have you ever listened to music from the seventies?"

She shook her head.

"One word: *disco*."

We both faked a body-quaking shiver and laughed.

Amy's expression changed suddenly and she grabbed me, turning us back away from the gym. "Don't look now, but somebody's watching you."

"Derek?" I whispered.

She mouthed, *No.*

"Who?"

She rolled her eyes. "The other guy you're crushing on."

"What? I'm n—"

But she looked at me with such open disgust I had to shut my mouth.

"How obvious is it?" I muttered.

"Oh, I'd think everybody's figured out what's going on by now—"

"Oh, no—"

"Except for Sarah," she clarified.

I responded with a hearty, "Thank God!"

"Yeah, but that can't last—not the way he looks at you."

"I'll have to talk to him, then," I said in my most stoic tone.

"Yee-aahh."

"What?"

"Have you tried talking to him before?"

"Yes," I said firmly. And I had.

"And what happens?"

I blushed. "He kisses me."

She blinked and then said, "Well, then, maybe *I* should try talking to him," with a devilish grin. "I wouldn't mind being kissed by a guy like that."

"So, how *is* Marvin?" I asked, trying not to wince at the memory of my first kiss, but hoping to change the subject.

"He's here somewhere. Probably with an armload of flowers. Could be worse." She looked at me. "At least *I* have a date for Homecoming."

The suspense tugged my stomach in knots. "Is he still watching?"

Amy glanced over my shoulder. "Even worse!" she hissed. "He's coming this way!"

"Do we have time to get to the bathroom?" I asked. I was *not* ready to see Pietr.

"No—hey. Look, Jessie, it's Pietr!" Amy twirled me around to face him.

"Oh. Hey, Pietr," I said. "Hey, Sarah!" I brushed past him, hugging my best friend—the girl who had followed him across the gym's shiny floor like a shadow in stocking feet.

She was flushed, and I wondered if it was from keeping up with Pietr's long-legged pace or because of something he'd said to her earlier.

"You look beautiful!" I said with a smile. It wasn't a lie. Sarah seemed to glow, her pale blond hair luminous under the gym lights' lowest setting.

She had on a soft-looking powder blue dress that just came to her knees and had faint swirls of tiny beads around its scooped neckline, bodice, and hem. She was carrying a dainty clutch purse, the spine of *The Great Gatsby* just peeking out of the top. Even it seemed perfect for the moment.

Sarah looked like a fairy princess—too frail for earth, but too full of life for Heaven. Like she was just caught in our world but not meant to stay. I was envious.

"You look pretty, too, Jessica," Sarah complimented. "No." She tilted her head and looked me up and down, searching for a stronger synonym. *"Exquisite,"* she said. "Yes. With your long hair up and that necklace and dress, you look exquisite."

I blushed, realizing she wasn't the only one who'd looked me up and down.

"I've never seen that necklace before," Amy commented, leaning around me to block Pietr's blatant gaze. I suddenly thought the neckline of my top might be too revealing and my hand went up to the pendant that rested at my breastbone.

"It's a rabbit netsuke."

I saw Pietr's eyebrows shoot up in surprise.

"A what?" Amy asked. "Sarah. Is she making that word up?"

Sarah beamed at being deferred to. "Nope. It's a real word. From Japan."

"Holy heck," Amy said with a roll of her eyes. "Music from the eighties, a Japanese bunny, and a Russian guy? Did I ever tell you I'm a distant descendent of the Chippewa Indians? Only thing I got out of it was a few freaky bedtime stories, a couple dream catchers, and probably the family propensity to drink."

I blinked at her.

Amy shrugged. "Overall, my heritage isn't important in my life. I think things are simpler if we don't look too far back. I mean, seriously. Can't anything just be simple in Junction?"

I couldn't meet her eyes. Don't look too far back? Wasn't my past what made me who I was right now? Sure, I tried to look beyond it, but Amy sounded like she'd rather forget it altogether. I didn't have that sort of strength.

I fingered the pendant, relaxing at the reassuring feel of its carved surface in my hand and still near my heart. "My mother was born in the year of the rabbit, according to the Chinese horoscope," I explained.

Something in my voice made Pietr add, "Netsuke were worn by Japanese men—samurai warriors—to help balance things on their belts. Your mother must have had the heart of a warrior," he said, holding my gaze like an anchor.

I nodded. "She was pretty strong." Way stronger than my paltry smile. "Mom always said it was the weirdest thing—the way she got the necklace. She was vacationing with her family one summer on Coney Island and she walked into the tiniest shop on the boardwalk and saw this necklace.

"She asked the shopkeeper—this odd little lady—about it but realized she had left her money in the hotel room. But the woman wouldn't let her leave the shop without the rabbit." I shook my head, remembering how confused my mom seemed about the woman's intense reaction, even so many years later. "She insisted it was meant for Mom's family and that she should just take it." I shrugged, remembering how sweetly, how patiently, and willingly my mother had told me the story every time I'd asked.

"Mom finally accepted it and rushed out to find her parents, figuring she'd borrow some money and pay the woman back.

Then she could pay her parents back when they returned to the hotel. But by the time she found her parents, the shop was closed. They were heading home the next morning before it opened again. Mom wrote down the address and tried sending the lady money, but the envelope came back marked 'Address Unknown.' Weird, huh?" I smiled at them, hoping no one could see the tears pushing at the edges of my eyes, brought on by memories of Mom and her stories.

Amy grabbed me, though, steering me to the side of the gym, and said over her shoulder, "Go get some punch, you crazy kids," to Pietr and Sarah. Mercifully they took the hint.

"Look," she snapped, hands on my shoulders. "You need to get back in control of yourself. I know you're going through Hell. I get it. You lost your mom, and your dad's never really around. And that fruitcake sister of yours . . ." She shook her head, rolling her eyes. "Like I said. Hell. But."

"But," I repeated.

"But this isn't you—this weepy girl. Every time I turn around you're martyring yourself over something."

"Whoa . . . *martyring*?"

"Yeah. It's a frikkin' big word for me to be tossing around. *Thank you, Sarah*," she scoffed. "But it's the right word for what you're doing. You see something you want—Pietr—and you give him to the person who ruined your life."

"What do you—"

"Don't what-do-you-mean me. Sarah was driving the frikkin' car that night. She's not legal now, she sure wasn't legal then." Her eyes glowed grimly. "Her joyride cost you your mother."

"Stop it," I whispered.

"What? You don't want to hear it? What, not here, not now? *Crap*, Jessie! Wake up. She killed your mom, and you helped feed her in the hospital. You're so stuck on forgiving her, you've forgotten to forgive yourself!"

I covered my ears. Amy pushed me into the corner and pulled my hands back down.

"She had no one else," I protested. "Her parents were totally clueless, and her so-called friends were the first to ditch her. Believe me, when I went to the hospital that day, the last thing I imagined was helping her. But it was such an amazing opportunity . . . to give her a fresh start. . . ."

"Opportunity? Shit! You're still in denial! Sarah killed your mom, and you helped her learn to walk again. She killed your mom, you read to her so she was ready for school this year. She *killed* your mom—"

"Dammit!" I snapped, glad the music covered my sudden outburst. "Don't you think I know?" Tears slid freely down my face, slipping into the corners of my mouth. "I was *there*, remember? Mom came to get me and—and . . ." My feet slid out from underneath me, and I slumped in the corner. Amy followed me down, crouching before me, obscuring the looks of curious dancers. "But she's not the same Sarah now," I insisted.

"No, she's not," Amy ground out. "She's not *herself* at all."

Pietr was suddenly there, nearly knocking Amy over in his haste to reach me. "Jess—"

I glimpsed Sarah not far behind him, carrying cups for four. "Jessica—?"

Pietr slipped his hands under my arms and lifted me, hurrying me out the gym door. My feet barely touched the ground.

The last thing I saw was Sarah standing there, dumbstruck, cups of punch in her hands. "Jessica? Pietr—?" she called.

But we were gone.

He half-carried, half-pushed me all the way to the restrooms.

"Oh, *no*—" I protested with a sniff when I saw BOYS written

on the door. He opened it and shoved me inside. I stood in front
of a broken mirror while he checked the stalls.

Satisfied, he put his back to the door and slid down until he
was seated on the tiles, jamming the door shut with his body.

We had our privacy.

I focused on the mirror, only occasionally glimpsing him
out of the corner of my eye. "I guess I should have invested in
the waterproof mascara." I chuckled.

From the stony silence I could tell he was not amused.
"Don't," he said.

"Don't what?"

"Don't put that mask back on." He wasn't looking at me.
Instead, he studied the tip of his sock-covered feet. "You do
that, you know?"

"What?"

"Lie. Like it's nothing. Like lying will protect people. It
doesn't," he said—though I thought it was more of a confession.
"It just ruins things."

"I don't—"

"You lied about liking me. You lied about wanting me to
bring Sarah here. You're lying right now if you say that you
don't lie. And"—he looked up at me, eyes searching—"the big-
gest lie you're telling is *not* telling me what's really going on
with you and Sarah."

"The sin of omission." I shrugged. "So why do you want to
help me, when you know how willingly I lie to my best friend?"

"Because I know you," he said.

"How?"

"I just do." He shrugged. "And I know lies can't last." He
paused a moment before asking, "So what's got you so wrecked?"

"Look. I'm just a mess, okay? I'm going through some stuff
and I'm not doing it gracefully."

"You're skirting the issue."

"What issue?"

"What's the problem between you and Sarah?"

I looked at the door.

He shook his head. "You aren't going through this door until I have some answers."

So I told him. *Everything*. About the car accident and my mother's death, about helping Sarah recover and hiding the truth of what she really was like before the accident. About not telling Sarah she *caused* the accident . . . I even confessed that the best friend I loved so much I really hated sometimes, too.

He listened while I poured my heart out. And, oddly, that was what I needed.

"Is she dangerous?" he asked softly.

"What?"

"Is Sarah dangerous?"

"I don't—" I rubbed my eyes. "I don't know. She's so different now. She was cruel before. Vicious. She was definitely dangerous *then*."

He looked at his hand, turning it over silently. He seemed to be making up his mind about something.

"What are you thinking?" I asked, unsure I really wanted an answer.

"Hey!" Someone bumped against the bathroom door.

Pietr reached up from where he still sat and rapped the door with his knuckles. "Bathroom's closed!"

I was glad he'd answered. I wasn't ready to talk to anybody. Except Pietr.

Someone outside snickered, but their footsteps grew softer as they left.

"Wipe your eyes," Pietr suggested.

"How did you know *this* was what I needed?"

He shrugged. "You looked the way I've felt lots of times. Destroyed."

"You really know how to flatter a girl."

His mouth turned up at one edge, giving him a crooked smile. I liked it. But that corner soon fell back in line. "There's something I'd better tell you, too." He seemed to reconsider as soon as he said it. But it was already too late. "It's only fair," he muttered.

I leaned against the single sink.

"My parents are both dead," he said, so softly I suddenly found I'd moved to crouch by his knees, my hand on his left leg. He didn't look up at my face, but focused instead on my hand. I thought about pulling it away but couldn't.

"The people in the office—"

"My brothers and sister."

"Oh." I sat. "What happened?"

"I—" He shook his head. I understood. Sometimes there were no right words. So I sat there beside him on the cool tile floor and gave him the time he had so willingly given me.

I finally broke the silence. "So, how long ago . . ."

"Almost a year."

"Promise me something, Pietr," I said.

"What?"

"That now that we both know . . . that since we understand . . ." My voice cracked before I got it back under control.

"What?" He reached up and touched my cheek.

"That on the anniversaries of their deaths—"

"We'll be around for each other?"

"Yeah. It probably sounds cheesy," I blushed. But I realized I wasn't alone in my grief. Pietr had been through it. He was *still* going through it. It was somehow more profound knowing that it wasn't just me. Just my family. I mean, I always knew that death was the great equalizer. Everybody died eventually. It was universal. Common. But that evening it all became real to me. And Pietr understood.

"*Nyet*. It doesn't sound cheesy to me." He pressed his lips together. "Only, I don't take promises lightly."

CHAPTER FOURTEEN

I looked away. I couldn't say the same thing. But this was a promise I intended to keep for as long as he let me. It was tough finding someone who really understood. Who really *got* you.

It was almost as if he could read my reluctance. He straightened. It was like I was watching him mentally rebuild a small section of wall. "It doesn't matter so much that they died early, I guess. We don't tend to live long, anyway."

"Heart disease?"

He nearly choked. "Not quite. Well, maybe in a way."

"I've seen how you eat," I pointed out. "You totally wolf down your food. You should try eating a salad or two. Not so much *'meat.'*" I put the last word in quotes with a dig of my fingers.

This time, he did laugh. "I think you're okay to go back to the dance."

"Yeah." I checked myself out in the mirror one last time. My eyes were still puffy, but I'd wiped away most of the blurred mascara. I touched my hair, making sure the mousy brown mess of it was still stable. *Something about me should be stable,* I thought. I looked at Pietr as he rose to his feet. Even when his presence made me feel totally out of control—when he caught me crying and dragged me from the gym—I still felt secure. Anchored. "Let's go," I agreed.

"You do really look exquisite," he said as he opened the door for me.

I would have replied but I saw Sarah sitting out on the bench in the hall, three carefully arranged cups of punch beside her. Amy stood behind her, sucking down the contents of the remaining cup like someone returning from the desert.

Amy motioned to me frantically, her hands telling me she'd *tried* to keep Sarah away and—what took us so long? Frustration pinched her features.

Sarah watched us emerge and I thought I saw in her expression a glimmer of her old self. The thought terrified me, so I did the only thing I could: I rushed forward and hugged it right out of her.

Sarah pushed me back, her eyes lingering on the details of my face. I felt plain and dull beneath her speculation. "Why did you fall apart back there?" she asked.

I moved a cup of punch aside and sat next to her on the bench. "I don't know exactly what did it," I said. "I think sometimes it gets to be too much."

Sarah nodded. Her gaze shifted to Pietr. I read suspicion there and I hoped he did, too. "Why did you two need to be *sequestered* for so long?"

I moved between them, blocking Pietr from Sarah. I looked at her, hoping my eyes were filled with a look of honesty and blind friendship—like I thought they had before the dance. "I needed some privacy—some time without people staring at me, so I could babble insanely and cry rivers. Pietr just knew."

Sarah blinked at me. I thought I saw the spark of something ignite in the green depths of her eyes. But she blinked again and it was gone. "He's smart—I *told* you." She beamed.

"It's not intelligence," he said. "I know something about what Jess is going through."

Sarah folded her hands primly in her lap. "Oh?"

Pietr groaned, a sound that seemed to rise from the depths of his soul. He rubbed a hand across his forehead, his eyes closed.

He'd said it once already. "Pietr's parents are dead, too," I said suddenly, as fast as a person ripping a Band-Aid off because a slow peel is like punishment for already being wounded.

His face relaxed. He nodded.

Sarah was on her feet, hands on his chest. "Oh, Pietr," she soothed. "I'm so sorry. I didn't know!"

He patted her hands. "I've barely been in Junction long enough to unpack. There's a lot you don't know about me."

His arm wrapped lightly around her shoulders, Pietr led us back to the gym. Amy linked her arm with mine, smiling when she saw everyone dancing.

"And we danced, like a wave on the ocean, romanced—"

"Come on," Sarah urged, her eyes bright as she tugged Pietr and Amy onto the dance floor. Attached to Amy, I followed, making up my mind. I would have a good time. Starting—now!

"We were liars in love and we danced—"

Pietr kept his eyes on Sarah—most of the time.

There were a couple of moments I caught him looking at me with nearly the same look Jenny had been giving Derek. It was unnerving.

I turned, dancing more in Amy's direction.

Amy pointed to the speakers and I searched my memory. "The Hooters," I said, naming the group.

We danced like maniacs, doing silly moves when "Girls Just Want to Have Fun" came on and sitting out when "Total Eclipse of the Heart" marked the start of a slow dance. Well, I sat out.

Marvin found Amy and dragged her onto the dance floor. Although I couldn't bear to watch them kiss (traumatized by memories of his rubbery lips back in fourth grade), I had to admit that otherwise they looked pretty cute together. Like they fit. And while Marvin watched Amy with a fierce intensity, he wasn't the only one looking at her. His hands tight on Stella Martin, Max watched Amy, too. I wondered if that might become a problem.

Sitting alone, I tried focusing on the line of boys standing in the shadows across the gym. If this dance was going to be anything like my last few middle-school dances, I'd spend most of the slow dances staring stalker-like at people I hardly knew.

When I was little I dreamed of going to dances. I thought I'd be the most beautiful girl there—the star of some social show. Now I just wanted to read a book. A good, quick-to-read vampire book. Something that defied the very definition of proper literature. Something simply *fun*.

My gaze caught on a couple dancing slowly into my field of vision. Well, not so much *dancing* as doing that weird slow-dance wobble. Derek and Jenny. I tried not to gag. They looked like they'd been glued together.

Dad told me when I was getting ready for my very first dance that there was a Junction teacher with a ruler who measured to make sure there was a proper distance between dance partners. I remembered that at that first dance I kept looking for the ruler, worried I was breaking some big rule. Now I *really* wanted to see that guy.

And then there was Pietr. Dancing with Sarah as if he might break her. He knew that she'd already had her brain scrambled once, so he was overly cautious with her. Nope, no ruler needed there. I sighed, relieved and frustrated at the same time.

Amy was suddenly in front of me. "Hey! You're not even paying attention!"

"Huh?" I had mentally drifted off, zoned out.

"You're missing some good music!" she proclaimed, snatching my hands off my lap and pulling me out of my seat.

"So what—?" I asked over the blaring music. "You're an eighties convert now?"

Amy grinned. "At least it's not disco!" she reminded me.

And we danced!

Another set of slow songs, and this time Amy sat out with me. "He looks bored," she said, motioning vaguely toward the dance floor.

"Who? Marvin?" Even Marvin had been asked to dance. I was feeling lower than low.

"Well, yeah. Him too. But I mean *your* guy."

"Derek?"

"No. God! I'm going to start carrying a chart," Amy warned. "Pietr."

"Oh. I hadn't noticed."

"You don't lie as well as you think you do," she said with a sniff.

"Ugh."

"Oh. Sarah doesn't look too happy."

I peered out onto the dance floor. Amy was right. Sarah

looked worse than unhappy. She looked straight at me, stretching to hold on to Pietr's shoulders.

My heart fell into my stomach and started jumping around like a fish fresh from the stream. I was the first to look away.

"That can't be good," Amy whispered, still watching.

I tried to look mesmerized by the floor. "Is she still glaring at me?"

"No. She's talking to him again." Amy leaned forward in her chair, following my lame ploy that there was something absolutely fascinating about Junction High's gym floor. She kept up the spy game. "Nope. She's mad." She poked me. "He's not trying to dump her now—not at the dance."

My heart stopped. "No—" But I wondered. Every time my dad had wanted out of something, he screwed it up so badly my mom quit asking him to do it. "Is he stepping on her feet?"

"What? No." Amy looked at me. "Sometimes I just can't follow your line of logic," she admitted.

"Way better that way. He won't break it off tonight. I told him he couldn't."

"Okay. I *definitely* don't follow your logic," she confirmed. She cocked her head, listening. "It's winding up again!" Amy shouted, as if I'd gone deaf since her last statement.

Pietr was before me, pulling me onto my feet. "Dance with me," he said.

Sarah was behind him, glowering at me. I hesitated.

Amy grabbed Sarah and headed to the dance floor. "Fast or slow?" she called.

Pietr had me by the wrist. I followed.

"I don't know!" I yelled to Amy.

But on the dance floor couples quickly formed and someone shut off a set of lights as a hint.

"Slow," Amy groaned, dragging Sarah back to the chairs.

I tried to go with them. I did. But Pietr already had me by the waist.

"Stay," he commanded.

"Fine. You've probably already doomed my friendship with Sarah, anyhow, by neglecting her during this dance," I said, resigning myself to reach up and rest my hands on his shoulders. "She's going to be jealous."

"I thought *I* always stated the obvious," he said, pulling me closer.

I couldn't help it. My eyes scanned the room. Nope. No rulers in sight.

"Who are you looking for?" he asked, all his Russian heritage returning and becoming audibly concentrated as he grated out that one name that seemed to irk him. "Derek?" His eyes narrowed.

I chuckled at the idea of Pietr, the popular and handsome—definitely handsome—new guy, being jealous of where *my* attention went. I leaned my forehead against his chest and sighed. "You wouldn't understand," I breathed.

"No," his voice rumbled in his chest, deep with my ears so close. "You're right." The words reminded me of Hunter's growl. "When it comes to you liking Derek, I can't understand."

I closed my eyes and tried not to think of anything but being close to Pietr, right then and right there.

"I wanna know—why can't this be love?"

Van Halen's song ended, and I dropped my hands away from Pietr's shoulders, taking a half step back.

"Wait," he said, tightening his grip on my waist. He looked thoughtful, peering at the ceiling as he listened to the first few notes of the next song. When his eyes next met my own, there was something different there—something sad and so completely lonely. . . . *"This* is my song," he whispered.

He pulled me close, his arms wrapping around me, hands resting at the small of my back. I didn't know what to do, so I leaned my cheek against his chest.

I could hear his heart beating. No matter how slowly we danced, it seemed to race like an old clock that had just been wound. I thought if we could both somehow slow time down, then we could be like this: close, together—forever.

I closed my eyes, listening to the song—his song—and his heart. At odds with each other. "Queen." I whispered the group's name, realizing it was from the album I'd looked at.

He sighed, a sweet, gentle sound. And I relaxed, resting against him and swaying ever so gently as he did. His heartbeat finally slowed as we danced, the tick-tock of a more reasonable clock. I wondered if it felt like time could stand still to him.

I thought that if this was what forever felt like, then *I* wanted to live forever.

"Who dares to love forever?"

"When love must die . . ."

He winced at the last line and I drew back, startled, looking up at his solemn face, his tightly closed eyes, and wondering what I still didn't know about Pietr. . . .

Sarah was almost between us at the song's end.

"He insisted on dancing with his guide," she explained, giving me her broadest smile as she put a hand on his arm. Possessively. "He said proper courtesy is very important to people of his background. What an interesting song, too," Sarah commented.

Forcing my eyebrows to stay level, I backed up. "It was by a group called Queen. Thank you for the dance, Pietr," I said, watching Sarah the whole time.

Amy put her hands on my shoulders and began to guide me away. "My mom's in the parking lot," she explained to Pietr and Sarah. "You two have fun!"

We slipped our shoes on and headed outside. "So," she said as soon as the school's doors closed behind us. "Do you think someone with Sarah's sort of head trauma can ever really return to what she was like before the accident?"

I was frozen, not by the autumn breeze playing with the hem of my skirt, but by the possibility. "I don't know."

"Well, we'd better hope not," Amy pointed out dryly. "Because if the old Sarah ever shows up and realizes how tight you are with her hunky boyfriend, then that cute little package you call *friend* is gonna want to absolutely kill you."

I hung my head, knowing Amy was right. Because of the original trio of Jenny, Macie, and Sarah, Sarah was the smartest. And the cruelest by far.

I had never been so exhausted after a dance as I was after Homecoming. It wasn't just that my feet hurt (they did), but it was the pain in my head and the ache in my chest knowing that I wanted Pietr more than ever. We shared heartache over the loss of family. We were attracted to each other and actually had significant things in common. But I'd pushed him toward Sarah and now he had to play the cards I'd dealt.

I was so stupid. As a writer, I knew if I'd been a character in a novel a good editor would have scrawled TSTL (Too Stupid To Live) on the manuscript pages. Well, maybe not too stupid to *live*, but definitely too stupid to *date*.

I tugged on my sleep shirt. The wind was picking up outside, throwing leaves around. But the scratching of leaves on my window wasn't what pulled me across the room to peer into the darkness outside.

No. It was the howling.

I'd heard coyotes. This was different. Richer, deeper, longer.

It was a sound that blended with the night and rose out of the shadows to stroke the starry sky.

I rubbed my arms, fighting the prickling sensation that raced across them. I knew almost instinctively that what I was listening to was a wolf. I wondered if it was what had been outside the barn the night before Pietr came to Junction High. Or if it had been what tore through the bushes and left a bit of its fur behind. Or maybe this was a second one—one wolf tracking the other.

I crawled into my bed, pulling the covers up and adjusting my pillows. I always fell asleep comfortably enough; it was only when I dropped into the nightmare that my body struggled to fight what my mind could not.

The dogwood tree was in full flower, pink petals spread wide, glinting in the sunset's brilliant blast of color. I remembered reading that its petals showed bite marks of the Devil— that Satan had bitten its flowers, enraged by the tree's sorrow at being used for Christ's crucifixion.

I pulled out my cell phone and hit send when Mom's picture popped up. "Yeah, I'll be by the dogwood," I heard myself confirm. "On your way? Awesome." I flipped the cell shut, looking at the tree's twisted branches again. At one time the dogwood supposedly grew as big as the oak. When the Romans crucified Christ, legend claimed the dogwood formed the cross. Christ, sensing its sorrow, promised it would never grow so large or straight again that it could be used for such a cruel purpose. And the dogwoods grew shriveled and twisted but also grew content.

A whisper of tires on cracked asphalt signaled the approach of Mom's sedan. I knew it now without seeing it. But in my nightmare, I always turned, watching her approach. I saw the car turn into the parking lot. And, like dreaded clockwork, Sarah was there—behind the wheel of her parents' Jag, tearing into the lot. On a joyride. And distracted. Tires squealed. Rubber burned as each driver saw the other—too late. The noise made me jump and cry out—though it was the same noise I'd heard every night since the actual accident. I screamed, choking on the smell of burning rubber as I ran straight toward the tangle of steel. 911. . . .

"This is 911. What is the nature of your emergency?"

"Car crash—at the parking lot by Fifth and Main," I panted. "Two cars—"

In the back of my mind a voice was shrieking—begging—why was the dream continuing? Why didn't it stop? Like it always stopped? Before the real tragedy? Before the truest part of the pain? *WAKE UP!* My mind screamed, but my body was rigid—frozen with shock at knowing what was coming and unable to pull me back from the horror I wallowed in nightly during the dream.

"What's your name?" the voice on the phone asked.

"Jessica Gillmansen. Two cars—two drivers . . . oh, God—it's bad. Please hurry . . . please, please . . . hurry . . ."

My hands were on Mom's door. Her face was bloody, her nose broken from impact with the steering wheel, but her eyes were bright. "Baby, I'm okay," she whispered.

I tugged on the door. It was stuck. I yanked up on the handle, growling when my nails folded back.

"I'm fine, Jess," she insisted. "The other driver—"

"Is—" I was barely stopped from saying "a psycho bitch" by the look in Mom's eyes.

"Is *hurt*, Jess. Check on her."

I tried the door again, throwing my whole weight against it

and cursing my inability to open it. I ran to the other side. The passenger's door was folded almost in half from the impact.

"Stop that," Mom demanded. "They'll need the Jaws of Life to get me out, baby. Go. Check on *her*." She fixed her eyes on me, willing me into obedience. "You've gotta do what you can do, Jess. Go. *Now*. She's somebody's baby." The ferocity in her eyes—the sheer strength shining out—made me obey.

I raced to Sarah's door. She was unconscious. *Stupid, selfish bitch*. Barely bright enough to wear a seat belt . . .

Mom was yelling out her window, "Pull her out, Jess. Get her out of there."

"Mom—" Even then I was argumentative.

"*Now,* young lady!"

"Shit!" I popped open Sarah's door and undid the seat belt. She fell limply into my arms. Thank God she was a frikkin' featherweight. . . . I lifted, carrying her awkwardly toward the sidewalk. A crowd was gathering, pouring out of the local movie rental place. "Help me!" I shouted.

I distinctly heard someone warn, "You get sued savin' lives." Everyone looked away, their feet rooted to the sidewalk.

Where the hell was the emergency crew? I turned to the wreck, a strange new smell stinging my eyes and nose. Not rubber burning, not—*oh, shit* . . .

The sedan caught fire with a *pop* and a *bang*.

"*Mom!*" I shrieked, heading toward the flames. But someone knocked me to the ground—kept me from getting there. I fought against them, blindly—fiercely, kicking and punching, scratching and biting. Even though I knew it was too late. My heart had burst, broken, knowing I'd saved the wrong person. The most vicious girl at school lived, and I let my mother burn alive. . . .

Pinned, I screamed uselessly. The fire trucks arrived, lights flashing, sirens blaring. And still I screamed. The ambulance pulled up. Medics poured out, announcing what I knew long before the sedan was snuffed. "Dead."

The living weight on top of me shifted, pulling me into a seated position. "Stay with me," he whispered, wrapping his arms around me to keep me from rushing forward—from trying to find something still burning to set myself ablaze and join my mother in eternity. "Stay," he urged. I began to cry, my voice long gone. I ducked my head against his chest, snuffling and sobbing as he stroked my hair and said soothing words.

I raised my streaming eyes to glimpse my savior and Derek looked down at me, doing his best to smile reassuringly—as if it would all be all right—but even he came up short. I cried even harder then.

CHAPTER FIFTEEN

It had been nearly a week since the dance, and I was struggling. Pietr's almost constant presence didn't help. Every morning his brother, Alexi, dropped him off to do chores. Pietr always looked good at school, but he looked even more amazing with the tousled appearance of someone fresh from bed.

Our goals never included mucking the stalls in the morning, we just aimed at feeding and watering the horses, turning them out if the weather was good and trying to avoid kissing each other. Some goals were more achievable than others.

Pietr tried breaking up with Sarah three times that week. She made it impossible. Each time he tried she acted so sweet and looked so sad. . . . He needed to be vicious to break her heart. I even called off one of his attempts, seeing Sarah so close to falling apart. As little as I knew about Pietr, I knew he wasn't naturally cruel. And I certainly didn't want to be the one who made him something he shouldn't be.

So each time I saw them together my heart broke a little bit further apart. He kept his distance from her as much as he could.

But there was a distance festering between Pietr and me, too. The only place it seemed we could be ourselves was at the farm. When Pietr showed up Saturday morning I finally felt it had been worth fighting through the week to reach the weekend.

"Hey, Dad!" I yelled up the staircase. "Weird Wanda's here!"

Pietr looked at me, rising to escort me from the breakfast nook to the door.

We'd finished chores early and he'd looked hungry. Well, not *just* hungry—famished. So I fried up some bacon with eggs fresh from our Barred Rock hens. The eggs were so rubbery they bounced off the spatula and onto his plate, but Pietr didn't seem to notice.

I'd offered him a selection of chocolates from the continually restocked tin on our table and although he admitted to liking chocolate, he said it did not return his feelings and he could no longer dally with unrequited love. Such an odd boy.

Spending so much time with Pietr meant that he was always close. I had begun noticing subtle differences between the way he acted at school and the way he was with me.

At school, he always had that chain he'd worn since his second day Junction High. But he never wore it when it was just the two of us. I asked him about it. "It's a magic chain. A buffer to keep girls at bay—it puts a damper on my obvious charms." He'd smiled. What a smart aleck.

"So why don't you wear it around me?" I'd asked.

He shrugged. "You seem nearly immune to my charms, but I'll admit to wanting to use any shot I have with you."

I'd rolled my eyes and pointed out it was a good thing I was wearing my muck boots. Because the manure was sure piling up fast—and it had little to do with the horses. Then I'd added, "Well, my pietersite worry stone is a buffer against you, too." I held it up with a grin.

"Do you always carry that?" he asked, no longer as flippant.

"Almost always," I assured him, holding my chin high.

"Huh." He rubbed his jaw, staring at the stone. "And you still kiss me."

"It's a *worry* stone, Pietr," I reiterated. "And kissing you only worries me more," I sniped before dodging a handful of hay.

Pietr also didn't seem quite so obsessed with the time when around me. When I mentioned it in a phone call to Amy one night, she quipped that he wasn't worried about the time because he was *making time* with me.

Being alone with Pietr so frequently meant I had to be on my guard even more so I wasn't hauled into a corner of the barn and kissed until I reminded him we had a *working* relationship.

He'd assured me once he absolutely agreed. He *was* working on our relationship. As often as he could. And then he kissed me again to prove it.

"Weird Wanda is Dad's wannabe girlfriend," I said with a roll of my eyes. There were some things I still didn't want to discuss with Pietr. Wanda's ongoing attempt to snag my dad was one of them.

Hunter and Maggie leaped up from where they lounged under the table, waiting for food to drop, and decided it was time to follow Pietr. It was weird. Pietr followed me; my dogs followed him.

"Oh."

"Yeah." I opened the door, and there she was: Wanda McGregor. She'd arrived in town about a week before Pietr's family did. She volunteered at the school, she worked at the local library—to me, she seemed always underfoot. To Dad, she was interested and available.

"Hi, Jessie," she said with a smile.

"Jessica," I corrected. I glared at her, thinking she looked well rested for once. The lines around her eyes were less obvious. Perhaps they'd been pulled tight by that ridiculous blond ponytail she always wore.

Wanda measured me with her gaze, probably figuring I was the only thing standing in the way of her happiness with my father. If that was true, she needed to watch out for Annabelle Lee before she got blindsided.

Pietr nudged me forward, grabbing his jacket. Wanda stepped back in surprise. For the briefest moment I thought I saw fear in her eyes, but she straightened and schooled her features into a look of mild curiosity instead.

"Who's your little friend?" she asked.

Pietr bristled and moved to my side. He stared at Wanda with a ferocity I'd only seen him give Derek.

The rumble of a growl built in Hunter's throat.

"I swear," I said, turning to Hunter and tapping his head, "You'll be carted off to obedience school for real if you keep this up." I looked from Pietr to Wanda and back, considering a reply. "He's—"

"Nearly six feet tall," he said. Very evenly.

Hunter fell silent. So did Wanda. But she watched every move Pietr made like he should be on display at some zoo.

Then she did that thing she *always* did. She reached up and plucked some speck off Pietr's shoulder.

He raised an eyebrow.

"Wanda does that," I mentioned levelly. "Touches what she shouldn't."

She returned my belligerent gaze, adding a shrug. "If you want to walk around with hay and stuff on you . . ."

Pietr faced me with a nearly inscrutable expression. "That science assignment," he said.

"Yeah. About dogs." I scratched Hunter's head.

"Actually all canines."

Did I see amusement in Wanda's eyes when Pietr corrected me?

"Anyhow—" I said, looking back at Pietr.

"Study date at my place tomorrow." He sighed.

"Wait . . . am I invited?"

"Not yet. And not by me. But call Sarah as soon as you can and wiggle your way into coming," he suggested. "You're smart. I'm sure you can make her want you there with a few choice words."

"Maybe I shouldn't . . ."

"I want you there." He kissed my forehead.

"Fine."

Down the drive Alexi's car honked for him. He headed out at a jog, waving to me until Wanda stepped into the doorway, blocking my view.

"Guys can be such dogs," she said. "I mean, seriously." She rolled her bright blue eyes. "He's got some poor girl coming over on a study date at his house and he wants you to manipulate her so you can come over, too?" She shook her head.

I tried to ignore her.

"What's he trying to do—build a harem?" She stalked to the foot of the steps, ponytail swishing with every stride.

"So what, Wanda? Are you trying to tell me I can do *so much better* than him?" I asked, glaring.

She looked me up and down. "No. I'm not saying *that*."

Ouch! No, I definitely did *not* like her.

She continued. "I'm just saying you'd better prepare yourself, because guys can be complete *dogs*."

Dad bounded down the stairs, two at a time, placing a peck on both Wanda's cheeks. "Mornin', Sunshine," he greeted her while tossing a look of warning my way. "So what are our plans this morning?"

She opened her jacket and pulled out a gun. "Need to sight this baby in."

Dad whistled. "That's a sweet piece, Wanda. Target practice sounds like a good idea to me."

"Yeah," Wanda agreed, looking my way for just a moment. "I have the feeling I'm going to be doing some serious shooting soon." She smiled in that way she so often did—the smile never daring to touch her icy eyes.

"Serious shooting?" I grunted. "What? Library having bigger problems with overdue books than we'd ever expect?"

Dad chortled but narrowed his eyes at me as he guided Weird Wanda out the door. As soon as they were out of sight, I was on the phone with Sarah and wondering, in the back of my mind, if Wanda could possibly be right about guys being dogs. I determined I'd find out on my own.

The next day Amy, Sarah, and I were packed into the Luxom family car with Sarah's parents and headed down a quiet street at the outskirts of Junction, on our way to where Pietr lived.

We crossed the Manido River where it began to turn back on itself and I realized Pietr's area of town was essentially on a small peninsula of land. If the supernatural things I read about in novels were real, a flowing river would make Pietr's neighborhood one of the safest around. I sighed, realizing I already felt safe around Pietr. Frustrated but safe.

I had followed his suggestion and called Sarah, playing up how freaked out *I* would be if I were visiting the guy I liked *and his family* at his home with *no backup*. Five minutes into the conversation Sarah told me to hold on so she could text Amy. If she was going to Pietr's place, she'd insisted, she wasn't going without *plenty* of help.

I hadn't lied—I *was* freaked out by the idea of being in Pietr's house and meeting Pietr's family and *I* had Amy as a second set of ears and eyes. Mr. Luxom pulled the car up in front of a yellow-ocher and green-umber Victorian house, complete with a wraparound porch and a dramatic . . .

"Look at that *turret*," Sarah whispered, awed.

Yep. A dramatic turret. I was amused. For Sarah, the girl who lived in the eight-bedroom, six-bathroom house on the top of Junction's highest hill, to be stunned into staring silence was a tremendous thing. The house *was* beautiful.

"Isn't that the Queen Anne we looked at when we were first engaged?" Mrs. Luxom asked her husband.

"Hmm. Kristen, that was so long ago I barely recall," Mr. Luxom replied, utterly uninterested.

I was surprised that as long as I'd lived in Junction I'd never noticed the house before. I *tried* to be observant.

"Everybody out," Mr. Luxom announced. "Remember, sugar-plum, you can just call us when you all are done studying."

"No problem, Dad," Sarah whispered without giving him a glance.

We hopped out of the car.

"Pietr!" Sarah exclaimed, dashing up the porch's steps to fling herself into his arms.

He caught her easily and waved at Amy and me.

"Nice place," Amy whispered to me as we headed up the herringbone brick walkway. "Not hurting for money, I guess."

"Hmm," I agreed.

We climbed the wooden stairs and were quickly in the porch's shadow.

"Nice house," I said.

"*Spahseebuh*. Thanks," he said. "Glad you all could come."

I saw him stiffen suddenly. There was noise inside, and he paused, his hand on the doorknob.

Then I heard it grow more distinct. Arguing.

"Then where the Hell's it all coming from, Sasha?" There was a heavy thud. I imagined someone being shoved up against a wall.

Another solid thump, as if the roles had been reversed.

I looked at Pietr; his face was set, as hard as granite. "This a bad time?" I asked.

He shook his head, smiling welcomingly, although I thought I saw a muscle in his jaw twitch. "Just sibling stuff," he assured me. But he didn't turn the doorknob.

"Our parents were honorable people, Sasha—"

"And they left us with *nothing*!"

"So what are you doing? And *who* are you doing it for? This all came at a price!"

"*Life* has its price, you son of a—"

"Don't dare—"

I jumped at the sound of things crashing. Something shattered. I hoped it didn't include jaws or ribs.

Pietr reached over and jabbed the doorbell's button hard. Twice. He shouted into the door's window. "*Round two!* Get to your corners!"

I could see nothing; the window was covered by a lacy curtain. Things grew quiet inside.

Pietr chuckled, but it wasn't the sound of someone comfortable with the circumstance. "My brothers, Alexi—*Sasha*—and Maximilian." With a shrug, he cleared his throat and reinforced his smile. "It can be difficult—three brothers under one roof." He held the door for us, and I took another look at his face before ducking beneath his arm to enter. I was not reassured.

Just inside was a wood-floored foyer—a *real* foyer—worlds away from what we called a mudroom at my house. The walls were done with a chair rail and slender wainscoting; a definite air of old elegance lingered in the space.

Picture frames dotted the walls. There were some images I recognized from my earlier world cultures class: St. Basil's Cathedral, with its amazing onion-dome roofs, the long, redbrick expanse surrounding the Kremlin, and the severe and spartan architecture of Lenin's tomb.

There were also things I was totally clueless about, including a picture featuring an enormous cannon and some folk art images captioned in what I guessed was Cyrillic. I wished I could read them. There were several mirrors, but no family photos. And everything seemed straight. Angular. Sharp. Nothing round or curved could be spotted as we followed Pietr along a path of perfectly spaced Oriental throw rugs and into a sitting room.

I recognized Pietr's family immediately. His two brothers were straightening their shirts and fixing their hair. Obviously recovering quickly from their scuffle. Perhaps it was normal with so much unbridled testosterone in one place. Behind them the girl sat up in her seat, looking as if nothing was out of the ordinary. Which made things seem even stranger to me.

Pietr began introductions. "These are my brothers: Maximilian—"

Looking just a year or two older than Pietr, Maximilian smiled at us with bright blue eyes and blindingly white teeth.

"Max," he reminded.

"Max," we all murmured in consensus. He was handsome by almost anyone's definition. He had a welcome smile and eyes that glowed with mischief; his hair was a shade or two darker than Pietr's and curled at the ends, giving him a boyish look that only magnified his charm.

"And this is Alexi, our eldest brother, and guardian," Pietr added.

When compared to his siblings, Alexi seemed a bit of a surprise. Max equaled him in height, Pietr matched him in leanness, and their sister outshone him in poise. Alexi was, in fact, the least impressive of the family, but there was still something about him that spoke of dominance and power. He was to be respected—of that, I had no doubt.

Both Max and Alexi wore necklaces nearly identical to Pietr's chain. I wondered if it was a Russian thing or a Rusakova thing, or even one and the same.

"Lovely to meet you ladies," Alexi said, giving a gallant bow.

Pietr pointed to each of us in turn. "Sarah."

"I have heard much about you, Sarah," Alexi intoned.

Sarah beamed and introduced me. "Jessica."

"Very nice to meet you," Alexi said to me. As if he'd never heard my name mentioned before.

I forced a smile. It, like the surroundings, felt awkward at best. I could understand him not remembering me from Pietr's first day at school, but shouldn't he have heard *something* about me?

Pietr introduced Amy. Max had already recognized her.

"Ah, in French *ami* means 'friend,'" Alexi said with a charming flash of teeth.

"Don't get any ideas, buddy," Amy quipped, smiling in return.

Alexi laughed, a deep, throaty sound. "What wonderful girls, Pietr," he congratulated. "Very lovely and certainly very smart."

Behind him the girl cleared her throat.

"Oh, *da*," Alexi said apologetically.

"Our sister. The beautiful Catherine."

"Pietr's twin," she announced.

We must have all gasped. She laughed, the dark curls framing her face bouncing. With her high cheekbones, strong nose, and bright eyes, she looked like she could have stepped right out of a book of ancient myths and legends.

"I can see there is much our Pietr hasn't told you." She laughed again, but I felt there was an edge to her laughter somehow. I was immediately struck by the fact I couldn't recall seeing her in school other than that very first day. "Sometimes it is best to maintain a sense of mystery, is it not, brother?"

Pietr smiled in agreement, but it was a simple smile, not heartfelt. I wondered what Pietr was holding back from us—what mystery he might still be keeping from me.

"Well, make yourselves comfortable," Catherine said, motioning us to sit. "I will make tea for us." She smiled graciously and rose, ghosting from the room with a grace I mentally reserved for ballerinas. Perhaps that was why I'd never noticed her around. Whereas Pietr was the sun, attracting a multitude of noisy worshippers, Catherine was as quiet and soft-footed as the moon as it slid across a midnight sky.

Pietr barely waited for his twin's invitation, falling into the middle of a small couch.

"What an adorable little *loveseat,*" Sarah said as she curled up beside Pietr, placing her backpack on her lap. Amy flopped onto his other side, and I was left standing by a marble-topped table covered with everything from amazingly detailed lacquer boxes to painted eggs depicting St. George and saintly women.

Pietr looked at me, but his expression was guarded. So he hadn't told his family about me. Me—the one he constantly manhandled into dim corners to steal a kiss from. I fought down the rage growing inside me, knowing I couldn't strangle him in front of witnesses, so I'd better busy my hands else-where. I snatched up one of the many knickknacks on the table.

It was one of those Russian nesting dolls, and seemed to somehow match the décor in the room: seemingly old-world European thrown into an American small town. "Cool nes—"

"*Matryoshka*," Sarah corrected as if she were making some weird preemptive strike.

"It doesn—" Alexi began, but I adjusted my grip, gave it a twist, and opened the first of the wooden egg-like dolls.

"Doesn't open," Alexi finished, on his feet. There was a gasp from the other family members; Pietr's eyes seemed to glow.

I blushed fiercely. "I'm sorry," I whispered, even my hairline red with shame. "I didn't know I shouldn't . . ."

Alexi's hand was heavy on my shoulder, his eyes on the *matryoshka* like I held a ghost. "*Nyet*," he said. "We all tried. We could never get it to open."

Catherine stood in the doorway, a platter in her hands covered with cups, cookies, cakes—all surrounding a stunning porcelain teapot. Staring, her mouth wide, she began to tremble.

"It's probably like a jar of peanut butter," I suggested, trying to dismiss the strange way the Rusakovas stared at the thing in my hands. "You know: You loosened it, and I get credit for my super-powerful strength because I'm the one who tries it one more time."

The teapot and cups rattled on the platter in Catherine's shaking hands. Max took it from her and set it aside on another small table. "Sit," he told her. She did, eyes never leaving my hands.

Alexi put his hand out, and I placed the *matryoshka*—man, sometimes I *did* despise Sarah's new way with words—in it. He put the first one on the table, closing it again, and gave the second one a twist. He tried, effort pinching his features.

"No good," he said, handing it to me.

"Huh." I gave it a twist; it popped open easily.

Another gasp.

The hairs on my arms stood up. "See, like peanut butter," I insisted.

Alexi lined another one up. "Next," he commanded, his voice oddly imperative.

Catherine was whispering, "Our parents had this made before we were born. They said a strange little woman in a tiny shop at Brighton Beach described it in some silly fortune-telling she did for them." She caught her breath and clasped her hands together, remembering the tale.

"They felt compelled to follow her description, even having it detailed in the style of the Sergei Posad *matryoskas,* but they never told us any more of what the instructions entailed. Or what was inside. It's been the family puzzle. We tried so often to open it—with no results—we presumed it wasn't able to be opened but was just a single, solid figurine."

Alexi kept accepting the smaller, hollow wooden dolls, lining them up and demanding I open the next. There were already three dolls on the table. I paused, looking at them. "Weird. They kind of look like each of you, don't they—except the first one," I amended.

"Our mother," Max said soberly.

"Oh. So this must be Catherine," I said, holding the doll and looking at Pietr's twin. There were definite similarities. I wrinkled my nose. "You were born first?" I asked.

"By two minutes," she confirmed.

"Ouch."

Sarah stood. She put her hand under my face. "Let someone else have a try," she said. She didn't say it gently, or happily, or—I handed it to her as if it had changed into a snake in my grasp.

"So this should reveal Pietr, right?" Sarah asked.

Everyone nodded, faces set, expressions ranging from curious to grim. Pietr just seemed to have frozen into a statue—cool and distant.

Sarah gave Catherine's doll a twist. Nothing. She applied more effort. She shifted her grip. Still, it didn't budge beneath the determination of her will or the strength of her slender hands. She grunted, trying one last time and looked at me in total exasperation. Defeated, she handed it to me again. "That's the last one," she said. "I guess they weren't expecting twins."

I spun the doll between my two hands and heard a little whine as the two halves parted. "For once, you're wrong." I winked at Sarah and parted the pieces. "Peanut butter," I proclaimed, watching Amy's and Pietr's faces.

The Rusakovas gasped at what was in my hands even before I peeked.

"What?" I asked, looking down as Alexi set up Catherine's doll beside the others. "Huh. Well that's gotta be a surprise," I admitted, holding the tiny wooden doll up to the light. "It looks like a wolf," I said. "I mean, I guess the hair color and eye color matches you, Pietr, but otherwise, I don't see any similarity," I said with a teasing smile.

No one else in the room smiled back.

"Well," I said, still holding the tiny wolf, "if you think *that* was impressive, you should see how fast I can solve my dad's old Rubik's cube."

Still, no one moved or laughed. Tough room.

The Rusakovas stared at me as if I were some sort of enigma. I examined the wolf again, hoping to give them time to pull themselves back together. Seeing them so visibly stunned had me shaken, too. "Oh, cool," I said. "The wolf opens, too. . . ."

CHAPTER SIXTEEN

"What?!"

Although I'd never lost their focus, it seemed the stares of the Rusakovas doubled in intensity—if that were even possible.

"The wolf opens, too," I insisted. But I hesitated, seeing how they watched me. It was as if I had magic in my hands. Like I'd change their world forever depending on what I found.

"Maybe I shouldn't," I whispered, but Pietr sprang off of the loveseat and stood before me, shadowing me, his head down, face so close his breath warmed my cheeks to blushing.

"Open it." It wasn't a command, and not quite a plea—but something suffering in between. His tone squeezed at my heart.

I met his eyes. They shimmered, the uncanny ring of gold that surrounded his pupils seemed like the sun just caught on the far side of an eclipsing moon, threatening to burst free. The ocean-deep blue of his eyes quivered. I was breathless before him. "Sure?" I asked. I would not open the wolf unless he was certain. Strange as it was, they seemed intimately connected.

He nodded, one quick jerk of his head.

"Okay," I agreed, hoping the single word might tame the wildness that crept around the edge of his glittering irises. With one swift move, the deed was done, the wolf opened, the contents spilled into my palm.

Pietr looked at Alexi.

Alexi and the other Ruskovas closed ranks around me.

"What? What is it?" Sarah asked from behind the wall of bodies.

With his index finger Alexi gently rolled the cream-colored heart over in my open hand.

"A charm in the shape of a heart." He squinted, lowering his face to study the pendant. "It appears to be white amber."

"*Royal* amber?" Catherine whispered. I knew I was missing something. Something big.

Pietr snatched the heart out of my hand. The look he gave me—gave us all—was one of total trepidation. He spent a moment examining the heart. Then he held it directly in front of me so I couldn't help see the creamy, swirling detail of it.

A shadow fell across the surface of the amber heart. A shape emerged as I focused, crisping its edges as I glanced from Pietr's face back to the pendant. "Oh," I said, catching my breath.

Carved deep into the heart was a simple but unmistakable silhouette of a rabbit.

"Well. Isn't that interesting," I commented.

I focused on breathing. On thinking.

Pietr gave me a look that nearly stopped my heart.

I wondered if he expected me to say right then and there

that the strange little woman must have known—that we were somehow destined to be together—that we should give up our charade of mere friendship for Sarah's sake. Just because I wore a netsuke rabbit, my *mom's* old charm, to the Homecoming Dance and now there was some crazy rabbit carving in a heart—arguably a *wolf's* heart? I couldn't do it. I wasn't even seventeen. How much fresh drama did I need?

"So," I said, barely skipping a beat, "we need to go over that stuff on canine biology, right?" I pushed between the dumbstruck Rusakovas and landed on the loveseat between Amy and Sarah. They looked at me, questioningly, and I rolled my eyes—the promise it wasn't important, but I'd tell them later.

The Rusakovas stood frozen in place for a long moment more before they all looked at one another. Catherine murmured, "Pour some tea, Max. I don't trust my hands." Mute, Max did as she requested, pouring and passing.

Seeing the delft, cobalt blue and gold onion-dome roofs decorating the teapot, I tried making small talk. "That's a beautiful teapot, Catherine."

"It's Lomonosov porcelain," she responded crisply. Shutting me right down.

I took a long sip of tea before balancing the cup on my knee and moving my backpack onto my lap.

"Oh, Catherine," Amy said. "It looks like one of your tea bags burst." Amy shook her cup to swirl the tea inside.

"We don't use bags," Catherine corrected.

I glanced at her. Her expression suddenly changed.

"Is everyone finished with his or her tea?" she asked, sweet once again.

We nodded, not knowing what else to do.

"Excellent," she said, rising. "Alexi, please take Amy's and

Sarah's cups, I'll take mine, and"—she reached out, snagging mine—"yours."

Max held his out for her, too. "Here."

"You are on your own," she snapped at him. "Let's leave them to study." Her tone made it clear the words were no simple suggestion. Sharing a conspiratorial look, Alexi and Max followed Catherine from the room.

Pietr's tea sat untouched on the table.

He still stood in the room's center, his back to us. I knew he was thinking about what I'd done. I had blatantly dismissed the importance of opening the *matryoshka*—not having a clue as to *why* it was important—and I wondered how long it would take for him to forgive me.

Reaching into my backpack to retrieve my science book and papers, I hoped he *would* forgive me. "'It's a Dog's Life,'" I announced, reading the worksheet's title. "People used to say dogs aged seven years for every single year. Although it is important to recognize that canines live at a faster speed than humans, the ratio of seven to one is not completely accurate."

"Pietr," Sarah said. "Come, sit down again, please."

It took a moment, as if he hadn't immediately heard her, but then he turned and came to sit with us. At Sarah's feet.

I tried not to notice how obediently he followed her directions, and I simply continued: "Experts have decided that at one year of age a canine is as physically mature as a fifteen-year-old human and at two years a canine is comparable to a twenty-four-year-old. By the time fourteen human years have passed, a canine's body is equivalent to an eighty-year-old human."

"Pietr, pay attention," Sarah scolded. "This may be on a test."

Pietr stopped playing with his shoelaces and looked up. But certainly not at me. "Go on," he said.

I did. "Other than the obvious impact aging has on canines physically, what other impact might such rapid growth, development, and age have?"

"Well," Sarah said, "if we exclude the physical, we're still left with the mental and emotional, right?"

We nodded agreement.

"So, mentally," Amy said, "what impact would compounded aging have?"

"Wouldn't they, like, start forgetting stuff? Perhaps go senile while we still thought they were young?" Sarah attempted.

I nodded supportively. "That sounds good." I jotted it down. "And emotionally?"

"If they know it's happening"—Amy toyed with putting her thought into words—"I mean, if they can make the comparison to us, wouldn't you think they'd feel jealous because of how fast life's passing them by?"

"*If* they can make that comparison. So"—Sarah looked at each of us for consensus—"jealous?"

"Wouldn't you be?" Pietr asked her.

"I don't know," Amy jumped in, reconsidering. "I mean, I'm not jealous of whales and they can live over a hundred years if they aren't hunted. But I look far better in a bikini." She winked. "Maybe I'd be all 'Live fast, die young, and leave a good-looking corpse.'"

Pietr snorted. "I can't disagree with you. Live life fiercely," he added.

Amy said, "Sounds like a good motto to me!"

Looking at the worksheet and textbook, Pietr asked, "Can we close this up for now? Let's go four-wheeling."

"Seriously?" Sarah asked. "Four-wheeling?"

Pietr nodded, getting to his feet and closing her book definitively. He shoved it into her backpack just below her copy of *Fran-*

kenstein. "Our property backs up against an old wood lot. We get to ride because the owners think it discourages trespassers."

"I'm not"—Amy looked at Sarah and me—*"we're* not dressed for that."

I looked at her outfit. "Sorry," I said with a smile, "can't you wash those clothes, Amy?" I understood her hesitancy. We'd all knew about accidents on ATVs and none of the three of us had ridden before. I'd heard plenty of four-wheelers zip and hum around the edges of our farm. They were loud, obnoxious-sounding, and always looked dirty. So riding one sounded much more interesting than continuing biology.

Pietr smiled, watching us bicker. "You can slip into the family mud suits if you want," he suggested.

"Mud suits," Amy said with a groan. "Jessie, this really doesn't sound like—"

Appearing in the doorway, Max cleared his throat. He already had helmets under both arms and looked to be suited up. "Wanna go for a ride with me?" he asked, looking at Amy.

I saw her blink a few times, but she stopped protesting and looked at me for help. I was not the help she was hoping for. Riding ATVs was far from what I'd been expecting as part of this study date. But it was an opportunity I wasn't about to miss. The rest of the science assignment could wait.

"Let's suit up," I said, grabbing her by the waist.

"Can I ride with you?" Sarah asked Pietr. The question drained the lightheartedness right out of him.

He nodded. "Of course," he said, taking her hand and striding past me.

Amy looked at me, giving a single *I can't get over this* blink of disbelief.

I shrugged. *What else could I do?*

I'd pushed Pietr at Sarah so much he seemed to have finally relented and accepted that his place was with her.

I was getting exactly what I wanted.

"Wait," I said. "Okay, Pietr with Sarah, and Amy with Max—I've never driven one of these, either. Who's driving me?"

Catherine hopped into my line of sight, much cheerier than when she stole away my teacup. "I'll take you. I'm a far better driver than *any* of the boys," she added, eyes glittering in challenge. Max growled a few words as Catherine handed us each a worn and speckled jumpsuit. They felt a little awkward, none an exact fit, but I wouldn't have to explain anything to Dad if my clothes weren't muddy at all.

Out the back of the house and down the porch's steps and I wondered how Dad'd feel about me doing something as dangerous as four-wheeling. I tried not to dwell on his fears. Besides, seeing the way the landscape suddenly dropped away at the Rusakovas' backyard, I had fears of my own.

We were guided to the front of a three-car garage and the Rusakovas started their ATVs, pulling them up in front of us. The air hummed and vibrated with the sound of their engines. They were different from what I'd imagined. Chrome made their metal guts gleam, and I thought they looked like alien insects with their glossy green, blue, and red bodies.

"Hop on!" Catherine shouted, and I snugged a helmet on and settled behind her as we jockeyed for position to be first down the hill. "Now *hold* on!" She laughed. I barely got my arms around her waist before we tore off, ahead of the boys, screaming down the trails, rocketing down the slope.

I had never associated the word *nimble* with an ATV until I was riding behind Catherine. She handled every lump and curve with such a sense of assuredness that I knew she'd driven this path a million times, even though they'd been in town only a short while. She was reckless—but man, could she drive!

She brought us to a slithering stop at the slope's bottom so we could watch the boys' descent. She reduced the engine's roar to a purr and turned to look at me. "Why aren't *you* dating Pietr?" she asked.

It felt like I had to pull my teeth out of the back of my mouth to answer. "He's dating Sarah," I replied, loud enough for her to hear over the engine's idling. I was completely aware of how fast the other two pairs of riders approached.

"He likes you," she said in a way that told me she knew that I already knew.

"I have to do what's right for Sarah," I tried to explain, but her eyes cut into my own. It was eerie. She and Pietr shared the same haunting and haunted eyes. She pinned me down with them.

"And when will you do what's right for *you and Pietr*?" Catherine asked.

"I just have to do whatever I can for Sarah. If it means letting her date Pietr—"

"Sacrifice is only noble to a point," Catherine stated. "Eventually sacrifice equates to lost opportunity." She adjusted her helmet. "Besides. I've always thought martyrs make for very dangerous friends. Who can possibly guess when their desire for self-sacrifice will also endanger those around them?"

The other two ATVs pulled up, and Pietr shouted, "What are you two waiting for?"

Catherine laughed and, yelling, "Not *you!*" she launched us ahead of them again—playing a muddy, jolting game of cat and mouse.

I loved every breathless second of it. My spine became rubber during the ride and when Catherine and the boys finally pulled up together I exhaled in relief. I had been watching over her shoulder as we went and I toyed with the idea of asking her to let me drive us back.

Following Catherine's example, I pulled my helmet off. Pietr stared at me with far more interest than he had even meeting me the first time. I tried to excuse the shiver sliding down my spine with the sudden surge of autumn wind, but I knew it was because of the way he watched me. Maybe I had mud on my face (I had it nearly everywhere else). I wiped it with a gloved hand.

That was when I really felt mud streak across my forehead. I looked down at my gloves, realizing I'd just spread it from my thumb. Pietr gave me his most uneven smile but glanced away as soon as I looked pointedly in his direction.

"Shall we head back?" Catherine looked toward the slope.

"Let's take a break," Max suggested, pulling a packet out of his jacket. "Jerky?" he offered.

Amy's eyes twinkled dangerously and I knew she barely bit back a clever quip.

The Rusakovas reacted to Max's suggestion ravenously. *We* were still trying to work our stomachs out of our throats from the jostling ride.

I focused on encouraging my legs to work and got off the ATV. Amy and Sarah did the same and we walked toward one another, knees filled with jelly. The Rusakovas watched us, their eyes hot on my back. "What a day!" I said loudly to the girls.

Amy took the hint immediately. "Yeah, too bad we have to head back home so soon."

Sarah nodded, watching me. Weighing me before she smiled in her happy-Sarah way. Still, something was only thinly veiled in her eyes. Only slightly hidden in her willing agreement to follow my coded suggestion.

Pietr watched the whole exchange. I felt his disapproval

and frustration as if he were standing beside me. "I'm going on a quick run," he said, voice tight.

I turned to stop him—to point out we needed all three of them to get us back to the house—but the look he gave me was full of heartbreak. I had been a constant disappointment to him today. I couldn't blame him for wanting to race away when I was the one calling a halt to the day's activities.

"Pietr—" Catherine called, but he'd already turned his ATV around and raced away.

She looked at me apologetically. "He's difficult sometimes. Moody." She ran her hand through her hair, shaking tangles out. "They used to believe twins had severed souls, you know?"

I shook my head.

"I wonder if sometimes they weren't correct. I'm so often happy, he's so often grim." She shrugged.

We heard the roar of Pietr's motor grow dimmer, weaker—more distant.

I tensed.

"He's rounding the far end of the trail," Catherine narrated, her eyes blank as she listened. "He'll be back in a few minutes."

As she predicted, the noise grew, strengthening again.

"He's a bit of a pessimist. But I guess he has reasons to be." Her glance shifted from me to Sarah and back again. "Life is complicated, *da?*"

Even Amy agreed. Heartily.

We could hear the clean growl of his ATV's engine as he started back toward us, we saw both the ATV and him grow larger as they approached. He focused on the trail, his ATV hugging the curves and rocketing up the bulges and jumps so he could catch some air before smacking back down to earth. It wasn't a horse—just horsepower—but I totally respected the skill with which he rode.

And then he looked up, took his eyes off the path to stare at me as the engine whined. I screamed, "Pietr!" But it was too late. The ATV vaulted into the air. There was a sickening crack and crunch as his helmeted head hit a low-hanging tree branch and he was swiped off the ATV and hurled to the unforgiving ground with a *slap*!

"Oh, my—"

"Holy—"

Max and Catherine wasted no time on words; they soared down to where Pietr lay like valkyries riding ATVs instead of wind.

My lungs were nearly bursting, my legs burning when I got to the site of the accident. Sarah and Amy were right behind me. I could hear one of them crying. Catherine had his helmet off, his head on her lap. His eyes were closed and he looked peaceful, even as a halo of blood spread around his head, staining Catherine's mud suit and leaking into the earth.

"Ohhh—" My stomach twisted, knotting. "Call 911!" I yelled at Sarah. She unzipped her mud suit and fumbled for the phone that had never before been far from hand.

Max was suddenly beside her, snatching the phone away and looking at Catherine for support.

I stared at them both, agog.

"Max," Catherine said.

There was a look that passed between them—a long pause full of subtext—as Pietr's life leaked out of his head and into the mud. His chest barely rose and fell now. . . .

It seemed his breathing was stuttering. Stopping.

I was frozen.

Pietr was dying.

CHAPTER SEVENTEEN

Phone in hand, Max jumped to his brother's side. "Give me the count, Cat," he ordered, digging his fingers into his younger brother's mouth. "Airway's clear."

Catherine slid out from under Pietr's head, tilting it back. "Go," she said.

Max knelt at Pietr's side, hands stacked on his brother's breastbone. He pumped up and down on Pietr's chest as Catherine counted rapidly to thirty. Max paùsed, and Catherine pinched Pietr's nose closed and breathed twice into his mouth. Then Max returned to his job.

My knees weak, I fought against the fear swimming in my gut, fought for focus. "Need to stop the bleeding," I whispered. I circled Pietr's prone form and knelt beside his head. There was a gash about three inches long arching over his left eyebrow. But it didn't take a big head wound to bleed a huge amount.

"Direct pressure," I reminded myself, unzipping my mud suit and wiggling out of my shirt as quickly—and modestly—as I could before zipping back up. No one spared me a glance. I rolled my shirt up tightly, pressing it over Pietr's forehead.

And I prayed. I prayed Pietr would live. I prayed he'd forgive me. And, at one moment when Max exchanged a frightened look with Catherine, I even promised God that if He—or She—let Pietr live, I wouldn't lie about my feelings for him again.

There was a cough, Pietr's chest heaved, and his head jerked underneath the pressure of my hands.

"Thank God," I whispered. "One more ride . . . risking your life . . . you selfish son of a bitch . . ."

Max and Catherine's heads snapped around and they faced me, eyes narrow, lips tight. Like I had insulted their heritage.

Sarah was at his side, holding his hand. His eyes peering up at the nearly nude branches of the autumn trees, he said, "Jess . . ."

"She's here, Pietr," Catherine soothed. "She is helping to staunch the bleeding."

"I'm bleeding?" he whispered. His pupils were dilated. He wasn't completely back yet. "Jess is trying to stop the blood?" He chuckled.

The hairs on my arms stood straight up at the eerie, distant sound of it.

"Doesn't she know I'm—"

"Utterly delirious?" Catherine asked, talking over him with determination. Again she shared a worried look with Max. "I'm pretty certain she knows," she said, following the statement with a trilling laugh.

Max shook his head. "Let's look at the wound."

I carefully removed my bloody shirt from above Pietr's eyebrow. It peeled away with a sound so much like Velcro parting I nearly wretched.

The bleeding had stopped.

"Could be worse," Max said.

"He nearly died," I said, stunned by his lack of concern.

"*Da*. Yes," Max agreed, his eyes latching on to mine. "But he didn't."

"He could have a concussion," I said. "He at least needs stitches. He should go to the emergency room."

"We don't use doctors," Catherine tried to explain.

"What?" I wondered if my brain had gotten scrambled when Pietr's had.

"We don't believe in them," Max stated.

"What?" I demanded. "I promise you—they *do* exist."

Catherine laughed. "He doesn't mean it *that* way."

Pietr groaned, sitting up.

"I'll be fine," he insisted.

I moved around to stand in front of him and, stooping over, I looked at his eyes. His pupils were fine.

"I heal quickly," Pietr said shyly.

"You also bleed quickly," I admonished. "Why weren't you watching the trail?" I'd shot right past fear and into outrage.

Pietr sighed.

Max helped him to his feet.

"We don't count it as a real week unless Pietr's done at least one stupid or reckless thing to endanger himself," Catherine said with a smirk. But there seemed to be something beneath it. Something dark and true.

"Well—" I was having a tough time searching for the words, I was so angry. "Well . . . that's just plain *stupid*!"

Catherine was helping get everyone back on ATVs. She paused, though, realizing Pietr, Sarah's driver, was temporarily out of commission.

"I'll drive him," I growled. "I watched what you were doing. We'll go a little slower, but we'll get there okay," I promised.

"Sit down now," I commanded. "Put that helmet back on. I won't have you scrambling your brain any more today."

Sheepish, Pietr obeyed. I straddled the ATV before him and started the engine.

"I'll follow with Sarah," Catherine agreed. It seemed she wouldn't challenge me. Sarah glared at me, angrier than ever.

Max led the way, and we lurched forward a few awkward times before I got the right feel for the ATV. An arm slipped around my waist, and then another came around the opposite direction, and Pietr held on to me, his chest warm where it pressed tightly against my back. A tangle of emotions stirred my stomach as we climbed the slope to the house on Pietr's bright red ATV.

Cresting the rise, I saw Max yank his ATV to a stop and rocket off it, nearly flying onto the porch. In the thin shadows of afternoon a broad-shouldered man stood nearly toe-to-toe with Alexi, arguing. The man seemed to be in his forties, his salt-and-pepper hair cropped close to his chiseled face. He looked like he'd been handsome once, but the strong jaw, sharp cheekbones, and Roman nose I imagined once turned heads now made him look hungry, mean. No. *Cruel.* His jaw jutted forward, and his brow lowered brutishly over his eyes.

Alexi's hands clenched and opened almost rhythmically at his sides.

Max was beside his brother in an instant, and I swear he bristled in anger, more beast than man. I cut the engine and jerked my helmet off, desperate to hear.

Pietr tensed behind me. Listening to the ruckus on the porch, I focused on keeping Pietr from following in Max's footsteps.

"Step back, whelp, we're all marked men here," the unfamiliar man growled.

"Max, cool it," Alexi warned.

But Max pushed. "Why? Is this the guy you're dealing with? O.P.S.? Russian Mafia? Is that who's financing—"

"Shut. The. Hell. Up." Alexi spit each word out like poison.

"He's frisky—this one. Temperamental. Perhaps you've been in the U.S. too long," the stranger declared, an accent thickening the swelling self-righteousness in his voice.

As Russian as the Rusakovas were, they were still United States citizens. The contempt with which this man said *U.S.* made me wonder if *he* was.

"Our hearts are Russian," Alexi stated, cool again. "Our endurance is great."

I signaled to the girls to stay focused on Pietr. Better we not be noticed. Catherine and Sarah were with me, but I noticed Amy kept glancing toward Max, worried as much as intrigued. I couldn't blame her. If I'd been dating Marvin, I would have easily been tempted by Max. Marvin was just lacking something.

"Catherine, what's O.P.S.?" I whispered.

Behind me Pietr answered, "A business name the Mafia jokingly registered under in Russia. They are two different faces of the same coin."

I heard the man laugh. "Good, Alexi. Now call off your dog before I tear the saber off his shoulder with my teeth." Again, he laughed.

Pietr quaked with anger on the ATV, but I grabbed his wrist. Sarah grabbed his other hand. In unison, we said, "No. Don't go."

I looked at her. For a moment we were in total agreement.

"It could make things worse," I added.

"You could get hurt," Sarah said.

Pietr glowered.

"And you're in no condition." Catherine caught his eyes for the barest of moments. "He knows we're right."

"So just do what you promised, Alexi, and deliver the goods as soon as they're marketable. Then everything can be happily ever after for you."

I peeked over my shoulder at the trio.

The man smiled, showing every tooth he had. "But if you cross us, Alexi . . ." He curled his fingers, leaving just the index finger and thumb straight. Like a gun. He jabbed his index finger into Alexi's temple and said, "BANG. *Vwee pohnehmytyuh menya?*"

To his credit, Alexi never flinched. *"Da. Yah, pohnemyoo."*

"You'd better understand," the man confirmed. He walked down the stairs nonchalantly, following the walkway back around to the curb. A sleek silver car with heavily tinted windows waited for him; a slender man in the driver's side flicked a cigarette out the window. The mystery man came with money and a sharp-eyed chauffeur. None of this seemed good.

Russian Mafia, Max had suggested.

"What the f—" Max glared at his elder brother.

Alexi shoved Max in the shoulder. Hard. "You are far too eager to discover a truly unpleasant truth. Following me like some hound—" He glanced in our direction before shouldering Max toward the door. "Inside, dumb-ass."

Max spun around him, taking the steps in a single bound and racing over to us. He held out Sarah's cell phone to her. "You should go home now."

She snatched it back, flipped it open, and made the call. "Ten minutes," she said in brusque reply.

Max rejoined Alexi and disappeared into the house.

"Just enough time to get changed—my shirt," I realized.

"I have it," Catherine confirmed. "It's seen better days, I'm certain." She grabbed me by the hand. "Come with me. You can borrow something of mine."

And as fast as the accident had happened, I was wearing a top of Catherine's and climbing into the backseat of the Luxoms' car, my shirt in a plastic grocery bag, tucked in on itself to hide the dark red stain of Pietr's blood.

"Soooo—" Amy looked at me. "That certainly rates up there as my most exciting study date ever." She folded her hands in her lap. "How about you, Sarah?"

"Yes, Sarah, what was Pietr's family like?" her mother asked from the front passenger's seat.

"They were very nice," Sarah replied.

It seemed to be enough for Mrs. Luxom, who simply said, "Well, that's wonderful."

But Mr. Luxom peeked at Sarah in the rearview mirror, his eyes skeptical. "Don't discount nice, sweetheart. There are very few nice people in the world anymore. The business world has the least of them," he muttered, refocusing on the road.

"I don't think she *was* discounting—" Mrs. Luxom began, but he cut her off.

"God, Kristen, sometimes you can be so dense. I *had* to marry a natural blonde."

Mrs. Luxom went back to quietly staring out her window.

Amy looked at me for confirmation, and I nodded *yes*, because the Luxoms were generally at odds with each other. Under her breath Amy asked, "So why do you think they didn't want to take Pietr to a doctor?"

Sarah jumped in, speculating. "Perhaps they're from one of those religious sects that believes God will heal you if He wants to."

Sarah's parents just continued driving and staring, one stoic, the other stiff.

"I don't know," I said. "Maybe they're in the witness protection program," I suggested. I could definitely imagine Pietr being part of some heroic story line that required bringing mobsters to justice and paying for it with a life on the run.

Amy went the other direction with her logic. "Maybe they're a family of wanted criminals, and going to the doctors would signal the cops and the place would be swarming with police. . . ."

"Maybe they don't have any insurance," Sarah countered.

"Oh, my," Mrs. Luxom exclaimed, suddenly tuning in to our discussion. "Did they *look* poor?"

I put a hand on Amy's knee before words spilled out of her gaping mouth.

"No, Mrs. Luxom," I assured. "They didn't seem poor. But people don't have to be poor to not have insurance."

"Well, what do they do if they get sick, Jessica?" she asked, quite flustered to know how some in "the other half" lived.

It had been rumored for years that Sarah's mom was merely a "kept woman," but I had never imagined that meant *kept* from reality.

I could see Mr. Luxom's eyes roll in the rearview mirror's reflection. He portrayed himself as a man of the world and probably viewed his wife as a trophy. Pretty and moneyed, but not of real substance.

"They hope they get better," Amy retorted.

"Or they go to a free clinic," Sarah pointed out.

"Oh, I've written a check to support one of those," Mrs. Luxom said, comfortably settling back into her seat.

"Or," Amy concluded grimly, "they take out a loan against their mortgage if it's a big problem like an important operation. Then they hope the interest rate doesn't crush them and that they can get back to work fast."

I looked at Amy, suddenly remembering the major back surgery her dad underwent two years ago. Did she speak from experience? She avoided my gaze, finding a dozen fascinating things outside that caught her interest.

Sarah continued, almost dreamily, "Maybe he's like one of the characters in your books, Jessica—a *vampire*—and his family knows they'd go utterly and undeniably insane with hunger being so close to the hospital's blood reserve." She sighed wistfully.

"A *vampire*," Mr. Luxom snorted. "Then send him to work for me. The business world is full of bloodthirsty types!" He laughed then—so loudly we recognized the cue for us to laugh, too. So we did.

But I knew that as little as I really understood Pietr and his family, he certainly was no vampire.

We turned down Main Street. It was always my favorite part of any ride. Main Street was the redeeming feature that both split Junction in half and still united it, making it somehow feel like a community.

Although Junction couldn't boast a long or even an often-bustling main street, it was still interesting. Lined with its artists' co-op, free-trade and organic stores, restaurants, bagel shops, and continually burgeoning cafés, it had even recently added a bookstore selling brand-new books in contrast to the used books store on the street's opposite side. To me, Junction was the epitome of a college town.

I enjoyed looking at the window displays, especially when a holiday was coming up. And since traffic on Main Street rolled by at only twenty miles per hour, there was time to look.

"Ugh. It's not just confined to the mall," Amy sighed. "Halloween's been vomited all over town."

I didn't mind. Halloween signaled that my birthday was just

around the corner. And as weird as my birth date was, I still looked forward to it.

Passing Summer's Café, I gawked. Sitting at the window table was Weird Wanda. And a guy that was definitely not my dad. Was he that cop—Officer Kent? He wore khakis and a rumpled polo shirt. Plain clothes made people look so much different than a uniform—it messed with my perception. At a glance all I could tell was they were deep in conversation. Driving past I saw her hand him something. A key? A note? I strained to see, turning in my seat. Something rectangular gleamed like glass between her fingers before it disappeared into his. A microscope slide?

Stuck in my own neurotic musings and wondering if I should mention spotting her to Dad or not, I didn't really witness the rest of the drive until the car turned up the long driveway leading to my house.

"When are you going to get this driveway paved, Jessica?" Mr. Luxom asked, adding, "The gravel is hell on a car's under-carriage."

"We don't plan on paving the driveway, Mr. Luxom. Asphalt leaches some nasty stuff we don't want on our farm, and cement doesn't always hold up." More important, it was too expensive for us to consider—but I'd never willingly admit that. I shrugged instead. "Sorry."

Mr. Luxom brought the car to a stop and announced our arrival. We laughed again. Right when we should, and nearly convincingly.

Amy and I stepped out. Sarah followed us with a "Just a minute, please, Daddy," to her father.

I froze, watching as she turned. She put her back to the car, her face stone, her eyes all flash and fire. "So what's *really* going on between you and my boyfriend?" she demanded.

I swallowed hard. When Pietr had lain dying in front of me, I'd made a promise. I swallowed again. A promise to *God*. Surely there weren't many loopholes in a contract like that. Did I confess here, then, on my gravel driveway, as her parents waited in a running car?

"Is Pietr your *boyfriend*?" Amy asked, ready to help out however she could.

"Yes, he is, *you little*—"

"Whoa!" I said, between them both. "There's no reason—"

"I can't believe you," Sarah fumed. "Pietr's the *reason*. A very good reason," she hissed.

"There's nothing—" I began the lie, words falling out of my mouth against my wishes.

"Everything okay out there, dumpling?" Mr. Luxom called out the skylight.

"Fine, Daddy," Sarah sang back. "Pietr's the best thing I have—" she snapped, just as angry as a moment before.

"I thought it was the promise of a Beemer for your eighteenth birthday," Amy tossed into the mix.

I shot her a look of warning.

Sarah ignored Amy, focusing her most intense glare on me. "*You're* trying to steal him away," she accused, every word filled with bitterness.

I sighed. "No." At least I could be honest about that. "I'm *not* trying to steal him away."

"Then what is it between you two?" she demanded.

"Look. She keeps trying to push him your way and he keeps coming after her harder and harder," Amy revealed. "It's not totally her fault."

"You think you have to *push* him my way?" The fire had died in her eyes, replaced with an iciness I'd seen only before the accident.

That first day I'd visited Sarah in the hospital (for reasons I still don't totally understand) I was moved by the warmth and fear in her eyes. She couldn't remember a thing then. A few names. Some spotty stuff about a handful of places.

Jenny and Macie came to see her briefly, but when they saw how broken her body was, they took advantage of her momentary weakness. She was suddenly no better than dead to them. Jenny won over Derek, and I got left with the opportunity to save Sarah. She was like our psych teacher, Ms. Wyatt, said: *tabula rasa*. A blank slate.

But standing outside the Luxoms' running car, Amy and I were no longer talking to the Sarah I'd tried to recover from the remnants of her broken brain. The ice was once again thick in her shimmering eyes. I was face-to-face with the Sarah who saw no point in redemption because she never felt the need for shame. I recognized her easily. I *remembered* this Sarah.

CHAPTER EIGHTEEN

Sarah laughed at me. "Do you *really* believe you're any competition for me?" She took in the farm, the house—everything I felt was a part of me. She laughed again, cruelty unmistakable in her voice. "Do you think *this* will hold his interest? A muddy farm with shabby horses and a double-wide as a house? *This* is all you are, all you'll ever be: a hired hand, a manual laborer for people like *my* family—if *we'd* ever even hire you. It's not a matter of how much you know or read, it's a matter of *class* and *breeding*. And you don't have either."

As I prepared to retaliate verbally, something changed in her eyes and I saw such a crippling sadness, so much tragic remorse. . . . All the hatred and anger seemed to dissipate like fog cleared by an unexpected breeze.

"God, Jessica," Sarah murmured. "I don't always know what I'm saying anymore," she confided, tears in her eyes. "It's like something's come loose in my head. I hear these things—like someone else's voice—and then I realize *I've* said those same things, that it never *was* someone else. It was always me. God, I'm so sorry, Jessica. I didn't really mean it. Not one word."

I nodded, feigning forgiveness. Her words had stung. And I knew in her heart she *did* mean it. Not *just* one word. *Every* word. She just didn't realize. Yet.

I'd been such a liar. The Sarah I'd been so intent on helping—on *creating,* after the accident—wasn't the real Sarah at all. I'd kept things from her—her past cruelty, her manipulations, her verbal and mental abuse of so many at school. The way she'd happily earned her peers' fear and hatred as if it were some sick award.

I had protected her, shielding her from the students who would have gladly taken the opportunity to kick her while she was down, while she was trying to find her place again. She'd grown to be so different in such a short time that not even Jenny and Macie noticed her unless it was to torment her. Just like they did everyone else.

I had truly hoped that with time and work, Sarah's place would be with us. But it seemed my hopes were crumbling as fast as my best friend Sarah's control.

I grabbed her by the arms, not knowing what else to do. "Sarah, we all have moments when we say horrible stuff, when we act without thinking," I assured her. "It doesn't mean we're horrible people." I needed to believe that myself. I couldn't bear the fact Sarah—our Sarah—was slipping away and would once again be the beautiful but demonic angel who terrorized an entire school. "It just means we have to try to be better."

"I *am* trying," she said. "I *promise.*"

I hugged her, blinking back the threat of tears. Promises weren't all they were cracked up to be. If I'd been willing to go back so quickly on a promise made to *God*—even in the heat of the moment—how could I dare think Sarah would hold firm to a promise made just to *me*?

Sarah got back into the car and Amy and I silently walked the brief remaining distance to my house.

"Hey, Dad!" I shouted, masking my mood as I shoved the door open.

"Hey, kid!" came the regular reply.

Amy and I entered the kitchen.

"Yo, Mr. Gillmansen!" Amy exclaimed, giving Dad a stinging high five.

"That's: Yo, *dude*, to you, young lady." He grinned. "How'd the study group do?"

"Dramatically," Amy proclaimed, falling into a chair.

Dad's forehead wrinkled as he thought about the proper interpretation. "I'm hopin' that's dramatically well. . . ."

"Well." I smiled, setting the bag with the blood-covered shirt on a chair and sliding it under the table's edge. "We did get some of the science worksheet done."

"Hmm. That's somethin', I guess. The fact that any of you girls got anything done with that Pietr boy in the same room . . . Even Wanda's been askin' about that boy."

"Ew," Amy said.

"Not like that." He chuckled. "Just the normal nosy-woman routine: 'Hey, who's that boy Jessie's with—' "

"Come on, Dad, you've got to get her to stop calling me that."

"Why? I call you that."

"You're my *dad*," I protested. "You get to take liberties with my name. But not many," I quipped before he started getting too creative.

His head snapped up and he looked at us suspiciously as if he'd just remembered something. "You didn't go into Pietr's room at all, did ya?"

I blushed. "No, Dad. We sat in the den."

"More like a sitting room," Amy specified.

"A sittin' room. That's a pretty fancy place to have for a boy throwin' hay to our horses." He winked. "Looks fit, though, doesn't he, Jessie? Like he can handle hard work."

I poured myself a glass of sweet tea.

"Your father asked you a question, *Jessie*," Amy said. Reveling in it. "Doesn't Pietr look *fit* to you?"

I blushed again, giving her my wide-eyed *I can't believe you* look from around the refrigerator door. "Yes," I said coolly, heading to the table. "He looks fit to me."

Amy took the tea from me and drank a sip. "Might even say he looks like a healthy, red-blooded American male," she said with a grin.

"Well, then, you oughta stay clear of him," Dad said, stirring additional sugar into his own tea. "I used to *be* one of those red-blooded American males. Got into a fair share of trouble, too."

"So, Dad," I asked, trying to steer him from the topic of Pietr—and blood, "what did you do so far today?"

"Hmm. More target practice with Wanda. Sightin' in another beautiful weapon."

"She seems to have quite a collection," I said.

"Yep. And that Wanda's got a dead eye."

"Ewww . . . ," Amy said.

"No," I laughed. "Not *literally.* Dad means she's a good shot."

He nodded. "Not as good as you coulda been, Jessie, but nearly always dead-on."

"Could we not talk about that?" I asked. I picked up the bag and started from the kitchen.

"I just think if you have a talent for somethin'—"

But we were down the hallway and headed for the promise of a mercifully loud laundry room.

"So why didn't you keep shooting? Weren't you supposed to train, like, at the Olympic Training Center?" Amy asked once the laundry room door was closed and she had me trapped.

I shrugged. "What? And leave all this?" I tried a smile. "Seriously. I think I gave up enough for the sport already. Leaving my friends—no thank you." The conversation closed as the washing machine door did. Solidly.

Monday morning was nightmarishly slow. There was no sign of Pietr to help me with the horses. I spent the time I should have been focusing on my chores focusing instead on where he was and *how* he was. *Why didn't I call him to see if he's okay?*

"Where's that boy of yours?" Dad asked as I searched through my backpack, trying to make sure I had everything I needed for school.

There was no point proclaiming he wasn't *my* boy. "Didn't show," I muttered.

"Not real dependable, is he?"

"He's dependable."

"Probably better he didn't show. Saves me a few bucks." He took down his favorite coffee mug. "They're startin' layoffs at the factory."

"What?" I looked up at him, stunned. "Are you on the list?"

"Not so far. I'm a pretty important cog in the works over there, ya know?" He poured some coffee. Stared at it a while before taking a sip. "But we better start tightenin' our belts in case there's no holiday bonus and no raise in the new year."

Tightening our belts? I was already clipping coupons and stretching everything we had to keep the horses in hay and grain. "Okay," I agreed.

The bus honked.

"Better run for it," Dad suggested as I bolted out the door and raced down the driveway.

I bounced up the bus's steps.

"Almost missed it," the driver warned.

I didn't even nod acknowledgment as I headed to my seat. There, with only a modest Band-Aid over his left eyebrow, was Pietr. I flopped down beside him.

"Stitches?" I asked as the bus heaved forward.

"*Nyet.*"

"You're kidding." It should have taken at least a couple.

"Must've seemed worse with all that blood." He shrugged.

I gulped. *Everything* had seemed worse with all that blood.

"*Eezvehneetyeh.* Sorry if I freaked you out. I guess I'm accident prone."

"I'd call it reckless. Selfish." I hugged my backpack.

"Are you going to push your new motto now: We don't just live our lives for ourselves, or whatever?"

"Well, we don't," I protested. "If you had been killed—" I gulped at the thought. "How would Max have felt?"

"Like he'd get a second chance at having my room."

"Okay, maybe not Max. Catherine. She would have been devastated," I said with authority.

He shrugged.

"You affect people, Pietr. Don't you realize?"

"I don't affect some as strongly as I *want* to," he muttered, beginning to turn away.

I wasn't letting him shut me down so easily. "You didn't show up to help today."

"*Eezvehneetyeh.* Alexi had to race off somewhere with the car. I didn't really have much choice."

"Well, you may not have a job for long," I snapped.

"If you want me to say *eezvehneetyeh* again . . ." He looked at me, his eyes narrow.

"Saying sorry won't do it."

He leaned toward me, his breath hot on my face. It was dizzying being so close and not being kissed. "I've done everything you want me to. I act like we're just friends, I date Sarah, I try not to take it badly when you totally blow off a huge omen in the shape of an amber pendant—"

"An *omen*? Who even talks that way?" I shook my head in frustration and peered past him and out the window. *How much longer until we got to the school?*

"Look, it's cool that I was able to open those wooden things for you," I began. "I seriously don't get why you couldn't, though. And it's neat that inside the wolfy one was a heart-shaped pendant with a bunny carved into it." I was rambling, but I was on a roll. Maybe I shouldn't help myself to Dad's coffee.

"But all it is," I continued, "is simple coincidence. I mean, sure, it's weird, but hearts and rabbits are both popular symbols. And, frankly—unless there's some crazy secret you aren't telling me—the fact the heart came out of a wolf has nothing to do with you. I mean—really. It's not like you're a wolf or anything; right, Pietr?"

I shook my head for him. "No. Of course not. So what does that leave?" My fingers tapped my chin. Yes, I was being mean, but he had nearly *killed* himself in front of me yesterday, and I certainly wasn't in the mood for any nonsense about omens today. The bus rolled to a stop in front of the school. "Oh," I said in epiphany, "if you're not a *wolf,* are you a *werewolf,* Pietr?"

He blinked at me. "Yes."

CHAPTER NINETEEN

"Ugh!" I stood, slinging the backpack over my shoulder. "You are absolutely infuriating! *Impossible!*" I stomped my way out of the bus, pounding my feet down the gritty stairs and jumping off the final step and onto the sidewalk.

Pietr was right behind me.

Sarah, Sophia, and Amy were standing there, waiting on us.

"Mornin', sunshine," Amy piped up, noticing my scowl.

"Is something wrong?" Sarah asked.

I waved a hand over my shoulder toward Pietr. "Pietr's being difficult."

"Oh," Sophia said, watching us both.

Sarah hugged him. "You look like you're doing well," she said. "You had us all so worried! You should give me your phone number so I can check up on you."

"There's nothing to worry about," he assured. "I'm tougher than I look."

I pondered the fact that I had Pietr's phone number and his girlfriend didn't. Sarah slipped her hand into his.

A whistle sounded two sharp tweets, and Coach Mac shouted, "No public displays of affection."

Rebuffed, Sarah pulled her hand back, head down. I looked down the sidewalk toward Coach Mac. Not five feet beyond him Jenny and Derek were locked in a fierce embrace, kissing as if he were a soldier headed to war. Already incensed, I shouted, "Hey Coach, to your right!"

His head swung around and he spotted the two lovebirds. He said something to them, quietly, so as to not draw attention. They pulled apart and Jenny's mouth moved, questioning. Coach responded with a jab of his chin in our direction. Jenny's face twisted with anger; Derek just smiled.

"Nice job," Amy reprimanded. "One more reason for Jenny to hate you. You know, considering your IQ, you're really socially retarded sometimes."

"Thanks," I said, glaring. "It's just not fair. Derek can publicly ram his tongue down Jenny's throat, and Sarah and Pietr can't even hold hands?"

I ditched the bunch of them then, needing the solitude of library research to calm back down. I ransacked Google, thinking about the weird stuff I'd collected so far. Russian Mafia, wolves . . . *cool!* I'd missed something. Probably that day Derek had come in to renew "World of Sports." But who could blame me considering how tight his jeans had been.

I clicked on the link and mouthed the words *Phantom wolves of Farthington? Two distinct sets of footprints found.* Bingo! That at least was something decent about today. I hit print, grabbed the paper, and headed to homeroom.

Amy didn't waste another word on me until second period. We were broken into groups and, pulling our desks together, we were told the assignment: "Choose a quote that summarizes your life."

Sarah blinked and put away *Dr. Jekyll and Mr. Hyde*.

"I don't know," Amy confessed, raising her hand. "Ms. Wyatt, do you mean our life up until now, or what we think our future will be like?"

Ms. Wyatt merely smiled and said, "That's why this is introduction to psychology—here, we ask questions." Then she danced away, her poet's shirt and long, flowered skirt flowing around her. "To quote Mary Oliver," she called from the opposite side of the room, "tell me, what is it you plan to do with your one wild and precious life?"

"Well, frankly, I haven't really thought much about it." Amy held out the list of quotes, daring any of us to take it.

Sarah did, of course. "I've recently had quite a bit of time to be *introspective*," Sarah pointed out. She ran a finger down the list, carefully examining each phrase.

I raised my hand. "Ms. Wyatt, can we have another list to share?" I asked.

"The school district recently adopted a policy encouraging conservation and recycling." Ms. Wyatt danced away again.

"I think that means *no*." Amy pouted.

"Oh!" Sarah's eyes were wide. "I found mine!" Carefully she wrote something in her notebook.

"What is it?" I asked. I tried to sound interested. And frankly, I was curious. . . . Considering how crazy she'd been acting, maybe I could decipher something from her choice of quote.

"By A. Powell Davies: 'Life is just a chance to grow a soul.'" Sarah sighed. "I like it. I think that's true. It's like that idea that life's not a destination but really a journey toward enlightenment."

Across from me, Amy's expression matched Pietr's. Cool and distant. They were merely observers of the moment.

"That's a great one," I agreed, silently hoping Sarah was on the path to growing a soul—to understanding and compassion. Instead of heading down the path toward destroying her peers.

She passed the paper to me. I leaned across my desk, holding the paper so Amy and Pietr could catch a glimpse, too.

Pietr glanced at the list and then sat back in his seat. "Mine's on there."

"What?" I asked. "You already have a quote for your life?"

He shrugged.

Sarah's hand took his. "What is it, Pietr?"

"'My candle burns at both ends; It will not last the night; But ah, my foes, and oh, my friends—It gives a lovely light!'" He said it all in a way I knew he'd said the lines many times, out loud and in his heart. "Edna St. Vincent Millay," he added.

"It's beautiful, Pietr," Sarah said with such gentleness it made me twitch.

"It's tragic," I snapped, staring straight at him. "You're talking about death. The quote's supposed to be about *life*."

"It's on the list," Amy pointed out.

"I don't care. It doesn't make sense," I hissed. Yesterday's events rushed over me in sudden and brilliant shades of red. "Do you *want* to die, Pietr?"

He blinked at me and then turned to look at the classroom's clock. He turned back, fixing his dazzling eyes on mine. "I want to live. *Every moment*," he responded sharply.

"He wants to live life fiercely, Jessie. Don't you get it? Live like you're dying." Amy peered at me out of the corners of her eyes. She sighed. "Maybe you should choose another quote, Pietr," she suggested.

I turned on her. "He doesn't have to choose another quote, Amy, he needs to think about what he's saying. He *never* thinks about what he's saying."

Pietr's fingers began to drum on the desk.

From across the room I felt Derek's eyes on me. I'd nearly forgotten he was in the class, I'd been so fixated on Pietr.

Amy raised her hands in mock defense. "Fine, fine." She looked at Pietr then, a hint of mischief in her eyes. "Shame on you, Pietr—being an adolescent male who may not have *totally* thought out the potential impact your words would have on a"—she looked at me and rolled her eyes—"*moody* teenage girl. Pietr, you are truly an exception to the rule."

Sarah was laughing.

"Ladies, ladies," Ms. Wyatt scolded in her teasing way, "Let's get our focus back. How many here have a quote?"

Sarah's hand was a rocket launching. Pietr's was slower—sullen, even—but no less assured.

"Good, good," Ms. Wyatt beamed at them before rounding on us. "And, girls, what are you considering?"

"'Life is so constructed that an event does not, cannot, will not, match the expectation'," Amy griped.

"Ohhh. A lovely pessimistic view from Charlotte Brontë," Ms. Wyatt said with obvious approval. "And you?" She faced me.

I looked at the paper again, looked at Amy, and then at Sarah. Sarah was smiling at me with such a look of utter support, the flash and fire of yesterday replaced with simple good will. It was like we hadn't argued at all. And I believed if I could save her from herself, I would. No matter how long it took. "There." I pointed. "Number five."

Ms. Wyatt squinted. "Hmm. Albert Einstein." She read it slowly. "'Only a life lived for others is a life worthwhile.'"

Pietr and Amy just looked at me levelly. Sarah beamed.

We darted out of intro to psychology, passing Derek in the hall. I swore I heard him say to Pietr, "Live like you're dying?

Life's too short to have it all, isn't it?" Pietr just pushed past as Derek grinned at me. In lit we had a rousing discussion of *Romeo and Juliet*! The topic of doomed love, lies, and naïve teenage relationships rubbed my nerves raw.

I tuned out, wishing I couldn't hear any of it. Didn't we all know by now that Romeo and Juliet had been doomed from the get-go by the nastiness between their family and peers? That their attempts to avoid Fate and find some cheery happily-ever-after ended in a tragic and bloody way because of poor communication? I didn't need to dwell on it. Not right now.

Pausing at my locker, I found a note taped to it. I immediately called home. "Yeah, one of my reporters dropped the ball. Yep. The curse of being an editor—no glory and all the headaches. No, Dad, I'll call when I need you to get me. Yeah. Okay, bye. Yep. I love you, too, Dad."

The rest of my day was spent splitting my attention between the article Sophia and I would need to write and paying attention (mostly) in class. There was no time to spend on Pietr, although I sneaked a few glances at him as he sneaked glances at the clock. We didn't even say good-bye to each other; I didn't say much to any of my friends all day.

Sophia was already waiting by the faculty lounge when I got there. She straightened her collar so even less of her was visible. It was strange how she hid in her clothes. She had really great skin.

"Hey, Soph. Anybody in there?"

"Mr. Miles came out a minute ago. I think it's empty now."

"Cool, let's get this done," I said, pulling the door open and revealing what most students never saw. I skirted the vending machines and mini-fridge, sitting at the round table.

Sophia slipped some coins into a vending machine and set us up with chips and soda. "Brain food."

"I can definitely use some. Okay. Let's throw together something that reinforces the idea what's on the inside matters more than the outside."

Sophia, one of the prettiest girls in my circle of friends, said, "So lame."

"You say that because you're beautiful inside and out." I grinned.

She stuck out her tongue at me.

"It's not such a bad thing," I conceded. "Yeah, it's a lame teacher topic, but occasionally we do have to do what they say. It *is* a school newspaper."

She rolled her eyes. "So, let's brainst—"

The door swung open and Derek and Jack, deep in conversation about football plays, stepped in for sodas.

Sophia looked at me, eyes wide. Her hand moved to her neck.

"Hey," Derek said, glancing at Sophia before settling his gaze on me. *Me.* My heart sped up.

"Derek," Sophia forced the word out between her clamped teeth. "Jack."

"Yo."

Jack inserted his coins and—"Daaamn"—smacked the machine a couple of times before it released his soda.

"Jessica . . . I wanted to ask—." Derek began, but Jack punched him in the shoulder.

"Get your drink, dude. My mom'll be out front in a minute."

Derek's lips twisted and he shot Sophia another look.

"You'd better get your drink, Derek, so you don't miss your ride," she suggested. Something threatening crept around the edges of her tone.

"Yeah." He turned around, bought his drink, and paused at the door. "Later," he said. To me.

"Yeah," I agreed as he left.

I sank into my chair. "Sophia. What the heck was all that about? I mean, I know you two went out . . ."

But it was a taboo subject. Sophia glared at me to reinforce the fact.

"Fine. I'll drop it."

"Good." She seemed a shade paler. Her shoulders dropped and her eyes softened before she jotted some phrases down on the brainstorming paper, her pen sliding across its surface effortlessly. Her phone chattered across the table a moment before she snagged it. "I have to go. Here are a couple things to help." She shoved the paper at me and looked toward the door. "Think they're gone?"

"Probably."

"Good." Sophia left then, too.

With a groan I looked at the paper.

Beauty's only skin deep.

Everybody has ugly days.

We're all made of the same stuff underneath.

Acting right is better than looking right.

Realize what makes you special beyond looks.

Evil can look pretty on the outside.

I read her brainstormed list twice. Then I ran my finger down the left-hand column of letters. *What?* BEWARE. Beware? Beware what? I jumped up, knocking over my chair as I headed to the door. Did Sophia realize what she'd written?

And then, my hands pressed to the door, I heard it, a faint clicking on tile like a dog padded along up the hall. And the whuffling. The sound of something big scenting, searching . . .

Hunting. In the high school. I turned the deadbolt and fumbled for my cell phone. The clicking and breathing got louder.

It was coming.

Open, my cell phone scanned for a signal. It found nothing. I held it out. I held it up. I paced the space in front of the door, tilting the phone, cursing the phone. . . .

Nothing. Except the steadily growing noise of the beast approaching. That was when I noticed the window.

Junction High had been around for years. Okay, easily several decades, maybe a half-century. It used to be one story and handled kids from Junction and a couple of smaller nearby towns. If you dared call them towns. As Junction grew, the school changed, but slowly. In pieces, slow starts and sudden stops.

The door to the faculty lounge looked like solid wood. So it was old. Sturdy. A single long, thin window ran near the knob, reinforced with metal wires that cut smart diagonals just below the glass surface. *Holy crap*, I realized as my feet moved my reluctant body closer, *I'll see it* . . .

My hands rested on either side of the window, my face so near my breath fogged the window's middle.

And then it was there. Slipping by the window, a ridge of dark auburn fur stretched like a saddle mark across shoulders so high they were easily halfway up the window. I gasped, realizing its sheer height.

It stopped, hearing me. Right on the other side of the door I leaned against. My heart stopped, too, as the thing turned and a pointed ear pricked in my direction. It nearly bent in half as it circled back—my face still firmly pressed to the warming glass in horror. Hot breath puffed beneath the door. With a snort that toasted my toes, it assessed me. Then it was off, streaking down the hall, I with only a look at its thickly furred back.

I collapsed onto the floor, my back resting against the door. What *was* that thing?

Hours after the creature was gone and I was safely home my brain replayed over and over the moment the beast crossed in front of that narrow window, adding a frightening prelude to my standard nightmare.

CHAPTER TWENTY

Still exhausted when I woke the next morning, I did everything robotically. I did my chores without Pietr (he'd probably given up on helping me), never speaking to the horses. I got changed, never worrying about matching my clothes. I ate breakfast, never tasting it, and stumbled down the aisle of the bus, falling into the seat next to Pietr, limp as a—wet noodle? A rag doll? Sure, both were clichés, but there was a reason for that. They were fitting. Unlike my T-shirt, I realized.

A leftover from last year, it clung to parts of me that simply hadn't existed then, and—I felt a faint draft of air circle my waist. Terrific. The terrible tee also revealed my stomach whenever I leaned any direction. I tried to tug at its hem to lengthen it and heard a *pop.*

Pietr glanced at me.

I blushed. Fabulous. Somewhere, a seam waited to betray me.

Pietr brushed against me, leaning forward to catch my backpack as it flopped off the seat. Inhaling deeply, he straightened and peered at me—and around me—like he was confused by the air itself. He looked past me. Down the aisle.

"Expecting someone?"

"No. Where were you last night?" he asked, his voice so low I leaned in to catch his words.

"School. Working on a story."

"The phantom wolf thing?"

"Oddly enough, no."

He tilted his head. "Why 'oddly enough'?"

Would he think I was nuts if I told him what I saw last night in the school's main hall? I mean, whether I wanted to or not, I really did like Pietr. *Really.* Should I risk his feelings changing toward me by telling the truth? I shrugged. "Oddly enough because it seems I'm always working on that story," I said. *Ugh.*

He nodded, but I still read questions darting through the depths of his brilliant blue eyes. My only question was: How many more lies could I tell before I got caught? Okay, not my only question. I also wanted to know how I could switch out of the terrible tee.

The bus finally came to a wheezing stop, brakes grinding. Everyone rose in unison and began to shuffle out.

"What the—" I knocked into the underclassman in front of me and felt Pietr, hot as noon, bump against me.

Someone had stopped on the bus steps.

"Move it, Stella," someone else admonished, but Stella was stunned.

I followed her gaze.

A swarm of police officers mingled and muttered on the sidewalk. Officer Kent stood at the group's edge, carrying his ever-present cup of coffee, eyes flickering from the uniformed officers scratching their heads to our bus number. Lucky thirteen. He separated himself from the group as we got off the bus.

"Strangest thing—"

"I just don't know what sort of—"

"Can't be a—"

"Not a dog, either—"

Kent was beside us, eyeing Pietr. "Rusakova. I presume your siblings are—"

"Driving separately," Pietr stated.

"Hmm. Glad you're still making it to class." Kent looked Pietr up and down.

"He won't be if he gets stopped here," I snapped, grabbing Pietr's arm.

Kent glared at me, but stepped aside and I tugged Pietr closer to the school's doors before I released him.

"*Spahseebuh*. Thanks."

"Yeah. You're welcome. Don't know what came over me," I admitted. "What the heck was that about?"

Stella circled us, hopping from one foot to the other, eyes bright as she assessed Pietr. "Did you do it?"

"Do what?" His expression seemed blank.

"Shred the Guidance Office!"

"What?" I gasped.

"Someone or some*thing* got in there and tossed the files around," Stella explained. Her interest in me as a suspect had waned. She probably wanted to congratulate the guilty rebel. My question and tone ruled me out.

Sophia, Sarah, and Amy joined us.

I peered between their shoulders at the gathering crowd of students clogging the hall leading to Guidance.

Sarah nudged closer to Pietr. "Weren't you and Sophia here late last night, Jessica?"

Stella's eyes popped.

Sophia shook her head and whispered, "I left before five."

Amy crossed her arms and squared off with Sarah. "And as pissed as Jessie may be at Guidance's fumbled attempts to help her, she would *never*. I swear, Sarah, it's like you don't know her at all."

Sarah's face fell just the slightest bit.

"Geez." I rolled my eyes. "Besides, I wasn't the only one here. Derek and Jack were in the building, too. We saw them before Soph headed out."

Sophia stayed silent. I thought of the strange note hidden in Sophia's brainstormed list. Did she know—had she somehow known? Was normally quiet Sophia—the same normally quiet Sophie who utterly snapped at Derek last night—was she connected to the shredding of the Guidance Office? I shook my head, my feet dragging me behind my peers and into school.

So why "BEWARE"? Rubbing my forehead, I shoved the question from my mind. Sure, Sophia had changed during eighth grade, but to presume she somehow knew something— had tried to warn me about something roaming the school . . . it would mean the world was a far weirder place than I'd thought. I was barely ready to deal with my own issues. Questioning the way of the world—that was too much.

In the middle of lit, Pietr passed me a note. It was brief and, for a moment, puzzling.

Can you keep your promise? Today is the day.

I thought about the date. My promise? Oh. *Crap.* I scribbled back.

Your parents?

He nodded and my stomach clenched. I knew it was coming up—he'd said that much—but I'd forgotten his parents had died on this date. *Crap, crap, crap!*

He watched me. There was only one way I could answer.

I nodded and turned back, pretending to listen to what Ms. Ashton said. "Shakespeare speaks of Romeo and Juliet as being 'a pair of star-cross'd lovers' in Act One's prologue. Romeo also says, 'My mind misgives some consequence yet hanging in the stars' as he's on his way to the Capulet party—where he meets Juliet. So, for your writing assignment tonight, answer this: Are these two kids doomed by destiny? Are their lives and ours part of some huge cosmic plan, or do we make our Fate and create our own luck? Five hundred to one thousand words," she concluded as the bell rang.

I groaned, knowing lit had just passed me by in a haze of words. So I let math do the same the following period. Lunch was far from spectacular, and although I nodded at the appropriate moments and said, "No way," and "Uh-huh," at all the right times, I had no sense at all of what we discussed.

Art replaced gym, and I struggled to regain my focus for the beginning of a pottery unit I heard we'd be starting. But Mrs. Hahn greeted us at the door with a frown. "Don't get too settled," she announced. "We have an assembly. Set your stuff down, I'll be locking up," she assured.

There was a mix of hoots of pleasure and sighs of disappointment at the news of a blown day of class. I didn't need to look to see who did which, the division of jocks and nerds usually made it clear. A couple guys were hanging around the sink as we started setting our bags down, and I heard the water turn on, but didn't think anything of it until Mrs. Hahn shouted and I was soaked as collateral damage from their impromptu water battle.

My shirt was dripping. Mrs. Hahn glared at the unrepentant boys. "Clean up that mess," she ordered. She looked at me in disdain. "You'll need to change into your gym shirt, I guess."

I just looked at her blankly, thinking that as angry as I was, surely the water would turn to steam and evaporate right off of me at any moment. Which would only further shrink the terrible tee. Great.

Pietr's eyes were glued to me as much as the back of my wet shirt was. "Here," he said, pulling off his sweater and leaving just a T-shirt underneath. He tossed the sweater to me.

Sarah nobly ignored the entire exchange, chin up.

"Thanks," I muttered, racing to the restroom. It took only a moment to yank off my shirt and replace it with Pietr's sweater. As I quickly checked my hair in the mirror, I noticed how his sweater swallowed me up, large at the neck, long on my arms and hanging below my hips. Like a winter wind playing through pine branches, Pietr's scent was interwoven with the sweater's variegated yarn. I inhaled deeply, trying to catch some sense of him—to understand his reckless ways.

Nothing happened. My life wasn't filled with magical understanding and epiphanies, just tragedy and stale struggle. I reached into my pocket and rubbed my worry stone.

Although my outfit certainly wasn't any sort of fashion statement, it was better than wearing my gym shirt. And far more comfortable than the T-shirt I wrung out in the sink. I'd hand it down to Annabelle Lee as a work shirt. If she ever *worked*.

I pushed the sweater's sleeves up above my elbows to open the door and rushed back to class. Mrs. Hahn had halted the class's questionable progress for my return.

"Get in line," Mrs. Hahn said, pointing to the line's head. I followed her instructions, standing right in front of Pietr to lead the unruly line.

"Thanks," I whispered again, just over my shoulder. "What's the assembly on?"

"An antidrug message and demonstration."

I nodded.

It was a quick walk to the gymnasium and even from the hall I could see we were nearly the last class to arrive. A banner was angled above the gymnasium's doors proclaiming LIVE FREE, NO DRUGS FOR ME! The bleachers nearly overflowed with uncomfortable and shifting students.

VP Perlson was standing beside a state police officer, chatting and eyeing the K-9 unit seated obediently nearby. A remarkable-looking German shepherd, its regal profile and thick ruff of fur on its chest made it appear majestic; I thought about how shabby Maggie and Hunter would look beside it.

"In and to the left," Mrs. Hahn instructed, pointing to one of the few open areas on the bleachers. I watched the dog, wondering how it could be so calm with so many anxious kids around. Hunter would have been peeing on members of the front row while Maggie barked encouragement.

Cute, I thought, noticing the crisply folded sky blue bandanna around its neck. It made it somehow look less threatening. I wondered if it was intentional when demonstrating a K-9's abilities to students. Earn their trust, impress them with its prowess and then, when their guard was down, search their lockers!

And then, as if it knew I was thinking about it, the dog turned and looked at me. Its head tilted, ears perked, it tipped its glossy nose, angling for a scent.

It stood. Facing me.

CHAPTER TWENTY-ONE

The officer put his hand down firmly before the dog and I saw his mouth form the single word: *Stay.*

The dog sprang forward, unbidden, yanked the leash free from the officer's hand and—

—charged.

Its ears flattened, its long mouth opened, teeth glistening, eyes fixed on the most certain target of its life—me. I couldn't move.

My mind struggled to grasp the speed at which everything was happening. . . . At that moment I had the rather mundane thought the cheery bandanna was awfully misleading. . . .

The dog's muscles bunched as it launched into the air. It was like seeing some nature show where the lion goes straight for the throat. I didn't feel like I was there at all. My mind couldn't accept there wasn't a television screen wedged between myself and severe bodily harm.

Teeth snapped as it soared toward my face, a taunt urging me to run—to give it a challenge. But my feet were stuck to the gym floor as if I were mired in freshly set cement. And then the world before me blurred and I saw an arm thrust out just inches in front of my nose. The move stirred the loose strands of my hair. An open hand connected with the dog's broad chest and hurled the snarling beast away, tossing it as if it were an angry child's discarded doll.

The dog yipped, landing gracelessly on the slick gym floor. It charged again, barreling toward my protector, not heeding the officer's orders. I turned my head to see who endangered themself on my behalf. My world moved. So. Slow-ly.

The dog was nearly upon us when Pietr dropped into a runner's sprinting position, his face at the same height as the dog's oncoming jaws.

My eyes widened, witnessing and wonderstruck at the insanity of it—

And then, nearly nose to nose, Pietr grinned at the dog, his lips sliding back to show his amazingly perfect teeth, his eyes cool and fixed.

In the space of a single heartbeat, I thought I saw Pietr's teeth lengthen.

The dog yowled, feet scrabbling to stop its progress in panic, its eyes wide with a sudden fear that matched my own. With a howl of terror it turned, lost its footing once, and scrambled madly away, leaving a trail of yellow liquid. The K-9 unit didn't stop its retreat until it was safely on the other side of its handler's legs. It cringed there, trembling and whining.

Beside me Pietr straightened and stood, running a hand through his hair. My eyes flicked from his calm expression to the awestruck spectators. The whole student body seemed frozen. Stunned.

Behind me I heard someone softly whisper, *"That* was totally bad-ass."

Pietr had saved my life and earned himself a reputation.

The state police officer thought so, too. He said something to Perlson and I watched the VP approach as Mrs. Hahn got the rest of the class seated.

"Come on, you two," he said to Pietr and myself. "We need to do a thorough search. That was a *drug-sniffing* dog."

I had to agree with the statement, if not the inflection. Whatever the quivering canine amounted to now, it *was* a drug-sniffing dog just a few minutes before I crossed the gym's glossy threshold.

"So, Pietr, you haven't been with us but a brief while and already we're headed to my office," Perlson commented as he ducked out of the gym and headed down the hall. "Miss Gillmansen"—he looked in my direction—"I sincerely hope you aren't interested in joining my frequent fliers club."

"Mr. Perlson," I began, "I honestly don't know why that dog freaked out."

Perlson eyed me skeptically. "It was a *drug-sniffing* dog. One would presume . . ."

I stopped dead in the echoing hallway. "Mr. Perlson. I know my behavior's been—"

"Erratic?" Pietr offered a bit too helpfully.

"Yeah. Thanks for *that*." I refocused, chewing my bottom lip. "But I don't—I haven't *ever*—done drugs. I have enough in life messing me up without looking for ways to *get* messed up."

Perlson examined my face, my posture, weighing my words against my body language, and I thought I saw his eyes soften a bit. "I think we need to conclude this in the privacy of my office."

I nodded, stepping in front of Perlson and deciding to lead the way to whatever Fate had in store. Pietr easily stretched his legs to keep pace, and in a moment we were just out of easy earshot of Perlson.

"What the heck *was* wrong with that dog?" I asked, still facing straight ahead. "K-9's are so well trained. . . . It's beyond bizarre that it acted that way."

"My sweater. I told you," Pietr said in a tone that made me think this was all absolutely normal for him. "Some dogs like me and some dogs don't."

I kept my feet moving forward as I fought the impulse to turn, reach up, and strangle Pietr. Even the rare dog that didn't *like* me had never tried to rip my throat out. I shoved the office door open, sort of hoping it would spring back and catch Pietr by surprise, but it merely wheezed slowly toward closing. Another disappointment in a string of them.

As grateful as I was he'd saved me from the suddenly crazed dog, still I was ticked he wasn't telling me everything. He was *lying* to me. That really got on my nerves.

I stopped at the door to Perlson's office and he stepped between us, opening it.

"Take a seat." He leaned on his desk, arms crossed as we sat, settling mutely before him. "We need to wait for a police officer of some variety," he explained. "Used to be that any teacher or administrator could do a search. But now?" He smiled grimly. "We wait for someone with additional legal authority and hope you're only carrying drugs and not bombs."

I slouched forward, playing with the hem of the sweater Pietr'd loaned me. It was so large it draped across the middle of my thighs.

"Is that the new style?" Perlson asked, looking with suddenly discriminating taste at my mismatched outfit. This from the man wearing a tropical orange polo shirt.

"There was a water fight in art," I explained. I looked up at him, answering the unasked question as it surely formed in his mind. "I didn't start it."

"Collateral damage," Pietr assured.

"Did you—?" Perlson appraised Pietr.

Pietr shook his head. "I loaned her my sweater."

"Hmm," Perlson said with a crisp nod. I could see he was thinking. I just didn't know *what* he was thinking.

It wasn't long before Officer Kent arrived, drinking a cup of coffee, radio rumbling on his hip. "Strangest thing," he said to Perlson, at first ignoring us. "Seems the dog couldn't get itself back together. It just lay with its chin on Officer Paul's boot, whining." His lips pushed together, making a line that was white along its edges. "Paul said he's never seen anything like it. His K-9's always done amazingly well. Seems worthless now."

He finally spared us a glance. "Okay. Let's start with you, big guy. Hmm. Rusakova," he remembered. "Switching from long bouts of truancy to drug dealing?"

Pietr said, *"Nyet,"* the word sharp.

Officer Kent shook his head and motioned for Pietr to stand. "Turn your pockets inside out."

Pietr obeyed, reaching into his pants pockets and pulling them all the way out, the linings winging out at weird angles.

The officer snorted and looked at me, too. "Your turn."

I had to tuck the sweater's very bottom into my mouth to reach my pockets. I tugged them out with a little effort.

"Shoes and socks," the deputy instructed.

I popped them all off, making a mental note either to stitch up the hole in my left sock or toss out the pair altogether. Going with the theory that no one was going to see it, anyway, was *obviously* not working.

"Hmph," the officer said.

"Are we done?" Pietr asked levelly.

"Nope. Put your shoes and socks back on. We'll head to the

nurse and she'll have you strip to make sure nothing's tucked into any undergarments. Normal procedure," he assured.

"Great," Pietr snarled the word.

"What?" I teased Pietr as I hopped back into my sneakers. "Didn't you always dream of being *normal?*"

He actually laughed. "Hardly. Normal is so—average." He chuckled, retying his shoe. He looked at me then—this recent addition to our school, this guy who had just saved me from a lunatic dog—and the smile on his lips finally reached his eyes again. I hadn't realized he'd been smiling without them for the past few days—until now. The transformation was remarkable.

I smiled, too, blushing.

"Come on, you two," Kent snapped.

Together, in more ways than we had been even just this morning, we headed to the nurse's office for a strip search, Kent frowning between us.

Opening the door, the nurse glanced at Pietr briefly, but her eyes stayed on me. She grunted. Yeah. She'd definitely pegged me as trouble. I doubted this visit would change her mind much. I smiled at her, anyhow.

She shook her head and disappeared into the room's back. Referred to as the "nurse's suite," the name definitely conjured images of larger, homier spaces. The reality was the suite was one of the smallest rooms in the school, with one sink, an old soap dispenser, a rescued refrigerator, a dilapidated desk, and two poorly designed closets. And five filing cabinets, none of which matched another.

The nurse wheeled out two metal frames sporting curtains I was pretty certain dated from before either Pietr or me were even a spark in our parents' eyes. Schools always got stuck using things that reminded me of the old war movies Mom and Dad used to watch, sitting on the couch after Annabelle

Lee and I were supposed to be asleep. Constant budget cuts made schools even more like the war zones they so easily became.

The curtains were positioned to mirror each other, and the nurse pointed. "You. There. You. There."

We took our places.

"Take off all your outer garments," she instructed.

Officer Kent mentioned looking through our lockers and left as we obeyed. Shoes and socks again. Jeans. Pietr's sweater.

I laid it all on a chair behind my curtain. The door opened again.

"How's everything going in here?"

"Fine, Officer Paul," the nurse muttered. "What? God." The nurse coughed. "What is that smell?"

"Sorry. My K-9 hit my boots."

"It peed on you?" she asked, scandalized.

"It peed everywhere," he admitted.

"Well—" I heard her shoes squeaking as they carried her between our curtains. "I can't stomach that." She reached the room's opposite end and I heard her grunt. I peeked out as a window squealed open and a breeze blew in.

Suddenly the curtains were not sufficient for maintaining privacy. Each peeled back, flapping. And I was looking at Pietr. Looking at me.

With a *yip*, I yanked my curtain back into place, hands shaking as I held it solidly across the frame.

"Oh!" I heard the window slam shut. "You!" She surely meant the state cop. "Out!"

The door opened and closed again.

I heard Pietr laugh, saying, "'Pay no attention to the man behind the curtain'!"

I was trembling. But chuckling at his well-timed *Wizard of*

Oz quote. I remembered once reading that when a person blushes, all of their exposed skin turns pink. I believed that like I never had before. Because standing there in only my underwear, I felt as if I were on fire.

The nurse bustled over and shook her head, this time in apology. She rummaged through my clothes before hastily giving me the okay to put them back on. That was when I finally let go of the curtain. I began to laugh. Across the room and again firmly behind his own curtain, Pietr echoed my laughter.

How bad could it have really been? I mean, I went swimming every summer, and each year as I grew, the suits I had to choose between at local stores seemed to shrink. Surely what Pietr had seen hadn't been more than what he'd glimpse at any beach—right?

I heard a similar rustling of clothes and knew Pietr had gotten the okay, too. And what did seeing Pietr nearly naked make me think? That he was a boxers, not a briefs, sort of guy? So what? Seriously. It was bizarre, but I knew that seeing Pietr like that, no matter how amazing he looked—it couldn't change anything between us.

The curtains were wheeled away, leaving Pietr and me doubled over, tying our shoes, unexpected mirror images. I laughed again, now at the absurdity of it all.

Officer Kent reported our bags and lockers were clean and he simply didn't understand why the drug-sniffing dog had flipped out. Pietr shrugged, acting like he, too, was clueless.

But I knew it had to be something to do with him. I just couldn't figure out what.

"Hey! You dropped your ID," I said, picking up the card.

"Thanks. It must have fallen during the search," Pietr said, putting his hand out.

But I took a moment to look at it. "Wow. You actually look okay in *your* ID photo. Except for the massive red-eye issue." I looked even closer. "Your eyes almost *glow* red."

"The flash caught me by surprise—it was rough." He chuckled. He moved his outstretched hand, probably trying to get my attention.

And just as I was getting ready to hand it over, his birthday caught my eye. "Your birthday's just around the corner." I eyed him suspiciously. "You'll be *turning* seventeen? You look older."

"Yeah. I've heard that before."

I set the card in his palm as Officer Kent delivered his next piece of great news. "Your parents"—his eyes snagged on Pietr—"*guardians*, have been called and should be in the office waiting."

"You're kidding." I knew he wasn't. "What did you tell them?"

"The truth."

My jaw was set. Kent could easily tell I needed more information.

"That there was an incident involving a drug-sniffing dog."

"*Not* that I was nearly the *chew toy* of one?" My voice cracked in disbelief.

Officer Kent turned. "Let's get this over with."

The news easily threw me into a black mood. So did the fact that Pietr's birthday was just days away and he'd never mentioned a word of it to me. "Are you having a party?"

"What? Oh. The birthday. *Nyet*. We don't really do that."

"Are you a Jehovah's Witness?"

He laughed and my mood lightened. "*Nyet*."

"So what are you going to do for your birthday—how are you going to celebrate?"

"I don't think it's much to celebrate," he said.

His tone seemed different. Heavier. Haunted.

"My birthday's on the first. I always have some sort of bash," I added. "I'll invite you. It's not long from now, either."

"Some cultures say November first's a magical day. A day the dead come to visit," he said thoughtfully.

I had to keep moving forward—the office just in sight, Pietr nearly on my heels—but my feet almost tangled beneath me at the thought of what some believed might greet me on my birthday. A reunion with the dead? *That* I most certainly wasn't ready for.

At least Pietr didn't have to worry about *that*.

My father was leaning against the office counter, looking stern. Beside him was Alexi, looking equally grave.

As we entered, VP Perlson emerged from his office. "Officer Kent."

"Vice Principal." Kent turned to look at Dad and Alexi. "A drug-sniffing dog"—he looked at me and noted my crossed arms and jutting jaw—"*charged* Jessica and then came after Pietr. As a result, we had to search them and their belongings."

"Wait," Dad said. "Do the dogs usually *charge* people?"

"It was a highly unusual situation," Kent admitted. "Anyway, there was nothing on them or in their possessions, so they're free to go."

Dad reached out and hugged me. My feet came off the ground in his exuberance. "I couldn't believe it when they called," he said. He set me down and turned his attention to Officer Kent. "Was the dog doing a scheduled search?"

"No, the K-9 unit was part of an antidrug assembly and demonstration."

"Sounds like a scared straight method if I ever heard one." Dad patted the top of my head. He looked at Alexi and Pietr. Addressing Alexi, he said, "You don't seem real concerned about all this."

Alexi shrugged. "My entire family has strange run-ins with dogs," he said. "Some dogs like us, some dogs don't." He turned to Kent. "So do they return to class now?"

Perlson answered. "I think that could be potentially disruptive to the student body. Most of them saw the dog's reaction. It's probably best to take them home today and have them attend school normally tomorrow. It should give things time to settle down again."

We all nodded. I'd gladly do whatever it took for things to settle down.

Walking out to the parking lot, I said to Pietr, "So, you may not be celebrating your birthday, but how about going with all of us the Friday night of the fair? Then for your birthday on Saturday it'll be like you already celebrated." I smiled, doing my best to be inviting and finding I didn't *need* to try anymore.

The time spent together went a great distance to lightening my mood and again changing my attitude about Pietr. Yeah. The time and the fact he'd probably saved my life from an insane dog. "So, will you come to the fair?"

"Okay."

And I felt better. About most everything.

I slumped into the car, thinking about Pietr's note in my pocket. There was no way I could ask Dad to let me hang out with Pietr tonight, not after all the weirdness that had just gone down. And the thought of asking Dad to let me stay over—it was laughable, really. I resigned myself to the fact I'd have to sneak out. What was one more lie among many?

I rubbed my eyes, hoping this wasn't going to be the straw that broke the camel's back.

Dad said very little on the way home, but it didn't surprise me. Dad seldom chatted, and frankly, what would you say to an innocent kid who had nearly been mauled by a drug dog?

We made it through dinner and homework, but when Dad suggested we watch television, I started getting antsy.

Annabelle Lee studied me carefully. She knew something was up, and she wanted me to know it, too. Sitting on the couch, she yawned and stretched, putting her book down. "I'm exhausted," she said suddenly. "I think sleep sounds good."

I responded with a well-timed, "For once, I agree with you. Today's been exhausting." I gave Dad a quick peck on the cheek.

He looked at both of us and glanced at the clock. "I guess it's not a bad time to turn in. Early, but I'm pulling a double tomorrow. Don't wake me for breakfast."

We nodded, and flipped off the lights before climbing the stairs and heading to our respective bedrooms.

In my hip pocket I felt my cell phone vibrate. I snapped it open. A text from Pietr.

2nite

I replied: *ASAP*

I turned off my lights and sat, waiting in the darkness. I heard my father leave the bathroom, walk down the hall and into his room. His door clicked shut.

BCNU, I typed. *BFN.*

CHAPTER TWENTY-TWO

Quiet as a cat, I crept down our stairs and out the door. I raced across the open space between the house and the barn, sure that if there was any place I'd be seen, it was there. Inside the barn I paused to suck in the sweet smell of hay and musk of horses. My heartbeat slowed as I readied my ride.

"Come on, sweetie," I soothed, slipping the bit into Rio's mouth. "Just a late-night ride." I put the saddle blanket over her back, tugging it to the edge of her withers. She snorted and shook her mane. "Hey," I said, "one more request. If you need to take a dump, please do it now. I really don't have time to clean up once we start out, and leaving a big clump of horse poo on the sidewalk will sort of let everybody know we were around."

Rio snorted again.

"Ooo-kay," I said. "If you really don't have to . . ." I hefted the saddle onto her back and cinched the girth. I tugged at the saddle, adjusting the girth strap again. I led her out of the barn, into the crisp night air. She twitched but stood steady as I slipped a foot into one stirrup and hoisted myself up. "Here we go. G'yup," I said, giving the reins a little flick.

We moved out at a trot, two dark figures joined in one secret purpose, ghosting along the edge of the trees where shadow and moonlight warred.

We made good time. The streets and sidewalks were empty, most houses lit with only the blue glow of television as people wound down the night. I sometimes caught whispers of what must have been conversation or television shows and commercials. The only other noise was the steady clopping of Rio's hooves on asphalt and concrete as we made our way across the corner of town. We crossed the bridge spanning the Wanido River, and the steady clatter of Rio's hooves was muffled by the lapping of waves against the old bridge's concrete feet. Down the old block we went, marveling at the dimly lit Victorian and Cape Cod houses, and most important—Pietr's home with its warm, inviting glow.

Catherine was seated on the porch stairs. Rio walked right to her and blew in her face, throwing Catherine's dark hair back in a gust. Catherine laughed at her antics, and I wasn't sure who she spoke her next words to as she got to her feet. "Thank goodness you're here." She rubbed Rio's nose. "If he would only talk to me." She shook her head, looking at me. "But he won't. So I hope you are what he needs right now."

I dismounted and looped the reins around the porch banister. "He's not doing real well, then?"

"You can imagine," she suggested, suddenly serious.

"Yeah."

"What will she need?" Catherine asked, stroking Rio.

"Oh." I removed her saddle and saddle blanket. "Some water—if you have a bucket to spare."

"Sure," Catherine smiled.

"Does anyone else know I'm here?"

"Not yet, but they will," she said, her tone ominous.

"Is it a problem?"

"We'll find out soon enough, won't we?" But she winked. As if that would make any of this easier.

Chewing my lower lip, I entered the house, leaving Catherine outside.

Pietr was waiting just beyond the foyer, sitting on the bottom step of their large staircase. His furrowed brow relaxed when he saw me walk in and close the door.

"How are you?" I asked.

He tried a smile. "Fine." It was the closest he'd come to lying to me. He stood, taking my hand to lead me up the stairs.

"Where are we going?" I asked, the words breathy—and not because of the anticipated climb, either, although the house was immense. It seemed almost bigger inside than out.

Pietr looked over his shoulder at me. "To my room. Where'd you think?"

My heart crawled toward my throat. Wasn't this exactly what my father had always warned me about? Going to a guy's *room*? What *was* I thinking? I tugged my hand out of Pietr's. "I don't think—"

He raised an eyebrow at me and I realized all signs of the ATV accident were gone. *Man*, he was like frikkin' Wolverine from my dad's comic book collection.

"What do you think's going to happen in my room?" he asked, sorrow replaced by obvious intrigue.

I stuttered—my brain on hold.

Catherine rushed up the steps, jabbing me with an elbow. "I gave her water, and don't worry, nothing interesting could *ever*

happen in Pietr's room," she assured. "It's the most utterly cere-
bral place in the house." She squeezed past us then, footsteps
fading above us. I heard a door open and close.

Pietr frowned.

"Lead on," I commanded.

At the top of the steps were four doors. One, open, was obviously a bathroom. I heard music coming from the one on the
far right, a light shining under its edge. "Catherine's," Pietr confirmed, pointing. "Max's. Alexi sleeps downstairs."

He opened the other door and pushed an old light switch.

The sudden light illuminated Catherine's strange statement
quite clearly.

"Umm . . . you must read a lot," I said, seeing the shelves
packed with books. There were no visible walls, just shelf after shelf of book spines, some new, many faded with age and
wear. They were a mix of English, Russian, and a few other
languages—German, French, and something else. A single
window looked out over the lawn, wedged between the shelves
like a single awkward eyeball in a cyclops skull.

He flopped onto his bed and moved a book aside.

"Is that—?"

"Not *Romeo and Juliet*," he proclaimed. *"The Merchant of Venice."* He shrugged.

"Did you know that's the first written thing that has the
name Jessica in it? She and Lorenzo are the Romeo and Juliet of
that story. Well, sort of. So. Reading Shakespeare. And not for
school."

"I read when I have time. I've been told it's very Russian of
me."

"Hey—I read, too," I said. Okay, maybe a bit too defensively.
"Wow—some of these are pretty heavy: philosophy and stuff,"
I mentioned, noticing a few titles. Yeah. And I was knee-deep in

vampire novels. I looked at him as he lounged, leaning on his pillow, watching me with curiosity coloring his bright eyes.

He nodded. "I think a lot about that stuff."

"Yeah?" I said, perching on the corner of his bed. I tried not to think about the fact I was sitting on a guy's bed. In his room. And should not be thinking anything at all romantic was going to happen. "What sorts of things do you think about?"

"What makes a man a man."

I choked on the topic. "If you asked half the junior class, they'd probably say it's having sex."

"*Da,*" he said, twisting his lips around in thought.

"What do *you* think makes a man?" I asked.

"His deeds. His responsibilities and reactions."

"Okay, I'd agree." I tugged at one of my shoelaces. "What else do you think about?"

"What makes a man a monster."

I stared at him for the longest time, the cogs in my brain slipping as if the very mechanism of thought was breaking down. "And what have you decided makes a man a monster?"

"The same things."

I nodded. Slowly. "Heavy stuff." I picked at a wrinkle in the comforter on his bed. "What about Ashton's question in lit? Were Romeo and Juliet screwed by destiny or their own doing?"

He chuckled. "You're asking if I think we really get to choose in life."

"Sure."

"I don't think we get as many choices as we should."

"Huh. That's an interesting way of answering. So is your destiny set in the stars?" I giggled.

Again he didn't answer directly. "I know how my story ends, if that's what you mean."

"Happily ever after?"

Again he avoided me. "Too soon."

"That's a safe enough answer," I conceded. I licked my lips. "So. Are you okay?"

He leaned over, lifting my chin with his hand, so I saw the pain glittering golden in his eyes. "I'm getting better," he claimed.

So we made small talk, quietly avoiding the topic of that very thing that brought us together: death. I pulled my legs up and tucked my feet beneath them, sitting cross-legged. "Here." I patted my thigh. "Put your head here."

Silently he obeyed. I ran my fingers along his forehead, tracing the faint worry lines there, trying to brush them away. He sighed, a sound that seemed to come from the deepest part of him. His whole body relaxed then, his breathing evened out, and I knew he had fallen asleep.

It wasn't long until my leg did, too. Pinned beneath the crushing weight of his head (who would have guessed it could feel so heavy?) I tried to regain feeling in my leg and foot. *Nuts.* I slipped my hands under his head and lifted as I scooted awkwardly away—and right off the bed. Suddenly on the floor, I blushed when Pietr's eyes popped open.

He grinned. "You okay down there?"

"Yeah. Hey. Want to go for a ride?"

He sat straight up. "Sure. ATV?"

"Nope. Tonight you're riding with me. Come on." I jumped to my feet, my knee buckling beneath me, my leg still tingly.

Pietr laughed, grabbing me and looping my arm across his neck. "There will surely be questions about this tomorrow," he smirked.

Sure enough, Max glanced up as we made our way down

the stairs. He paused, a smile twisting his lips. "What can you possibly do so quietly that winds up with her limping?"

My ears burned at the implication, but Pietr snarled at him in my defense, "Get your mind out of the gutter."

Max shrugged. "Just don't let Sasha find her here so late."

Pietr followed me until we were standing beside Rio. "Okay, let's do this." I quickly explained what I was doing and why as I saddled her, mounted, and kicked my feet out of the stirrups so he could use one to vault up behind me.

He mounted like a pro.

"Have you ridden before?"

"Not really. Got up once and got thrown right off. Not the sort of ride I was expecting," he admitted wryly.

"I promise this one won't be so shocking."

He wrapped his arms around me as I slipped my feet back into the stirrups and whispered into Rio's ear.

She took off like a rocket, tearing around their house and only pausing in the backyard when I tugged faintly on the reins. Pietr's arms were so tight around me I had to focus to breathe.

His breath skimmed my ear, "You lied," he reprimanded teasingly. His grip relaxed and I was able to laugh.

I patted Rio's neck. "I just like to show her off a little."

"Don't do that again," he insisted.

"What? Race her around your house?" I quipped.

"No," he murmured. "Lie," his tone changed. Went serious.

I turned a little in the saddle to look at him. "I won't lie to you," I breathed.

He just stared at me. Nodded.

"Is there an easier descent to the woodlot?"

"Mmm. *Da*," he said, relaxing against me once more. It was weird, reading both Rio and Pietr's bodies at the same time, feeling the interplay of muscle tightening and loosening. It was one of the reasons I liked to ride bareback at home.

You really knew your horse and its moods once you understood the subtle twitches just below its skin. There was no subtext, no lying, not with my horses. Pietr pointed around me and I guided Rio down a much more gentle path than the one we'd descended on the ATVs.

I looked up once, amazed at how much light pierced the ragged tree branches. "So what is it?" I asked, pointing to the moon with a quick motion of my head. "Waxing or waning?"

"Definitely waxing," he confided.

"How do you know?"

"I just do." I felt him shift, shrugging, I guessed.

"I don't look up at the sky that often," I admitted.

"You should. Life's short."

I sensed an urgency in his voice and felt a slight tightening of his muscles. "Yeah. Is that why you skipped off to Europe last year? Because life's short?"

He sighed, and although he was behind me, I knew he was smiling. "*Da*. We saw and did just about everything over there."

There was an odd note to his description. I let the reins go lax in my hands, allowing Rio to pick her own way around the woodlot.

"Just about *everything?*" I asked. "Define." It was even easier to be tough with him when I wasn't looking at him. When he couldn't see my face.

He sighed again, but this time it was the sound of someone caught red-handed. Someone who knows he'll be held accountable. "Um." He paused, surely gathering his thoughts. I tried to keep the tension from straightening my spine to the point he'd notice. I knew what *everything* meant to me, and I was hoping . . .

"I've done a lot in my life," he said finally. "Remember how I said we Rusakovas don't tend to live very long?"

I nodded, mute.

"Well, because of that, we try to pack a whole lifetime of experiences into a few brief years. We try everything once—some smart stuff, some pretty stupid."

"So is it the chicken or the egg?" I asked.

"What?"

"You said Rusakovas tend to die early. And that you all do some pretty stupid things. So which came first? The dying young, or the stupid behaviors that get you killed? Young," I emphasized.

He chuckled. "I never thought about that. Huh. I don't know."

"You might want to think about that before you whack your head into a branch again."

He groaned.

"Wait. You said you did just about *everything*?" I asked, wondering if I'd used the right inflection.

"*Da*. Everything. Oh." I felt his body tense in realization. "You're asking about sex."

CHAPTER TWENTY-THREE

"Sure. Sex," I responded casually, heart wedged in my throat. "If that's what *you* want to talk about." I tried to sound uninterested. And totally nonjudgmental. It was way tougher than I'd thought.

"Wow. Okay. Let me explain."

I waved my hand in the air over my shoulder. "No. If you don't want to—"

"Wait, Jess. You're getting the wrong idea. I've done a lot of other stuff." He paused. "But I haven't done *that*," he clarified.

I tried not to let out a sigh of relief, but my backbone relaxed against him, betraying me. "And why not?" I asked before I could shut up. *Dammit.* What if I didn't want to know? What if it was just lack of opportunity? I was momentarily tempted to cover my ears with my hands and begin to sing.

"I know people who have seriously done everything. *Seriously,*" he reinforced. "They actually seem less happy."

"Oh. So you're waiting."

"Yeah."

"Until what?"

He laughed. "I have *never* had this conversation before. . . ."

"Until marriage?"

"Maybe."

"Until—" I pried.

"The right person."

"And what if *she's* not ready?"

He shrugged. "Then I wait some more."

"And what if she's not so—innocent?" I nearly squeaked.

"Oh. If she's not—like a virgin?"

"Touched for the very first time," I stated.

"Huh?"

"Never mind. Eighties music thing." I blushed till my bones went red.

"I think she's innocent," he stated. "I don't know about the virginity thing, though. It doesn't matter, anyhow. Innocence has almost nothing to do with virginity."

I thought about it for a moment. "Huh." I stretched in the saddle, yawning. "Ready to head back to the house?"

"Sure. But Alexi's bound to be home, so let's park the horse out back."

"No problem." I giggled, setting Rio into a jog.

Catherine evidently had the same idea. The water bucket was out back and the house was quiet, nearly completely dark as we climbed the stairs once more to Pietr's room.

"You know," he started. "She would have liked you." He looked at me with measuring eyes. "My mom," he clarified.

"Oh." I took a seat on the bed again and he grabbed a chair snuggled under his desk.

He straddled it, arms stacked on its back, and rested his chin there. "She was strong. Like you."

"I'm not strong," I protested.

He snorted. "You don't give yourself enough credit."

"Tell me about her," I urged.

"My dad—he was more like me. Always doing something stupid."

I opened my mouth to protest, but he shook his head.

"He'd rush into a situation to help and when he'd made a royal mess of it, Mom would get things fixed. She insisted he blame her for things so his reputation was never dirtied." He sighed. "She said, 'The man's name goes on—it should be clean.'"

"Then I guess she did a good job. I've never heard anything bad about the Rusakovas—"

He quirked an eyebrow at me and I sighed, hands in the air. "Okay, okay, I've never heard *anything* about the Rusakovas."

He chuckled and then went solemn again, but gently. "Did you think at all about today's date?"

"No," I admitted. "Why?"

"I would have thought with your fascination about the Phantom Wolf of Farthington story you'd have instantly realized today was the day all that came to a head."

"Wait. What?" And I thought about it. "Crap! You're right!"

"Of course," he said.

"So they died the same night?"

"*Da*. No obituaries in the papers, either."

My mouth gaped.

"The staff apologized for misplacing them," he mentioned as if it were enough.

"Wow. So how . . ."

"My father was—I don't know—drunk? He was acting very strange. He got into a fight, Mom stepped between them and . . . they were dead."

"Murdered," I suggested.

He shook his head. "Supposedly self-defense."

"No trial?" I whispered.

He smiled so sadly I felt as if someone were wringing out my heart. "Our family is only recently legal here. The people who killed them probably came over on the *Mayflower*. The U.S. does better than many countries with its trials, but justice isn't blind, and people are still judged for being different."

I nodded.

He turned in the chair, pulling open a desk drawer and producing two candles and a book of matches. "I'm told that in Russia, most of our people don't spend much time in church, but they do light candles and pray." He looked at me, seemingly embarrassed. "Do you pray?"

"Before every math test," I assured.

He laughed again. "I thought I might light these and just say some words. . . ."

"Go for it. As long as you're not sacrificing animals, I'm cool."

He struck the match and lit the first candle before tilting the second to share the first's flame. He blew out the match and simply said, "Mother. Father. I miss you every day. I try to live as you wanted and follow the rules you taught. And I know you are not far from here or now."

Behind him, my hands settled on his shoulders. "Well done," I said. Because it was well done. And I had nothing worth adding.

He snuffed the candles, rolled down the covers on the bed for me, and took a pillow and blanket before curling up on the floor to sleep. Like the most faithful of hounds.

———

That night, sleeping in Pietr's room—on Pietr's bed—there was no nightmare. But there were no dreams for me, either.

At 4 A.M. the alarm went off and I hopped off the bed and bent over, kissing Pietr's forehead as he rose from the floor. "I've got to go," I reminded him. "My dad'll kill us both if he learns I slept over."

He grunted and helped me gather my stuff and go downstairs. As the door closed quietly behind me, I saw Max step over behind Pietr and snarl, "Alexi noticed something was up, so I covered your ass. But don't let it happen again. You'll make liars of us all—and for what?"

Without another word, Rio and I headed home.

As we entered the barn, my father's voice boomed, "So. Got somethin' to tell me?" I jumped. Rio snorted. Like she knew we'd be caught in a lie eventually. Damned horse sense. Dad stood, stoic and shadowed, under the hayloft, staring at us.

"Dad, I—"

"Where were you?" He folded his arms. "I called Amy. She tried to cover for you. I told her I wasn't happy she was lyin', either."

I focused on stripping Rio and brushing her mane. Finally I stepped out and closed her stall door.

"I know you weren't at Sarah's. You never go there without backup. I can't blame you for that." His jaw worked as he considered what to say next. "Sophia's not really an option anymore, either, is she? Darn near mute most o' the time."

I still refused to look up.

"Just say it, Jessie."

"I was at Pietr's," I whispered.

"God *damm it!*" he shouted, hurling tack off the wall and

onto the barn's floor. "Don't you know what sleeping with some boy—"

"Dad! D*ad!*"

He kicked over a bucket, cursing nonstop.

I grabbed at his flailing arms and nearly got knocked to the floor. He caught me just before I totally lost my balance.

The rage in his eyes was replaced with heartbreak. "Jessie, what would your mama say?"

"She'd ask what happened at his place, Dad." I trembled, but knew I was right.

He groaned and sat down heavily on a hay bale. "What *did* happen, Jessie?"

"Nothing."

"Don't lie to me now." He refused to meet my eyes. "I knew I shoulda never hired that boy. Probably connected to the wrong sorts . . . dammit, this is my fault, too. If he hadn't been round you so much . . ." He shook his head, glaring at his boots as he berated himself. "You spent the night with a boy who looks at you like you're his world. That's *everything* a father worries about."

"It wasn't like that," I tried to explain.

"Then what's it like, Jessie?"

"We rode Rio. We talked for hours. He fell asleep on the floor. I fell asleep on his bed. *Nothing* happened."

"Why, Jessie? Why'd you sneak out?"

"He needed me, Dad."

"The wrong ones always say that, baby," he whispered. He rubbed his forehead, trying to paw away wrinkles. "It's like a lure to y'all. A big tough guy sayin' he needs you—you think you can help him work through somethin'—like you have some power—and then what? You wind up pregnant. No reputation left. No future of just your own. You're stuck in Junction with a guy who gets a job at one of the only two factories still runnin'."

My breath caught in my throat.

"Your mama wouldn't want the same thing for you."

My mind reeled. "Dad—nothing happened."

He wouldn't look at me now.

"Dad. Mom *loved* you," I stormed, realizing this was as much about him and Mom as it could ever be about me.

"Yeah. We got lucky with that at least."

"She *wasn't* stuck here," I insisted.

He stood suddenly. Brushed off his jeans. "Don't do somethin' stupid with that boy of yours, Jessie. Boys like that—they don't have a future. I want you out of Junction as soon as graduation's over. And no lookin' back."

CHAPTER TWENTY-FOUR

"You look like you were put through the same hellish blender I was," Pietr greeted me as I slumped into the bus seat beside him.

"Nice. Again with the compliments." I rolled my eyes, forcing a smile, and looked over his shoulder and out the window. The bus sputtered and limped forward. Trees bumped past, a few farms, and then we edged into suburbia. "Yeah. Dad caught me coming back in."

"It was bad."

My throat tightened. "Yeah. You?"

Even looking past him, I noticed the way his knuckles whitened on the seat back in front of him. "Alexi says nothing good will come from my involvement with you."

"Oh. He prefers Sarah." It wasn't difficult to imagine. Sarah was beautiful, bubbly . . .

"*Nyet.*" Now it seemed it was Pietr's turn to look past me. "But—with Sarah, things are simpler. She and I . . ."

Just the conjunction linking them stung.

His brow creased. "I don't want the same things from her that I want from you."

"Oh." I swallowed and opened my mouth, but it took a moment—a long moment—to push such a seemingly simple question out. "What do you want from me?"

His eyes caught mine. Held them, the faceted depths of his sparking with a fierce inner light. "Understanding."

"Your accent's not bad at all. I'm sure plenty of people understand you."

His hand was heavy and hot on my own. "That's not the understanding I mean, and you know that."

Over the next few days, Pietr learned understanding was not easy to find. And forgiveness, from me, at least, was still in short supply. Especially when Sarah started telling me about the *other* study dates—ones I *wasn't* invited to. Sarah was moving forward quickly with Pietr and was happy to give me the blow-by-blow of what happened each time she visited him.

I knew when he smiled at her, when he laughed, when they held hands, when he looked into her eyes. . . . She even texted once about a kiss. I discovered how indestructible my clunky cell phone was when I threw it against a poorly matched picture frame. I came up with a quick excuse for Dad when he raced into my room absolutely worried. But there was no fooling Annabelle Lee. Thankfully she just didn't care enough to talk about it.

Pietr also seemed to know when Sarah called. He called almost immediately afterward, equally quick to follow her flowery descriptions with logical explanations. Explanations that always seemed laced with his own grating frustration at his inability to slip free gracefully of the relationship I had pushed him into.

By the end of the next week, everyone in Junction was focused on the upcoming town fair. The fair was a big deal in Junction. It brought in outsiders and showed off small-town Americana. The shift in focus also made it easier to obtain library passes here and there to do a little additional research. It seemed I'd found all the real gems about the Phantom Wolves of Farthington and I was ready to give Google a rest when something caught my eye. A retraction had been printed in a local paper about the situation. I hopped right to it.

Yeah. Huh—that *was* different. Although the final articles regarding the Phantom Wolf—wolves, they'd realized—had claimed both beasts were dead (shot, killed, sent to a lab, and then to the taxidermist famed for stuffing Roy Rogers's horse Trigger), one guy disagreed with the official story. It appeared when he'd been interviewed originally he'd stuck to the party line.

Yep, two corpses, he'd said. But then he'd demanded a retraction be printed. He claimed he hadn't gotten the payment he'd been promised for just going along. So he'd grown a conscience (or developed a bitter streak—sometimes hard to tell the difference when it came to whistleblowers) and decided to tell the public the truth. Yeah. On the bottom of page eleven. That showed how highly the reporters thought of him.

Two wolves shot. One taken by him, the other taken somewhere else. And he doubted it was dead, he said. He transported a male, but he swore the other was a female. He referred to her as *the bitch* several times in the brief article, and I wondered if it was because of her gender or because of the rumored damage she'd inflicted protecting her mate in the last moments of their standoff with the cops.

Either way, it was interesting and worthy of my bulletin board and speculation, so I printed it.

Although most of the week's talk had been about the upcoming fair (because, really, what else was there to talk about in Junction?), I wasn't prepared. I mean, I knew what I was wearing, knew what time we'd meet and where. . . . But I wasn't prepared to potentially have fun publicly with Pietr. Last time we'd all been together, his idea of fun had ended in bloodshed. And he'd almost died.

After that whole mess with the drug-sniffing dog, it'd been harder to convince Sarah there was nothing "special" between us. Matters weren't helped by the fact that Sarah's parents had heard about "the drug incident," as it had become known around town. Why it wasn't just as easy to say "the *dog* incident," I'll never know. Dad said it was like selling newspapers: The headline was all that mattered, not the facts below.

Sarah's parents first came to me about the rumor they'd heard. They wanted assurance I wasn't doing drugs—I was *so* important to their daughter's recovery and growth. The toughest moment came when I realized by defending my innocence I was also defending Pietr—reassuring them he was okay for their daughter to date.

I could have said, "I have my suspicions about him." But they wouldn't have been drug-related. And *suspicion* wasn't quite what I felt about some of the odd things I'd noticed about Pietr. *Suspicion* was too negative a word. I truly trusted Pietr, but even *that* I didn't quite understand.

So when school was dismissed early for the fair, I didn't know what to expect. In fact, the last thing I expected happened. Dad announced it was necessary to Annabelle Lee's socialization to attend the fair. Only thing was, he was pulling an extended shift. So Annabelle Lee's appropriate socialization became *my* assignment. I knew exactly what Dad was doing. Chaperoning by proxy.

Annabelle Lee met me as the halls were emptying, ready for the walk to the park. Occasionally pausing to snatch up a new bit of text from the paperback edition of *War and Peace* she carried, she was a very slow traveling companion. By the time we arrived at the fair, the gang was already milling around the senior class's booth. Colorful palm trees, mustard yellow sand, and a turquoise ocean shimmering with glitter glue decorated the hand-me-down concession stand. The beach theme clashed garishly with the naturally modest town fair setting. Feeling the autumn breeze pick up, I thought the seniors were as overly optimistic as they were underinspired.

"Hey," I greeted everyone.

"Hey," Annabelle Lee mimicked. Almost perfectly. She glanced again at her book.

Sarah held out a cup of warm mulled cider to me—the first blatantly nice thing she'd done since Pietr loaned me his sweater.

"Thanks." I took a long sip, slowly turning to look at the fair and the bustling crowd of people. The smells of fresh French fries and vinegar warred with hamburgers and hot dogs. Down the slope beyond the main stage was the rides area with its pulsing lines of large colored lightbulbs, the sight punctuated by the occasional shrieks of riders. Cables and extension cords stretched and crisscrossed between rides like lazy snakes. Yes, even compared to the rides, the senior stand looked cheap.

"What's up first?" I asked.

Sarah smiled up at Pietr, tucking her latest read more firmly into her purse. Huh. *The Catcher in the Rye*. "How about the Ferris wheel?" she suggested. "We can see the whole fair from the *apex* and decide then."

Amy, just behind the pair of them, looked at Sarah and then at me. She rolled her eyes.

Annabelle Lee stifled a snicker.

We bought our tickets and headed down the gravel path past the indoor art and flower arrangement competition and beside the John Deere tractor display. Near the rides the scent changed, food giving way to the smells of animals and fresh manure. Yes, there was nothing quite like a small-town fair.

Sarah grabbed Pietr, bounding up the Ferris wheel's ramp and tugging him into a seat with her. As they sat, so did Annabelle Lee, wedging herself between them and bringing her book back to nose level, looking like quite the chaperone.

I almost missed her smirk. "Annabelle Lee—" I warned, but Pietr chuckled, plucked off her ill-fitting hat, tousled her hair, and set the hat back on her head. As the safety bar came down across the trio's laps, I noticed neither girl seemed very pleased anymore.

Pietr winked at me.

I rode with Amy. She asked, "So has Sarah totally flipped her lid yet?"

"What?"

"Sarah," she whispered, eyeing their basket warily. "Has she lost it? Snapped? Blown a gasket? Blown a fuse? Gone round the bend—off to the loony bin—a few fries short of a Happy Meal—you know, cuckoo?"

"Amy!" I nearly laughed at her rapid-fire list, but didn't because I knew I was dealing with a serious issue.

"No. She has these weird moments—times when I think she must be dreaming of where to hide my body, and then it's like"—I waved my hand in front of my face and grinned—"back to happy, loving, word-a-day-calendar Sarah."

"You both need your heads examined." She looked out over the fairgrounds. "So what are you going to do?"

I leaned over the safety bar, rocking the seat. "I *don't* know. I think I need to keep going on like she can be my best friend— like she'll never go psycho again. Maybe if—"

"If what?" Amy snorted. "If you believe hard enough for *both* of you? This isn't some movie, you know. There's no hero on a white horse, no way to clap and bring fairies back to life. It's like you're expecting some sitcom moment where I smile at you and say, 'that's crazy enough, it just might work.'" Amy shook her head. "Holy crap, Jessie. Step back from the ledge. You've been playing with fire since the accident. You can try to tame it, make it good and useful, but the moment you aren't careful anymore, fire will *burn* you."

"She's my best friend," I defended.

"Look, I understand keeping your friends close and your enemies closer, but every time you say she's your *best* friend, I get the urge to slap you."

"Oh." I thought about it a second. "She's *one* of my best friends? Amy, I never meant . . ."

"Yeah. I'm okay with it. You occasionally put your foot in your mouth. And chew. And sometimes you seem to take time to even swallow." Amy sighed.

My face prickled, surely crimson.

"And I know what you mean. But, Jessie. Sarah's not herself." She studied her hands on the safety bar before adding softly, "Not yet."

The ride stopped and we got out.

I smiled at Sarah and Pietr. They were holding hands. Pietr pulled out his cell phone to check the time. "So, where to?"

"Let's look at the animals," Sarah suggested.

She would suggest that. Anyone who wasn't around animals every day would never imagine it was dull to see them all again—just in a more confined and unnatural setting.

A familiar couple caught my eye at the edge of the shifting crowd. Ugh. Jenny and Derek, hand in hand by the popcorn.

I didn't get it. Jenny had Derek and yet she always looked so miserable. He was joking with her about something, but she just looked like she'd burst out bawling any moment. She struggled to smile, but it looked completely forced.

Some girls were never happy even when they had what they really wanted.

I tried to remain upbeat. "Okay, you guys lead," I said. Amy made faces behind Sarah's and Pietr's backs again.

"Hey." I realized our group was one person short. "Where's Annabelle Lee?"

Pietr blinked. "She was just with us," he said.

I scanned the crowd. "Yeah, but *now*?"

"Restroom?" Amy asked, heading toward it. I raced after her. We pushed ahead in the line, blanketing apologies as we popped our heads down at each stall door to check shoes.

"Annabelle Lee!" I yelled, peeking at pair after pair of unrelated shoes. "Annabelle Lee?" But she wasn't in any of the slightly slanting stalls. We raced out the building's other side and back to Pietr and Sarah.

They were deep in discussion.

"No, she wouldn't go to look at the chickens *or* the rabbits," Sarah said.

Pietr looked at me, worry clear in his eyes. "Nothing?"

My heart raced. I scanned the crowd again, wondering why she'd ditch me—or what could cause her to ditch Pietr (whom I was starting to suspect she was also crushing on). My anxious eyes stopped, stuck on something lying loose on the ground by the Ferris wheel. I gasped. "Oh, no."

Annabelle Lee's hat lay in a crumpled heap, abandoned. I pointed in silent horror at the lonely hat left on the ground by the ramp.

Pietr snatched it up. He recognized it, too. "Would she just—"

"I don't know." Annabelle Lee might not mind messing with me, but she'd never run off. It wasn't her style.

Sarah and Amy hugged me, and Pietr—well, Pietr put the hat to his mouth and nose, striking a thoughtful pose. But I got the distinct feeling he was *smelling* Annabelle Lee's hat.

I watched through tear-blurred eyes, mid-hug, as Pietr searched the crowd. His expression suddenly changed. "Follow me," he murmured.

CHAPTER TWENTY-FIVE

Taking Amy and Sarah by the hand, I followed Pietr through the wandering crowd, an awkward chain of girls following the strangest guy I'd ever met. We wove our way through the mass of humanity, barely seeing more than a body or two ahead of us. Pietr changed direction, his head snapping to the left as we did a quick hairpin turn. Then another. A few more yards and yet another sudden turn. If I hadn't noticed how often he looked over his shoulder to check our progress, I would have thought he was trying to lose us.

I'd seen Hunter scent after rabbits and squirrels—it was amazing how similar his focus was to Pietr's right then, like they experienced the same thing. But I didn't question, didn't stall—there would be time to ask him later about the *how*. Right now I was just fixated on the *where*.

And then I saw her, looking frightened and out of sorts by the funnel cake stand.

"Annabelle Lee!" I shouted, dropping Sarah and Amy's hands.

I ran to her, hugging my little sister like she'd been gone for days, not minutes. "Are you okay?

"Oh, Annabelle!" a familiar female voice called from nearby. "Thank *God* you're here!"

I turned, releasing Annabelle Lee and staring at Wanda, her ponytail swinging. She looked from Pietr to Annabelle Lee, to Pietr, to the hat still in his hand and back to Annabelle Lee, her expression relieved and yet smug. "I was so worried when I realized I'd gotten separated from you."

"Separated from *you?*" I demanded. "How did that happen? She"—I turned back to stare at Annabelle Lee—"was supposed to be with *me.*"

"Wanda saw me standing by myself at the Ferris wheel and offered to get me something to eat—so fast you wouldn't even miss me," Annabelle Lee qualified. "But we got separated in the crowd."

"You *never* ditch me again. You want to go somewhere or with someone else, you tell me. I freaked out," I admitted.

Sarah and Amy nodded emphatically in unison.

Pietr scrunched the hat back down over her head.

"If it hadn't been for Pietr—" I began, but he put a hand on my shoulder.

"I just figured she'd be hungry," he said, his eyes skipping to Wanda's face before returning to mine. "I'm *starving.*"

"Fine, let's get food," I agreed, pointing everyone toward the French fries. "And *you,*" I said to Wanda, "should *certainly* know better."

Almost apologetically she said, "I'm learning, Jessie."

"Jess-i-CUH," I insisted.

She smiled. "I'm learning."

The whole time she was saying it, she never once looked

at me. She focused on Pietr like a hawk spying a mouse far below.

We walked away and were out of her sight quickly enough. "What was *that* about?" I asked him, keeping my voice low.

"Seems like an unfortunate misunderstanding—"

I gave him the Big Blink. "No. Really." I touched my nose and pointed to Annabelle Lee's hat.

"I've told you before," he muttered.

"Well, try it again."

"Not here," he whispered. "Tomorrow night. You and me."

By the end of the fair, Pietr and I had subtly arranged to meet Saturday night. The night of Pietr's seventeenth birthday. It had all been done in quiet, stolen moments.

Beside the colossal ketchup and mustard pumps, I asked, "Tomorrow night?" And he said, "At eight." I pushed the pump, quickly becoming collateral damage from a ketchup-y spray.

Pietr handed me a napkin, smiling.

I realized something. "No good. Too much like a date. Dad would be suspicious," I pointed out. Actually, *no*. Dad would be primed to kill if he thought my friendship with Pietr had evolved even further since spending a night in his bedroom.

Pietr shook his head, "Something's gotta give, Jess."

We next met anointing our fries with the malt vinegar shakers. "Has to be nighttime," he insisted, "and it could take a while."

I threw him a scandalized glance, followed by, "I *knew* you were a vampire."

He snorted. "*That* would be simple."

"A slumber party, then," I suggested.

It was his turn to look scandalized. "I don't do pillow fights," he said, looking as if he was drawing a moral line.

And that was how we worked out the details of our lie.

Over common condiments. It was deceptively simple. I would tell Dad I was going to a slumber party at Sarah's immediately following a study session at Pietr's. That way, Alexi and Pietr could pick me up and we could bypass Sarah altogether. And I would be with Pietr—in the forest—all night long. I couldn't stop my heart from thundering around my chest at the thought.

It would be a tough sell, getting permission to be out all night so close to Dad catching me. But it had to work. I had to know the strange truth behind Pietr's uncanny ability.

Until then, all I could do was hope was our deception *was* simple enough to be believable.

Pietr called later that evening and, after we both messed around on our computers, he worked with me to firm up plans for his birthday. Until Alexi stormed into his room.

"What are you planning, Pietr Andreiovich Rusakova?" I heard Alexi snarl.

"I'd better go," Pietr stated.

"Pietr, wait—is everything—"

The phone clicked. Pietr was gone.

I held it to my ear for another moment, anyhow, thinking of the venom in Alexi's tone. Even with Pietr's parents gone and choices exceedingly limited regarding guardianship, I still thought Alexi was only barely the lesser of two evils when compared to a foster parent arrangement.

I hit redial.

Busy.

Dammit. What was going on over there? And then I thought about the Skype channel Pietr had opened earlier that evening with me. My computer had reverted to its screensaver mode while we had talked on our phones, lounging comfortably around our respective rooms. But if Skype was still running, I might be able to hear *and* see through Pietr's Web cam. I just needed to make sure he couldn't see *me*.

I leaped over to my computer and plugged in my headset. The channel was up. I pressed a few keys and made sure Skype was set for me to spy. Pietr and Alexi were still arguing. Pietr sat on his bed, Alexi pacing tight circles in front of him.

I wedged a knuckle into my mouth. I couldn't risk falling into the argument myself and focused on the fact I was just watching. . . .

"It's none of your business, Sasha." Pietr might have looked as if he were pouting, but his sullen expression hid emotions coming to a boil.

"Everything here is my business, whelp," Alexi said with a sneer, leaning over Pietr. "This family is all any of us has. That *girl*"—he pointed to the discarded phone—"already knows too much."

"That *girl*," Pietr retaliated, "is very important to me. To all of us, if you ask Catherine."

Alexi snorted. "Just because Tsarina Ekaterina read something in some tea leaves, you would have this stranger be a risk to us all?"

"I would have that *stranger*—Jessie, to you—*understand* me."

"Shit, Pietr!" Alexi snapped. "It doesn't work that way. Have you forgotten who we are?"

"*What* we are," Pietr corrected, eyes narrowed.

"Whatever!" Alexi's arms waved above his head, his face flashing through at least three shades of red. "She knows too much! She's too close to *you*." He thrust an accusing finger in Pietr's face. "If she finds out the truth . . ." He began to pace again, holding his hands tightly behind his back.

Pietr's expression was so hard Alexi pulled his finger back immediately. "Jess needs to know," Pietr insisted.

"And when she freaks and tells everyone?" Alexi asked, his tone cold again.

I leaned closer to the computer screen.

"She won't." Pietr was adamant.

"I don't *know* that." Alexi turned away from Pietr. "I could forbid you from seeing her."

I shoved my knuckle farther between my teeth.

Pietr was on his feet. "You wouldn't dare . . ."

"I've dared more than you can imagine for this family," Alexi countered.

"I won't obey," Pietr swore.

Alexi faced him once more, nose to nose. "You know you won't be *able* to disobey, Pietr."

"I will fight you with all that I am."

"For some girl?" Alexi laughed. "Ohhhh. Are you *in love*, little brother?" he mocked.

Pietr blushed. *Blushed!*

I sat back in my chair, dumbfounded.

"You wouldn't understand," Pietr grumped.

So what the heck did *that* mean? Was he in love or not? Crap. *Ask the question again, Alexi,* I willed the figure on the screen.

But he didn't. *Nuts.*

Alexi ran his hand through his hair. He reached into a pocket and pulled out a cigarette and lighter.

Pietr glowered and Alexi pocketed them both once more.

"Put her to a test," Alexi finally suggested.

"What? What test?"

Alexi paced the space before Pietr's bed, rubbing his chin in thought. "It must be dramatic. Something that will prove undoubtedly she is tied tightly to us in her loyalty. That she trusts *you* unerringly. If she passes, things continue. If she fails—well, it won't matter much then. Those who fail tests of faith leave quickly enough on their own."

"And how would you test her?" Pietr asked, suspicious.

Alexi grinned and picked up one of the few things (excluding the multitude of books) that decorated the bedroom. I squinted at the computer screen.

He smiled, considering his idea. My stomach churned as I imagined what it could be. But Pietr would keep me safe, wouldn't he? The only way to learn Pietr's strange secrets (and I felt certain there was more than one) was to prove my loyalty. To show my absolute trust.

"This test will be quite fitting to our heritage," he grinned.

"I doubt breaking out the vodka for a drinking game's appropriate," Pietr scoffed, trying to lighten the mood that even in my room across town brought both darkness and chill.

"You must learn more respect for our people," Alexi warned. Then, an instant later, he smiled again. "You have studied our classics, *da*?"

"Of course," Pietr said, his head tilting in speculation.

Pietr caught the thing Alexi had been holding. "Then you know *that* may be far more than it first appears."

Pietr held it up, his eyebrow rising when he next looked at his eldest brother.

A model train. *What?*

"Come." Alexi replaced the tiny train and tweaked Pietr's nose. "Smell that?"

Pietr winced. "Who couldn't?"

"Cat baked cookies," Alexi said with a smile.

"Oh, God," Pietr whispered.

"I know, I know," Alexi agreed. "But we *are* her brothers. We must be supportive." He shrugged. "I will explain the test and all will be as it should be in the end."

He wrapped an arm around Pietr's shoulders, and although Pietr hesitated, he allowed his brother to lead him out of the room—and out of Skype's earshot.

I wondered what Alexi was plotting. And made a mental note to avoid Catherine's baking if at all possible.

Shutting off Skype, I clicked over to Google and ran a search. Train+"Russian Literature"+symbolism. Up popped references to *Anna Karenina. Nuts.* Someday I would seriously need to read that book.

"Jessie!" Dad called from someplace downstairs. "Dinner. Now!"

Pietr was smart enough to ask my father's forgiveness for encouraging my secret overnight visit. After Pietr explained about his parents' deaths, Dad actually said if he'd known *that,* things would have been a little different; that death impaired everybody's judgment, and he was sorry for Pietr's loss. One little discussion (and the fact that Pietr helped with the Saturday morning chores for free) went far toward fixing things between the two most important guys in my life.

Unfortunately, I knew I'd have to risk that fragile trust all over again to unravel the puzzle that surrounded Pietr.

It wasn't long after morning chores that Dad let me go for a ride with Pietr. I never specified horses or ATVs, and Dad didn't ask details. He had to pop by the factory and fiddle with some machine, anyhow. He informed us that we had an early-afternoon curfew and to use our cell phones if we even thought about asking permission to change the plan.

Pietr pulled the ATV to the edge of the path. Although I'd grown up in Junction, I had no clue where we were at the moment. I wondered if we were even still *in* Junction or somewhere beyond its gerrymandered borders. He cut the engine and turned to me quietly, the solemn expression on his face making his eyes cloud and turn stormy gray. "I would have never asked this of you, Jess."

My heart hammered. Ask what? Where were we and why choose this place for my test of loyalty? "I know. I understand." What a lie.

Pietr called me on it. "*Nyet*. You don't," he whispered, his normally crisp voice raggedly edged and profoundly accented with a distinctive Russian rumble. "But you will. Soon."

"What do I have to do?" I asked, glancing around. Now the engine was silent, I heard water. And something else. Not quite like wind, not rain . . . I jumped when a train whistled in the distance, the sounds connecting to answer my curiosity.

"Alexi will meet us soon. Put this on. I'll carry you."

Normally I would have scoffed at his naïve belief he could just tote me around. I threw hay bales and rode bareback. I was no wisp of femininity. But there was a quality to his voice that suggested he'd find a way to lug me along—even if I was loaded with bricks. I took the bandanna he offered. I must have looked as confused as I felt. "Put it on—?"

"A blindfold," he confirmed.

Well, *that* was reassuring. I hated putting the things in my hair, and would face any test of courage blind rather than gagged. I was a talker, after all. I got gifted with gab whenever I grew nervous. I was both a talker and a writer, an expressive girl . . . *Oh, God,* I realized. *I'm freaking out.* I blinked a couple times, my brain stuttering. *Breathe.* . . .

"We can leave," he offered.

But I knew as honest as he was being, I couldn't leave. I didn't dare. Leaving now would mean I couldn't be trusted. That I wasn't brave. Or worthy. Crap. *That* didn't matter to me. Suddenly I realized I didn't know what leaving would really mean except that things between Pietr and me would change. Forever.

I put on the blindfold, turning so Pietr could tie it tight. Full of worry, Pietr's face was the last thing I saw. *Stupid heart. Stupid girl.* I wanted to make a joke of it all, but before I could find any words, he picked me up and held me in his arms as if I were nothing.

My head on his chest, I marveled at how fast his heart raced. It seemed unnatural anything could pump that fast without exploding in a final fit. A breeze stirred the hair near my face and as careful as he was, the subtle twitches of his muscles telegraphed the whole story of our run back to me as I lay like a very solid sack of flour in his grasp.

Every rock he balanced briefly on or leapt ably off of was known to me. Felt by me. I knew when brambles snared his jeans, heard them hiss as he tore straight through, making his own path. He carried me up sharp inclines and down rapidly slanting hillsides. He was fast. Remarkable and surefooted.

"Ow! Dammit!" I snapped, more in fear than pain when my shoes whacked against a tree trunk at his amazing pace. My toes tingled and I curled against him more tightly—a more compressed sack of flour in his arms.

"Eezvehneetyeh," he whispered, breath stirring my bangs and warming my face.

He was forgiven. Of course.

He suddenly stood me up; points of rock bit into the thin soles of my sneakers. Gravel? I gasped, panting a moment from the excitement of the run we'd shared. His breathing told me he was not at all winded. He shifted on the stones as another set of footsteps approached.

"So. We are all here after all."

Alexi.

He sounded disappointed. "She can't see anything?" He surely tested my vision, but I couldn't tell how. "Good," he said, satisfied. He paused.

The train whistled again, sounding closer.

"The test is simple," Alexi assured coolly. "Stand right here—still—until Pietr comes for you. Keep your hands at your sides. Do not move. Do not make a noise."

I wanted to ask what to do if my nose itched—say something to lighten the mood—but I couldn't guarantee the steadiness of my voice. Refusing to sound like a coward, I nodded.

"You can back out now," Alexi tempted. "You can still be with Pietr, still visit."

"But you would not let me be with him tonight if I *do* back out," I clarified. *Yep,* my voice was shaky. Great.

"There are some things you do not have to know," Alexi suggested. "Not every riddle needs a straight answer. You can go home. Be happy and safe without knowing everything."

The lure of knowing Pietr's secret was too great. I straightened, raising my chin in absolute indignation.

Alexi snorted. "This will all be over in a few minutes."

"I don't think—" Pietr began, but Alexi snapped at him.

"*Horashow.* Good. Don't think. Obey your brother."

Two sets of footsteps crunched away from me. Then a set came sprinting back.

"It'll be okay," Pietr promised. "Just stand still. No matter what."

I nodded.

He kissed me. For a moment I forgot where I was and just kissed him back. Then his lips withdrew and the gravel ground and growled as he raced away. And, just like that, I remembered my predicament. Acutely. The blindfold helped. I might kiss with my eyes closed, but most of my life was lived with my eyes wide open. Even when I was being purposefully left in the dark.

Alone and blind, I tried thinking about other things. The weather. Yeah. Brisk breezes, leaves falling and crunching beneath feet. Yep. Still autumn. *Done.* Trying to think more distracting—more involved—thoughts, I imagined riding Rio through jumping practice. But I couldn't shut up my yammering mind. It ran in frantic loops: *Why are you here? Where is "here"? What do you really have to prove?*

There was gravel under my feet. The train's whistle sounded again. Louder yet. Definitely closer. Okay. I chewed my bottom lip. Gravel under my feet. An approaching train . . . *stupid girl!* I flinched at the realization. I was standing blindfolded on train tracks?

The blood poured from my head, arms, and chest, pooling like molten lead in my feet. I was petrified in terror.

The gravel shimmied beneath the soles of my feet, chattering against wooden sleepers and metal rails. I felt suddenly disoriented. The train, the tracks . . . Alexi's words to Pietr as I watched via Skype: "She knows too much already!"

What if Pietr believed I'd be fine but Alexi had decided to get rid of me? My heart caked with ice. If I died here, now—flattened by a train—would anyone even wonder about the circumstances of my sudden death?

I tried to swallow the sudden lump filling my throat. Surely Alexi knew about the teen train track suicides. Maybe he figured this was a good way to get rid of me—an emotionally unstable teenage girl (wasn't *that* phrase redundant?)—without too many questions being raised.

My guidance folder *did* have a red paper clip marking its pages, after all. Maloy already had his doubts about my willingness to suffer life too long beyond my mother's tragic death.

What if Pietr's secret was too dangerous to dare comprehend? My brain sputtered, jumping to a scene from *The Matrix,* one of my dad's favorite movies. If this were my red pill–blue pill moment, would I choose the comfort of my bed or the journey down Wonderland's rabbit hole?

CHAPTER TWENTY-SIX

My stomach fluttered and stilled. And I knew. With certainty.

My fingers twitched at my sides. There was a grating noise, a steady rattle. *Stay still, stay still, it'll be okay.* Metal clanged and clattered against metal, scraping, whining and growling—building into a deafening roar.

My jaw ached, my teeth clenched as I willed myself to remain immobile. Pietr wouldn't let me get hurt. Not ever. Louder than any thunderstorm it came. The train hurtled toward me, groaning, squeaking, clanking—I wanted to cover my ears at the noise, but I had to stay still. . . . *Breathe. Just breathe.* . . . The soles of my feet tingled as the behemoth shook its track and swallowed the distance between me and—

"Ugh!"

The impact slammed me to the ground, knocking breath and sense out of me. Something heavy held me down. Heavy and hot. Had the train hit me? Was I bleeding out? *Damn blindfold.* But I'd been slugged from the side and whatever pinned me down and kept my arms at my sides was breathing. And cursing.

Inventively.

My blindfold was yanked away and I yelped, the knot tearing hairs out of my head. I blinked in the dazzling sunlight. Pietr lay atop me, his head haloed by the most spectacular sky imaginable.

"That bastard Sasha!" he growled and raised himself off of me.

I turned, watching as the train rushed away—on an alternate track?

Pietr pulled back, resting crouched on his heels. "Are you okay?" He stuck out a hand.

I took it and sat up, my eyes locked on his. "It was on a different track." The words were much clearer than my head.

He looked to his right and I followed his gaze. Alexi stood beside us, his face red with rage.

"*Da*," Alexi said, his eyes not on me at all. Each word carefully weighed and timed he explained, "It switches tracks a few yards earlier."

"I was safe the whole time." I laughed. It was a distant noise. Brittle.

"*Da*." Alexi crossed his arms. "You should have left. Given up. Anyone with common sense would have." He literally growled in frustration, his hand raking through his hair, his eyes latching on to Pietr's. "I think we've learned something here."

"*Da*. That you ask *too much* of people," Pietr snapped, tugging me to my feet.

Alexi shook his head. "*Nyet*. That your little girlfriend has more trust in me than you have in me—*my own brother*." He turned and stormed away.

I was stunned.

Pietr, though—Pietr was pissed. He spun, poised to spring after Alexi. "You—"

I grabbed his arm. Stopped him in his tracks. All the anger, the fear—it washed right out of his eyes and he looked at me, ready to kill for me as fast as he'd die for me. His look of open loyalty stung. "Don't," I said. "I'm okay."

"Are you?"

"Yes." I took a step to prove it and my knees buckled. Laughing, I pulled myself back up by his arm.

"Jess?" His voice cracked.

"I'm just shaken." I looked up at him and smiled. "Um. You did so well carrying me before—"

And before I could get another word out, he was cradling me against his chest. I looped my arms around his neck, lacing my fingers together and resting my head against him, sucking in the wild scent of him, filling my brain with whispering woods and muted meadows. Peaceful places far from train tracks.

"See ya, Dad!" I yelled up the stairs. Sleeping bag and backpack slung over my shoulder, I rushed the door. "Be back tomorrow morning—I've got the cell!"

Returning from my test of faith, I'd taken a nap and woken up feeling absolutely remarkable. Triumphant.

The amber heart pendant bounced against my chest, and I tucked it into my shirt's neckline. Pietr had given it to me to wear for him whenever we weren't around Amy or Sarah. So I had decided to wear it tonight.

For Pietr's seventeenth birthday.

As the door swung shut I heard heavy footsteps pounding down the staircase after me. "Jessie—"

I saw Alexi's car in the driveway, positioned to steal me

away from home and rocket me closer to understanding the mysterious Russian soul that comprised Pietr. I sprinted to the car, yanked open the door, and threw my stuff inside. I was buckled in by the time Dad caught up to us.

"Hey." He tapped on the window. Alexi rolled it down. "Where's the fire?"

I laughed. "Did I forget something?"

"A hug and a kiss for your old man." He peeked in the car. "Oh, I guess y'all are off to pick up Amy and Sarah next," he said, giving my cheek a peck.

Alexi didn't skip a beat. "They seem to study well together."

Wow. Alexi was the master of the subtle subterfuge! I wondered how many lies *he'd* told. And more important, how many times he'd been caught. Actually, what he'd just said wasn't really a lie—when we *were* studying, we *did* study well together, but even saying that didn't have *anything* to do with *if* we were really picking the girls up or not.

"Yeah," Dad was saying, smiling at Alexi. "That's a good thing. Well, you learn lots of stuff tonight, Jessie." He snaked an arm inside the car and gave my shoulders a squeeze. "I love you." He paused and fixed his eyes on mine. "I trust you."

"Ahhh—" I blushed. When were parents supposed to stop hugging their kids in front of their peers? There had to be a law about it somewhere. . . . "I love you, too, Dad," I said as Alexi closed the window and we drove away.

We'd had a little father-daughter talk about trust between what was for me one lie and then another. Dad had sent Pietr out to the horse barn to tidy up and then explained how he really did want to trust me again. I explained how his allowing me to go on a ride with Pietr demonstrated that he *could* trust me. I mean, hadn't we gotten back before our early-afternoon curfew? Dad conceded and said the study session and sleepover at Sarah's was okay as long as there were adults present. Alexi was driver and escort of part A, I explained, and Mrs. Luxom would certainly be home during part B. So Dad put his trust in me. And I was going to throw it away and hope I didn't get caught.

Besides, I knew Dad was working another double.

"So," Alexi started. "It seems you two have gotten me to lie for you. What's so important that you'd need me to do that?"

The town was a blur. We sped through Main Street, every traffic light green like I was meant to learn Pietr's strange secret even faster than I thought I would.

"Well?" Alexi prodded.

I saw Pietr turn to face him from the front passenger's seat. He said nothing, but it seemed almost enough.

"Pietr," Alexi demanded.

"It's my birthday, Alexi."

"So you are going through with it. I had hoped a few hours would make you smarter." Alexi looked at his younger brother and then flicked his gaze to the rearview mirror. He stared at me a moment and I wondered how he could possibly see the road at the same time. "How old are you?"

"She's almost seventeen, like me," Pietr interjected before my mouth even opened.

Alexi laughed at that. "Almost seventeen, *like you*?" He laughed again.

Chilled suddenly, I zipped my jacket up higher.

"You still don't get it, do you?" Alexi barked the words at Pietr. "She's not like you—none of them are like us. We come from a different *world*—"

"*Nyet*, we don't," Pietr muttered angrily. "We just live a different life."

He sounded so hurt that no one but his family was like him. I sat forward, straining against the seat belt. "If it's about having Russian background—" I tried, "I'm learning about the Russian culture for a history project."

Alexi jerked the steering wheel, pulling the car to the road's edge so fast I gasped and held the seat before me. He adjusted the mirror to gaze at the amber pendant I wore. The Rusakova family pendant Pietr had given me. *"Are* you?" A blaze of blue glowed in his eyes.

I nodded slowly. It wasn't as if I didn't feel safe in the car at that moment with Pietr and Alexi, but still a sense of dread burbled up in my stomach.

Alexi spoke slowly. "Have you read about the Cold War?"

"Yes," I confirmed, held fast by his sparkling gaze.

"And do you know how desperate our people were to gain some advantage over your people—what they were willing to try—willing to do?"

"Stop it, Alexi!" Pietr demanded, his voice so loud it rattled the car windows.

Alexi pounded on the steering wheel. "You are being so stupid!" he snapped.

But Pietr had cooled again. "Not stupid. Selfish," he admitted.

"*Nyet.* Stupid. Utterly, irrevocably, f—" He glanced at me in the rearview mirror.

I could swear I heard his teeth grind together.

"Stupid. Taking her out into the woods tonight—"

"It's supposed to be a nice night," I defended. Weakly.

Alexi laughed. "This is not the time," Alexi warned. "Taking her out tonight. *This* time." He paused and changed tactics. "Catherine is celebrating alone."

Pietr was unmoved.

I was being talked around. Like I wasn't there. And although I knew they weren't speaking Russian, still it seemed the words they said didn't have only the meaning I expected.

Turning to Pietr, Alexi curled his upper lip in a snarl. "I guess she'll learn everything tonight, though, won't she? You're playing with fire, little brother," he warned, "And you risk burning our whole family."

Pietr blinked once. "Will you stop me?"

Alexi squeezed his eyes shut and his jaw clenched. *"Nyet."*

"Are you sure?"

"Are *you*?" Alexi challenged. His tone, though, was resigned.

Pietr's look was enough answer.

Alexi readjusted the mirror with a *snap* and slammed his foot down on the accelerator to emphasize his frustration with the squealing of tires.

But the battle was over.

We rode the rest of the way to Pietr's house in a thick buffer of silence.

Their home seemed different, less inviting. Or maybe Alexi's attitude was throwing me off.

Up the stairs and to Pietr's room we went. There was a book on his bed. I picked it up. "What's this?" I asked looking at the title. *"Bisclavret?"*

He snatched it out of my hands. I swear he blushed. "It's a retelling of a traditional French poem. In English," he clarified. "And in modern-novel form." He tucked it away on one of his many bookshelves.

"French poetry?" I raised an eyebrow. "Is it *romantic*?"

He pulled it right back out and passed it to me.

I grinned at him. "You're reading a romance."

He glared at me and took the book back. *"Nyet,"* he snapped. "I'm reading a werewolf story. About revenge."

"Really? Give it back," I demanded. "Maybe I should read it."

"When I'm done. The werewolf stuff's getting interesting

now." It was only another moment before he assailed me with a question.

"What do you think makes a man a monster? Be specific."

I was caught off guard for a moment. Huh. He wanted to revisit our last very private conversation. I plunked down on the bed and pursed my lips in thought. "I don't know." I tried to weasel out of answering.

"Liar."

"Fine." I crossed my arms. "What makes a man—or woman—a monster is his or her ability to hurt people."

"Everyone can hurt someone," he pointed out.

"Agreed." I paused, regrouping. "His *willingness* to hurt people—or animals—" I added quickly.

"A hunter willingly *kills* animals."

"Good point." I groaned. "You really need to know this right now?"

He nodded and flopped onto the bed.

I rolled the words around in my head again. "Sarah would be *much* better at this," I said before I could stop myself.

"But I wouldn't care as much about her reply."

"Okay, here I go again," I warned. "His *willingness* to gleefully hurt people and/or animals." I looked at him, hoping for some visible seal of approval. "How was that?"

"*That* was more like I was hoping to hear," he whispered, his eyes soft. Calmed. He looked out the window. "And just in time," he said, rising from the bed. "Turn around, please."

"What?"

"Turn around. I'm not dressed for our hike," he explained.

"Wow," I said, obeying, "and modest, too!"

He chuckled. Cloth rustled as he changed. "Okay," he finally announced.

CHAPTER TWENTY-SEVEN

I turned back to face him. *"Well.* That's very Bohemian." He was wearing a simply constructed, loose-fitting shirt with a wide T collar over baggy pants.

"You don't like it?" He sniffed discerningly; I knew at that moment my approval meant absolutely nothing. The outfit was important somehow.

"I like anything *you* wear," I asserted.

"Oh, *horashow,*" he said, leading me back out his door and down the steps. "Then you'll definitely love the lucky football jersey I wear for the Super Bowl—hasn't been washed for years!"

"Whoa. Even I, with shirts stained with both blood and ketchup, have my limits," I responded. He picked up his jacket and hung mine around me.

Catherine bounded into the room. She frowned. "You will need a scarf," she informed me. "Here. Take this one of mine—and do not lose it. It's my absolute favorite."

"Thanks. I'll take good care of it," I promised.

"Good." She grinned and then stretched up on tiptoe to kiss Pietr's cheek. *"Za udachu,"* she whispered.

He kissed her forehead in turn, replying, "For good luck."

I noticed she was dressed in an outfit similar to what Pietr wore. Both looked homemade. "Oh, Catherine." I dug my heels in to pause as Pietr dragged me out the door into the first taste of evening. "Happy birthday!"

Startled, "I hope so," was all she said before the door closed and Pietr pulled me toward the woods.

He led me onto the trail, away from the house, down the slope, out the edge of the woodlot that was their family's frequent racetrack, and into a thicker stand of trees. The trail narrowed, branches and brambles tugged at my pants legs and snagged at my jacket.

I lost Catherine's scarf once in a wrestling match with wild berry canes, but Pietr plucked it right out and scolded me gently with "Now, we can't have you losing this scarf. You'll need it tonight."

"I actually have my own scarf, too," I remarked, tugging a long mess of colorful fabric out of one of my coat pockets until it seemed I was performing a magician's standard never-ending handkerchief trick.

"That'll come in handy." Pietr chuckled, winding the scarf loosely around my neck until nothing between my nose and shoulders showed.

I sputtered.

He laughed.

We walked up a brief incline, doubtless a deer path, before the woods opened before us, thinning and becoming less dense. Less wild.

Pietr paused at the forest's fringe and looked out at a spot of meadow. We were on the crest of one hill, but nestled at the feet of three others.

The sky was as immense here as above my horse ring at home, but the emerging stars seemed even closer to earth, as if I could pluck one right out of the sky. The sun and stars seemed to be fighting a beautiful war, the glowing ball of fire slowly retreating as it stained the sky an impassioned pink and dared the stars to pierce its bloodied path.

Although we hadn't walked far, it was as if we'd entered an entirely different world. A magical realm. Being with Pietr, alone beneath the materializing stars, stole my breath away.

He maneuvered so he stood before me a minute, blotting out the sky. He seemed lost in his own strange thoughts.

I broke the silence. "'In such a night as this,

When the sweet wind did gently kiss the trees

And they did make no noise, in such a night

Troilus methinks mounted the Troyan walls

And sighed his soul toward the Grecian tents,

Where Cressid lay that night,'" I whispered, remembering Lorenzo's lines from *The Merchant of Venice*.

He grinned. "Not *Romeo and Juliet*," he surmised. "*The Merchant of Venice*." He seemed to search his memory before responding.

"'In such a night did Thisbe fearfully o'ertrip the dew

And saw the lion's shadow ere himself

And ran dismayed away.'" He added the next portion.

I raised my chin. "I am no Thisbe, scared of a lion," I challenged.

"And I am not Pyramus," he confided.

I shook my head, letting my hair catch in the rattling breeze.

"Perhaps I am Psyche," I teased. "Ready to discover your secret identity, dear Cupid! You *did* promise to tell me how you found Annabelle Lee," I pressed.

He nodded. "So are we Cupid and Psyche?"

"Well, we're not Romeo and Juliet," I insisted.

"*Nyet*. Never. We're not so naïve. Lorenzo and Jessica?"

"I don't know. They were greedy. Besides, can you save my soul?" I joked, not suspecting his tender and devastatingly earnest response.

"I'm afraid the best I can offer is a try at healing your broken heart. Do you trust me, Jess?"

"Yes," I said without hesitation. How could he even ask me that when we'd already come so far together—he'd done ridiculous things on my behalf, saving me from a crazed dog, saving Annabelle Lee from Weird Wanda. Whatever all *that* was about. It all meant so much to me—*he* meant so much to me already—that I'd lied to my father to be here, alone with him, on this night.

His eyes were closed, his features drawn tight by a pain I couldn't fathom.

"Did I say something wrong?"

"Hmm." He opened his eyes, letting them glitter into my own for a breathless moment. If he had asked me then did I *love* him—I would have probably responded with equal fervor. There was something about him. . . .

"This isn't some simple question I'm asking," he whispered, pressing his forehead to mine to peer into my eyes as if he could divine some destiny in their depths. "I need to know if you totally trust me. Totally and *completely*."

I opened my mouth to respond, but he pressed his fingers to my lips, silencing me with his nearly searing touch.

He pulled his face back from mine, searching the darkening

horizon. His breath steamed against the cool air, scalding my cheek. "Because if you even have any doubt—*any doubt at all*—you can still make it back to the house and call your dad. The path's simple and short."

He glanced back down the trail toward his home, calculating. He nodded. "If you have any doubt at all—go *now*," he urged, eyes sparkling like cut crystal.

I swallowed. I *did* trust him. *Absolutely.* But the way he was talking—the concern that etched his handsome face—I was suddenly afraid, too.

"Do you want to go?" he asked.

"No." And I wrapped my arms around his neck, burning up wherever our bodies touched as I pulled him closer to kiss him—melting against him. In that moment, there was no Sarah, no lying, no fear, just him.

Kissing me with lips that threatened to brand my own.

He pushed me back against a tree trunk, kissing all the while, a strange desperation in his lips' attentive touches. Then he broke free of my embrace and stared hard at me. "Do you trust me, Jess?" he implored one last time, an odd huskiness to his tone.

"Yes," I insisted.

He shrugged out of his coat, draping it around my shoulders, and carefully unwrapping my absurdly long scarf from around my neck. He nestled Catherine's scarf at my neck instead, and, leaning forward, his breath hot by my ear, he tossed my scarf around the tree's trunk, twisting it first around the tree and then me. He tied it, securing it snugly around my waist. I must have looked puzzled, because he kissed the tip of my nose.

"Trust me," he murmured. And then his tone changed and I heard an urgent warning color his voice as darkness skittered and crawled close around us. "And no matter what happens—*don't run.*"

He turned from me, and, hand in hand, we watched the moon slide over the mountains to the east: white, full, and haloed.

In the distance I heard a wolf call, the sound clawing at the air, far richer than the crazed yipping of coyotes. It haunted the horizon, threading between the trees as it rode the brisk fall breeze and I thought briefly of Farthington. But looking at Pietr, feeling how he squeezed my hand, I couldn't imagine being safer.

And then he let go.

I shivered.

He fell to the ground, writhing suddenly at the forest's edge, bathed in the shifting and milky moonlight.

That was when I started screaming.

"Pietr—Pietr!" I tugged against the scarf he'd cinched to both the tree and me. It had been a simple knot he'd tied—in only a scarf, right? So why did it stump me, rooting me to the tree at my back? I struggled—desperate to go to him. He convulsed—body quaking and fevered—suffering some sort of attack—

I reached into my jacket pocket, fumbling for my phone. I flipped it open, dialed 9—

"*Nyet!*" he groaned, and for an instant I saw his face. He looked fiercely at the phone in my hand. His eyes as bright as the full moon's light and as red as in his student ID, they shone like the predator lights we used to keep hungry animals away from our birds. "*Nyet,*" he ordered, somehow making the word hiss.

I gaped at him, the phone a worthless lump of technology in my trembling hand.

His face twisted, contorting in agony, and changed—there was an audible popping like joints coming undone as his face began *lengthening* somehow—I started screaming all over again, my phone falling to the forest's soft floor, all but forgotten.

He jerked away from me, face hidden, and I wondered if I renewed my struggle with the scarf, how fast I could make it to the house for help.

But his words came back to me: *"And no matter what happens—don't run."*

"Pietr . . ." The curled body on the ground no longer moved—no longer twitched or trembled. "Pietr!"

The moon seemed to spotlight him where he lay, and I watched in amazement as he twisted and shrugged out of the loose-fitting outfit. Only what revealed itself wasn't Pietr at all, but a huge and broad-shouldered wolf.

It scented the wind, not even conscious of me at first. It reminded me of the way Pietr scanned the fair's crowd searching for Annabelle Lee. And then it caught my scent and swung its heavy head to look at me. Its ears flattened against its skull. It snarled, lips peeling back to showcase a line of wickedly curving teeth, each at least the size of my thumbs.

I stayed perfectly still. Tried to remember to breathe.

And my mind shot back to that evening at the school and the beast that roamed the halls—wrecked the guidance office. Could it have been Pietr? But the markings, the colors . . . No. This was a different beast. Thick gray and silver fur seemed a trap for starlight, his pelt glittering as much as his eyes.

This one was even different from the one that shoved me to the ground that rainy night, leaving human footprints in the mud.

"Pietr?" I whispered, my brain misfiring at the idea the huge wolf before me could be the guy I'd been kissing just minutes—*was that all it was?*—ago.

It snorted, brows lowering over lantern-like eyes. Stiff-legged, it walked toward me and sniffed again, sucking down the scents on me with frightening eagerness. Then its ears pricked up and it raced off—toward the heart of the forest.

I sighed, thankful it had the unexpected gift of a short attention span. I slid down the tree's trunk, bark wrenching at the two jackets and shirt I wore, scraping my back. I winced. The scarf that chained me to the tree descended sluggishly with me. My back would be a torn-up mess in the morning. *If* I made it to morning.

I heard a rustling in the bushes to my right. "Pietr?"

A wolf emerged—or—I thought about the wolves I'd seen in zoos and nature shows. These weren't the same. Not only were they larger—they were also . . . dammit. I couldn't find the right word. There was something somehow indescribable about them. It was as if the bulk of their bodies was oddly divided between broad shoulders, a heavy head and paws so wide they seemed perfectly designed to hold the earth. They certainly weren't wolves. And yet that was the only word that even came close to describing what they *were*.

I noticed immediately this one *wasn't Pietr.*

It was smaller. The eyes were different, the attitude more excited. It approached, ears down, mouth trembling as saliva dripped from its jaws. The expression was the same Hunter and Maggie got when I cooked sausage for breakfast. Only colder by many degrees.

It was hungry.

And I was still tied to a tree.

CHAPTER TWENTY-EIGHT

It approached, a steady growl emanating from deep in its throat.

I stayed still—what else could I do?—and watched its nostrils flare as it sucked down my scent. It towered above me as I sat there. Its shape shadowed me, the starry sky overhead embossed with the sharp silhouette of a wolf. The creature paused, its nose at Pietr's jacket. It blinked, snapping its teeth.

Did they know each other? I closed my eyes and thought, *God, please let them be friends.*

Its nose was at my neckline—my *neck*—the beast's breath as hot as summer's first sunburn. Encountering Catherine's scarf, it yipped and hopped back, legs straight but full of spring.

I willed my eyes open again, watching as it approached once more, its mouth closed, eyes wide. It sniffed the scarf again. It whined, licked my face and bolted away, joyful.

"Catherine?" I called after it.

I leaned my head back against the tree trunk and shut my eyes. A family of wolves? I corrected myself—*werewolves*? I laughed, unable to figure out if I was laughing because I wasn't dead yet or because I'd finally lost my mind. I decided it might be a little of both and determined to stay still, wondering what would happen next.

I must have dozed off, the surge of adrenaline and fear—oh, yeah—*definitely* fear, had left me drained. I was startled awake by the sound of something large moving through the brush and crumbling the dry autumn leaves beneath its feet.

"Catherine?"

Nothing.

"Pietr?" Something big pushed through the brambles and padded forward, the crunch of autumn's discarded leaves like an earthy afterthought as it stalked through the strongest shadows.

I pushed with my legs—my knees were loose, as if they connected my leg bones with rubber bands instead of cartilage. With a groan, I forced myself to stand. I would meet whatever approached while on my feet.

I felt the amber heart hanging near my throat but thought of my mother's netsuke rabbit sitting on my bureau at home. "Mom," I whispered to the night sky. "I need your strength, your vision. Mom," I begged. "I need you. . . ."

The moon had crested high above the seemingly bearded western horizon of forest. A fine silver plate with a rabbit etched into its surface, it threw remarkable light everywhere but where I really needed it.

I realized I had already lost *hours*. . . .

The beast stepped out of the shadow, something dangling from its mouth. The creature looked at me and cocked its head. It whined, a sound as chilling as it was mournful.

"Pietr," I breathed.

The wolf dropped the thing it carried by Pietr's abandoned shirt and nosed a bloody and awkward way into the clothing. It lay there a while, its back to me as it shivered in the dark. I thought surely dawn was close, ready to throw better light on the situation.

"Pietr," I whispered. *What if he was hurt?*

And then the lump—the thing that had so recently been a wolf—rolled over, became Pietr, the *human* Pietr, again.

Slowly he turned to face me, his eyes hollow—sorrowful. He was still Pietr, but different, wilder and sadder, on his knees before me.

Words seemed to come slowly for him now, as if the brain of the beast and the brain of the boy jigsawed awkwardly together in the first few minutes after transformation.

"*This* is what I am, Jess," he hissed, quaking like a lowly penitent soul. In his left hand he held the shredded and bloodied corpse of some small forest innocent. I tried to see beyond it, to focus on Pietr, his soul broken, voice ragged, but my eyes returned to the limp remnants of the anonymous animal in his shaking hand, my brain spinning as it tried to make out what the creature had once been.

"How can you ever care for someone—some*thing* like *this*?" he demanded. The mess in his hand quivered as his body shook in self-loathing.

I swallowed hard, my brain rioting as I suddenly recognized the animal in Pietr's hand. My treacherous scarf fell loose at my waist and I dropped to my knees, face-to-face with Pietr, my gaze holding his. I could be his anchor, I promised myself as I took the rabbit's mangled remains from him and gently laid it on the ground.

I swallowed again, my throat tight and dry. I felt the amber heart tap against the hollow spot at the base of my neck. I took Pietr's face in my hands. "Pietr." I paused. Searching for the right words I stumbled and stuttered. "I-I—"

He tried to look down. To look away.

"No." I made the single word sharp, demanding his attention. He looked at me again. It was the only time I'd read fear in Pietr Rusakova's eyes.

"How—?" he asked again, letting the word fall between us.

"I don't *know* how," I admitted. It was true, and we both knew this was one thing I couldn't lie about. Pietr, my friend, my hero, my loyal and utterly kissable companion was a *werewolf*—an abomination. "But."

His eyes sparked for a moment, and his hands grabbed my own, pressing them harder against his face.

"But I'll learn a way," I promised.

"I am a monster," he protested.

"Hush now." My mind leaped back to our earlier conversation. *What really was the measure of a man? And what made a man a monster?*

A branch snapped in the woods. "Catherine?" I said, but no one came forward. No voice responded. Even though I wore two jackets, a shiver shook my spine.

Had we been watched, and if so, for how long?

Another *crack* sounded, and I whipped toward it. "Catherine!" I cried.

"Oh. She's here," a voice replied from the darkness.

Pietr tore out of my grip and spun to face the intruder.

I shuddered. I'd heard that voice before, but where?

"I must say—bravo! 'All the world's a stage, we have our entrances' "—the man from the porch, the man who'd threatened Max and Alexi, stepped out of the woods—" 'and exits.' And it seems a few of us play twice as many roles." He was the one Max had identified as O.P.S.—Russian Mafia. He snapped his fingers and nearly a dozen other men ghosted out of the forest. Their faces shone in the illusory moonlight: a mix of awe, shame, and anger.

Held between two of them was Catherine. Head down, hair a tangled mess, she was bloodied—definitely beaten, but not done fighting. She still struggled against her brutal captors. She kicked, she bit, she flailed, and to her credit, the men—as big as mountains beside her—flinched again and again beneath the unending ferocity of her quick and wild attacks.

"Hold her tighter, Grigori," their leader demanded, and one of the guards squeezed her arm until she squeaked. "*Da.* We have your Catherine," the leader assured us. "I feel as if I've stumbled into a new imagining of *Romeo and Juliet*. He's a werewolf, she's—*not*. . . . Not just two different households, two different worlds."

I grabbed Pietr and held him by the shoulders, gluing myself to his burning back. "You are no *monster,* Pietr," I whispered. "*He* is the monster."

I knew how futile my efforts were. Knew more clearly as Pietr's powerful muscles slipped and slid beneath his fiery flesh. If he wanted to go, he'd go. "Wait," I demanded. "Think."

He nodded, slowly, but I felt his muscles bunch and coil, filled with heat from his transformation. In a heartbeat he'd spring into their midst. His gaze was pinned to Catherine and a growl boiled up within him, vibrating its way into my palms, jarring my fingertips.

"There are too many of them, Pietr," I whispered, my mouth at his ear.

He knew I was right. But that alone couldn't drain the fight from him. And I noticed that the men, these "marked men"— mafiosos—were already banged up. Catherine had fought as hard as Pietr was prepared to.

They still caught her.

My grip on Pietr tightened, fingers roasting on his fevered skin. My palms sweated for a multitude of reasons.

Pietr looked up at the moon in a way that made me wish I'd read werewolf stories instead of wasting so much time on vamps . . . Could he—?

"Don't even think about it, boy," their leader snapped. "Remember that *Romeo and Juliet* is one of Shakespeare's tragedies. I already have Catherine. You are quite outnumbered—even if you Change. It would be a quick fight and we don't want things to end *badly*." He smiled. "We only want what was promised to us."

Moonlight glinted off gun muzzles. *Crap.* They were well armed. And I was armed with nothing. . . . Wait. I quietly reached around behind me, fingers rooting through rattling leaves to find my cell.

Careful now, I thought, bringing it around to where I could see it. Fabulous. Now that I had the phone, who would I call? Ugh. I'd never thought an association with werewolves would actually limit my options. Of course, I'd never thought of an association with werewolves at all.

Thankful my cell was a cheap model that gave little light, I nestled closer against Pietr's back. His heart pounded so strongly mine tried to match it. My skin prickled and I felt sweat bead beneath my shirt at Pietr's proximity. With a breath, I flipped open my cell and tagged the Rusakova house phone.

Someone picked up. And, at that moment, I became amazingly brave. Or stupid. Both, actually. I stood, the phone hidden, cupped in my hand. "And just what is it you think you were promised?" I snapped.

Pietr stood, shielding me, arms out. He probably thought I'd lost my mind. Maybe I had.

The leader cocked his head, preparing to address me.

My hand out in front of me, I shook my head with an arrogance I had never before mustered. "Don't *even* talk to me until you tell me your name. Because, right now, you wouldn't like what I'm ready to call you." I hoped he mistook my trembling for the shake of anger and not fear. My teeth nearly rattled.

He blinked at me. "I am the wolf at your door—"

"I've never seen *doors* in the *back end of the old park,*" Pietr replied with an authority that strengthened me.

Thank God he was a quick study!

I glanced at the phone. The light blinked off. Done. The Rusakova phone had hung up. I just had to hope that Alexi or Max had gotten the call and knew what to do.

I sure didn't.

"You may call me Nickolai, little girl. Who is she, Pietr? Is this the newest hope of muddying the bloodline? I wouldn't do it, you know? They tried to breed the wolf out in Mexico." The way he said *wolf* made me believe it was a proper noun. "And look what happened. You should accept your Fate, revel in your power. Each of you is a most glorious monster!"

Pietr shook before me, enraged.

"The wolf inside you is meant for a great destiny—one a proud child of Russia would never deny." Nickolai walked slowly toward us.

"We are no longer *just* children of Mother Russia," Catherine snarled, her struggling renewed. "Our family now includes an uncle named Sam," she growled. "Where was dear Mother Russia when we were nearly discovered in Farthington?"

Nickolai flew at her, grabbed her, and shook her by the shoulders. "Mother Russia is *always* with you—she is in your blood, you ungrateful bitch!" He slapped her so hard the *crack* of impact even rocked Pietr.

I felt a subtle shift in him as I stood so close behind. He'd seen something beyond the line of armed men. My hands dropped from his shoulders and I took a half step back. Pietr took that moment, while all focused on Catherine, to drop to all fours and *change*. Far faster this time—I barely saw a flash of bare flesh before he was a huge, angry Wolf. He charged across the meadow, leaves flying in his wake.

He sprang up.

The mafiosos' eyes popped.

A gun rose, glittering, to pluck the Wolf from the air with a single shot and I screamed. Nickolai swung around, cuffing the overly eager Grigori, and shouting as he spun just out of the Wolf's path. The Wolf touched ground for a heartbeat before ramming his broad, furred shoulder into another mafioso, sending him flying into the forest. There was a *crunch*—like flesh and bone meeting wood—and I knew that man wouldn't rejoin the fight.

Another Wolf soared over the wall of armed men and I realized he was what Pietr had seen seconds before his transformation. This one was broader still, with darker markings and a leering grin. Eagerly, he tore into the men, his long fanged mouth grabbing one by the leg and whipping him out of view. In the midst of the madness and falling men, Catherine broke free.

For a moment her eyes locked with mine. She looked at me almost apologetically. And then she shouted, "Run!" and she, too, switched into the very form I had learned to fear in fairytales and fables. Savagely empowered, her howl—a bansidhe's battle cry—tore at the gathering clouds and she struck out with gleaming teeth and claws.

I did exactly as she commanded. I ran back across the meadow and into the tree line. But then I stopped. Anyone with any common sense would have kept running. I *got* that. But instead, I climbed a tree and wondered why no shots had been fired.

I understood, my stomach knotting, as Taser cables sliced through the crisp night air.

They weren't here to kill the werewolves. They wanted them alive. Taser tips lodged in Wolf flesh. A *sizzle* and the air lit up—shades of violent electric blue. Desperate to tear the darts out, the Wolves' teeth flashed away from their attackers to combat the cables carrying the current.

My fingers dug into the tree trunk, lichen crumbling to dust under my nails. I wanted claws. I wanted teeth. I wanted to help somehow. . . .

The blue shockwave knocked them to the ground. Immobilizing Catherine, Pietr, and the other Wolf. They struggled in slow motion, their responses dulled, muscles quaking.

"Again," Nickolai demanded as he stood and brushed himself off. The *zip* of electricity delivered another blow. I'd never thought Tasers could deliver more than one jolt. But these did. Nickolai grinned. "Again." And another. Until, finally they lay there, Catherine, Pietr, and Max, quaking, their forms shivering somewhere between man and beast.

Nickolai surveyed the scene. And realized someone was missing.

I heard him yell, "Where is that girl? You and you—Grigori—find her!" I hugged the tree so tightly I became one with its trunk, snuggling into it where the shadows of its knotted and gnarled neighbors wove tightly together in the gloom. Who would have guessed that years of playing flashlight tag with Amy, Sophia, and Annabelle Lee might come in handy against the Russian Mafia?

Dazed, his mafiosos stood, looking at him a moment.

"Get the girl!" he demanded. "She knows too much!"

Dammit. Why did people keep presuming *that,* and if it was true, why the hell couldn't my GPA reflect the fact?

CHAPTER TWENTY-NINE

Grigori and his companion raced past, just below the branches holding me. Did they expect a victim so terrified she ran blindly, thrashing through the forest? I was the other sort of terrified. My brain wasn't working fast enough even to make flight possible.

I needed a weapon. The forest floor was littered with sticks and branches big enough to knock a guy's head off, but that required getting close to someone's head without getting shot. Nickolai may have wanted the Rusakovas alive, but I was no Rusakova.

I heard a thin and reedy whine and looked away from the bodies in the field, unable to watch them writhe as yet another bolt of electricity shot into them. They had already taken horribly unnatural amounts of current. The fact they still lived shocked me with equal doses of hope and fear.

Nickolai was speaking again. Thank God he was a talker, it might just buy us time. I only hoped time was what we needed. "This was not the delivery I had hoped for, but—"

The whine grew louder and I recognized the sound only when Alexi's ATV roared onto the meadow and skidded to a halt. I thought for an instant that I heard something else even farther out. But Alexi yanked off his helmet, stepped off the ATV, and immediately had everyone's attention.

"Ah, Alexi. I was just about to mention your obvious development of cold feet. . . ."

"I never get cold feet."

"Then what would you call it?" Nickolai snapped. "Did you forget your part in this deal? Did you forget who pays your bills? What side you're on?"

"*Nyet*. I have forgotten nothing. But I have remembered things you would rather I forget." Alexi's look alone could have killed the remaining seven men. I wondered why he hesitated—why didn't he Change and attack?

"Then you surely remember that you are not like them." Nickolai stuck a gun to Alexi's head. "At all."

Alexi paused in his progress forward. "I've never forgotten that."

"Would you have ever told them, I wonder." Nickolai smiled cruelly. "That you are not their brother—only their keeper? Like the man who shovels dung out of cages at a zoo?"

Alexi flinched.

I noticed the bodies between the two men tightened, necks craning as they strained to look up at their eldest brother. Their guardian.

Max snarled, lips drawn back, "You bastard! You were going to sell us out?"

Nickolai grinned. "Go ahead, Alexi. Tell them the truth. For once," he urged. He verged on laughter.

Suddenly I understood how Alexi could lie so convincingly. He'd been practicing for years. And seeing what all his lying led to . . . I shivered, staring at the mess in the meadow. In the short while I'd known him, Pietr had always been honest. Until I'd made a liar of him, too.

Dammit. How did anyone untangle a mess of these proportions? How could everything ever go back to normal now? Once trust was gone . . . I bit my lower lip and tried not to think of my dad and the last two phrases he'd said to me. Instead, I focused on the disaster directly in my line of sight.

And I noticed how Pietr, Max, and Catherine, now merely human, slowly moved, slowly adjusted their positions, all the while letting their fingers subtly work at the taser darts. Barely flinching, they worked them loose from their damaged flesh and held them so the wires never went slack. So no one noticed.

"Tell them, Sasha. Tell them you are the grandson of the scientist who helped *create* their species. The man who dashed their hopes of normalcy and built them to self-destruct early. What is their lifespan now? I imagine it's further compressed by their parents being full-bloods. It must be quite the countdown. Tick-tock, tick-tock," he said with a sneer. "Do they hear it start ticking when they turn thirteen, I wonder? Quite the life sentence!" Now he did laugh, letting the noise bounce across the meadow.

"Sasha," he addressed Alexi coldly with the nickname. "You must tell them!" He laughed again. "Tell them that when the USSR revoked his funding and put the children he'd created into state-run orphanages he disappeared, only watching from a distance. He was sure he was right—sure the transformation would take. . . . But they didn't turn until later, did they?"

Nickolai shook his head. "He left them at the mercy of strangers. And such a pity, really. So many lost in those first years. He couldn't track them all. So he married, right, Sasha?" Nickolai leered at Alexi.

Alexi denied nothing.

My stomach seized. I was going to be sick.

"If he couldn't track and find all of his own creations, perhaps he could persuade—or create—others to assist him. But his wife was no fool. She only gave him one child—that blasted and meddlesome girl—your mother. You're nothing but the son of a Coney Island con woman."

Alexi went rigid at the mention.

I blinked. Things were starting to reorder themselves in my head. My brain tried to make sense of the insanity before me.

"So we became *werewolf* hunters!" Nickolai chortled. "Bring them back, train them up, reclaim the real Mother Russia with the dog soldiers the USSR threw away." He nudged the muzzle of his pistol into Alexi's temple. Pietr flinched at his feet.

"We were all thrown to the wolves, weren't we? These men"—he motioned to the remaining mafia members—"started as good, honest men. We returned from serving our military—a proud tradition—and what was there for us? Nothing. But the O.P.S.—it welcomes all hard workers. It has a vision, including reclaiming all discarded souls—even werewolves."

"Aaah!" I yelped feeling rough hands close on my ankles, dragging me from the safety of the tree branches. I hit the ground, hard, the fall jarring every bit of bone in me.

The pain, stunning as it was, made me acutely aware of the men now glaring down at me, smirks twisting their lips and raising their eyebrows. They grabbed my arms, wrenching me to my feet. I pulled against them, shoulders popping at the effort. I flailed. I kicked. I struggled as valiantly as I could. It was like I'd done nothing. "Aaarrgh," I growled, and threw myself against one—using all of my strength.

"Ah—it sounds as if the girl will be joining us shortly. Perhaps there will be more compliance now. So, Sasha, let us have what you've been receiving payment for all along and you won't die here in the dirt like the simple man you are."

My captors never reacted to anything I tried. I hadn't even managed a pale imitation of Catherine's efforts. In disgust I went limp between them, trying at least to summon the annoyance of dead weight.

Without hesitation they began to drag me across the meadow.

A huge vehicle crashed through the brush at the meadow's northern edge, brambles across its bumper as it barreled into the middle of everything. It careened to one side suddenly, ramming into a mafioso with a *crunch* as the impact sent him flying.

My captors reacted to *that*. They dropped me to grab their guns.

"What have you done now, Sasha?" Nickolai demanded, his hand tightening on the pistol's grip.

I scrambled away as the doors of the SUV snapped open and Wanda and Officer Kent—*Holy crap, what a strange, small world,* I thought—jumped out, guns firing.

Pietr rolled, wrenching the taser out of a man's hands and sweeping Nickolai's feet out from under him as he pulled the trigger. The shot went wide and Pietr was a Wolf again, Catherine and Max following suit.

"Get down, you bastards!" Wanda shouted.

"Shit! It's Farthington all over again. They're like *her*, aren't they?" Kent yelled.

"Talk less—shoot more!" Wanda commanded.

The Mafia turned their attention, and their bullets, on the— cops? What the hell were they? I needed a chart to keep things straight.

Alexi lay on the ground—dead or unconscious, I couldn't

tell. He wasn't alone. Near him there were several bodies and across him lay a Wolf that gleamed silver in the starlight.

Oh, God—I was running before I could think anything but *Pietr*—

"*Shit!*" Wanda took me to the ground, covering me with her body as she dragged me toward the scant protection provided by the SUV. "Is everyone in Junction here?" she muttered, firing a shot that took down a Mafia member. "If you don't have a gun—*and you'd better not*—hug the hubcaps and hope for the best," she said, targeting another man.

"Pietr—" I insisted.

"Will be fine," she retorted. "They can take a hell of a beating and be one hundred percent in a day."

As she aimed for another Mafia member, Kent dropped, hit, on the other side of the SUV.

"Crap. I always have to do *everything*," Wanda griped. "Stay here." She slid under the SUV and tugged Kent to safety underneath it.

I saw her check him, roll him over, and quickly search him. He was still breathing, punctuating each careful breath with a curse that threatened to set the air on fire. Just on the far side of the SUV his gun twinkled, half-covered in leaf litter.

The Mafia was dropping all around us, some dispatched by Cat and Max, some taken out by Wanda. Separated from me during the firefight, Grigori was steadily advancing on Wanda like something out of a black-and-white horror flick.

I scrambled under the SUV, heading for the gun—as did Wanda. She rolled out just in front of me and, her gun on Grigori, reached behind her for Kent's. It was just out of reach of her grasping hand. And I knew, as she must have, that she needed it. We'd both been counting. Wanda was nearly out of bullets. And nearly out of time.

Grigori fired a shot and Wanda gasped, rocked backward by the impact. Blood spread from her shoulder and she smacked her hands together, steadying her pistol with a two-handed grip. She pulled the trigger.

Grigori took a half step back, touching a spot on his arm where blood seeped up and stained his sleeve. She'd grazed him. He grinned. And adjusted his aim.

I grabbed Kent's gun, pulling it free of the rattling leaves that dotted the meadow. The sights glimmered for a single second, Grigori's eyes widening in realization. His index finger twitched as the muzzle of Kent's gun flashed, hot and dangerous as any fire.

Grigori dropped, eyes rolling back. He coughed, blood dribbling out of his mouth and then he was still. Dead.

I dropped the gun. I had killed a man.

"You little bitch—" I swung around in time to see Nickolai raise his gun and snare me in his sights. No time to cry out—I closed my eyes—and nothing. What? My eyes popped open. Nickolai staggered, his legs tangling, pistol dropping . . .

. . . as his head landed on the ground with a *thump*. About two yards away from his limp body.

Pietr, the Wolf, balanced precariously on his hind legs, claws covered in gore, the soft fur of his chest spattered with the same blood that streaked his muzzle. He looked at me, eyes wide and wild, and then he dropped down to all fours.

I began to breathe again. Just before I vomited into the leaf litter.

"Come on," Wanda urged. She winced. Blindly, I turned and helped her to her feet. "Get Kent . . ."

The meadow was eerily quiet, except for the occasional gust of wind rustling leaves and the ragged breathing of the werewolves and cops. Together Wanda and I dragged Kent out from under the SUV and awkwardly pushed and pulled him into the back of the vehicle.

Catherine and Max were dressed and beside Pietr, who crouched near Alexi, his eyes closed. As human as they seemed now, I noticed something feral about them for the first time. Something about their eyes and in the lines of their faces seemed to promise the beast within was never far from the surface.

Werewolves! my mind howled, faced with the facts.

Pietr's eyes snapped open, and he struggled to find words. "Jess—"

I stayed still. Watching. Stunned.

Catherine looked at me, worry filling her eyes. "She's still here." She turned back to him. "Put on some clothes first," she said, shoving his pants at him.

They all turned as Alexi groaned and slowly stood. Cat jumped in front of him and smacked him so hard his head rocked on his neck.

"Catherine!" Pietr growled, but Alexi put one hand up as he rubbed his jaw with the other.

"It's okay." He looked at her, shamed. "I deserve worse." He put his hands out in front of him, looking at Wanda, expecting to be handcuffed.

She shook her head. "It's complicated. And I'm still bleeding. Let's get the hell out of here. Alexi, take Catherine home on the ATV. She'll keep you in check, I'm sure. Max, you drive. You two"—she pointed at Pietr and me—"backseat."

Doors closed, Wanda made a call. "Yeah. Clean up on aisle one. Location—" She looked at a GPS unit on the dash and read the coordinates. Then she handed the keys to Max to start the SUV. "Okay. We don't have much time," she explained. "The severe pruning we just gave that Mafia branch will be noticed."

I took Pietr's hand and shuddered, trying not to think about what made it damply crimson.

Wanda continued. "They will send more men. Soon. Things won't get better until they get waaay worse." Pietr slid closer to me, his body still hot from the Change, warming me against chills that had nothing to do with the breeze swirling around the vehicle. We bumped back along the path it had carved earlier. "I want to bring you all in to our local headquarters. We can hole up safely there; plan. *Crap.*"

I closed my eyes, exhausted, but all I kept seeing was Grigori and Nickolai dropping. Bleeding. Dying. As if it were etched into the insides of my eyelids. I resigned myself to living with my eyes open as often as possible.

Wanda was still rambling. "Nobody outside my team will ever believe this. Crap. *I* barely believe this. A family of were-wolves!" Wanda laughed hysterically, ponytail dancing, her shoulder wound nearly forgotten in the afterglow of adrenaline. "Good thing we had your phones tapped." She sighed. "Thank goodness *that's* become easier."

I fumbled in my pocket and pulled out my pietersite worry stone. "I think I may have been carrying this for you as much as I rub it *because* of you," I remarked, holding it out to Pietr. "It's for helping with change and transformation, right?"

He looked at me, his eyes glowing. "Keep it," he insisted. "I have the feeling we'll all be dealing with big changes."

Wanda continued as I again pocketed the stone. "Now, the most important thing to remember is that none of this happened. The Rusakovas need to stay here. In Junction. Nobody leaves. Nobody moves, unless I know about it first—unless you have my *permission* first," she corrected. "We'll make this the new epicenter of the action. We can protect you, keep everything hush-hush. You'll just need to be willing to eventually do your patriotic duty for Uncle Sam at some point . . . but that's a while from now. *Shit.*" She pounded the dash with both hands. "If you knew how hard it was to find you!"

I looked past her and out the windshield as the SUV thudded along, Kent groaning (and still cursing) in the back. Out of the corner of my eye I saw just the edge of Wanda, the rest of her obscured by her seat and my position. There was something strangely familiar about that hair, that shoulder—the very edge of her face and amazingly determined jaw.

And all the blanks in my head suddenly filled in. Two Phantom Wolves in Farthington: one dead; one MIA, according to the retraction. Pietr's mother defending his father. The auburn-colored beast at my farm, roaming the school halls, tearing Guidance apart while hunting answers . . . What Kent said before the shooting started . . . *Werewolves!* The CIA swamped with files as an agent with pale hair pulled tight in a ponytail watched. . . .

I said the one thing capable of dividing our strange alliance before I could even stop myself. When I'm nervous, I talk. And sitting in an SUV with werewolves and the CIA has an uncanny way of making a person nervous.

"Oh shit, Pietr," I hissed. "Your mother's alive. And Wanda and Kent know where she is."

Max hit the brakes.

The glove compartment flew open, a box of microscope slides tumbling out. Max moved so fast they didn't even reach the floor. Cradling the curiosity, he touched them with amazing delicacy for a guy who could shift into a raging beast. "You've been hunting us a while now, haven't you?" Max snarled at Wanda.

He tossed a slide to me and one to Pietr. They were labeled with names and dates. My slide, my name, this year. A single strand of hair plucked off my shoulder.

Pietr's slide: "My mother," he whispered. Another hair sample. The collection date was clearly visible. Two years ago.

Werewolves. The CIA and the Russian Mafia.

I knew I was *definitely* going to need to talk to a professional, after all. Some things you just can't handle on your own.